MARDI GRAS MADNESS

A ZEKE MALONE MYSTERY

XAVIER DeSOTO

Black Rose Writing | Texas

The author grants the final approval for this literary material.

First printing

This is a work of fiction. Names, characters, businesses, places, events, and incidents are either the products of the author's imagination or used in a fictitious manner. Any resemblance to actual persons, living or dead, or actual events is purely coincidental.

ISBN: 978-1-68513-057-2
PUBLISHED BY BLACK ROSE WRITING
www.blackrosewriting.com

Printed in the United States of America
Suggested Retail Price (SRP) $25.95

Mardi Gras Madness is printed in Calluna

*As a planet-friendly publisher, Black Rose Writing does its best to eliminate unnecessary waste to reduce paper usage and energy costs, while never compromising the reading experience. As a result, the final word count vs. page count may not meet common expectations.

Cover Design by Laura Foust

COMMENTS ABOUT
MARDI GRAS MADNESS:
A ZEKE MALONE MYSTERY

"Xavier DeSoto is a **NEW AND EXCITING VOICE** in murder mysteries."

"A masterful **NEW ORLEANS NOIR MYSTERY**."

"Grabs you and doesn't let you go."

"*MARDI GRAS MADNESS* will keep you guessing till the **PULSE-POUNDING ENDING**."

"The tension never lets up."

"A stunning debut novel...**ELECTRIFYING**."

"The story simmers like a pot of Cajun gumbo—**DELICIOUS READING**, savor every page."

"**A TOP-NOTCHED THRILLER** that explores the dark underbelly of New Orleans."

"A treat for murder/mystery fans."

"**AN EXCELLENT GRIPPING MYSTERY** that keeps you reading till the last page."

"**FUN TO READ**..."

"*MARDI GRAS MADNESS* IS QUITE THE ADVENTURE! You just never know what part of this beautiful and historic city you'll follow Zeke Malone into...You'll be on the edge of your seat until the end—when you'll be wanting for more Zeke Malone!"

"First, Zeke Malone has the task of solving the murder...before finding that his dead wife was involved. A story full of **TWIST AND TURNS** you didn't see coming."

"**FUNNY IN PARTS...SAD IN OTHERS**...mystery and action throughout—MARDI GRAS MADNESS has it all."

"First, his wife is killed...**THEN ALL HELL BREAKS LOOSE.** Non-stop action till the end."

"Xavier DeSoto has created a new unique fictional detective: **ZEKE MALONE IS A DELIGHT. TOUGH AND TOUCHING.**"

"**REFRESHINGLY FUNNY** with action that will leave you breathless. Definitely a gripping thriller! Can't wait for the next Zeke Malone Mystery to be released!"

"**JAM-PACKED** with a sympathetic detective, Zeke Malone...you'll root for his every move."

"A novel just made for **MYSTERY AFICIONADOS**..."

"**THE CHARACTER DEVELOPMENT IS TOP NOTCH!** One of the things I most adore about this novel is how disappointed I was when it ended. I will be rereading this novel until the next novel because I already miss the characters!"

To Angeles (Cookie)—the only one who stuck with me—regardless.

No animals were harmed in the making of this book—
but many kittens were had!

MARDI GRAS MADNESS

A ZEKE MALONE MYSTERY

PART I

CHAPTER 1

Had I known it was going to be such a day, I may have stayed in bed. But who can predict the future—good or bad? I sighed and rolled out of bed.

"Zeke Malone, someday, you're going to get yourself shot," Jane said.

Every morning, it began, as most things do, with a complaint. And not just any complaint, mind you, but objections from the woman with the grass-green eyes. And the only lady I had ever loved. I sat up, sighed again, and stared out the window. From our second-story apartment, past the wrought-iron balcony, I could see the top spires of the Mississippi River Bridge, cloaked in a gray, low fog.

"You could always get yourself another job," she said.

I yawned with sleep. "Yeah, like what?"

"You aren't that dumb. There are lots of professions you could go into."

"Such as?" I stood up, stretched, and put on my shorts.

"Anything. You could drive a bus, sell shoes, go into private practice as a—"

Just then, my phone started playing "*Who Shot the Sheriff*" on the bedside table. It was Bull. "Hello?"

"You got a college degree." As if I weren't on the phone, she kept talking. "You even enrolled in Loyola's school of law to be an attorney. You said—"

In a futile attempt to quiet her, I said, "Shhh. You'll wake Carla."

She climbed out of bed, slipping a nightgown over her forever gorgeous body. "Why do they always call you?" She was loud with sweeping-arm gestures, too loud for this time of morning. Bull said such open displays were "exposing your ass for others to see."

"Could you please?" I scooted into the bathroom, phone to my ear. "They need me."

Following me, she stopped by the bathroom door. "You bet your ass they need you. It's always you."

"Will you shut up?" I tried to kick the door shut with one leg, but she blocked it with her hip.

"If that's Bull, tell him to haunt someone else."

I covered the mouthpiece. "Quiet, dammit." Back to the phone. "Yeah, yeah, I know where."

"Tell Bull to kiss my butt!" she said in a loud voice.

Hurriedly, I scribbled down an address onto the pad I kept on the toilet tank and hung up. I glared at her.

"Well?" Her hands-on-hip.

"I gotta go."

"One of these days, you're going to get yourself shot. And what will I do without you? What will Carla do?"

"That's what you get for marrying a cop!" I said, lathering my face over the scar on my chin. "And Bull said, 'Hello, back.'"

"I should get a divorce," she said, her grass-green eyes blazing.

She shot me the bird when I left.

•   •   •

Maybe the fog had me on edge. Or maybe it was because I just had a fight with Jane, or because Mardi Gras came early this year and the street barricades for the parade routes were already up, making me late.

But mostly, I hated being late to a crime scene, joining my partner of seven years. The investigation scene was a service alley for trash collection and deliveries, running between two abandoned warehouses. Overhead, a tangle of electric and telephone lines hung from poles leaning like the Tower of Pisa.

"Zeke, over here!" Already on the scene, Bull stood, shouted, waving me over with his hammy hands from the sunless alley. Detective Bull was perhaps six-four or -five, making him four-and-a-half inches taller than I was, and fifty, maybe, sixty-pounds heavier. His nose had been flattened and straightened from his boxing days in the Navy. In point of fact, he was the best detective I've ever known. However, Jane's assessment was that Bull would make a good circus bear with a fez, juggling balls, and a little training. But she didn't know him like I did.

As I entered the alleyway, I saw two men slumped against the dumpster, looking as if they had just stretched out for a nap. Already, I knew they were dead. Deader than door nails, as Dickens had said. That was, of course, in violation of Louisiana ordinance R S 14:107, namely, vagrancy in public places. Not that the dead guys cared.

That morning, a thick fog had swirled in from the river on little cat's feet and curled around the base of the dumpster, giving everything a wet, depressing feel. All thoughts of an easy investigation left me.

But still, I got on with it, and took a deep breath of frosty air, reeking of urine and wet garbage, ducked under the yellow police tape, trying to keep my new L.L. Bean Duck shoes dry. Nearby, white and speckled pigeons pecking at garbage took flight while I skipped puddles. The Forensic technicians were gathering samples, while a CSI photographer snapped photos of the stiffs.

There was one corpse with his head thrown back, mouth open in an Edvard Munch *Scream*. Blowflies circled his head. And the breakfast I ate this morning, toast and coffee, wanted to crawl out of my throat, but I looked away, and took some deep breaths. The blowflies, unable to tell the difference between an open dumpster and an open mouth, took advantage and tried to fly into the corpse's throat.

The other dead guy's head had dropped forward, his chin on his chest, one hand outstretched in a puddle of water, the needle sticking out of the crook of his reed-thin arm.

Though I knew better, and knew he'd bristle, I went ahead and asked, "Did you check their clothes for ID?"

From his position, crouching like a simian over the bodies, Bull grumbled, "Let's just do the job." That was his favorite mantra, and the first thing he told me when I became a detective—*"Just do the job. And forget about all the bullshit!"* It was clearly the best advice I had received about the job.

About two hours later, working the crime scene, my phone played *"Come To The Mardi Gras"* by Professor Longhair, interrupting the gloominess of my work. Fumbling it out, I said, "Hello?"

"Hi," Jane said. "You still pissed about this morning?"

"No, I'm not—pissed." Since we'd nearly finished, I signaled Bull and walked towards the mouth of the alley.

"You could have fooled me the way you stormed off."

Over by the dumpsters, Forensics packed their bags and were getting ready to leave. It was clear that everyone had finished as the ambulance guys stretched out the two bodies—like mannequins—and zipped them into black body bags. Now, the blowflies returned to their normal fare in the dumpsters. I turned away, the sour taste still lingering on the back of my throat.

"You okay?" she asked.

"Yeah, sure. Why?"

"Oh, by the way you—something bothering you?"

I hesitated. "It's nothing." Following old habits, I never shared the details of my work with Jane.

When we first started going together, Jane would ask, "What did you do today?"

"Oh ... same old shit. Nothing," I'd say. Most of my job is routine—mostly boring.

Did she believe me? No—her arched eyebrow told me. "For all I know, you put on your uniform, go sit in the park with your buddies."

"We could," I grunted.

"Or sit in Tastee's eating doughnuts and drinking coffee." She rolled her eyes.

I grunted again. "That, too."

Finally, after stonewalling her a dozen times, she quit asking. That's the golden rule—Don't talk about it. Maybe that's why cops' wives are always filing for divorce 'cause we keep it inside. Our unspoken motto is: *What Happens on the Job, Stays on the Job.* Obviously, Vegas has nothing on us.

Just then, a cool wind blew down the alley from the river, and I felt its chilly breath on my face and neck. The swamp-water gray skies thinned in the morning sun.

Then I changed the subject. "Your brother picked Carla up for school yet?"

"Yeah, he did. Mark's chaperoning the class to the children's museum," she said.

Carla is mute. Nothing wrong with her vocal cords, but she just doesn't speak.

The quiet hung between us for a moment. "Did you fix her hair in those fancy French braids?"

"Yes, the way she likes it." Then, she seemed to hold her breath for a beat before asking, "You remember what today is, don't you?"

"Hmmm. That's a good question."

"Perhaps there will be a good answer?" She only waited two seconds before saying, "God, you're slow."

"No, I'm not," I protested. "It's our third wedding anniversary."

"Are. You. Sure? You don't sound very certain. If I recall correctly, you forgot our first year anniversary—some detective you are."

"Funny. That's Detective First Class. And, if I remember, you didn't say a word for a week."

"Hoping you'd remember on your own."

"I remember taking you to Commander's Palace with champagne and flowers to make up for it. Cost a fortune."

"You got laid that night, didn't you?"

"Hmm. Yeah." Yet still, my pulse quickened. "And I took you out again two weeks later."

"Can you blame me? I'm not one to prevent a man who wants to *atone* for his incompetence."

"Atone?"

"Repent. As in 'make up for guilt'," she said.

"I know what it means." I had to laugh. "But c'mon, atone for my incompetence?"

"Guilt is a better word. We all have something to hide. People are seldom what they seem," she said. "And you're no exception."

"You seem to know a lot about that," I said.

"I've looked inside people and seen blackness." She drew out the last words. "Knowledge unlocks doors."

"And modest." On that point, she was correct. It was true, she knew a lot. As an art dealer, she was one of the go-to persons for art collections in New Orleans. She had developed a list of wealthy, high-class clientele, seeking advice on investments—from Dadaism, French Realism, to Modernism, Cartoon Pop-ism. -Isms, I had never even heard of.

"You can't imagine." Her voice was barely above a whisper. On that point, she was also correct. Secrets seemed to swirl around her like the mist creeping in from the river. Although we had known each other for five years, screwed for four, married for three, Jane never discussed her past with me. *Never.* Whatever her memories were, they haunted her, and her alone—and did not include me. Early on, she gave me a stern warning, *"If you love me, you will not ask."* I loved her, so I did not ask. Our marriage had endured a lot.

Then, her voice changed directions, lifting like the pigeons in the alley. "Do you remember what the Third Anniversary gift is?"

"Let's see. Three years? That's wood, right?"

"Wood?" She laughed. "You're kidding me, aren't you?"

"Apparently, I am." I loved her laugh. Beginning with the first time I met her and heard her deep, throaty laugh, I wanted to hear it again. And again.

"No, not wood. You're ice cold." She waited.

Very often, we played the Hot/Cold game with each other.

She gave up. "It's pearls."

"Pearls. Huh, I knew that. Are you asking me to give you a pearl necklace?"

She laughed again, "Boy, you are slow. No, I'm asking for a million dollars," she said. "But, you're getting warmer."

Bull walked over beside me, and we watched as they wheeled out the men on gurneys with concertina legs. The bodies jiggled under the black plastic bag with every bump.

Bull arched his eyebrows at the phone.

I mouthed, *Jane.* He said, "Okay, I'll wait by the car."

"Who's there with you?" she asked.

"Bull."

"Tell him I'm sorry for calling him a *motherfucker* this morning."

"You didn't call him that."

"Well, I was thinking it."

I shouted to Bull, "Jane says *Hi!*"

Bull turned and nodded.

"Bull says he loves you," I told her. "And aren't you lucky? I think I might have some pearl beads left from Mardi Gras." I followed Bull to his car.

"Ice cold, Magoo. Mardi Gras beads won't get you laid tonight."

"Hmm. You want the genuine article? Can't promise a necklace, but will pearl earrings do?" Nearly a month ago, I bought a pair from Kay Jewelers, and hid them under my socks.

She laughed. "Now you're getting hot. You still picking me up at noon?"

"Noon? Lunch? Well..." I glanced at Bull. He narrowed his eyes, wagging his head. There was a backlog of cases. He held up his index finger. "Uh, I still have work to do. How's one o'clock?"

"No. Make it twelve."

"You're called pushy a lot, aren't you?" I got into my car and started the engine.

"I prefer the term *decisive*," she said. "And you, what name do you prefer besides *slow*?"

"Hmm. Believe it or not, *slow* is okay with me."

She laughed. "Try to make it at noon. One's okay. I've got a surprise for you."

"Am I getting lucky at noon?"

"Dirty perv, no, you're not. At lunch, you get a meatball po'boy."

$$\bullet \quad \bullet \quad \bullet$$

I swerved in and out of traffic on the I-10 in my black Ford Mustang, 390 GT, the same car Steve McQueen drove in *Bullitt* on the streets of San Francisco. Because it was two-fifteen and I was running one hour late, I gunned her hard to make up for lost time to pick up Jane. Listen, most cops love the sound of a hyped-up engine, and the thrill of speed, and the vibration up the seat into their butt. Me, I guess I'm no different. I love it.

I exited at the Canal Street Cemeteries and saw the same guy by the light, panhandling for change. He'd worn a groove into the grass where he limped daily, rain or shine. Unshaven and uncombed, he wore army camo fatigues and carried a cardboard sign. Was he ex-military? Or just a guy faking injuries? This being New Orleans, his existence confirmed the American Dream doesn't reach everyone.

Cutting through City Park, I saw the Lin Emery kinetic artwork, rotating on a twenty-foot pole like mythological steel knives cutting into the stubborn Louisiana air. As I steered closer, I spotted a blue-and-white cruiser parked at the curb with a patrolman crouched down beside the open door.

Immediately, I pulled over across the street and leapt out. But something about him screamed rookie since he was peeping over the cruiser's hood as if he were playing hide-and-seek. If anything, experience taught me to move slowly, to not startle him. When he detected me coming behind him, he whirled, pistol pointed at me.

"Whoa! Whoa!" I shouted, raising the palm of my hands, then flashed my gold detective's shield. He was young and baby-faced, eyes round as Rex doubloons, with a buzz-cut we used to call a flattop.

"I'm Detective Zeke Malone. Take a deep breath." He stank of sweat and fear. "What's going on?"

His voice trembled with dread and emotion. "It's... it's. I was walking in the building when I saw him," he stuttered.

There was a sudden twinge of apprehension in my chest because the building he was referring to was the Whitney Museum, and Jane was inside delivering a George Rodrigue *Blue Dog* for the president's office.

"Okay, take it easy. Who's him?"

"Him. A man with explosives."

Fuckity. Fuck. Fuck. My heart rate increased. Boy, do I hate when guys want to blow themselves up. Bits of brain, skull, shit stuck to the wall. Crap that would make the most devoted fans of *Game of Thrones* gag. Who knows what goes through their mind? Probably their way of saying to God, "You ain't firing me. I *Quit!*"

"Slow down," I instructed. "Where were the explosives?"

"Strapped to his chest," Buzz-Cut said.

Shitty. Shit. Shit. More crappy news. "Where was he?"

"Next to the elevators." His face was pale.

Needless to say, my heart thumped in my chest as I fumbled out my cell and punched the speed dial for Jane. Stay locked down. I wanted to warn her. After six rings, it went to voicemail. I tried again. Voicemail: "Lock yourself in the bathroom. Open only for the police." And I ended with, "I love you."

The rookie said, "He looked like a boy."

"A boy? Did this ... Bomber Boy say anything?"

"Yeah. 'Get out!'"

"Okay. Have you called it in?"

"l ... uh, l ... no." He looked as if he might pass out.

l told him to go back to my car and notify dispatch. "A 10-79. Got it? A 10-79. Tell them what you told me."

"Yes, sir. 10-ninety seven." Buzz-Cut scrambled away from me on all fours.

"No! it's a 10-79! A 10-79." *Damn rookie shock.*

Scanning the lower and upper windows, l saw no movement. And l listened for a moment—no sounds except the creak of the polished sculptured blades slicing the air. Typically, in police procedural TV shows, the Good Cop waits for backup. Patrol cars scramble, and tactical units arrive, and SWAT sharpshooters take up positions. When the negotiations fail, a hail of bullets takes out the armed perp, all in fifty-two minutes or less.

Now, I'm still not sure why I ignored the cardinal rule to wait for backup. Probably, it was that Jane was in the building and not answering her cell phone. How do you explain that Matters of the Heart don't have explanations or a reason?

"Aw, to hell with it," l said, checking my Glock 22, and leaving the safety of the patrol car even as Jane's words echoed in my head: *Zeke Malone, someday, you are going to get yourself shot.*

The voice in my head, the one who tells me when I'm about to do something stupid, was screaming: *Bloody Hell. You idiot!. Get back to your car!*

In my lifetime, I've done stupid sometimes. Other times, I've done nutty. But usually, I don't do them together. My main objective was to get inside and check on Jane. Slipping my earpiece into position, l clicked on the Bluetooth, and edged towards the building.

The front door was the revolving type. Beyond it lay the lobby, and still l saw no activity. Taking a sharp breath and exhaling, l pushed through the doors into a foyer. It was hushed as a pin-drop. The entrance smelled of floor polish and fresh paint. On my right, a man in a business suit and a woman in a red dress hid behind a guard's desk. We locked eyes. *Where?* l mouthed. The man raised a finger and pointed to the left. Left meant the elevators.

Moving quietly, I flattened myself against the smooth-icy marble wall, taking deep breaths. I held the Glock's muzzle down. Explosives. *Damn!* What if I set off a bomb? I tucked my pistol into my belt at the small of my back.

There was a rustling sound—a shuffling of feet from the hall. Okay, here goes; I peeked out and around, and my eyes took a second to adjust. There was a figure pressed against the elevator doors—not a boy, but he was young, all right.

And just then my blood ran cold—under a mishmash of wires, he wore a sleeveless big-game-safari vest; the bullet loops stuffed with sticks of pale-red dynamite.

In his right hand, he held a detonator the size of a roll of quarters.

A block of ice slammed into my stomach by what I saw next. I stopped breathing. *Stupid and nutty be damned.* I stepped out, putting my hand against the wall to keep from collapsing.

His eyes bulging with fright, the boy flinched and jerked his right arm towards me. His thumb quivered over the black button.

Standing next to him was a woman—his left arm in a choke-hold around her neck.

It was my Jane.

CHAPTER 2

The overpowering fear I felt was as pure an emotion as I possessed—the sight of her stabbed into my heart like a spear. Bomber Boy's lips were moving, but I heard nothing. My heartbeat drummed in my ears like a bass drum.

Jane stood frozen, eyes wide. In his hand, Bomber Boy's thumb trembled above the detonator button. He clung to Jane, as if she were a life preserver keeping him from drowning.

His voice finally burst through the thumping in my ears, and his words came through. "See. See," he stammered. "She's okay. Go ahead, Lady, tell him."

Jane nodded. "I'm ... I'm alright." Fear made her voice high and shaky.

Incredibly, from the time I spotted Jane and heard her voice, it took all of maybe fifteen seconds. But during that time, my mind raced through a thousand scenarios. How do I move her out of harm's way? Shoot him? Bring up my pistol? And where do I aim? His forehead, his face, his heart? Pray his hand doesn't convulse and trigger the bomb.

And I knew not a damn one would have worked. Then, I started operating on all those years of training. That's when Muscle Memory took over, and Detective Bull's voice whispering in my ear—*Just do the job.*

I willed my pounding heart to slow down, my breath to calm down, and my mind to focus. *Just do the job.* Deal with it. As my body relaxed, my senses heightened. Suddenly, I could hear shouting outside the building. Looks like Buzz Cut got through. Unbelievably, I could hear the rasping of Bomber Boy's breathing. Even from across the space between us, I smelled the fear radiating off him in waves.

Not wanting to think negative thoughts, I couldn't help but realize it was a big mistake coming in here, and a miracle if we got out here, and a bigger miracle if I didn't get us killed. But, when I spoke again, my voice was calm, steady, despite the horrid scene before me. "Good. Let's keep it calm."

Beneath the vest, he wore a white t-shirt with baggy khaki pants, immature-looking—No, it was actually more than that. I focused in on his features. His face was taunt and twitchy, shiny with sweat, black hair plastered to his forehead. He was the kind of kid in the diner who washed dishes but would never progress beyond busing tables and taking the garbage to the dumpster. Short for his age, he was maybe eighteen or nineteen. And but for the dynamite strapped to his chest, he didn't look dangerous. Just simple and scared.

"What do you want?" I began. "Are you trying to commit suicide?"

"No, no. I no wanna kill myself."

I leaned against the wall. "Well, what then?"

"Money." The word popped out of his mouth.

Is this what this is? A stick-up—in a museum? That made little sense. But nothing made sense, and now wasn't the time to figure it out. *Stay focused.* I stepped out farther. "How much?"

"What?"

"How much money do you want?"

"I want … a million dollars," he looked around, licking his bottom lip. "In unmarked bills," he added, as if repeating instructions.

"Wow, that's a lot of money. What are you planning to do with that money?" I forced a smile and threw out, "Buy a yacht?"

"No, no yacht." He pushed back his shoulders. "I buy a house for *mi mama.*"

"Good for you," I said. "She'll be proud of you."

He carried himself with a sort of childish embellishment, his chin tilted up with exaggerated nods.

"A million bucks? That will buy some fancy house, no?"

He grinned widely. "With a front porch, so she can sit in her rocking chair *en la tarde*. A big garden to grow tomatoes and bell peppers."

"And chickens," I added, remembering my grandmother's house in Boutte.

"Yes, chickens and a mango tree, and..." He didn't finish his thoughts, his eyes staring in the distance. Into a future that would never be.

"Sounds like it'll be a wonderful house," I said gently, taking one more step out.

All at once, a voice crackled in my ear. "Malone, what the *fuck* are you doing in there?" I couldn't believe it. Jojo Turner, head of Homicide, was speaking in my earbuds.

"Get the hell out of there!" he shouted.

This has to be a mistake! Of all the commanding officers, it had to be that sleaze jerk. He knew as much about police procedure as a monkey knew about brain surgery. How did he ever get to be Captain? Now, not only did I have to deal with the Bomber Boy, I also had to deal with Jojo, the *Cool*. We had a history, and it wasn't always good.

I held up my hand in a wait-a-minute gesture towards Bomber Boy. "Hold on, I need to talk to the coordinator." Turning my head, I pointed at the black earbud in my ear.

His eyes grew large. "Who's that?"

"He's the guy who's going to get you the money. Right?"

Quickly, Bomber Boy tightened his grip on Jane and swiped his face with the back of his hand, still holding the detonator. He shifted from foot to foot. "Okay. But no funny business."

I pressed my index finger to my ear as if it were an intercom button. "Jojo, he has a woman with him. A hostage. He wants a million. You got that? A million," I said in a loud voice for the benefit of the boy.

Jojo hesitated, then shouted. "What in the Jack Schitt are you talking about, Malone?! Are you crazy?"

Pleasantly smiling, I continued in a business as usual manner. "Yeah, that's right. A woman hostage. He insists—one million dollars." I nodded at Bomber Boy as he shook his head up and down vigorously.

Turner shouted, "Zeke, get the hell out of there! Our hostage negotiator is on his way! Let him handle it."

"No!" I blurted. "He doesn't want tens and twenties. I'm handling this. We don't need—"

Jojo cut me off. "What the hell, Malone? Move out of the way, damn it! SWAT is getting into position."

"No. Don't do that. He's got a woman with him." My throat shrank.

For several moments, Jojo didn't speak. Then his voice deepened, and I could almost hear him grinding his teeth. "Malone, I'm giving you an order! Move your ass *out* of there!"

"Afraid I can't do that, sir. I've got things under control here." My heart tripped in my chest. I wasn't turning this over to a negotiator. Not now. I needed to figure out a way to deactivate the detonator. But I needed time.

Then for some reason, my mind started flashing doomsday scenarios, but I shut them off. Concentrate. *Just do the job.*

Jojo's voice ratcheted upward. "Malone, I said—"

This was not going well, so I yanked the earpiece out. There was only one goal now, *Get Her Out.* I turned to Bomber Boy. No more bullshit. "You know, this is a terrible idea. But I have to tell you, you're going to die."

He cocked his head to the side like a confused dog and held my gaze.

"You're not getting out of here alive unless I help you."

He smacked his lips and opened his mouth to speak, but closed it, saying nothing. For a minute, he stayed silent, blinking. "Why would you help me?"

"Because of her. The lady. You don't want to hurt her, do you?"

He looked away, angry. "I will if I don't get what I want!"

"Come on. Your *madre* didn't raise you that way. Look at her." He needed to see Jane as a person. Not as an anonymous piece of meat. Not as a hostage.

"Look at her!" I shouted, instantly worried I'd pushed him too far.

His head pivoted. His eyes blinked rapidly, trying to comprehend my words and their meaning.

"Lady, what's your name?" But Jane said nothing. I imagined, too afraid to speak. "Tell him your name." I said more forcefully.

That got through to her. "It's ... Jane," she said in a tiny voice.

"Jane. Very good. Jane, say hello to—What's your name, pal?"

He looked back at me. "They—they said not to give my name."

There it was again. Someone else giving the instructions.

"Alright then. Say hello to Jane."

He mumbled something under his breath to her.

"Now, isn't that better? I know you don't want to hurt her," I repeated. "What if she were your mother? I'm sure she's someone's mother."

That seemed to hit home, and he nodded.

"Ma'am, do you have children? Tell him about them."

She struggled to get the words out. "My daughter is—twelve-years-old."

My mind called up a vivid image of Carla sleeping this morning. I kissed her head, feeling her warmth beneath the locks of hair. She brushed hair from her face with the back of her hand before snuggling into her pillow. My throat closed, but I forced myself on. "What's your little girl's name?"

When she spoke again, her voice had taken on a more resolute tone, low and steady. "Her name is ... Carla."

"There you go. Now, do you want to rob Carla of her mother?" I asked.

Staring down at his feet, he shook his head.

At a more rational time, I might have come up with another course of action. Yet this was the one I chose, and as I spoke, I could not overcome the sense of dread, though I knew it was the only plan I could think of to get Jane out. "Right. Here's what we're going to do. You let Jane go, and I'll take her place. Fair enough?"

His face jerked up. "You?"

"Yes. Me."

He narrowed his eyes. "How do I know you're not trying to trick me?"

I locked eyes with him. "You've got my word."

Perhaps Bomber Boy realized he had gotten in over his head. Perhaps, he realized he had made a big mistake. Or possibly, all he wanted was for this to end so he could go home to his mother. Whatever was going on in his mind, I was not privy to. He took in a deep breath, blew it out. And now, suddenly he muttered quickly, "Okay," looking drained and defeated.

I felt weak with relief, feeling my heart hit a fast drumbeat, but determined to have this come to an end. After a moment of hesitation, I said, "Alright, first, lift your finger away from the detonator."

He did not move. His mouth hung open, eyes riveted on his trembling fingers.

"Off the button," I commanded. "What if your finger slips? We're all dead. And then your mother won't get her house with the porch. No garden. No chickens in the backyard. *Nada*—"

He moved his thumb aside and gripped the detonator till his knuckles turned white.

"*Bueno*. I need to inform the money man she's coming out." I pointed at my earbud.

He shot a sideways glance at her, then at me, barely able to get the words out. "Okay, go ahead."

I slid the earbud back in. "Jojo, you got that? The hostage is coming out."

Jojo was silent for a moment before his voice came back on with an odd tone I couldn't quite fathom. He growled low, as if speaking through clenched teeth. "Do you have your police-issued weapon?"

I closed my eyes. My pistol still pressed against the small of my back. "Yeah, but that's absolutely not going to frigging happen. We're making a swap! The hostage is coming out."

"Get out! Snipers got him in their sights!"

I couldn't believe my ears. I didn't know whether to cry or scream. "No, don't. Please." I opened my eyes, fighting to control the tingling in my hands, my chest. I had a bad feeling about Turner. *Terrible.* "Jojo, don't do this," I pleaded. "Let me handle it."

"What's going on?" Bomber Boy asked, his eyes darting back and forth like a trapped bird.

"Just working out the details." I calmly told the boy, as I craned my head and scanned the outside, through the glass doors, at the parking lot.

I realized the same thing happened midway through my rookie year—a call from a bank of an armed robbery-in-progress. By the time we pulled up, three guys came sprinting out, firing their weapons. Everyone ducked for cover, but I leaned over the hood of my cruiser, took aim, and took out two. I turned my service revolver towards the third robber, but he was having none of it. He threw down his weapon. It was my first genuine success as a patrolman. It secured my reputation and got me on Detective Bull's radar, later my partner.

But that's history now. This was different—Jane was involved.

When I turned around, red dots were dancing on his chest. Without thinking, I stepped out, blocking their aim, knowing they were on my back. The hair on my neck stood up.

Jojo shouted, "Are you nuts?! Move out of the way!"

"I have this under control. She's coming out. His thumb is off the trigger."

"Then take your shot, Malone. TAKE YOUR SHOT!"

I couldn't. Now, my breath is coming fast, near panting. Oxygen fading and my brain is *fading*. My vision focused on Jane's face. Her skin ashen. Her eyes—the ones I loved—grass-green with specks of gold.

"TAKE YOUR SHOT!" Jojo screamed. "TAKE YOUR FUCKING SHOT, YOU MORON!"

The red dots slid up to his forehead like glowing drops of blood. I stepped again to block the shots before they fired but it was too late. It felt like a Mack Truck hit me. The bullets spun me around like a top off-center, like a pirouette of death, and slammed me into the floor.

The shuffling of feet echoed in the hall. I forced my eyes open. Bomber Boy was dragging Jane towards the stairwell exit. She glanced over her shoulder, and our eyes locked for a moment—she mouthed, *I love you,* before the door slammed shut.

I tried to lift myself but blood squirted from my shoulder. Sprayed from my neck. I fell back and began crawling.

Before I reached the staircase, I heard shouts, breaking glass.

And then, the thing I had dreaded most—*Gunshots*—BAM, BAM, BAM!

Followed by an explosion in the stairwell. A blinding white light blasted out the window of the exit door.

"No! No! No!" I thought, or maybe I screamed.

The last thing I remember was fire and thick black smoke shooting out the window like the exhaust of a jet, with acrid fumes choking me. Feeling lightheaded and seeing a sudden vision of Jane's face, saying, "Poor, dear. It'll be okay."

Then darkness. As I thought I heard her call my name from a great distance.

CHAPTER 3

TWO YEARS LATER
A WEEK BEFORE MARDI GRAS

The two year anniversary had come and gone. Not the wedding anniversary. Her death.

Since that day two years ago, there wasn't anything I hated more, and I mean anything more maddening, more irksome, than having to wait for someone. Never was in my DNA, but since losing her—it's been worse—but there I sat, on a hard-backed bench in Jackson Square, waiting. Unlike two years ago, this day was a typical Louisiana Hot morning, one week before Mardi Gras. Still, I hadn't started sweating under my blue, lightweight sports jacket just yet.

High above me, I watched an amoeba glob of black birds dive-bombing out of the sun, like Kamikaze pilots, towards the Pontalba. Just when it looked as if the flock would crash into the roof, they swooped into the branches of the crape myrtles, cackling like the birds from the Hitchcock film.

I recall little about the weeks and months after the explosions. It's all a big blur. In fact, my first memory was waking up six weeks later in a hospital bed, disorientated, achy, groggy, and in pain. A doctor told me the bullets shattered my shoulder and nicked my carotid artery. I lost half my blood. The left side of my neck, a patchwork of stitches, clamps and dressings. If you ask me, it's a good thing I don't remember.

By the time I regained consciousness, Mark and Doris had buried Jane in a family mausoleum upriver from New Orleans, near a small river town called Edgard. I never visited. To my shame, not even once.

Had Jane lived, she would have been dressing Carla in her school uniform—blue shirt, beige skirt, shiny patent leather Mary Janes. Braiding her long hair in the special French braid that reached the middle of her back. The one only Jane knew. If she had lived ...

Now, I was feeling a mixture of irritation and worry, missing the comfort of my service weapon, a Glock 22, that hung from my belt. There was something primitive about the weight of a weapon riding my hip, but I turned in my badge with my gun when I resigned. Years ago, I had a cousin that lost his foot in an accident. He said he could still feel the toes, feel the itch, the cramps. Phantom pain is the term he used to describe the itch. Couldn't scratch it.

At first, I thought this was ridiculous. How can I have phantom pain for a weapon?

"Come on. Come on," I muttered while waiting for the lady who today took her sweet time. Pretending to read the Times-Picayune, I asked myself, "Why am I here?" Bills. There are bills to pay. And the money for this gig was too good to pass up. The shit we put up with for a buck.

Jackson Square buzzed with the usual clot of Mardi Gras tourists gawking at the homeless derelicts sunning, and schoolboys chasing pigeons. A clown in over-sized shoes, red fright wig, and Polka Dot bloomers, fashioned balloon dogs for the children. Nearby, a gang of college revelers had a head start on the celebration, sitting and dozing on the grass.

I waited twenty minutes when, out of the corner of my eye, I realized I was being watched—the balloon clown stood at the end of the bench. I ignored him. He took a moment to gather himself, then strode towards me, shoes flopping. Yet, hoping to avoid him, I reopened my paper and ducked my head into the Sports Section to read about the Saints. Now wasn't the time for distractions, and I sure didn't feel like talking, especially to a clown.

No such luck.

"Aren't you Zeke Malone?" he asked, unplugging his red rubber nose from his face, revealing flesh-colored skin underneath. It contrasted with the white greasepaint and candy apple red lips. He was slender as a tent pole under his baggy Pagliacci outfit. Slung over his shoulder was a beat-up leather tote decorated with tassels. Deflated balloons and a Clarabell horn peeked out.

Ever since the explosion, I've been hard of hearing in my right ear. But he had a loud voice. I lowered my newspaper and gave him a hesitant smile. "Yeah, that's me."

He shuffled his feet before thrusting out his hand. "I'm Fred LaForge. Do you remember me?"

Underneath the face paint, I couldn't place him, but his features looked familiar. He leaned forward, pumping my hand, looking as sincere as a clown with purple hair could look.

"I used to be a cop," he said.

Now, it all came back to me like a sour taste. "Sure, Fred, sure I remember." Then, I had just made detective when he joined the police. He was an awkward rookie who never should have qualified or been allowed on the force. However, the NOPD was desperate for new recruits. And, if memory served me, he got his partner shot and almost got killed himself. Not wanting to appear too friendly, I didn't invite him to sit, but he plopped down next to me on the bench anyway. His purple gag shoes were at least size eighteen, and he splayed them out in front of us.

So much for looking inconspicuous, an ex-cop and a clown sunning themselves on a bench in the morning sunshine. Then, he started reminiscing about the good old days and how he missed them.

"It's all good, unless they shoot at you," I said.

"Yeah, right, I didn't like the shooting part." He told me how he took a bullet in the line of duty. Filled me in about what he'd been doing since leaving the police force and his lousy pension. Reduced to earning money working part-time jobs as a Balloon Artist around the Quarter. Now, he called himself Noodles. I nodded my head at Noodles now and then, trying not to encourage him.

That's when she entered from Decatur Street past the wrought-iron gates close to Cafe' du Monde. Her name was Kitty Fowler, and she wore a white silk dress above the knees, a white blouse, and a yellow sun hat that flopped over a corner of her face. Two joggers nearly broke their necks, trying to glimpse her long, tanned legs. With a strut like that, she would draw stares anywhere in North America. Remarkably, Kitty looked like the freaking double of Michelle Pfeiffer. When she walked by, men stopped listening to their wives, heads craned around, paused in mid-bite of their beignets and Lucky Dogs. A few whistles and catcalls echoed through the Square from the yellow hard-hats repairing a water line.

Meanwhile, my unwanted companion continued babbling about his injured leg as she strolled across the open space. She glided like a runway model, circling Andrew Jackson, sitting astride his rearing stallion. Then, she exited the Square, crossed the pedestrian walk area, and entered the doors of St. Louis Cathedral, just as the tower clock beneath the middle spire struck eight o'clock. The Cathedral's triple steeples overlooked the French Quarter, towards the Mississippi River, all the way to Algiers Point on the West Bank.

I couldn't afford to lose her. "Look, uh ..." Having forgotten his name already.

"Fred. Fred LaForge," he said, looking a little disappointed.

"Right, Fred. I'd like to sit and talk, but I've got an important meeting," I said, fake-checking my watch.

"Let's get together sometime." He stood with me.

"Sure, anytime." I said, hurrying away.

"Here's my card." So he followed me a few steps, pushing the card into my hand. "If you ever need an entertainer for your party, I'm your man. Or should I say—clown? I've got other costumes, as well."

That's the trouble with surveillance, getting distracted, which means you hurry to catch up and still try not to get made. I hustled out of the Square to the open stone-paved plaza in front of the Cathedral. Already, street musicians were warming up, tarot-card readers and fortune-tellers unfolding their tables, and artists hooking their canvases on the fence.

A few tourists milled in the door, and I cut ahead of them into the sanctuary. I paused and from the back tried to spot her in the shadows. She was nowhere to be seen. *Damn. Had I lost her already?* Silhouetted in the sunny doorway wasn't the best spot for my eyes to adjust to the dim cavern of the church. I stepped inside. Noise echoed off the high ceiling murals, making voices garbled, while the interior smelled of incense and wax candles. It seemed ten degrees cooler than outside.

Still unable to locate her, I walked along the back pews, scanning the middle benches. A dark-haired man and a woman with a Spanish mantilla over her hair knelt in the midsection while a classroom of children on a field trip wiggled and squirmed among the aisle rows.

She couldn't have just vanished.

Then, I allowed my gaze to drift towards the front of the church, where I spotted her kneeling at the altar. Her white blouse almost glowing in the gloom, her yellow hat bowed.

There were empty seats on the back benches, and I slid into one next to the stained-glass windows. When Kitty Fowler left, I figured she wouldn't notice me, and I'd continue the tail without detection.

What puzzled me was why she'd come here. Locals seldom come here to pray. And she was a local, not a tourist. Look, people aren't always what they seem. Making a pilgrimage to the "Big Easy," to commune with God, especially with Mardi Gras a week away, doesn't make much sense. But what do I know? Some of the exciting things about New Orleans, the French Quarter in particular, is it draws all types—tourists, artists, panhandlers, saints, and the proverbial sinners alike. When I was young, the Quarter used to be one of my favorite hangouts, but not anymore. Too many terrible memories. Right now, my thoughts drifted to Jane—she would be choosing her jewelry for a Mardi Gras ball, maybe even the pearl earrings she never saw. Since her death, I hated sitting still, like now, in the shadowy cool Cathedral, too many bad memories.

Uh-oh, she's on the move again.

The attractive blonde in the yellow sun hat stood up. But instead of returning to the back, she lingered in the front, seemingly admiring the statues, and crosses, and rows of flickering votive candles. After a moment, she strolled to the right side and vanished behind a large stone column. I waited for a minute, but she did not reappear.

The next thing I knew, the creak of a door opening and banging shut told me she exited by a side door.

Oh shit! I hurried to the front, rounded the column, and saw a heavy wooden door with a lighted red EXIT sign above it.

I paused inside the door, realizing I might blow my cover if I went barging out. But with no time to waste, I pushed the emergency exit open and stepped into the bright morning sunlight. Immediately, the door slammed shut behind me, and I stood in the medieval-looking flagstone alleyway, leading to Royal Street.

When I looked left and right, she was not in sight. And unless she had Usain Bolt speed to dash sixty-yards in six-seconds—in high heels, no less—she had pulled a Houdini on me. She had evaporated into the humid air.

Believe me, even in the spookiest parts of the *Vieux Carre*, people don't dematerialize like ghosts. *Was she still inside?* The door wouldn't budge even as I yanked and shoved against it. I debated running around to the front and re-entering the Cathedral. *Think?* Unless the door I heard opening and shutting was not the side exit, but behind the altar. That meant she entered the fenced-in St. Anthony Garden, behind the building, with the statue of Christ.

Ready to curse myself if she slipped away, I hurried along the spiked, ten-foot-tall fence that ran around the garden, scanning for her.

No one. Crap! Had the two year layoff dulled my police skills that much?

Surrounded by the Quarter, St. Anthony's Garden is an oasis of quiet behind a tall wrought-iron fence. The space contains rose bushes, clipped hedges along red brick pathways, and concrete benches for meditating. The funny thing is, I've never seen anyone on the grounds. In the center of this park, stands a statue similar to the Christ the Redeemer in Rio de Janeiro. A mini-me Jesus on an elevated pedestal, hand outstretched with a benevolent smile. Now, he seemed to reproach me for my carelessness. I was thinking—*what will I tell the husband? Your wife is lost.* I stopped and clutched the cast iron bars like a felon gazing between the bars of his jail cell. *She has to be in there somewhere.*

That's when a glimmer of white caught my attention—her white skirt—on the ground barely visible, behind rows of red rose bushes. I took a few steps along the fence for a better view. Her yellow hat slouched over her head. If she was playing hide-and-seek, she was the best I'd ever seen because she was deathly still.

CHAPTER 4

Within twenty minutes, St. Anthony's Garden was swarming with policemen.

Almost instantly, the cops strung yellow POLICE LINES DO NOT CROSS tape, crisscrossing the garden, strung from the iron fence and alley like spider webs.

She laid face down in the trim grass. Her sunglasses caught in the spindly branches of a boxwood bush about six feet from her head, as if she'd flung them off when she fell. One of her three-inch slingback heels lay beneath a flowerless rose bush. The white dress had hiked up to mid-thigh.

To my surprise, the lead detective investigator of the homicide was my old partner—Detective Bull—from the Eighth District. It had been two years since we last spoke. He visited me a few times in the hospital when I was in a coma, and later, after I woke up. But I turned him away since I didn't want to see anyone.

Bull squatted over the body of Kitty Fowler like Sasquatch in a suit on his haunches, brow furrowed in concentration. He had not changed at all, still talked with the dead, trying to communicate with the increasingly rigid Mrs. Fowler.

His appearance, however, had changed little, except for one thing. His hair was still a mess, and his shirt looked as if he didn't own an iron. But he had grown a thick mustache that hung down on both sides of his mouth like bicycle handlebars, reminding me of old, grainy photos of Pancho Villa, serious, unsmiling. With department approval, he later said.

I stood off to the side, watching, replaying the events leading up to finding her body. Old habits die hard, I suppose. Can't teach an old dog ...

Of course, no matter how many times I've seen dead bodies, brutal death always surprised me. One time, when I pissed off my unit commander, Jojo Turner, he reassigned me to the Ninth Ward. A typical sweltering summer night might include a drive-by shootings, stabbing, and a broken beer bottle jabbed to the eye. You name it, I've seen it all. But the surprise of death never went away.

For an instant, as I stood near the body, an image of Jane's body torn to lifeless pieces, blood-splattered, popped up and jolted me. My heart drummed. Though only for a second, mind you, as I clenched and unclenched my jaw muscles, and shook it off hard, just as the psychiatrist had suggested. It's called Changing the Trigger Points, Dr. Lucy in the Sky lectured. "Choose a substitute for your disturbing thoughts." So jaw and fist clenching it was. "It is a gesture that might be a throwback to our reptilian brains, a desire to bite someone," she said. I suppose she's right. She also said, "Try pulling your head out of your ass and concentrating on the task at hand."

Bull rose, stretched. I heard the creaking of his knees from ten yards away. Placing his fist onto the small of his back, he walked backwards, never lifting his gaze from the woman. He turned towards me, but he wasn't seeing me. Instead, he gazed over my shoulder at the statue of the New Orleans' Christ.

Bull walked to the fence and looked back, studying the layout.

A woman detective approached him and began speaking. I couldn't hear the conversation. Pretty but unsmiling, with a stern expression, lean and dark, not short, but she stood about two-heads shorter than Bull. She wore a black suit, a gold detective shield dangling from her neck. I could see the bulge of her gun under the coat. She finished talking, then left, putting a cell phone to her ear.

"Who's that?" I asked when he stepped back.

He turned to watch her exit the garden. "Who? Birdie?" He looked at me. "She's my partner."

"Birdie? Is that her name? How is she?"

"Yeah, Detective Bertha Birdsong. *Birdie*. She's okay."

After a moment, he cleared his throat and gestured to the dead lady. "So, why were you following her?" He pulled his compact notepad from his inner coat pocket.

"I told you, the husband hired me to follow his wife."

"Why?" His beefy hands scribbled notes.

"Dr. Fowler, her husband, suspected she was unfaithful, carrying on an affair."

We all stood looking down at her. She was a looker, all right.

"Go figure," Bull sighed.

Outside the fence, a back SUV with a blue light flashing, the word Coroner on the door, drove past police barricades and parked on Royal Street. A short, balding black man in a white lab coat and a metal case slung over his shoulder made his way inside the Cathedral and into the garden. His name was Michael Jordan, head of the coroner's office.

"I'm surprised to see you here, MJ. Didn't know you made house calls?" I said.

"You know how it is, shorthanded for Mardi Gras," he said. "Good to see you, Zeke."

So, if you haven't guessed by now, his mother named him after the phenomenal Michael Jordan, probably the greatest basketball player of all times. I hoped she wasn't too disappointed because MJ, that's what we called him, was the polar opposite. He was short, skinny, and memorable for his starch-white, stiff lab coat, and glasses that looked like aviator googles. A couple of antennas and he'd look like Doctor Ant. And a great friend of Bull's and mine.

MJ and I spoke for a few minutes. Then, MJ, with the help of the EMT technicians, turned the body of Kitty Fowler over, and the CSI photographer snapped pictures.

A dark circle of crimson, four inches wide, had stained the center of her white blouse, spreading around a neat hole you could cover with a quarter, like a bullseye. Even in death, she was beautiful.

MJ shook his head, staring down at her. "Jesus, she probably never knew what hit her."

While MJ did a preliminary investigation, Bull returned to questioning me. "So, she was fucking around?"

"Boy, you police sure know how to toss around fancy legal jargon," I said.

"Fucking-A," He twisted his head, looking up at the sky. "I think I learned it from you."

I shrugged. "If you say so. Glad you learned something from me."

As the CSI photographer continued to take photos, the sun slid behind clouds, and a damp breeze drifted in from the river. The shrill, whistle-tunes from the steam-calliope on the *Riverboat Natchez* wafted in— *Take Me Out To The Ball Game*—-mixed with the rhythmic chug-chug of the tugs.

With the gentle wind, the scent of lilacs, her perfume, rose to meet me. Jane sometimes wore that fragrance, and a familiar ache stabbed at my insides.

Bull continued. "So, you followed her, and she ends up shot."

"He paid me to follow her, not be her bodyguard," I said.

Bull re-read his notes from the flip-pad. "Now go over it with me again—I know, I know," he held up his palm. "You told me already. But you know the routine?"

Of course, I knew the routine. I'd worked homicide before. Having witnesses repeat their story, over and over, might reveal a remembered fact that could lead to solving a case. The trick was to listen. Bull was well read. He loved Sherlock Holmes' quotes: *Nothing's more deceptive than obvious facts.*

Now, I was on the other end of the shovel. I sighed, recounted my story once more.

MJ interrupted us, wanting to know if we were going to the Half Moon tonight.

I wasn't ready to socialize yet. "Sorry," I said.

"Well, I have to go. They found a body in the swamp in New Orleans East," he said, throwing his double-top specimen case over his bony shoulders. He returned to his black SUV and sped off.

Bull started in on me again. "Why didn't you wait outside the Cathedral instead of inside?"

"Should I have expected her slipping out the side door? Because Dr. Fowler said she'd go in the Cathedral but never came out."

He cocked his head. "Her husband knew this?"

"Yes, he did."

"He had her followed before?"

"Yes, he did. By his cousin."

Bull rolled his eyes. "Wait, don't tell me. An amateur, right?"

"Worse. His cousin's a Jefferson Parish Honorary Sheriff. Even doctors make mistakes."

"Hmm—so she sneaks into a church to cover an illicit affair. Smart." Bull shook his head.

"Alleged affair," I corrected. "Makes sense to me, though. While she's inside, Mrs. Fowler gives confession and asks for forgiveness."

"Say two Hail Marys before the tryst and two Glory Bes afterward." He said. "This is getting interesting. OK, then what happened?"

"Like I said, I followed her out and found her dead."

Bull motioned for me to follow. We moved around the body, searching for evidence in ever-widening circles till we walked the edge of the garden inside the spiked fence.

Bull pointed his fingers like a gun. "The shooter stood outside the perimeter and—" He dropped his thumb. "Bang! Clean through the heart."

"Must have used a silencer." I offered.

"Did you hear anything?"

"Nothing," I said. "How could someone stand on the sidewalk, shoot a pistol in broad daylight and not be seen by anyone? The crowds are already here. Mardi Gras is in a week."

"You know, you're sounding like a policeman again?" Bull turned to me and leaned in. "And that worries me." He touched my arm. "You may have forgotten. You don't *need* to hang around anymore. Collect your fee and get on home."

That fact had not escaped me, and I understood. "I know," I said.

"You know, but will you?"

The bell on the Cathedral rang eleven times. Bull looked up at the steeple and stroked his Pancho Villa mustache as if he were caressing a cat's tail.

"Nope. I can't."

"You can't or won't?"

"Both."

Bull frowned, rubbing his chin. "You haven't changed? Have you?"

To be honest, I haven't. But I tell him, "I'd like to think so."

"I worked with you for too long," Bull said. "You're like a dog with a bone. Can't let it go. It's bugging you right now that Dr. Fowler hired you to watch his wife. And she ended up dead."

"I can walk away if I want."

He glared at me. "Ha! Now you sound like an alcoholic. Or a drug addict."

I grimaced. "I know."

"You know? You never walked away before—always were a hard-headed son-of-a-bitch. But I guess that's what made you good." He messaged his temple. "The best I partnered with."

"We made a good team," I added.

"Why don't you come back?"

The coroner's assistant rolled her body into the black cadaver bag. Her fish-white arm flopped out to the side, and the assistant tucked it inside before pulling up the zipper.

I wanted to look away but I couldn't. I took a deep breath and admitted, "Look I can't." Eleven-o-five in the morning, and all's *not* well.

Bull nodded.

Then, despite myself, I turned to him. "Look, Bull, this is probably not the right time to ask. Or the right place. And it probably breaks a dozen rules ..."

Bull frowned again, eyeing his watch intently as if it were broken. He shook his wrist and held it to his ear.

I fumbled for the words but steamed ahead. "Let me tag along. I won't be in the way. You won't regret it."

Bull lowered his arm, studied the open notebook in his hand and tapped it with his pen as if he were beating a small drum. He stopped, began kneading the back of his neck, his gaze fixed on me. "All right." He tucked the pad into his shirt pocket.

"You won't regret it," I repeated. I wanted to give him a big hug. But I didn't.

He coughed and cleared his throat. "Right, but just this time. To observe. Understood?"

"Damn right. Just like the old times," I said.

CHAPTER 5

A week earlier, across town in his Bywater art studio, when Martin Covert stood in front of his latest canvas and scrutinized it. Really scrutinized it, the painting made him want to puke.

He was tired of the dark swamps and his trademark purple alligators that adorned his canvas. Critics called it Pure Cajun—based on the old voodoo tales told to him by his grandmother from New Iberia—which was a lot of horseshit he used to sell his paintings to tourists because she died before he was born.

Martin Covert considered himself to be a talented artist. In fact, one of the best. After all, the critics praised his work. One even calling him a genius. *The next Big Thing to come out of South Louisiana.* Ahead of his time. The next Blue Dog. He had been the proverbial starving artist at the start of his career. The critics loved his art, but sales were few. Until an unnamed benefactor, his Patron Saint, started buying his works through a man by the name of Goldenstein.

Setting aside his brushes, he took a beer from the mini-fridge in the corner and chugged it down. Suddenly, his phone buzzed. *Oh great!* It was a call from Goldenstein, the neat and compact man who always wore a dark suit and tie. Goldenstein was the mysterious middleman for the even more secretive Patron Saint, a person Martin had never met and knew nothing about.

"Hello, I see you called me earlier, Mr. Goldenstein. My apologies, I was painting."

"Yes, I'm sorry. I had forgotten," Goldenstein said in his precise, unhurried voice. "You do not take calls while creating your art."

That was a lie. He told him that because he didn't want to be bothered.

Like a dream come true, the guardian angel bought the entire collection of his paintings, every single one of them, and now had an exclusive contract to purchase them all—and not on the cheap either. The collector, whoever he or she was, paid top dollar, securing Martin's future. But now, he'd had enough. He signed them all, but had gotten to where he gave them numbers instead of names. Now, this was his fortieth or forty-fifth one. He didn't keep track anymore.

"How can I help you?" Martin said, taking a gulp of beer.

"Do you have the next two paintings you promised?"

"Uh, yes, I've completed them." That was another lie. They were only half done.

"Good, then we can expect immediate delivery."

"I'm sorry, but they are not dry yet."

"That's all right. Your sponsor would like to view them now. Would you be so kind as to place them in traveling wet frames?"

"Well, yeah, I suppose—"

"Good. We'll be by to pick you up."

"Me?"

"Yes, he wants to meet you." And with that, he hung up.

Meet me? That's new.

That was part of the problem. Painting at someone else's demands, their timetable. But the money. Ah, the money. Too good to pass up. He could pay off his bills, care for his mother in her nursing home. But he longed for the good old days when he could paint whatever he wanted, whenever he wanted. Since he had not finished the canvases, he hurried to his art studio and packed the still wet paintings.

Before he knew it, though, someone banged on his door. *They can't expect me to have it ready.* The two goons stood outside the door. They gave Martin the creeps. The bigger one was tall with huge shoulders like bowling balls on a rack, and a round head, eyes and mouth where the holes would be. The shorter one was compact and muscular, with short blonde hair on a round face with liver-lips, reminding Martin of the photos of Nazi guards in concentration camps. Neither one ever spoke.

Behind them stood Goldenstein, dressed, as usual, in his conservative suit, tie, and collar. He looked like some type of professional, an attorney or accountant. He stepped forward between the two men, smiling. "Good evening, Martin. May we come in?"

Before Martin could answer, Goldenstein motioned with his head, and the two muscular thugs brushed past Martin into his studio. Martin hurried after them. "Be careful. They're still wet," he called. But they seemed to ignore him as they placed the two canvases into the wooden frames and fastened the clamps. They seemed to know what they were doing, covering them in plastic sheets, taping them closed.

"Very good," said Mr. Goldenstein. "Shall we go?"

Martin was still in his shirt, covered with paint spots. "But I need to change my clothes," protested Martin.

"It doesn't matter. Your benefactor wishes to see you. Immediately." Goldenstein said as Bowling Ball ushered Martin out the front door and the Nazi followed behind, paintings in tow.

They loaded the paintings into the back of a large, shiny black van with lots of chrome and blacked-out windows.

No one spoke as they climbed in.

"What's he like?" Martin asked, breaking the silence.

Goldenstein said, "You'll see."

They drove for an hour to a small wooden dock on the edge of Lake Bourne. A small, expensive looking speedboat with a roundhouse waited for them. Martin got out and followed the trim Nazi in the black suit. "Watch it," Martin warned the two men as they threw the paintings into a locker under the cushioned seats.

The skiff sped away. The boat twisted and turned through waterways, lined by high marsh grass, and overhanging moss-draped trees. Martin was lost and worried. Though Martin painted about the swamps, he seldom ventured into it, hated the water. Could not even swim. It grew dark as the last rays of the sun faded behind the cypress that lined the banks.

Soon, he saw a shallow lagoon lighted by spotlights. The boat slowed. A long wooden pier led up to a boathouse. Beyond that was a large, gleaming white mansion rising out of the foggy swamp like a castle in Disney Land.

The boat pulled up to the docks and Goldenstein leapt off. He led the way up the brick steps, through a manicured garden of rose bushes. Martin hurried to keep up.

Standing at the top next to massive columns was a figure all in white, like Colonel Sanders, if you will, but one who looked as if he ate a bucket of finger-licking chicken with every meal. His neck was an inner tube, and he looked as wide as he was tall. He held a drink in his hand and he smiled down at Martin.

"Ah, we meet, Martin," he said with a jolly laugh. "Welcome to my humble abode."

Martin was not sure if this was a put on, as the home was anything but humble, but he played it straight. "Thank you. It's a pleasure to finally meet you."

The colonel shook his hand with fingers like Vienna sausages. He placed his heavy arm over Martin's shoulder and gave him a warm squeeze. The short, dumpy man stunk of bourbon and sandalwood. Martin should have felt welcome, but something about the Colonel made him ill at ease.

"Martin, forgive me for getting started without you, but may I offer you something to drink?" he said, gesturing with his glass at a silver drink tray.

"Well, yes ... I—"

"Good, Goldenstein, fix something for our guest."

Goldenstein handed Martin an expensive, aged bourbon that Martin recognized from when he was a lowly art student slinging drinks. He downed it in two gulps, though he had intended to sip it. "I'm sorry. You seem to have me at a disadvantage," Martin said as the bourbon burned down his gullet. "You know my name, sir, but I don't know yours."

"Oh, forgive me. I usually keep it a secret except for my closest associates. I've given myself a new name—Theodore Onyx."

"Onyx, like the precious stone?"

"Yes, that's it, *exactly*," he said, leading Martin into the interior of the mansion. "Please allow me to give you a nickel tour of my home."

What type of nut was this? thought Martin. *Calling himself after an exotic jewel?* But he did not pursue the thought further, because his attention was riveted on the painting in front of him. To his astonishment, a Salvador Dali painting hung in the hallway—the missing *Woman at the Window!* He recognized it immediately. Not the one everyone recognizes, but the prequel he painted. Martin could not believe his eyes. He had read that it sold twenty years ago to an anonymous bidder for millions. And not seen since.

And here it was. Martin stopped in his tracks. "Is that the—?"

"Yes, it is." Onyx cut him off, giggling like a teenager. "The original. And not a copy."

Good God, this guy must be loaded. Unbelievable. Martin stared at the corpulent Colonel Sanders. His face was round with chipmunk cheeks, blonde hair, an unglamorous comb-over. And cherubic Kewpie doll lips as if from a medieval painting.

Martin scanned the room. It was then that he realized the statues and paintings displayed in the mansion were worth millions. There were paintings by Rembrandt, Monet, Modigliani, Picasso, and Kandinsky. And against the far wall, lighted by small accent lights, was a Vincent van Gogh. *No, it couldn't be. That one was lost since the Second World War.*

"You like?" asked Onyx.

"It's fantastic," muttered Martin. "How did you gather such a collection of the world's masterpieces and stay under the radar? I've never heard of you."

"On the sly, Martin." Onyx smiled. "On the Q.T. When I decide to pursue something, I usually get my way." He led Martin into an adjoining room, where sixteenth-century tapestries hung on the wall and the finest blue Dutchware sat on display shelves.

The entire mansion was like something out of *Citizen Kane*. "It must have cost a fortune," Martin stammered.

Onyx laughed and set his drink down on a marble table. "To tell you the truth, Martin, most of them I bought on the cheap. You see, they always say value is in the beholder's eye."

"I think it was 'love is in the eye of the beholder.'" Martin interjected.

"Love. Value. What's the difference? After an artist dies, the value either goes up or down. If it cannot stand the test of time, its value decreases." He paused and stared at Martin. "Or, the value increases—after he dies."

He led him through several rooms, all filled with splendors of the art world. "You see this all?" He spread his hands out in a casual gesture. "It means *nothing*. It's like collecting stamps or baseball cards. As a child, I collected plastic model airplanes. I had every conceivable WWII plane ever built. From the *B-52s Flying Fortress* to the *Flying Tigers*. They hung from my ceiling. Later, I collected coins, cars. Do you know what I did with them?"

Martin shook his head.

"I sold them to finance my next interest. My next collection."

They walked into another room filled with Roman and Greek sculptures.

"It all means nothing," he said, smiling. He turned to Martin. "But you. You are the one with value. For you are the creator."

Martin felt a warmth on his cheeks. "Thank you," Martin mumbled. "It's unusual that I hear such words of praise from such a collector."

The tone of Onyx's voice changed. He placed his hand on his Martin's shoulder. "But Goldenstein tells me you are tired of doing the purple alligators?"

Martin tried to keep the surprise out of his voice. "Uh, I ... not that I'm tired." But in actuality, Martin was *sick* and tired of the goofy 'gators. Purple! My god, it had been a joke when he started. The joke got out of hand. And too profitable to change. He'd been at a party with musicians and artists in the French Quarter. He drank till he blacked out. When he woke up the next day, there it was—a purple alligator hanging from a tree. He must have painted it after stumbling home, but had no memory of it. The painting sold faster than any of the others. It paid the rent for the month. What else could he do but paint another? It sold faster than the first. Now he found himself in the classic artist conundrum: do what you love and stay hungry and homeless? Or paint what you despise and grow fat in your own home?

Martin again slammed his drink back. He was feeling light-headed. "I ... I just wish to go in another direction," he said, his cheeks feeling flushed.

"Oh, that's too bad. I rather like the little purple critters. They were cute and your best sellers."

"Don't get me wrong, Mr. Onyx. I'll be eternally grateful for your support, forever and always."

Onyx frowned. "In fact, it's the one thing that you have done that will be your legacy."

That's a chilling thought. Martin wasn't sure how to reply to that. All he knew was that this fat man, in his too-tight white linen suit, was not smiling now. Onyx gripped his shoulder a bit too tightly and gave him a hard stare that sent a frosty finger up his spine.

The fat man continued. "One cannot be certain of what will live beyond his days. You've studied art, my friend. Van Gogh, in his lifetime, sold only two paintings—both to his brother."

Martin nodded, confused. *What point was Onyx trying to make?*

Onyx paused by a white marble statue of a nude discus thrower. The fat man crouched with difficulty in front of a Roman gladiator's statue. He put out his hands, stroking the statue's thighs, his face only inches from the figure's crotch. "What determines the value of anything?" He stared up at Martin. "Supply and demand. If there are a million widgets, but no demand, their value goes down. On the other hand, if there are only a few widgets, and the public wants those widgets, the price goes up."

Onyx grabbed Martin's arm and struggled to pull himself upright, his breathing raspy. Two black dogs ran into the room and began sniffing Martin's legs. His crotch.

"Supply and Demand. Art does not differ from baseball cards. Scarcity is the key that dictates the price. When is too much, too much? Won't you have another drink, Martin?" Onyx signaled to Goldenstein, who seemed to have a drink always at the ready.

Martin took it and gulped down the drink. *What is this old fool getting at? I need to get out of here. Now.*

Onyx said, "Are you sure you will not reconsider? The inventory would benefit from a few more alligator paintings."

"No. I must do this," Martin stuttered. "I must move on."

"Very well. I can't force you if you don't want to."

"Thank you, Mr. Onyx. I appreciate that."

"The two paintings you brought with you. You will leave them with us, of course?"

"If that's what you desire," Martin said. "But they are not quite done. I—"

"Oh, that's perfectly all right. They may be more valuable incomplete. The last purple alligators by Martin Covert," he said, walking away.

Martin wasn't sure what to do. So he just stood still.

Onyx said over his shoulder. "Mr. Goldenstein will take you back to the boat landing. It's been nice doing business with you."

Onyx disappeared through the doorway before Martin could say more.

Soon, Goldenstein appeared, and Martin followed him back to the boat, noting his hair was neatly combed and his back straight. The two thuggish guards sat by the boat. Nazi drove, while Bowling Ball sat, staring into the night, and the roar of the two outboard engines drowned out any conversation, so no one spoke.

Martin began sobering up as the cool wind hit his face. He tried to unravel what Onyx had said as they zig-zagged into the swamp. However, it seemed to Martin that they were going in the opposite direction from which they came. Martin had no way of knowing where they were headed. In the distance, to his relief, he saw lights through the trees. Yes, he was eager to get off this boat onto dry land.

The blonde one killed the engine, and the boat lurched forward, toppling Martin off the seat. The boat stopped, rocking side to side, while the darkness wrapped around them like a blanket. *Is there a problem?* Frogs croaking and night birds screaming in the trees. Mosquitoes buzzed his face.

He turned towards Goldenstein. "*What* are we doing *here?*" he cried.

No one answered. Martin peered into the darkness, heart tripping in his chest. Nazi turned on a spotlight, lighting the bottom of an upturned boat, floating about twenty feet away. A life preserver and oar floated next to it.

Mr. Goldenstein turned towards Martin. "Mr. Onyx was not happy when you announced you would not paint any more purple alligators."

"I'm sorry," said Martin as he felt a loosening of the bladder—he had to pee.

"He does not take kindly to those who betray him."

"Now, wait a second! I didn't betray him." Martin protested. "If he wants more purple alligators, I'll do more. It's just that—" Suddenly, Bowling Ball jerked him from his seat and threw him overboard. Martin struggled to get his head above water, but he was no match against the powerful arms that held him under. He gulped water, clawed at the arms, choking. Flaying his arms in panic, he tried to grab the side of the boat. Anything.

And then, Martin had the dark realization that this was it—he was going to die. As the darkness closed in, Theodore Onyx's words came to him: "The value of an artist's work goes up after his death."

CHAPTER 6

It had been over two hours since someone had put a bullet into Mrs. Kitty Fowler. Bull stood in St. Anthony's Garden behind St. Louis Cathedral, moving to the next stage of investigation: fact gathering. His eyebrows furrowed as he gazed at the spot where the body had lain between the flower beds. The grass was barely disturbed. MJ and the coroner attendants had already moved the body.

I lingered off to the side, working through new ideas and thoughts about the case. Yet, nothing came to mind. Bull had already okayed my tagging along, and I intended to make myself helpful.

"Maybe the bullet didn't come from street level. Maybe someone shot her from one of those balconies." I gestured upward at the two and three-story Pre-Civil War apartments with green hurricane shutters and wrought-iron balconies. On the riverside of St. Anthony's Garden was Pirate's Alley, resembling the narrow uneven cobblestone streets of Europe. It was also the home, for a short while, of the Nobel Prize winner for literature.

Bull said, "Doubtful that anyone stood on the balcony of William Faulkner's old apartment and shot her."

My eyes followed the metal spiked fence to the police barricades, which held back the crowds and street artists.

After a minute, he motioned me to follow, and we left the garden. Circling the Cathedral, we soon found ourselves on Royal Street. From behind the police barricades, we surveyed the art galleries, shops, artist studios, and apartments. In this part of the

Quarter, everything about the street seemed commercial, appealing to the tourists.

"Who do you think shot her?" Bull began.

"Don't have a clue."

"The husband?"

I shook my head. "If he planned on knocking off his wife, why did he hire me to follow her?"

As he ran a hand through his hair, Bull seemed to consider this. "He wanted you to be a witness?"

"He didn't need me to witness her death. We're sitting in the middle of the French Quarter. Plenty of working folk and tourists to see the action go down if that were his aim."

"The lover?" Bull asked.

I wagged my head again. "Oh yeah. And who might that be?"

"I don't know. You were the one tailing her."

"If she was having an affair, I never saw it."

"What did she do?"

"She dined out, went shopping, drove aimlessly," I tell him. "And then she returned home."

"You think she spotted you?" he asked.

I pursed my lips. "Doubtful. How is that even a question?"

"Sorry. Did she ever hook up with someone? Sneak off without you noticing?"

"Not that I observed. She was alone all the time."

Bull was about to say more when Detective Birdie approached him. "We've tried reaching the husband a dozen times. Still no answer. Hold on." She took the phone from her pocket, swiped the screen, and put it to her ear. Listened for a half-minute. "Thanks." And hit the end button. "Dispatch tried, as well. No answer." She flicked her ponytail till it flopped over one shoulder.

Bull tugged at his bottom lip for a moment and asked, "How about his office?"

"He's retired. We sent a car by his house to knock on the door." She shook her head, and the ponytail fell down her back. "No answer."

"Okay, Birdie, keep trying."

She nodded, as if he didn't have to tell her that. She was compact, more legs than upper body. Maybe she had been a sprinter in high school or college. Or maybe she had the genes. Or maybe not. The severe expression never left her face, as if to tell everyone that she was all business. I'd seen it with other women cops: *Don't underestimate me just because I'm a woman. Don't flirt with me; I'm not here to make friends, I'm working.*

She looked at me, wrinkling her brow, openly regarding me from top to bottom. "You used to be Bull's partner?" Whatever and whoever she was, she wasn't shy.

I nodded. "That's right."

"Yeah. He's mentioned you now and then."

"Now and then?"

"Yeah."

I said, "Good, I'm sure."

She took out her phone and answered. "Yes," she said, without answering me. I couldn't tell if it was a sneer or a snort as she turned and walked away from me.

Bull and I walked along the barricades, avoiding the man holding a microphone and a cameraman interviewing pedestrians. Instead, we spoke with three street artists impatient to hang their paintings on the fences. This was one of the peak times of the year for doing business. If they lost Mardi Gras sales, they suffered.

"How long?" shouted a tall man wearing a black beret and a paint-splattered shirt, like a French artist from *An American in Paris*. All he lacked was a pencil mustache. He guarded a pushcart piled high with canvases and brushes, folding chairs on hooks, and a red and yellow beach umbrella on top.

Bull stopped, furrowed his brow. "When we finish."

"This couldn't happen at a worst time," French Beret complained. "I'll go broke."

Bull exhaled. "Be patient." Softer. "Soon."

We approach the building facing the back of the Cathedral on Royal Street. It was a two-story Creole cottage, done up in the Old World French Quarter style. Small balconies jutted out on the second floor in front of wooden shutters. Fuzzy pea-green ferns hung from wicker baskets.

Two businesses occupied the building: a bookstore and an art gallery. A lanky policeman with a knobby Adam's apple told us the elderly owner of the Royal Street Books only came in on Mondays and Tuesdays. "Closed the rest of the week. We're trying to contact him."

Bull nodded.

Next door to the bookstore, the sign above the door read Le Chat Noir Art Gallery. Large gaudy paintings propped in the windows all with the same theme—the silhouette of a drunk man, bottle in hand, lurching against a crooked Bourbon Street lamp post. The background was the always-glowing-brothel-red. We jiggled the front door. Locked, but we noticed movement inside. Bull rapped on the glass panes.

"We're closed!" a man's voice shouted.

Bull rapped again.

A man, dressed in black, with an unhappy expression, appeared from behind a framed canvas.

Bull flashed his badge, and the man said, "Oh," with a look of surprise. He unlocked the door, and as we entered a cramped picture gallery, a silver bell jingled above our heads. Oil and acrylic paintings hung from the walls and crammed onto wooden racks. An assortment of canvases, ranging in sizes, from tiny miniatures to gigantic, ten-by-eighteen feet, were strewn across the gallery/studio.

He identified himself as the sole owner and artist of the *Le Chat Noir* Art Gallery. Said his name was *Clive, one name only*. He was a handsome man, mid-thirties, with a square jaw, the kind on male models in a Giorgio Armani suit in glossy magazines. Or in ads selling expensive Rolex watches—close-up of the chin and wrist only. This was only my impression, but his features were out of proportion. His forehead appeared smaller compared to the rest of his face. And he smelled of sandalwood.

I do not, in fact, start off disliking a person because of their appearance. However, as with his paintings, I disliked Clive on sight.

"How can I help you, Detectives?" He smiled, his teeth glinting in the overhead accent lights.

"You heard what happened out here?" Bull began.

His smile fell away. "Not really. They blocked the street."

Bull pulled his notepad from an inside coat pocket. "We're canvassing for details. Something you might have seen? Anything out of the ordinary?"

"As I told the policewoman earlier, I was in the back doing inventory and didn't notice nothing until the police arrived." He was tall, lean, and athletic, with jet black hair combed straight back— very stylish. A hairdresser took monumental pains to make it appear casual, making him look more like an actor than a painter. He wore a black pullover sweater, black pants, and a small oval St. Christopher's medallion around his neck.

"What's upstairs?" Never shifting his gaze, Bull motioned towards the ceiling with his chin.

"My storage room and I do portraits up there—sometimes."

"A studio?"

"Yes, would you care to see it?" He volunteered without prompting. "I could show it to you."

He led us through a door into a back-office cluttered with stacks of papers, a computer, printer, and a yellow mini-fridge. Mr. Coffee shared a desk with empty frames and shipping boxes. Swirled on the window ledge, a midnight black cat sat, watching people pass on the street. When we entered, it stood and stared at us with bold, green eyes. Two yellow spots above its eyes gave the illusion of a four-eyed cat. Clive stroked its head, and the cat sniffed at his fingers before licking them.

We climbed a steep and narrow staircase to the second floor. When we reached the second-story landing, Bull exhaled, and the owner unlocked a door.

"Sorry for the mess. I haven't used it for a while," he explained, stepping aside to allow us into his art studio. The aroma of linseed, oil paints, and the piney, sweet smell of turpentine filled the air. Like the messy office downstairs, his artist's workroom overflowed with wooden frames, blank canvases, easels, and assorted chairs. Shirts, dresses, and costumes hung from a metal-clothes rack on wheels, like bellhops use.

Bull scanned the room. "You said you do portraits up here?"

"It's been a while."

"Last time?"

"About six to eight months ago. Actually, it was from a photo." He fidgeted.

We made our way around stacks of cardboard boxes blocking the French doors leading to a tiny balcony. Peering through the slates, I saw the back of the Cathedral and the statue of arms-spread-Jesus in St. Anthony's Garden.

Clive straightened up a pile of paintings that had toppled over. "Who got shot?"

"How did you know about the shooting?" I asked.

Clive looked surprised by the question. "The policewoman who came around earlier mentioned it."

Bull reached down and righted a fallen stool. "Hmm, well, a woman died. You hear anything?"

"Who, me? Nothing. I was in the back room, unloading canvases. As I said."

Bull thanked him, and we clumped down the narrow stairs. The four-eyed cat was nowhere to be seen. We stood outside the Chat Noir surveying the street while Bull regained his breath. French Beret caught our attention waving at us. He mouthed, *"Please."* Putting his hands together as though in prayer. Bull sighed and waved at two police officers, who started taking down the barricades.

He turned towards me. "What are you going to do?"

"I hadn't thought about it," I said. When I was a cop, I hated leaving a scene without at least a few concrete leads to follow.

"Not that it matters now, since you aren't a policeman anymore," Bull said.

"I might go back to my office," I mumbled.

"You could." He nodded. "Have you tried calling him?"

"Who?" I asked.

"The President of the United States. Who do you think?"

"I already tried to reach the doctor by phone," I said. "But, like Detective Birdie said, *No answer.* As I see it, I've got three options."

"Just three?" Bull frowned. "Okay, what's the first?"

"I could go to the office."

"Go on. Two?"

"Or I could go drive over to his house on my own and investigate."

Bull cleared his throat. "What's your third option?"

"Or I could follow you to Dr. Fowler's house."

A shadow passed over his face. "Zeke, you've got a fourth option."

"What's that?"

"Since you aren't a policeman, you could forget about it and go home," Bull said.

I shrugged.

He gave a halfhearted shrug back. "You're still not gonna let it go, are you?"

"You cops think you know everything," I joked.

"Damn right." Bull shook his head and rubbed the side of his face. Then he sighed.

I sighed back.

"Okay," he responded.

"Okay, what?" I breathed deeply.

"Follow me to his house—but it's unofficial," he muttered. "You're still not involved."

"*Damn* right," I confirmed, almost cheerfully.

CHAPTER 7

I eagerly followed Bull's beat-up police-issued LTD as he turned off St. Charles to Washington, into an area called the Garden District. Two hundred years ago, this locale was home to the plushest pre-Civil War mansions of prosperous plantation owners, silk-stocking merchants, and successful slave runners.

Not surprisingly, Doctor Fowler's three-story, elegant antebellum home sat only a few blocks from historic Lafayette Cemetery Number One and just two streets over from Commander's Palace, the highly rated, four-star restaurant where the wealthy dine. And yet, only a few blocks from the river, where poor families sat on stoops living in a different world, living on welfare. Each block farther from the river, a home cost a half-million more to purchase.

I parked on a side street under a canopy of oak limbs.

Bull stood by the curb, looking at a Queen Anne mansion one block over, cloistered behind a spiked fence. "I've seen this place before. They used it in the movie, *Interview with A Vampire*. "That's Anne Rice's place, right?"

"Could be, don't know," I said.

As I observed the turrets and towers beyond the wall, I realized that wealth puzzled me. While growing up in Midtown, a working-class section of New Orleans, with double shotgun houses and corner grocery stores, my neighbors were cooks, brick-layers, bus drivers, and my uncle, a NOPD cop, who lived a block over. *Did I envy all this wealth?* Perhaps my answer was *No. Maybe? Yes. I just didn't know how to gain it myself, and it always evaded me.*

We walked up the curving redbrick steps to the stately home. The first thing that caught my attention were the six white Corinthian columns and the broad, wrap-around front porch. I could picture Scarlett O'Hara standing between the pillars and waving a silk-lace handkerchief.

I wasn't sure why I had come. Was I feeling guilty? Though I could have avoided it, I felt it was my responsibility to deliver the bad news. Rather than have a policeman knocking on his door with an impersonal, "Your wife is dead."

Things did not quite seem right; the house was quiet, no lights. Bull rang the doorbell, and we heard muffled chimes in the interior. No answer. After a minute, he pressed the bell again, before banging the golden lion-headed knocker. The thuds echoed in the house.

Bull walked to the edge of the porch and peered down the side. "You've been here before?"

"I have. Once, when Dr. Fowler first hired me."

Bull leaned back, scratching his lower back, looking up, as if he expected someone to shout to us from the balcony. Then he cupped his hands against the tall-glass windows. "Looks like nobody's home," he said.

I glanced around. "You think?"

"What's in the back?"

"A patio. Banana trees," I said.

Leaving the porch, we made our way along a narrow, shady walk between the house and an ivy-draped brick wall. I led the rest of the way in the dim alleyway, stepping cautiously, aware of too many stories of guys shot by jumpy homeowners with itchy trigger fingers. *But that's the world nowadays.*

A six-foot-high wrought-iron gate blocked our path, but it was unlocked. I hesitated before pushing it open and stepping through.

"Dr. Fowler?" I called out. The flagstone patio looked like a postcard picture courtyard in the French Quarter, complete with ten-foot spreading umbrellas, teak Adirondack chairs, palmettos, and cane palms.

We stood waiting for signs of life. Red and yellow goldfish swam in a koi pond under a 3-tier bubbling waterfall complete with water lilies. We circled a few gigantic, sand-colored terracotta pots with green, exotic-looking ferns.

The rear sliding glass door was open several inches.

"Hello!" Bull called into the opening. *Nothing.* We exchanged glances and stepped to either side of the patio door. Somewhere in the shadowy interior of the house, a TV played.

"What do you think?" I asked in a hushed tone.

"He isn't home," Bull said.

"Or maybe he's dead," I said.

"Maybe." Bull took a deep breath and let it out. "Somebody killed his wife, right?"

"Right."

"Hell, maybe they went for a twofer." He hitched back his coat, revealing his service weapon.

"He could be in there bleeding to death," I said.

"Could be. Only one way to find out." He loosened the trigger strap before sliding it out in one quick motion. He held it two-handed, close to his chest, barrel pointed upward. I slid the door all the way open. We stared at each other, both of us inhaled deeply, and nodded.

"Police!" he shouted. "If anyone's in here, show yourself." *Nada.* We stepped over the threshold, then side-stepped avoiding being silhouetted by the light. *You never forget old routines.*

To our left, we found an empty dining room with a dozen chairs surrounding a large oval table covered with a white lace tablecloth. Each place had three crystal glasses, plates, soup bowl, shiny silverware, and napkins folded like swans.

To our right was a kitchen. It smelled airy and was spotless. Rows of pristine pewter pots and frying pans hung from hooks in descending size. Everything looked new, as if never used.

Next, we entered a living room with windows for walls, looking out to the tree-shaded garden and three-tier fountain. The room was decorated in modern Scandinavia that seemed out of character with the antebellum exterior. The tables were of exposed silver metal pipes holding up thick glass, minimalist style. Chairs and lamps were beige leather. The white marble floor shined like ice.

The ground level was deserted, so we crept to the second-story on a carpeted, curving staircase. I hoped to God we would not find a bloody body. Still, I stepped through the open bedroom door, expecting the worst. Rumpled bed sheets hid no corpse, thank you very much. On the floor, a red, very short baby doll nightgown and a pair of black lace panties lay discarded. The clean, white-tiled master bathroom was empty. Likewise, in the second bathroom, with its pink-tiled bathtub complete with a sauna and hot tub.

Bull holstered his pistol, letting out a huge breath. "Well, what will you do now?" he asked.

Clamping my eyes shut, I inhaled the warm scent of her bath. I detected through the steam expensive bath oils and shampoo. And I didn't think of the dead woman lying face down behind the Cathedral. Nor of her missing husband. But rather, I thought of the nights Jane and I would bathe together, washing each other's back. "You know, every time I bathe with you," she said. "My breasts come out smooth as silk." Then we'd slip into bed and make love. I shook the images off.

Bull walked out into the hall, pivoted, and stared at me. "Well?"

"I'm going back to my office," I said.

CHAPTER 8

Because of the portly nature of his body, five-foot two, three-hundred and five pounds, Theodore Onyx fought sleep apnea and woke as if he were being choked by an invisible assailant. His breaths came in gasps, lungs crying out for precious oxygen. His phone woke him, but he was lightheaded and disoriented and couldn't answer for a few minutes while he sucked in enough air to become clear-headed.

Finally, he picked up his phone, his voice breathless, "Alright, alright, who is it?"

The even, unhurried voice of Goldenstein said, "It's me."

Sucking on a prednisone inhaler, Onyx then asked, "Well, how did it go? Was the job accomplished?"

Goldenstein pictured Kitty Fowler and the bullet that took her out, lying in the garden behind St. Louis Cathedral. "Yes, just as planned."

"No fuck-ups?"

"None that I can see." His informant had watched the police while that little squirt of a coroner worked over her body. "It was a clean kill. Mission accomplished."

Onyx's breathing had slowed down, and he relaxed. "Mmm. None that you could see? What about the ones you couldn't see?"

Goldenstein hesitated a moment. "It went off without a hitch."

"You sure?"

"She'll never interfere with the operation or open her yap again. At least not in this world."

"Who's covering the case for the police?" Onyx asked.

"Detective Bull. You know him."

"Bull. I know him alright." Onyx took a big gulp of water to clear his throat. "He's supposed to be good. He doesn't quit."

"Yes, but this one will soon go into the cold case files," Goldenstein said. "Unsolved."

Onyx was silent for a moment. "Okay. Call me if you think of anything else."

"... Okay."

"That didn't sound too certain. What is it?"

"Well, you remember the guy whose wife died in the explosion?"

"Zeke Malone! Yeah, that bastard," Onyx said, his voice all but shouting. "I should remember him. It's the only time I got busted for—"

"He's not a cop anymore."

Goldenstein could hear Onyx's loud breathing over the phone. "Then what's he got to do with it?"

"He was on the scene of the murder," Goldenstein said. "First one there."

"What the hell was he doing?"

"Apparently, Kitty Fowler's husband hired him to follow her."

"Hired him to ..." Onyx paused. "Yeah, go ahead."

"Malone is now a P.I. He was trailing her when she was shot."

"Why did the doctor want her followed?" Onyx said.

"I don't know yet. Maybe he was the jealous type? Or suspected her of fooling round?"

Silence.

Goldenstein asked, "Should we do anything?"

Onyx hesitated. "No, that might open a can of worms. Just keep your eyes open."

"On both?"

"Yes. Do nothing. Follow Detective Bull's progress, and as for that asshole Malone, leave him alone. He'll go away on his own." There was a pause. "Anything else?"

"No."

The phone clicked off.

CHAPTER 9

Since Dr. Fowler was not in his mansion in the Garden District, I left Bull to explore further, and I drove back to my office in the Bywater.

Nearly always Bull was right—I had difficulty leaving well enough alone. *Let it go. Yeah*, I thought. *Let it go.*

My office, in the Bywater, an area next to the Quarter, may not look like much, but it possessed a certain Crescent City charm. My workplace sat to the rear of a boarded up, hole-in-the-wall bar gone bankrupt years ago, a sign still said BEER-75 Cents. Finding my office meant cutting down a narrow, cobblestone alley, up an unreliable wooden staircase, holding an unreliable banister, to a landing overlooking a small inner-courtyard. Originally built as slave quarters, the building was over one-hundred-seventy years old. Demolished and remodeled over a dozen times since the Civil War. The building outlived the first owners, the Lusitania sinking, a fire on the first-floor, the War to End All Wars, WWII, Vietnam, and the unending Middle-East conflicts. Now, it served as my humble office in the twenty-first century.

Parking is on the street, unless you ride a bicycle. As I got out of my car, I saw a little girl driving nails into the creosote telephone pole with a small, blue-handled hammer. She was maybe eight or nine in cut-offs and a sagging t-shirt, tacking up fliers. Not very tall, she stood on a two-step kitchen ladder. On the ground, a stack of posters sat with a rock weighing them down so the wind wouldn't blow them away.

When I passed her on the sidewalk, she jumped down, gathered her posters, and ran after me.

I turned, and stopped, unprepared for her question.

"Have you seen a little dog around here?" she asked. She had large, dark-brown eyes. Chocolate eyes, and for a moment, she reminded me of my stepdaughter, Carla.

I shook my head. She handed me a flier. The photocopy was of poor quality. The dog was a mixed-poodle of some sort, with frizzy-white hair sticking out in all directions. Its two black eyes were like lumps of coal pressed into fur.

"No, I'm sorry," I said. "How long has she been gone?"

"She's a he. A week. His name's Wally," she said.

I shook my head.

"Wally's about that big." With trembling hands, she held them apart, showing a short distance.

"So, he was a little dog?" I said.

"Yes. I've had him since he was born. He loves doggy treats. Lifts his paw and shakes your hand. Are you sure you haven't seen him?"

We stood in the middle of the sidewalk, and two boys on bicycles swerved around us. "No, I have seen any dog that size."

Her lower lip quivered. "He loved to be hugged ..." Tears began running down her cheeks.

"Where did you lose him? This Wally?"

"Over there." She turned her head and pointed at a yellow shotgun double on the next block. A tall woman stood in the doorway watching us. Was she glaring? "I left the screen door open ... It's all my fault, Mama said. Serves me right for ..." She tried to stop crying.

"I'm sorry. I'm sure he'll show up. They all come home when they get hungry," I said. After a week, of course, I knew it was a lie. What else could I say?

She covered her face with her hands; some fliers tumbled to the sidewalk.

"I'll keep an eye out for him." I helped scoop up the loose papers. "If I see anything, I'll call you. That's your number at the bottom?"

"Yes, would you? Oh, thank you. Thank you," she said, taking my hands in hers. Tears had dampened her tiny fingers.

I wanted to pull them away. I wanted to apologize. But for what? What can you say to a child in distress? I told her, "It will be okay. Everybody loses something. You can always get another."

Why did I say that? As I watch her trudge away, bony shoulders drooping, I couldn't help thinking of Carla, and the mother she'd never see again.

My heart hurt, and I hurried from the street into the carriageway leading to my office, feeling a familiar sadness. My shoes clicked across the cobblestone alley into the courtyard with unkempt ferns and bougainvilleas. I clumped up the aged wooden stairs to the second-story landing, fumbling my key into the door. On the frosted-glass panel was stenciled *Crescent City Detective Agency.*

Walking like I hadn't slept in a week, I slumped behind my desk, trance-like, staring straight ahead at the empty office. Like in dream, a bottle of Jack Daniels materialized before me. I could almost taste the amber liquid passing over my tongue, the hot sensation bouncing in my stomach, and the blessed release it would bring. I had not felt such a strong need for a drink since … I clenched and unclenched my jaw, sat upright, and tried to shake it off. *Focus on the job,* I reminded myself.

The LSU clock on the wall hit the top of the hour and played the first bar of the "Tiger Fight" song which shook me back to the present. I inhaled and stared around, as if I had just awakened from a dream. Well, this is it, my little domain. A desk, a couple of chairs, a Goodwill couch, a filing cabinet, and a bathroom so small, my knees bumped the door when I sat down. And a coat-rack next to the wall where I hang my faded black-and-gold Saints windbreaker with my LSU and Astros caps. Through the window, over the flat-roof of the shuttered bar, I viewed the city skyline. Smudged thumbprints of gray smoke drifted over the river.

Think. Think, now where was he?

And for an instant, I couldn't be sure if I meant Wally, the white poodle, or Dr. Fowler. I inserted a K-cup into the Keurig, which sat on the salvaged gray filing cabinet. I put in my Saints mug and pushed "large-mug" button. What a marvelous invention. No more making a pot when all I wanted was one cup. I sat at my desk, waiting for the coffee, studying my day planner. I had cases pending, but nothing I couldn't put off.

When the coffeemaker quit hissing, I collected my cup and took my first sip, leaning against the cabinet. *Coffee—Good. Booze—Bad.* And then I pushed back my sleeves, like I was going to dig a garden, and slid open the drawer. Thumb, thumb—there it was, a hanging file labeled *Dr. Fowler.* Returning to my desk, I settled down to study the dozen yellow legal sheets of hand-scribbled notes. I gather them up and sat, sipping my coffee, and reading.

Then I found a note I had forgotten making: *Loves raising orchids. Greenhouse.* But where? I seemed to remember something about a burnt-out family plantation downriver from New Orleans? I Googled: *Plantations.* Too broad. Then the name: *Fowler* and *Plantations.* I got a hit.

It will probably yield nothing—a wild-goose chase. But I decided that anything was better than sitting here, thinking about a dead wife, a missing doctor, and a little girl's lost poodle.

CHAPTER 10

The Fowler Plantation would not appear on any of the tour guide maps along the Mississippi River. The old plantation originally sat about twenty-miles downriver on the West Bank of the river, and once had been one of the finest cotton, sugarcane, and slave farms in Louisiana. But, since the Second World War, the main building sat boarded-up, having lost its *Belle of the South* charm, looking haggard like Bette Davis in *Hush, Hush, Sweet Charlotte*.

However, fate was to intervene, and a dozen years ago, three young men under the influence of who-knows-what had the bright idea of breaking into the deserted Fowler Plantation in search of Voodoo ghosts. Inside a pentagon star, the ceremonial candles started a fire and the entire building burned to the ground. Only the greenhouse survived.

This was where I hoped to find Dr. Fowler.

I drove over the Crescent City Connection to the West Bank and wound my way along the lonely road that followed every twist and turn off the river. Hidden by trees and unkempt brush, I almost missed the turnoff to a rutted dirt road. My tires bounced and kicked up dust for two-hundred-yards before I spotted the black timbers piled on each other, like the charred bones of a dozen dinosaurs.

Beyond a cluster of scrub elms, palmettos, and ferns, I spotted the glass-cathedral roof of the greenhouse. The tire tracks lead me through the tall grass, where I parked and walked till I reached it. The muffled sound of classical music wafted through the tall grass and underbrush. I saw the slender figure of Dr. Fowler inside, dwarfed between rows of red and yellow orchids and ferns.

Knocking on the glass panes, he startled and turned, eyes wide. I had surprised him. Then he smiled and waved me in. He was a thin man in his mid-fifties, maybe early-sixties, with gold-wire-rimmed-spectacles and thinning blonde hair, parted to the side. He wore an olive-green apron with big pockets over a pale-blue dress shirt, sleeves rolled up. No tie. *What was a such an old guy doing with such a pretty young wife?* No wonder he hired me.

Placing a water-spritzer bottle on a potting table, he removed his gloves and turned down the music. "Mr. Malone, what a pleasant surprise to see you."

I greeted him, and what I had to tell him made my mouth feel like cotton.

"Do come in," he said. "I was just finishing up watering my 'babies' here. Most of what you see in this greenhouse are Phalaenopsis, also called 'Moth Orchids.' Did you know orchids take seven years to produce flowers? They are epiphytic, which means they grow anchored to other plants. But they are non-parasitic and draw nutrients from humidity and any rotting parts on the plants. Most people do not understand orchids. They assume orchids are difficult to cultivate, but I've found that if you understand what it is an organism desires, you can make anything thrive. This is as true in plants as in humans. Often, humans are much more mystifying if only because they aren't always transparent about their needs and wants ... Oh, listen to me!

"I am certain you have not traveled from the East Bank to hear my philosophies on life, humanity, and epiphytic organisms. Please come, let us have some iced tea," he said, caressing a purple flower. His fingers were long and smooth, the hands of a surgeon, with only a hint of a tremor. "Unfortunately, I have no maid out here, so you will just have to make do with tea from a thermos." He spoke with a soft southern lilt, but with very precise enunciation, no contractions, which was unusual for anyone who has lived in New Orleans for any length of time.

The sound of water splashing on tile echoed off the glass. My apartment could almost fit in here. The sweet fragrance of Moth Orchids hung in the moist air, mixed with the cloying, pungent odor of fertilizer.

"Do you like Mahler, Mr. Malone?" he asked.

I shrugged. "My wife used to love classical music. I tend more towards Dr. Longhair and his genre. The old stuff." I didn't go any further.

He looked at me and said, "You have news, I suppose? Otherwise you would not be here, I imagine." He turned off the water-spigot and then the music, leaving us in silence. His smile had deserted him.

"I tried to call but got no answer. I thought I'd catch you back here."

"Yes, it's my regular routine. I make it a practice to not answer the phone in the morning until after I have fed my flowers. They need lots of care, which I can do since I quit practicing medicine."

He turned and started removing his apron. "Now tell me, Mr. Malone. You did not just drop by to listen to Mahler and admire my orchids. Although I will admit, they are worth the visit."

I stared at him and took a deep breath. *Here it goes.* "Dr. Fowler, I'm afraid I have bad news."

He fell silent, apron still in hand.

"Your wife, Kitty, is dead." I held eye contact with him, wishing I could spare him the pain that I knew all too well.

He stepped back, and his eyes grew large behind his spectacles. *"What?"*

"I thought it best if I came and told you myself."

He began breathing hard. "When?"

"This morning—"

"This morning?" His eyes glistened with tears. "What are you talking about?!" A look of confusion on his face.

"Someone shot her." My voice sounded distant to me. "At St. Louis Cathedral."

He shook his head. "That's impossible."

"Dr. Fowler, I know this is difficult. But I saw the body ... saw her. It was Kitty."

He continued to shake his head, eyes wide. "When did you say this happened?"

"This morning, I was—"

"But, Mr. Malone, that is impossible because my wife just left the greenhouse not twenty minutes ago." His lower lip quivered. "You may have passed her on the way here."

I blinked.

CHAPTER 11

If Dr. Fowler's wife left half-an-hour before I arrived, who was the dead woman behind St. Louis Cathedral? And who, by now, was lying on a metal slab in the morgue? My thoughts were swirling so quickly it was hard to follow them.

After questioning Dr. Fowler for an hour, I backed out of the glass hothouse, smelling of fertilizer and expensive orchids. He said he was certain of the time she left. He had just turned on the radio to WWNO. "At the start of Beethoven's *Symphony Number Five*," he swore.

As soon as I got back into my car, I called Bull. "You will not believe this," I started.

"Where the hell you been, Zeke?" he cut me off with a sharp voice.

"I've been with the husband, Dr. Fowler. You best sit down for this 'cause you won't believe it," I repeated. "He swears his wife is still alive. And that we have the wrong corpse."

"Well, today is full of surprises, isn't it?" he said.

"Why? What do you mean by that?"

"I've got a surprise for you as well."

He stayed silent on the other end. Since I had worked with Bull for years, I could tell by the undertone of his voice that he was fuming about something. Though his style was blunt, he lived up to his name: Bull. And he did his job well. So I waited.

Finally, I asked, "Well, do I have to play twenty questions?"

"Just get yourself down here, *pronto*."

"Where are you? Or do I have to guess that, too?"

"The City Morgue. I've got questions." He hung up.

•   •   •

After Hurricane Katrina flooded the city, the coroner's office was under ten-feet of water, the morgue moved into an abandoned industrial park in New Orleans East, off Almonaster Road. Now the City Morgue comprised rows of refrigerated Reefer trailers and donated FEMA trailers parked behind a ten-foot-tall chain-link fence. That part of New Orleans, close to the abandoned Six Flags amusement park, has no subdivisions, no homes, only small storage facilities and light industry. The street traffic consisted of delivery trucks and drug dealers. It could get eerie during the day and grow more creepy by nightfall.

Soon, storm clouds had gathered in front of the sun as I drove through the minimum-security gate into the parking lot. *It might be a wet Mardi Gras this year.* The wheels of my car crunched the shells in the parking lot in front of the main building, a metal Quonset hut. The dampened roar of generators from the freezer units filled the air. How does the old saying go? People are dying to get in.

I entered the door beneath the sign: MICHAEL JORDAN, CORONER. Inside the lobby, green-plastic chairs line the perimeter and an unoccupied desk sat to the right with a clipboard for signing in. I had been here many times, but it never failed to make me uneasy. I walked through the double-doors into a short hallway. Frequent buffing had made the linoleum floor appear wavy.

Detective Bull emerged from a room at the far end. He paused, hitched up his pants, gave me a dirty look, and motioned me to follow him. "You sure took your *sweet ass time* getting here," he said when I caught up.

Something was eating at him, but I would wait him out till he was ready to tell me. Our footsteps echoed off the corridor walls. We clattered through a narrow passageway, similar to the type that connects subway cars, and entered another trailer before he turned to me. "Now, let me get this straight. You followed a woman this morning, right?"

"Right."

"She was Dr. Fowler's wife?"

"Right."

Bull said, "How did you identify her?"

"The husband gave me a photograph and a description: height—five-foot nine, weight—one-hundred-thirty-three pounds. Blonde hair." I pulled the photograph out of my pocket and handed it to Bull.

Bull studied it for a moment, and then gave me a long, deliberate look.

"What's going on?" I asked.

"Come with me," he said, entering a room with a push-down handle like a walk-in meat locker. Set to thirty-three degrees, the cold storage was freezing and stopped the decomposition of bodies.

Six corpses lay on gurneys side by side, covered with frayed off-white sheets. For a moment, I imagined Jane lying on a stretcher, covered by the same Charity Hospital sheets. However, I shook the image off. And yet, my knees still grew weak, and I took a deep breath of the freezing air.

Clouds of condensation plumed out of Bull's nostrils. He nodded at MJ, who wore a face mask, a heavy pea-jacket with a Saints logo, over his blue scrubs. Our old friend rolled a gurney over to us, the front wheels creaking.

"Do you want me to I.D. her?" I asked, keeping my voice even.

Bull didn't answer me, but nodded at MJ again. The outline of a woman lay beneath the sheet. Only a toe-tag stuck out. MJ folded the top of the sheet back, revealing her face. And I looked down.

Kitty Fowler's hair was different, a buzz-cut, the long blonde locks gone, like a woman who'd lost her hair to chemotherapy. Her crew cut reminded me of Sinead O'Connor, more than Michelle

Pfeiffer. The blonde wig lay on the gurney beside her long, smooth neck.

Her face was peaceful: a model's face with a sprinkling of freckles and an upturned nose. However, the lips and skin had an unnatural, leaden-gray paleness to it, drained of blood, that no amount of makeup would ever disguise. She seemed unconcerned. As Raymond Chandler said, "You don't care about the nastiness of how you died or where you fell," when you are dead.

Nothing was making sense. Was *this* the real Kitty Fowler? The wife of Dr. Fowler? Or did the doctor lie this morning?

Bull held the photo in his beefy hand, squinting, seeming to compare the corpse against it.

"Except for the lack of hair, it's her," I said.

Glancing at me, he nodded at the MJ, who then pulled the sheet to her waist.

Nestled between her shapely breasts was the neat, ugly bullet hole. Even in death, nothing sagged.

Then he pulled the sheet all the way to mid-thigh.

My heart stopped. I stepped back. "She's got—"

"Yep," said Bull.

She was beautiful, a gorgeous person—except—she had male genitals.

"Yep," he said. "She's got *balls* and a dick."

I stammered, "She … She … She's a man?"

Bull turned to me, his mouth pursing as if he had eaten something sour. "You were trailing the wrong woman," he said. "No, correction—the wrong man."

CHAPTER 12

After MJ rolled the gurney away, I stood there, cold as the surrounding air, staring at the outline of the body under the sheet. My mind tried to absorb what it did not understand. I saw the body, a beautiful face, curvy female anatomy. And yet, there was a penis. I took an unsteady breath and tore my eyes away from the stretcher.

Bull's dark eyes scanned the row of bodies for a minute. Then he motioned for me to follow him out of the freezer, where the burly detective hiked up his pants, his habit when searching for answers. "Well, don't just stand there. Talk to me." His brow knitted.

Though we had left the cold storage, I still felt a deep chill in my bones. "What can I tell you that I haven't told you already? Dr. Fowler hired me to follow his wife. He gave me the photo and her agenda where she'd be this morning."

"He told you?"

"Yeah, last week. Said he hated to bother me since it was near Mardi Gras. But his instructions were quite specific about where she'd be. So I stationed myself in Jackson Square, waiting for her."

"What did he say since she was with him this morning?" Bull asked.

I thought back. "He said, she changed her mind about going to the Cathedral."

Bull frowned. "You did not know she was a man?"

I shook my head. "No idea. I mean, you saw her. She … uh, he looks exactly like the photograph."

"So, you followed a Look-Alike, and this person winds up dead on your watch. How did that happen?"

I gave him that, not wanting to go over it again. "The question that's bothering me," I asked, "Is if the dead guy in there isn't the wife ... who the *hell* is he?"

Bull scratched his immense head. "The lab is running his prints right now. Hopefully, we'll have a match soon."

I kept reminding myself, *Don't blame yourself for any of this.* I had no reason to suspect an imposter. No way I could have spotted the differences. It was done. Yet, somehow I'd gotten myself right-smack in the middle of it all. You might say it was a big mess.

Still in a state of disbelief, I mulled this over as we walked the long corridor back to the front.

"Whoever shot him thought he was killing the doctor's wife," I said, lengthening my stride to match his.

He looked at me and took his time studying me until it seemed he'd decided about something. "Maybe, yes or no. Logical. But who would want Kitty dead? The husband?"

"Doubtful. Let's suppose he wanted her out of the picture." We were nearing the front door. "That would be motive, if she cheated on him. But then, why hire me to follow her?"

Bull shook his head, pushing the bar to open the door. "To act as a witness?"

I shrugged. "Makes little sense."

We exited the morgue into the humid Louisiana air, like walking into a sauna. We paused by Bull's beat up Gran Torino.

"When you left Dr. Fowler, what did you tell him to do?" Bull asked.

"I told him to go down to the Eighth District on North Rampart Street. And to wait for you."

"And what about the wife? The live one?"

I shook my head. "Damned if I know."

Bull paused. "I put out an APB on her when I realized the body on the slab wasn't her. Now I'm going to question the husband," he said, slumping into his car with a grunt of the springs.

For over seven years, I had known and worked with Bull, and so much of our communication was non-verbal. We had learned to talk without saying a lot. So, I had to conjure up words now. "Do me a favor," I said. "I want to listen to the interview of Dr. Fowler."

His Gran Torino started like a tank, and he sighed, giving me a tired look. "Why would you wanna do that?"

"I could tell you," I said, "if what he says doesn't match the facts."

Cranking up the air-conditioning to high, he seemed to think it over.

"Plus, you owe me," I said, leaning towards him, putting the weight of my body against the door so he couldn't close it.

"You going to bring that up again?"

"If I have to," I said, resisting his powerful tug on the handle. "Besides, they murdered somebody on my watch."

"Your watch ended two years ago. You're not a cop any longer, remember?"

He was right, but I shrugged. "That doesn't matter. I want to find who did this."

He took his time mulling it over.

"I have my reasons," I said, though I couldn't think of any right then.

Bull, with a scowl, mercifully did not ask. "Okay, okay, *Pain in the Ass*. But you can't be in the interrogation room. Stand behind the one-way-mirror."

I stepped back and he slammed the car door, threw it into gear, and sped out of the parking lot, crunching and flinging gravel. I hurried to my car and left in hot pursuit. Dr. Fowler was waiting.

CHAPTER 13

"Are you crazy?" Dr. Fowler shouted. "Why would I hire someone to impersonate my wife?"

"That's what we're trying to find out," Detective Bull said, stroking his Pancho Villa mustache. He cleared his throat and stared hard at the husband, before leaning forward on the metal table like a knuckle-walking anthropoid. Since I left, they had painted the Interrogation Room a battleship-gray instead of puke-green. But some things hadn't changed. The unpainted metal table was still bolted to the floor and a few straight-backed aluminum chairs faced each other. The furniture looked to be scavenged from a 1950s classroom.

I stood in the next room, staring through a one-way mirror, feeling strange since I was usually on the other side with the action. When Bull and I were partners, we played the good cop/bad cop routine. Bull always assumed the bad guy role. He was more suited for it with his intimidating size, snarling mouth, angry eyes, and bulky shoulders.

I acted the good cop—your friend, your pal, just trying to help you out of this mess, your Father Confessor. Since I left, it seemed my burly ex-partner had found no one to play the good cop—not even Birdie Birdsong—who worked well with him. I wanted to be in the room, but I could only observe as I had no official status.

The biggest obstacle to Bull's smooth extraction of information sat in a chair to the doctor's left, looking like a giant fluorescent lemon. Dr. Fowler's attorney—Zip Romero.

Zip Romero was the most effective and skillful attorney in New Orleans—the darling of the accused, and the dread of the judicial system, and the bane of the police. He wore a white linen suit with lemon-yellow socks, pale-yellow silk-shirt and metallic-gold tie. Although given to the theatrical and dramatic, driving a few prosecuting attorneys and judges crazy, he was the best. And only the wealthy could afford him.

Word on the street was, if you're guilty, call Emilio Zapata Romero, his proper name. But everyone called him Zip. He had a younger brother, a world-renowned surgeon.

I first met Zip after I first joined the force. In the Crescent City, he was the one attorney I feared most, but I respected him. I admired the way he never backed down and always fought for his clients. Although Justice is supposed to be blind—she isn't always—the lady with the blindfold and sword seemed to forgive Zip for his antics, and his outlandish sartorial outfits.

Bull stared at the husband, then his eyes slid towards Zip.

Zip nodded. "Why, Detective Bulardeaux, we meet again. Can't keep away from me, can you?"

"It's hard as hell, but I manage."

"You haven't commented on my new outfit. First time wearing it today. Do you like it?"

"Sure, if you like yellow icing on lemon cake."

In mock surprise. "You don't? Too sweet for you, huh?" He shook his head in disapproval and tried not to smile. "Oh, I see. You're a diabetic? How sad." He tsk-tsked.

"Nope, that isn't the reason. Your suit is … isn't exactly my taste."

Zip grinned. "I just simply love you macho guys. So sure of yourselves."

Bull's thick neck strained against his collar. Zip had gotten under his skin already. If I were still his partner, this is where I'd step in. As the good cop, I could deal with Zip, carry the conversation even further about his suit, diffuse the histrionics and tension.

Bull said, "Can we get on with the questioning?"

"That's why we're here, Detective. Oh," Zip held up his hand. "Just so we all know, I've advised my client not to speak to you. But … in the spirit of cooperation, he wants to be helpful."

"Wonderful. I asked your client a question."

"My, my, do tell. And what question was that? What with this fascinating wardrobe discussion, I forgot the question."

"I asked, did you hire someone to impersonate your wife?" Bull asked, staring at Dr. Fowler.

The doctor glanced at Zip, who nodded.

"No, I did not." Stating each word with emphasis, the doctor spoke as if he were on the witness stand.

Zip cut in. "But, please, Detective Bull, why don't you just ask my client if he killed his wife?"

The room fell silent for a moment. Then Bull asked, "Well, did you?"

"What?"

"Kill your wife?"

"No! Of course not!" Dr. Fowler said without bothering to seek Zip's approval.

"Now, wasn't that easy?" Zip smiled, placing his hand on the doctor's shoulder. "He denies he committed murder. Now, I am advising my client *not to say another word*."

"We're just trying to solve a homicide." Bull straightened up. "This morning, a person was shot who looked the same as your spouse, dressed the same, walked the same, and—"

Zip interrupted. "One thing I've learned is that when a wife is murdered, the men-in-blue immediately suspect the husband."

"It wasn't his wife."

"Then why are you questioning him?"

Bull ignored the question. "Dr. Fowler, you admit to hiring a private licensed investigator to follow your wife, correct?"

He turned to his attorney. Zip nodded.

"Yes, I did."

"Why?"

"Don't answer that." Zip crossed his arms and sighed. "Nice try, Detective, but this is a fishing-expedition. You are looking for a motive, a reason you can pin this death on Dr. Fowler. Why aren't you out trying to locate his wife? Instead of sitting here, wasting my client's time? If someone is attempting to kill her, as you said, who's to say he won't try again?"

"We left a patrol-car parked in front of your home. Your wife isn't answering her phone. We do not know where she is." Bull leaned in. "Does she do this often?"

"Do what often?" Dr. Fowler said, lips in a thin line.

"Disappear, so no one can locate her?"

Dr. Fowler shifted in his seat, gaze fixed ahead. He did not look at Zip, nor did he respond to the question.

Bull had scored a point, but he shrugged and emptied a red evidence envelope onto the metal tabletop. A stack of 8x10 glossies slid out. He pushed one towards the doctor with his thick index finger. "Have you seen this person before?" It was a photo of the man in the morgue.

Dr. Fowler and Zip studied the photograph. "No, never." The doctor grumbled before placing it down and sliding it back. "But she bears an uncanny resemblance to my wife. Was she the woman killed?"

I watched Dr. Fowler's face, looking for a tell, a give-away that would show he was lying. He wasn't. Police Interrogation is like a game of poker. You bluff, you fend, you search for the tell that will show you what is going on inside their head, something they are trying to conceal. Often, you act like their friend, other times, their worst nightmare.

"You sure you've never seen this person?"

Zip sighed. "Detective, Dr. Fowler just said he does not recognize this woman."

"Look at it again. And I'll rephrase my question. Have you seen this *man* before?"

"Man?" Dr. Fowler leaned forward, squinted at the picture. "Looks like a woman to me—with short hair."

"Have you seen this person, this *man*, before?" Bull repeated.

"No, I am certain I have never seen her before. Who is she ... uh, this person?"

"He's the man who impersonated your wife."

"Let me see that," Zip said, snatching it up to examine. "Why, that's Leslie Baronne, a female impersonator."

"You know him, Zip?"

"Personally, no. But I've seen him perform. He's the best drag queen I've ever seen."

"Where?"

"He performs in Carnival Balls." Zip looked up. "But mostly at the Oasis Club."

"Will I have to pull you in as a material witness, Zip?"

"I would *not* try that, Detective. Unless you intend to call every person who's been to the Oasis Club in the past few years. I'll file so many objections and motions, it will be years before you get a single deposition."

Zip stood up. "You know, Detective Bulardeaux, I think we've had enough. I'm going to pull my client out. He's finished answering your *asinine* questions."

Bull said, "Don't leave town. I may need—"

Zip Romero cut him off. "Need I *remind* you, Detective Bull, don't even think of questioning the doctor without my being present? Understood?"

Bull did not answer.

And with that, Zip took Dr. Fowler's arm, and they left.

CHAPTER 13

Later that evening, Goldenstein sat waiting for the phone call from Theodore Onyx. It was true: good news takes forever to make the rounds, but bad news spreads like wildfire. He straightened the knot on his tie and checked his fingernails. Then he checked his watch again. Any minute now. The call would come soon, but he wasn't sure when. He worked the crossword puzzle with his pen as he waited.

Finally, his cell phone buzzed. Goldenstein let it ring four or five times, sighed and answered. Onyx was all but hyperventilating and shouting. "What the *fuck* happened?"

"It was an unavoidable screw-up," Goldenstein said.

"A screw-up! That's an understatement."

"That's part of doing business with a third party. You rely on others. The shooter didn't know."

"But *you're* paid to know," Onyx said. "How did your man not know?"

"He didn't know."

Onyx sighed in resignation. "How did he kill a guy, for god's sake? The idiot shot the wrong person. Couldn't he tell the difference between a man and a woman? And Kitty Fowler's one hell of a good-looking woman."

"Kitty hired a cross-dresser. A man that looked like her. Same color wig. Same dress. Same features. Same—"

"Are you *kidding* me? It's like out of a Keystone Cop movie. This is fucking ridiculous."

"He was where Kitty was supposed to be," Goldenstein explained.

"My god, now we'll be the laughingstock of every snook and asshole that wants to pull a fast one on us. How can I run a business when everybody keeps screwing up?" His voice grew calmer now, as if he were thinking. "Who was he? This guy that looked like a woman?"

"I don't know his name yet. Kitty Fowler hired this ... this Look-alike to impersonate her."

"I should know better than to ask, but why?"

"So she could get away, disappear without raising suspicion."

"Disappear? Dare I ask why?"

"Do I need to draw a picture? So she could meet her lovers. I think she had a long list of them. What more can I tell you?"

"Don't tell me *shit*. You were supposed to know this. You make a ton of money off me. Crap, now I have to call my—call the director and explain what happened."

This was a revelation to Goldenstein. He always suspected someone else was above Theodore Onyx. Someone bigger, someone higher, that pulled the strings. Onyx's slip-of-the-tongue confirmed this. He threw out this question, hoping to find more. "So *who* do you have to call?"

"None of your business, asshole. What you need to concern yourself with is finding the real Kitty Fowler before she goes blabbing around."

"We're out searching for her right now."

"For Chrissakes, if she's found, and she talks, we're all in deep shit. Find her, *goddammit!* Make sure that she's got a pussy between her legs before you waste another bullet. And don't fuck up this time!"

Goldenstein was about to protest when he heard the click of the phone.

Since he only had a few words left on the crossword puzzle, he finished it. *Twelve Letters Down: SUBTERRANEAN.* Goldenstein was thinking. *Dammit. That's where she's gone—Kitty Fowler's gone underground. Now we've spooked her good.*

CHAPTER 14

"That's easy," said Bull. "Clint Eastwood dies in four movies."

"As usual, you're wrong," MJ said, shoving his enormous goggles that served as glasses up his nose.

The three men sat on their bar stools slouched against the dark oak cigarette-notched bar at the Half Moon Bar and Grill off Magazine Street. Zeke Malone hadn't joined his two drinking buddies, MJ and Bull, in over two years—not since Jane died. He had a strange feeling of *déjà vu*. He hadn't touched the hard stuff, not even a beer since he started counseling.

"Are you shitting me? Of course it was four," Bull said, counting out his fingers. "Clint Eastwood dies in one-two-three-four movies."

MJ popped cashews into his mouth, and said between crunches, "Okay. Name them, smart ass."

In the past, the Half Moon always suited the three friends. Yolanda, the barmaid, was friendly and had a crush on Bull, paying him extra attention he didn't seem to mind. The cashew nuts were fresh. And they stocked the Wurlitzer with old school songs. All three used to enjoy unwinding here. But it was different now. Everything was different. Jane was gone. Zeke felt an empty feeling in the pit of his stomach. Now, he wasn't sure he wanted to revisit the past.

"Let's see," Bull said, stroking his Pancho Villa mustache. "First, there was that one in the Civil War where the schoolgirls poisoned him."

"The name?"

"*The Beguiled.*"

"Correct. That's one. What's the next one?" MJ said, washing the nuts down with a slug of beer.

The game was *DEAD MAN TRIVIA*—MJ's creation, and the three men's favorite pastime. Even as a child, death fascinated MJ. As a coroner, he'd chosen the right profession and was a walking encyclopedia on how, when, why people died. And especially the who. Today, it was Clint Eastwood's turn: *death in his movies*, though not in real life.

Bull hesitated for a beat. "Next, Eastwood dies in *Unforgiven*. He won an Academy Award for that one."

MJ nodded. "For directing. Not acting. That's two."

The bar room smelled of hamburgers, and onions sizzling on the grill, and stale beer. The sound of pool balls ricocheting off each other clicked in the air. Now and then, someone would shove money into the jukebox and play music like Elvis' "*Hound Dogs*" or *Sweet Emma Barrett's "A Good Man Is Hard to Find,"* or some funky Delta Blues.

Above the big steamy bar mirror and the rows of whiskey bottles, hung a cheap reproduction of a smiling, naked girl reclining on a couch, her hand draped over her pubic hair. Zeke thought of Kitty Fowler. Or was it the impersonator? He blew on his piping-hot cappuccino in a chipped cup. He placed the cup on an unmatched cracked-blue porcelain Dutch saucer. Nothing in the Half Moon matched, not even the letters on the neon sign outside. The bowl holding the nuts was green Tupperware plastic. The beer and whiskey glasses behind the counter were of assorted sizes and shapes—glass, plastic, ceramic. A mug stolen from Pat O'Brien's. Another, an elegant fluted-stein, lifted from Commander's Palace. Maybe that's why the three felt comfortable in this Irish Channel bar. *Misfits fit in.*

MJ said, "And what else did Clint die in?"

"Don't rush me ... *Gran Torino*, when all the Vietnamese shot him," Bull said.

"Hmong, not Vietnamese," corrected MJ.

"Whatever. And the fourth was *Pale Rider*."

"You sure?"

"Yeah. No, wait ... " Bull bit his lip in concentration. "Yeah, four."

Bull sipped on a beer with a foamy head in a large frosted mug, Saints' logo stenciled on the side. He tilted back on his stool and finished it in a long swallow. A foam mustache attached to his upper lip. Using his sleeve, he wiped it away with a brawny arm.

"Wrong!" shouted MJ, as if he had just bested a kid on the playground. "Eastwood did not die in *Pale Rider*."

"What do you mean? Eastwood was called *Death*. He was dead all along."

MJ bounced up and down on his stool. "He wasn't dead. They called him *The Preacher*, the harbinger of death."

Bull turned. "What do you say, Zeke? Right or wrong?" Bull knew Zeke was uncomfortable and was trying to get him into the game—like the old days.

"While you two discuss it," MJ said, sliding off his stool, "I'm going to the john." He hustled away.

Bull stared at Zeke. "What's bothering you, Zeke?"

"Who, me? Why do you ask?"

"Oh, just the way you haven't jumped in—I left the last answer open for you."

"Yeah, I thought so," said Zeke.

"And?"

"Nothing. It just feels strange being back here with you and MJ. It's like old-times. But not really ..."

"Yeah, I get that," Bull said.

Zeke looked up and saw Bull's new partner strolling into the bar. She had slung her suit coat over her shoulder, wearing a tight, wrinkled-white shirt which looked as if she had sweated it through and then it dried out. Her badge was fastened to her belt.

Birdsong. Birdie, that was her name. She was slim and compact, carried herself light on her feet. Like a dancer, or a bird. Her nose was prominent, but not overly so—slightly out of alignment. She wasn't ugly, far from it. Some might even call her pretty.

"What's she doing here?" Zeke asked.

"Oh, you know. Since you've been gone, she sort of filled the third leg of the team. She's okay."

Zeke stood, while Bull remained seated.

"Sit down," she said. "Nobody gets up for a woman anymore. Besides, I'm a cop and no one gets up for a cop." She flopped her coat on the bar stool. Bull scooted over and she sat between them.

She was more attractive than he remembered from the crime scene. She looked more relaxed.

MJ returned drying his hands with a paper towel. "Hi, Birdie." He sat down beside Zeke.

Birdie waved at Yolanda and ordered a round of beer for everyone.

"Only coffee for me," Zeke said.

She glanced at him with a smirk. Or was it a half-smile? Zeke couldn't be sure.

She turned to Zeke. "You look as if you're the only sensible one here," she said, popping some cashews into her mouth. "But you can still be a pain in the ass." She said to MJ. "What are we playing tonight?"

"The death of Clint Eastwood in his movies," MJ said.

"That's easy," she said. "*Beguiled, Gran Torino* and *Unforgiven.* Only three."

Bull's mouth fell open. "How did you know that?"

"I was a movie buff growing up," she said. "My old man was a Clint Eastwood fan. We saw every movie he made—at least a dozen times."

"Okay, okay, I've got one," Bull cut in. "Not about death—but near-death. In what movies did Clint Eastwood get hanged?"

MJ jumped in. "That's a softball pitch: *Hang 'Em High.*"

"And?" Bull said, leaning forward.

"And what?"

"I said: movies. The *s* sound at the end means more than one."

"More than one?" MJ repeated through a frown. "There weren't any others!"

"Yep, another one. That's what I said."

Bull turned to Birdie. "What about you? What do you think?"

She shook her head. "I agree with MJ."

Bull said, "Give up?"

"Give me a minute." MJ took a big swig of his beer. "No, there is no other. Only one: *Hang 'Em High.*"

Bull made a buzzing sound. "Wrong! They hung Clint Eastwood in *The Good, The Bad, and The Ugly.*"

"You can't be serious?" MJ said. "That's one of my favorites. I've seen it a dozen times. They did *not* hang him!"

"Sure he was," Bull said. "Tuko put a rope around his neck and yanked it tight."

"Tuko dragged him on the ground," MJ sputtered. "That's not hanging!"

"Sure it is," said Bull. "He put a rope around his neck, pulled it tight—that's asphyxiation! Drag. Hang. It's the same thing."

MJ and Birdie shouted, "That doesn't count!"

"Sure it does," Bull repeated. He was about to argue some more when his cell phone buzzed. "Hold it." He got up.

"Yeah. Yeah. Okay, we're on our way," he said and clicked off.

All three stared at him.

"That was Forensics. They tracked down the next of kin to Leslie Baronne."

"Next of kin?"

"Yeah," Bull said. "His husband. A guy named Presley Baronne."

CHAPTER 15

Detective Bull and I left the Half Moon and drove back to the morgue to meet Presley Baronne, listed as the spouse of the dead man. We rode in his beat-up Gran Torino muscle-car, with its 429 cubic inch Cobra Jet engine, two doors and torn rag top. The car sounded as if it had a hole in the muffler.

"When are you going to get rid of this car?" I shouted to be heard above the roar. "You've had this one since ... since as long as I've known you."

Bull stroked his mustache. "I like it that way. So people will shut up and not bother me while I'm driving. Besides, why bother? It gets me from point A to point B. So long as I get my man, it doesn't matter what it looks like."

He was right. Bull had the best murder-clearance rate record of any detective present in the NOPD. Next to mine, of course. His arrest percentage went down when I retired.

The night sky had turned slate-gray with rain clouds, and a breakdown on the High Rise eastbound caused a traffic jam, bumper-to-bumper. Bull used his lights and sirens, and we exited at Almonaster Blvd. We drove by the abandoned Desire Housing Projects. A gray cloud of dust rose above the night demolition crews razing another box-like apartment complex; a hurricane fence surrounded the grounds. On the brick face of a vacant building was a sixty-foot graffiti mural of Martin Luther King, Jr., JFK, and Tupac, all standing over a dead body. Beneath, in large letters painted to look as if dripping with blood: BLACK LIVES MATTER.

When we pulled into the morgue parking lot, the car's tires crunched the oyster shells. The sky rumbled, and the floodgates opened as we ran to the main entrance of the morgue.

We walked down the tile corridor to a small green-walled waiting room. When we entered, a fragile man seated in a Salvation Army cushioned chair stood up, distressed look on his face. The pallor of his skin contrasted with the gold earrings and powder-blue suit with a white shirt open at the collar, looking like he came off the set of *Miami Vice*.

"Mr. Presley Baronne?" Bull asked

"Yes, that's me," he said, reaching out to shake hands. His fingers were soft and slender, around his neck hung a small silver Jesus on a jewel-studded cross. I'm no gemologist, but the diamonds on the crucifix looked real.

At least four rings adorned each hand and his hands shook. "This is about Leslie, isn't it?"

Bull glanced at me, then back at Presley. "Yes, I'm afraid it is."

Presley Baronne lowered his head, stiffened, and took in a deep breath. He clutched the crucifix as if it might ward off the answer to his next question. "She's dead, isn't she?"

"Yes, Mr. Baronne, I'm afraid so."

He sat down hard on the sagging cushion and stared at us. "There couldn't be a mistake?" he asked.

Bull shook his head. "No, I'm sorry."

He closed his eyes tight, took in and let out another big breath. For a few moments, he did not speak. We all sat silently. Then he looked up and said, "I'd like to see him."

"Yes, as his closest relative, we need you to identify the body." Bull's voice came out flat, matter-of-fact, a professional police interrogation technique. *Just the facts, Ma'am. Just the facts. Keep a wall between the person and yourself.*

We walked along the long corridor with the wavy linoleum, and through the connecting-passageway to the adjoining trailer. But instead of walking into the meat locker, we turned into a small room with a picture-window, where we lined up like fathers waiting for the nurses to roll out the babies in their bassinets. A gray curtain blocked our view.

The shaky little man was fighting hard not to show emotions, clenching his jaw and twisting his lips shut. He wanted to be stoic. It seems as if he were wishing it was a mistake, hoping for a miracle. As a cop, I'd seen his behavior many times before by family members, holding back the tears. They never believe their loved one was dead until they see the body. Was he praying? He squeezed his crucifix so hard, his knuckles turned white.

Bull rapped on the window and MJ, dressed against the cold, pulled back the curtain. He rolled over a stretcher, a clean white sheet draped over the body.

Bull nodded. And MJ lifted the sheet off the face and folded it to mid-neck. Presley Baronne stared and stood silent for a long while. It was then I noticed he had been holding his breath. He exhaled, the hope he had before—evaporated. I kept my eyes on his face, watching for a tell, to see if there was anything else there besides grief. Nothing, only what you'd expect. There was no *deus ex machina* in this room. He dropped his eyes to the floor, and they were wet. He released his hold on the crucifix and the trembling was more pronounced than before.

Bull nodded, and MJ covered the face before drawing the curtains.

CHAPTER 16

"Whatever I can answer, I will do so," said Presley Baronne in a shaky voice, as we sat around the cold-metal table in an intake room. Bull took notes and asked questions in his even tone, on the weird chance that this *husband* may have been involved in *his wife's* death, the guy in cold storage.

After a visible struggle, Presley Baronne regained control and answered our questions in a sincere and serious voice so that we had little doubt he was telling the truth. He explained that Leslie Baronne used cross-dressing talents as a professional dancer and part-time actor to earn a living. Leslie had bit roles in a long string of low-budget movies shot here now that Louisiana was the Hollywood of the South. Also walk-on parts in made-for-cable shows. Since then, his wife had performed in various nightclubs. But the main source of income was still the Oasis Club, the follow-up to Club My-O-My of ages ago. In addition, Leslie also performed at select Mardi Gras Balls and private parties.

Presley Baronne acted as Leslie's manager. "We married five years ago in Acapulco on the beach, under the moonlight," he said. "Leslie wore a loose-fitting chiffon dress with a real goddamn veil. Me in a tux," he laughed. "Can you believe it? She got so drunk, she puked all over our honeymoon bed. It was hilarious," he added. Then his voice broke, still shaking from identifying his wife. The flesh of his jaws jiggled, eyes leaking tears.

We gave him a minute till he quit crying. He took a purple handkerchief from his coat pocket and blew his nose. His eyes were red and raw, face sagging like soft dough.

Bull paused for a minute, reviewing his notes, his squat, block head with the drooping mustache poised over his pad. "Okay, can you tell me what Leslie was doing in Jackson Square this morning?"

"We were engaged to impersonate a woman."

He looked up. "Someone hired you guys?"

"Yes, to look and dress like this woman," he said, reaching into his coat pocket and taking out a photograph of a beautiful, blonde-haired woman. She stood like a model next to a fountain in a white dress with a yellow-sunhat in hand pressed against her thigh.

The photo was different from the one Dr. Fowler gave me. But the face was unmistakable. It was Kitty Fowler.

I asked, "You sure you never saw this woman before?"

"Nope, I never saw her," he said.

"Did Leslie know her identity?"

"She told me no."

Bull and I exchanged glances. Not only did I not understand this, I didn't like it. My eyes traveled back to the photograph. It was the same fountain in the picture-perfect postcard-patio of the Fowler's backyard.

Bull stroked his mustache. "So, how were you hired to impersonate this woman?"

"I never met the person. All I know is that a man handed Leslie an envelope stuffed with cash and a photograph of that woman. There were instructions on how to dress, where to go, and a timetable."

"By any chance, did Leslie get a name?" Bull asked.

"Nope. The guy didn't say a word. He wore a rubber Spider Man mask."

"Spider Man? Like in the ... movies?"

"Yeah. Just handed the envelope to Leslie and disappeared back into the crowd at a Mardi Gras Masquerade Ball. Must have been a couple hundred people dressed in costumes, in drag, and masked."

Bull raised his eyes from the photo. "And he paid you in cash?"

"Yes. All crisp one-hundred-dollar bills ... just like the time before."

"Before? This happened before?" I asked.

"Yes."

"When?"

"About six months ago. A man approached Leslie and handed over an envelope."

"With a Spider Man mask again?"

"No, Superman that time. The photograph, the same, though."

"And what did the instructions say?"

"Nothing unusual. Drive around the city. Go by the Lakefront and feed the gulls. Go to the New Orleans Art Museum. That kind of thing."

"Do you still have the envelope?" Bull asked.

He thought for a moment. "Maybe. It's probably still in my files. I can get it if it will help."

Bull instructed him to go home and bring the files to the Eighth District Station.

Mr. Baronne shook our hands, his fingers cool and soft.

"I'm sorry for your loss," Bull said.

After he left, we sat down at the uncomfortable metal table.

"What do you think?" I asked.

He shook his head. "This doesn't make any sense."

I held up one finger. "First, we have a man hiding his identity behind a rubber mask."

"Yeah. Someone impersonating a comic book character."

"Two. He hires a drag queen ..."

"A man who professionally impersonates women—and ends up dead."

"Three. Hired to impersonate a rich man's wife."

We left the interrogation room and stood looking out the front door. The heavy rain had passed and slackened to sprinkles now.

"So, let me see if I got this right," Bull said, stroking his Pancho Villa mustache. "We have an impersonator hiring an impersonator to impersonate someone else."

"Now, all we have to do is figure out who the impersonator is, and then we can find who the killer is."

CHAPTER 17

I see Jane's face in my dreams, in that crazy half-world between nightmares and wakefulness. There is fear in her eyes and Bomber Boy has his arm around her neck, like a choke-hold in a wrestling match. *Is this for real?* But there is nothing phony about this. She cannot get away.

I am rooted to the floor and unable to move, unable to help. Her eyes are bright with fear. Nothing happens when I open my mouth. The shouts die in my throat. I'm mute and dumb and too stupid to save Jane.

She whispers, *"I love you."* Her lips trembling, eyes brimming, and she emits a low moan from her chest—or is it me?

No. No. No. I want to scream, but I can't, even though I know what is coming next; I've relived this scenario a thousand times—as the side of her head disintegrates into a thousand pieces, I gain my voice and scream.

The voice in my ear is shouting, "Take your shot! TAKE YOUR SHOT!"

I jerk up into a seated position, shaking. My sheets were soaking wet. I've had this dream over and over. Yet, nothing stops them—nothing. I've tried booze, pills from my doctor, and pills from the street. Still, the nightmares persist, returning again and again.

All relief is temporary.

The unorthodox counselor assigned by the police department helped a little. I used to visit her twice a week. That was after they released me from the hospital. After the shock of the blast. When I could not work. When I couldn't sleep and jumped every time a car passed. And after I got drunk and wrapped my car around a tree in Belle Chasse. While I was still in the hospital, Jane's daughter, Carla, was taken in by my brother-in-law and his wife, Doris. Now, I can only visit under supervision.

Now, it's every other week with the shrink, but I skip as many as I attend.

The shrink's name is Lucy Baumgartner. A small sign by the entrance to her office says *Lucy in the Sky*, one of those sandblasted wooden signs with stars. Her face is comprised of concentric circles—a round face with round, white plastic-framed glasses that make her eyes more barn-owl-like, and a small mouth that forms an O when she isn't smiling. Her style was to tell jokes to get me to relax as she rolled around her office in a wheelchair with blue plastic seating and giant metal wheels.

She said she lost the use of her legs from a childhood accident but doesn't elaborate. Instead: "We're here to talk about *your* fucked-up life. *Not mine.*"

Her office is on the third-floor of a small industrial-style building with windows facing the Mississippi River. Today, she greeted me with the news, "I've written a new version of Tammy Wynette's '*Stand By Your Man.*' It's for paraplegics."

I walk in and take my usual place in an overstuffed armchair. Dr. Lucy sits facing me with her back to the windows.

She added, "I call it, '*Roll By Your Man.*' What do you think?"

"It should go right to the top of the charts," I said.

She smiled and wheeled back with two swift turns of her wheels. I gave her a perfunctory laugh, cross my legs at the ankle, and stare out the window. Behind her, I can see the tops of sea-going freighters gliding by as if they were right outside on the street. It felt like I was in a dream.

"How's it going?" she asked.

Not well. If things were different, I wouldn't be here. I'd be getting off work and going home. Jane would be waiting. "It's okay," I told her.

"Don't bullshit me, Zeke. You look like *shit.* How do you really feel?"

"Like shit."

She pursed her lips and stared at me with her large, magnified eyes. "Try not to be bitter," she said. "Try to be better."

This was one of her favorite phrases; she repeated it like a mantra. *Try not to be bitter, be better.* That was the best advice she could think of? *Be Better—than what?* Try not to be bitter because a lunatic blew up the person I love into little bits and pieces. The images come up at all hours when I least expected it. I could be watching TV, or taking out the garbage, or driving down the street when suddenly—BOOM!—I see her face. Watch her lips, breathing her last words.

And I felt helpless. Just like that day.

The doctor, this *Lucy in Disguise,* called it PTSD. "Just like the guys coming from Vietnam or the Middle-East." She fixed me with a wide-eyed glare. "We are all handicapped. The only difference between you and me is, I know I'm disabled—but I roll on, while you're stuck like a horse's ass in quicksand." She maneuvered her chair across the room and poured herself a cup of coffee, then pivoted. "You are disabled by the death of your wife—and unable to move on, unable to admit your disability. Your butt is stuck in a rusted-iron wheelchair in your mind. You see, your disability is your inability to move on!"

She's got a zillion of these saying, these plays on words. For example, "you don't understand a man till you've walked a mile in his shoes." Turns into: "until you roll a mile in his wheelchair." Or, "put your best foot forward," becomes, "put your best crutch forward."

"You're not drinking, are you?" she asked.

"No, that way is—it never helped."

"Progress, Little Luke. Progress. Now you're learning," she said.

Yet again, we discuss Jojo Turner's voice in my dreams. Jojo, who had it in for me since the Police Academy, is front and center. His voice berates me and I can see his blue dress uniform, gold bars on his collar, and his reptilian smile. *"You killed your wife as good as if you pressed that button."* He told me after I awoke from my coma.

Lucy Baumgartner told me when she was growing up, "We were so poor, we couldn't afford to live on the ground-floor. Our apartment was on the second-floor. Since I couldn't walk, I had to scoot up a flight of stairs on my butt to get home—one step at a time. I tell you, from the bottom step, those stairs look ten-stories high. The janitor even got a raise for keeping the steps *so* clean. But it was *my ass* keeping it spotless. I threatened to tell the super if he didn't give me a dollar a week."

She rolled her chair back and forth as she spoke, in eager anticipation of the next part of her story. Her next mind-broadening lesson to me. "You might ask, what did I learn from that?"

"How to blackmail people?" I replied.

"That, too. And I learned to do it with a smile." She goes into the next part, the punch line. "So you might ask, what did I learn from bouncing my ass-end up and down that staircase for two years? The big takeaway from it was ... ?"

She gives me a quizzical look. Then she does a drum roll on the armrest of her wheelchair. "Take-It. One-Two ... ?" She waves her hands at me with a come-on gesture as if she were encouraging a rather dull-witted student.

When I do not answer, she repeated. "C'mon, oh, obtuse Padawan, you can't be that dense. Take-It-One...?" Each word enunciated with a giant nod of her round head.

"Take it one step at a time!" I blurted out.

"That's it," she said with a wide grin, sitting back in her chair. "I knew you were making progress with my counseling." Her eyes narrow to slits behind her glasses as if she were observing a bug.

"When the task seems daunting, break it down into small steps. *That's* how you get to the top. You can do anything."

She leans forward in her wheelchair again for emphasis. "All you need to do is *roll one step at a time.*"

CHAPTER 18

Exhausted, I roll out of bed. It was five past nine.

Last night, around one AM, I woke up from a bad dream, but went back to sleep. Then again, at two, and every hour afterwards, the nightmares came again, but I barely remember them. The yellow sticky-note on the refrigerator reminds me of the ten-o'clock appointment with a new client. I even added: ZEKE, KEEP THIS MEETING.

Hurriedly, I put on some coffee and jumped in and out of the shower while it percolated. No suit today, too hot, just slacks and a pullover.

Things were quiet on the street at this time of the morning. Later, tourists would stream into the Quarter, looking for nightlife on Bourbon Street, or in the music clubs on Frenchman, or in the crappy dive bars.

The flier for the little girl's lost dog, Wally, was still tacked up on the telephone pole, tattered and fluttering in the breeze. I hurried from the heat and turned into the carriageway, my shoes clicking on the cobblestone alley. I checked my watch: *Good, only five minutes late.*

"Hello!" boomed a voice over the balcony on the second-story landing. I look up from the patio. The voice belonged to a sizable man dressed in an expensive business suit with a very red face. "You're late," he grumbled, holding out his corpulent wrist as if I could see his watch from the ground level. I ducked under the untrimmed banana leaves.

"Yeah, sorry."

The ten-o'clock appointment was with Malcolm Mudridge, and he didn't tell me what he wanted when he called. He stood with fat hands on his hips, sweating.

"I'm sorry I'm late, Mr ... Mudridge, isn't it?"

"Yes, yes, Mudridge," he said, taking out a handkerchief and wiping his face while stepping aside, allowing me to unlock the door.

Once inside, I flipped on the light switch, strolled over to the window unit, clicked it on, and stood in front of it for the first blast.

Frowning, he followed me in and his beady eyes scanned the room. "I hope this is not an indication of the type of work you do."

Unsure how to answer, I just ignored the comment. "Won't you have a seat, Mr. Mudridge?" I motioned him towards the chair as I went around the desk and sat down. We both wiggled in our seats, trying to get comfortable.

"Now, how can I help you?"

"It's my partner." He fell silent for a moment, as if trying to find his words.

"Okay, what about him?"

"He cheated me ... " Mudridge stared down at his hands. He was quiet for another long pause.

"Out of what?" I prompted.

"Money." He said, wringing his hands together. "No. More than that. He stole my good intentions, my excellent reputation."

"Why don't you start at the beginning? And give me all the details?" I said, pulling a yellow pad out of the desk drawer to jot notes.

For the next half-hour, he told me how he'd met this handsome-looking man, Rocky Stream, he called himself. Soon they became involved in more ways than just business deals, he told me in a low voice.

"We were buying old properties in the Quarter," he said. "Renovating them, then reselling it to rich out-of-town corporations. Tax write-offs where they could entertain fat-cat clients in the picturesque Old French Quarter. Rocky Stream oversaw the renovation, while I provided the finances. Everything was running smoothly until Rocky disappeared.

"I thought something had happened to him. It was unlike him to not answer my calls for more than a day," he said. "And then, I realized all the money was missing," Mudridge finished, sounding downhearted, staring at the floor, hands between his knees. "I have not seen him or the money in a month."

"How much money are we talking about here?"

"Ten million dollars," he said it as if it were a couple of hundred dollars.

"Ten mil..." I whistled. "That's a lot of moolah."

"I trusted Rocky." He lifted his eyes to me, glistening.

"Have you notified the authorities? The police?"

He snorted. "No, no, I can't do that."

"Hmm," I said. "Why did you come to me?"

"To find him, of course."

I chuckled. "No. I mean, *why* did you come to me?"

"You came recommended by someone," he answered, as if it were a silly question.

"Who?"

"I'd ... I'd rather not say." His brow wrinkled. "I want a quiet search, and I heard you are someone who can keep his mouth shut. If it got out that he stole investors' money, it wouldn't be any good for ... " He trailed off. Had he meant to tell me that? Had he just let the cat out of the bag—the money bag?

"So it wasn't your money?"

"Yes," he said, wide-eyed. Then thought better of it. "Well, no, not all of it. A part. I want him found."

"What do you do, Mr. Mudridge?"

"I'm a fund manager."

He keeps piling it higher and deeper. I leaned back in my chair and observed him over my steepled fingers. A very distinct feeling gnawed at my gut that he wasn't telling me everything. "All good and well, Mr. Mudridge, but he may be anywhere in the world by now. He could cover a lot of ground with ten million dollars—and be far, far away."

"Look, are you a private investigator or not?" He placed his hands flat down on my desk and leaned in.

"Sure, but … "

"Then find him. I don't care how much it'll cost. My only requirement is that you complete it without arousing attention. I want that son-of-a-bitch found." He tossed out the last words with a bucket of venom sloughing over the rim.

I was ready to turn him down. Something about him spelled trouble. Besides, chasing a guy like that around the world could be a long and tedious task with plenty of frustration. I doubted he had dealt me a full hand of cards. He was holding something back, tucked up his fiduciary sleeve, so to speak.

I told him my fees and then an estimated cost of hiring international agents if need be. "The cost to begin could be considerable," I told him. "Buying silence would be even more expensive."

"I don't care. Find the bastard!" He shouted, while pulling a checkbook from his inside coat pocket. He scribbled out the check. "Just find the fucker. I don't care what you have to do!" Mudridge stood, eyes bulging, and slammed the check down on my desk, before storming out of the office. He banged the door shut.

I picked up the check and saw that it was double the amount I asked for.

Dammit! I'm such a whore.

As crazy as it sounds, my first impulse was to tear it up and toss it in the trash. But then I reread the amount written on the check. I had to hand it to him, he didn't hesitate to cough up the money requested. Even though there was the possibility it was not his money he was giving me. I folded the check, placed it in my wallet intending to deposit it at the Hancock Whitney on my way home. I almost wished it would bounce, so I could refuse the case.

Leaning back, I contemplated the stack of folders in the inbox. The stack seemed to have grown taller since I last looked yesterday. I took the Mudridge notes describing his cheating-heart partner, put it in a file and shoved it to the side.

I sighed. Time to get organized if I was going to earn my fees. I fished the top folder from the inbox and flipped it open.

First: an offshore worker wanted his wife put under surveillance. He worked offshore: six weeks home, six weeks on the rig. After six weeks in the Gulf, he returned horny as hell. "And she said she don't want no sex no more." Shaking his head. "Now, that's a change. When we first met, all she wanted to do is fuck. That's why I married her in the first place," he complained. "Thongs! She never wore them before! Said they irritated her ass. Now, she's bought them! And I don't even get to see them on her. Can you imagine that?!"

Actually, I could imagine it but didn't want to. The photo he showed me was of a short, plump woman with a too tight, low-cut green dress revealing a yard of fish-white skin and tattoos peeking over the bra line.

I placed the file on top of the Mudridge folder.

Second: The owner of a small pizza business thought his employees were stealing money from the till. "Penny-ante stuff, but it still adds up," he complained. I advised him to put in a closed-circuit camera. "Do it with plenty of fanfare, so they'll all notice. Just the installation will be enough to scare them straight," I said. But he insisted. He wanted to prosecute. "Find 'em."

Third: A father thinks his son, in the tenth grade at Jesuit, was doing drugs. "He's getting it from the new kid down the street. Just moved in. I want him to stop."

"Did you report the new kid to the police?" I asked.

"What?! And get my son in trouble?"

Fourth: More of the same.

The fifth, sixth folders held similar, depressing jobs—clients wanted me to follow, photograph, spy, report, and exact revenge. More drugs, more thefts, more cheating. I was ready to sweep the entire pile off my desk into the trash can.

If it wasn't for the money, I'd ... I'd ... but I knew I would reach down and do the work. *"Just do the job,"* Detective Bull's voice echoed in my mind.

I had determined to get off my pity pot and *get on with the job* when I heard a noise by the door.

Someone was out there. I could see a silhouette through the frosted glass.

He, or she, didn't move. Only stood there.

A sudden fear gripped me, and I slid the desk drawer open as quietly as I could, and removed my weapon.

CHAPTER 19

The shadow behind the door did not move.

It was definitely a guy. *What's he waiting for?*

I propped my pistol on my wrist, aiming chest high, in case he kicked it in and came bursting through.

Still, nothing.

I tip-toed across the room to the door. Reaching down with my left hand, I gripped the knob, took a deep breath, and flung it open. I was ready to confront a thug or a gangster or—

What the hell!—It was Fred LaForge—without his clown makeup.

He had the goofiest expression, eyes wide, as if I had caught him peeping into a girl's bathroom.

"*Fred?*"

His face broke into a smile. "Yeah, that's me. Fred LaForge. You remembered me?" He dressed in a too-wide tie and a suit coat that hung a size too big.

"What the hell are you doing standing out there?"

"Uh ... nothing," he stuttered.

"Nothing?"

He blinked rapidly, then stared down wide-eyed at the gun in my hand.

I lowered my gun. "I didn't know who you were. You were there for over a minute. I could have shot you." He stood motionless. "Look, Fred, I've got some important paperwork I need to do."

"Oh sure, I understand," he said, but didn't budge.

I glanced over his shoulder. He was alone. "Okay, come on in," I said.

He carried himself with a sort of hangdog expression. Both shoes were scuffed, with one lace dragging the ground.

"I was afraid you'd forgotten me since we last met at Jackson Square."

"I remembered," I said, returning behind my desk and dropping my gun into the desk drawer. "How's, uh, how's Jocko the Clown doing?"

"It was Noodles, not Jocko. I was tiring of all the Bar Mitzvah and birthday parties."

"Too stressful, huh?" I said, slumping down in my chair, waving him to have a seat.

He took the chair, spine rigid, butt covering only the front half of the seat. I once again reviewed what I knew of Fred LaForge from my cop days. Graduated bottom of his class. Passed firearms training with the lowest passing score. Almost got his partner killed. And he got shot.

"How's your injury?" I asked.

"It's okay. Sometimes it aches when it rains or when the weather changes."

I rubbed the side of my face. "Okay, Fred. I know you didn't just happen to be in the neighborhood. What can I do for you?"

"It's that obvious?"

"Uh, yeah."

"I guess my standing outside your door—"

"A dead giveaway," I said. "And the coat and tie. What's on your mind?"

"What's on my mind? Ever since we met in Jackson Square, it's all I think about."

I said nothing.

"Since I was a boy, I always wanted to be a policeman," he admitted. "While other kids wanted to be Drew Brees, or play in rock bands, all I ever wanted was to be a cop." He rubbed his palms on his thighs. "I thought I'd tell you this upfront … You ought to know, when I was in the Police Academy, I admired you. You were my idea of a super-cop. Others pointed you out when I first arrived. 'See that guy there? That's Zeke Malone. He's the best,' they'd say. You were a role model to myself and a lot of other recruits."

I wasn't sure if that spoke good or bad of me, considering how things turned out. "Thanks, Fred," I said. "That's awful nice of you to say; that's flattering. But you still haven't answered my question."

"Your question: what brings me in?" He hesitated, as if trying to arrange his thoughts. "I don't know about you, but the short time I was a cop was the happiest time in my life."

I thought he might be exaggerating, but after looking into his doleful face, I knew he was serious. In addition, he had these sheepish brown eyes with a wistful look. A hangdog look. I wasn't sure if I should feel sorry for him or pity him. Fred was a screw-up. He nearly got himself and his partner killed.

But the crazy thing was this: as I sat there studying this poor Sad Sack, I realized I felt the same way. For the first time since I left the force two years ago, I realized I missed the life of a cop. Other than my marriage to Jane, being a detective was the most fulfilling thing I'd ever done. All the stress, the tension, the fears, the pounding heart—that was what I hated. But also what I lived for.

I wasn't about to share my feelings with him. So, I told him, "I get that."

Fred LaForge sat there with a thousand-yard stare on his face.

"Well, that's all very interesting. But as I say … " I held up my wrist and tapped my watch.

"Oh, sorry. I know you're busy." He stood, tugging at his ill-fitting coat, edging towards the door. Then he stopped, pivoted, and sat down. He'd decided to say his piece. "The reason I'm here. And I've been thinking about this a lot. The reason I'm here—is to ask for a job."

Oh, God! I was afraid of this. My first impulse was to tell him, *Hell NO!* and kick him out of my office, but his eyes gazed at me, reminding me of a puppy I once owned. "Well, I didn't expect that, Fred," I mumbled, trying to buy time until I could think of a reason to tell him goodbye without hurting his feelings. "And don't think I'm not flattered that you would consider working for me."

"Yeah," he jumped in. "I know you're a one-man operation. But everybody could use some help, right?"

I halfway nodded my head before I caught myself. "But the truth of the matter, Fred, is that I work alone, and the agency doesn't make enough money to hire an extra body, and—"

"I thought of that," he interjected. "What I'm willing to do is work for *nothing.*"

I blinked.

"See, I'll cover my own expenses," he added.

"Wait, not paying an employee is ... isn't that against the law? I don't know, Fred."

"Mr. Malone, I need this job. I'm going crazy being a clown." He leaned forward. "If I have to blow up another balloon or chase another snotty kid, well, I'd—I'd rather die first."

"Fred, I—"

"Come on, Mr. Malone. If it's a legal problem, pay me minimum wage. I'll only charge you ten—no, five hours a week."

I placed my hands on my desk, palms down, ready to push myself up and refuse him. That's when my hand knocked over the stack of folders, the pending jobs. They scattered on the floor. I looked down and thought of the offshore worker and his dumpy wife in her thong. The pizza shack with sticky-fingered employees in the cash register. And the newest one: Rocky Stream stealing money that didn't belong to his partner, Malcolm Mudridge.

I steepled my fingers, tapping my forefingers together, watching Fred stoop and pick up the files, stacking them on my desk. And I let him, never moved a muscle. *How much effort could it take to do surveillance?* Before I knew it, I started making up reasons *why* I could hire Fred. *Whoa, what are you doing?* I asked myself, trying to slow down my thought process. The crazy thing was that I felt sympathy for Fred. Those emotions always got me in trouble.

More rationalizations came to mind. I ran my thumb up the end of the folders like you would a deck of cards. *It doesn't take a rocket scientist to do a little snooping. Why, even a ... a clown could do it.* I set the folders aside and turned my attention back to Fred LaForge. I stared at him in a new light. Nonetheless, my brain couldn't shake the image of Jocko, no, Noodles The Clown—it stuck like flypaper pasted to the bathroom wall of my mind.

It was probably a bad idea. A very *big* bad idea, I told myself. *But what the hell!?* Against my better judgment, I nodded my head. "Okay, Fred. I'm willing to give it a try."

Fred leaped to his feet, reached across the table, and grabbed my hand. "Oh, thank you, thank you, Mr. Malone."

"Fred, if we're going to be working together, you gotta quit calling me Mr. Malone. Call me Zeke."

"I knew it. I knew it," he said, pumping my hand up and down like an old-fashioned water pump. "You'll never regret it, Boss. Never!"

I hope not, I thought.

CHAPTER 20

After meeting with Malcolm Mudridge and hiring Fred, I still had an early afternoon session with *Lucy in the Sky*. I could not miss this as I had skipped the last meeting, and that wouldn't look good on my report. She greeted me at the door with a joke about a Rabbi, a Protestant minister, and a guy in a wheelchair. "Guess which one got into heaven?" She said, rolling back and forth, barely able to contain herself before delivering the punch line.

I thought for a moment. "The guy in the wheelchair?"

"Nah. None of them. They were *all* assholes." She poured herself a cup of coffee in a plastic travel cup with a Nicholls State University logo on the side, stashing it in a cup holder taped to her arm rest with silver electrical tape. Today, she seemed animated, nervous, manic even. I flopped down in the plush armchair as she wheeled over facing me. *Does she have trouble sleeping like I do?*

The coffee smell was strong, depressing. Suddenly, I wanted to get out of there.

"So, how's it going lately, Zeke?" She asked, fixing me with her beady eyes behind her round glasses.

"Well, I'm *good*," I said, suppressing a tremble in my fingers by clasping them in my lap.

She frowned. "You always tell me that—*Good?*" She wrinkled her nose as if smelling the stench of shit. "What does that even mean? As in: *Good*, a streetcar didn't run me over? *Good*, I found Jesus. Or *Good*, I got laid?"

I shook my head. "No, none of the above."

"So, I'd like the truth," she leaned in. "You're not really *good*, are you, then?"

"No, I suppose not."

"Can you elaborate?"

"It's that no matter what I do. No matter how long it's been ... I can't let go of ..." I paused.

"Of Jane?"

"Yes."

She wheeled back and rolled over to the window with her back to me. After a pause, she said in a soft tone, "I know it's difficult to let go of someone you loved deeply."

I said, "No matter what I've tried, nothing works. The booze didn't, the pills didn't either. Yet, being sober is just as bad, if not worse, as being drunk. With the booze and the pills, at least I could check out for a few hours. But it always came back. Worse."

She wheeled around. "We've talked about keeping yourself busy. Doesn't that give you any sense of relief from the ... the depression? What about your agency? How's that going?"

"My P.I. firm is doing well. It's finally making money and serves as a distraction for short periods of time. I even hired an ex-cop to help me."

"You hired an ex-cop to help? Tell me more? What's his name?"

She wheeled in close, facing straight on. *I hate that.* "Fred. Fred Laforge. But, you know, I'm not sure it will work out."

"Why not? Are other people incapable of helping you?"

I shrugged, "Yeah, well, it's not that. I'm just unsure he will be a good fit. I work best alone."

"Well, Zeke, I think it's high time you let other people into your life. You've been alone since Jane died. It's time to be better, not bitter."

Oh, God. Here she goes with another of her wheelchair-is-like-life metaphors. "To what end?" I asked.

But she was straightforward in what she said next. "I think you'll be surprised how much you'll improve when you let others get close to you." She patted my hand. "Put the past behind you, start focusing on the present, and look to the future, Malone. You are one of those brooding types who really needs to open up and free yourself. Release responsibility for things beyond your control."

"Forget about Jane?" I asked.

She sighed and pulled back her hand. "Not forget, dummy! But realize you did not kill Jane. You are not responsible for her death. Bomber Boy killed her. You must rebuild your life from the rubble. No doubt, Jane was the love of your life. And she is someone you'll never forget." For a moment, Doctor Lucy seemed to melt into her chair as she wheeled away from me, a distant look on her face, staring at the floor. "But you have a responsibility to her memory to begin living again."

We both sat silent for several minutes. There were sides of *Lucy in the Sky* I knew nothing about.

Finally, she looked up, and said in a bright voice, but her puffy face betrayed her. "I've seen cases like yours before. You're facing backwards, clutching the past like a life preserver. You can't move on if you're looking back in the rearview mirror. Let new people in. It's the only way forward, Zeke!"

The only thought in my head and the only fear in my heart was— am I forgetting Jane?

• • •

Whatever was bothering Lucy in the Sky this morning was contagious. I went to my office with a jittery feeling in my belly and couldn't sit still all day. Finally, I jammed my paperwork into the desk drawer and went home. Later that afternoon, I paced back and forth, considering her words: *Let other people in.* I figured she was right. If I was going to get out of this funk, this permanent black hole I'd slipped into, maybe letting others in wasn't such a bad idea.

Letting others in? I thought about the last time I was at the Half Moon Bar, a week ago. Including Birdie, now the group had grown to four, and we all played MJ's DEATH GAMES. It was fun, but I just couldn't stay. I had had enough togetherness for one evening.

As I left, Birdie caught up with me by the front door. She said, "Why don't you call me sometime?"

I liked Birdie. We could be buddies, in a palsy-walsy kind-of-way, with MJ and Bull around. But could I see her in a romantic, more friendly way? Possibly. I didn't know. I couldn't answer her. I just stood there mute. Like the idiot I am.

She stuffed a piece of paper into my shirt pocket. "That's my number. Use it. Call me if you need me. Or just want to talk."

I was still silent.

"Or if you decide to take that stick out of your ass. Give me a ring," Birdie said, returning to the bar.

When I got home, I tossed the note into a wastebasket without ever reading it.

That was before my session that morning with Lucy in the Sky. I was way too restless to concentrate on reading or watching TV. With a fluttery feeling in my chest, I decided to call Birdie. I figured all she could say was no, so what the heck? I searched the wicker wastebasket for the paper with her phone number. At times like these, there's something to be said for being such a lousy housekeeper. I unraveled the wad of paper and smoothed out the wrinkles on my thigh.

With hesitation, I punched her number into my cell phone. It rang twice and jumped into the song, "*Who Let the Dogs Out.*" To tell you the truth, I was relieved, too, and about to hang up. The recording started telling me, "Sorry, I can't come to—" when her voice cut it with an abrupt, "What?"

I hesitated, trying to find my voice.

"Who's this?"

"Uhhh, it's me. Zeke Malone."

She hesitated, then she said in a softer voice, "I was wondering how long it would take you to call."

"Yeah, well, you said to call and—"

"What did you have in mind?"

"I thought we could ... could talk."

"*Uh-huh.* Do you want to come over to my place? Or do you want me to go to yours?"

• • •

Her apartment building was bright-yellow with white trim shrouded under magnolia trees off Canal Blvd. Birdie's apartment was one of those old Queen Anne charmers, strictly New Orleans, but it seemed to work. Front stairs led to an entrance on the second-level, that I took two at a time. *Settle down*, I told myself. The house had a wrap-around balcony overlooking the street, with hanging spaghetti ferns and sky blue hurricane shutters.

Shifting from foot to foot, I gathered my courage and knocked on the leaded-glass door, saw a light come on and a figure approaching. The door opened and there she stood, smiling, a wine glass in her hand. She wore a long, silky dressing gown with a loose cloth belt accentuating her waist. Her hair, usually in a ponytail, spread out on both of her shoulders down to her breasts.

Her eyes were bright. "Well, Zeke, come on in."

As soon as she shut and locked the door, she stepped in close, put her arms around my neck and we kissed. I responded by kissing her hard and long. We spoke no more as we made like in the movies— the camera tracks over the trail of clothing on the floor leading to the bedroom. The setting sun quivered through the lace curtains in purple and pink dance patterns, and she whispered, "What were you waiting on? An engraved invitation?"

We entwined ourselves in each other's arms like two sweaty wrestlers struggling to get a better hold. I bore down on her like a blacksmith banging on an anvil.

Afterwards, we lay there side-by-side, breathing heavy, going slower and slower, until she propped herself up on one elbow, facing me. "Boy, do you always fuck like you're chasing a criminal?"

·   ·   ·

After midnight, when I left her apartment, instead of going home, I drove around aimlessly. I could still smell her scent on me, and I buzzed down the window to get the full blast of the night. Eventually, I found myself near Lake Pontchartrain, parking along the seawall, listening to the Silver Bullet Band, one of Jane's favorites. Probably, if Jane had lived, she would be home, safe. Maybe with a glass of wine after she put Carla to bed. Maybe unwinding from another successful work day. At peace. Safe.

Twenty-three miles across the darkness of the lake, the lights from the North Shore twinkled like dim stars. And for the first time, I had difficulty remembering Jane's face. All her features were there, the wide set grass-green eyes, the straight lines of her jaw, her full lips. Her long neck.

But there was a fuzziness, a lack of details, as if someone with an airbrush had erased away the small lines around her eyes, smoothed over the slight indentation in her chin. It was like looking through the wrong end of an out-of-focus telescope. The green of her eyes were dull.

Yet, instead of feeling exhilarated at just having made love to a beautiful woman, I was empty like a knife had carved out my center.

The conversation with *Lucy in the Sky* came back to me. *Was I forgetting Jane?*

CHAPTER 21

The next day, I felt washed out, depressed. I drove to my office in the Bywater and sat in my chair, mulling over the events of the last two years. The last months. Days. My mind felt muddled and overwhelmed by the turn of events with Birdie. She was no longer one of the guys at the Half Moon. Our relationship had evolved to where I was uncomfortable. Why was I feeling guilty? Why did I feel as if I'd betrayed Jane?

I could hear the chug-chug of the tugboats on the river—and my eyelids grew leaden, and the next thing I knew, I had dozed off. It could not have been long; I awoke with a jerk. Noises roused me— footsteps on the slate tile in the courtyard. Then the creak of the rickety stairs. I blinked the cobwebs away.

The steps paused at the top of the landing, then to my door. The footfalls were heavy, as the person were tired. But not of a man—a woman. Another hesitation, followed by a sharp rapping.

"Come in. It's unlocked."

The door swung open, and a short, stout lady, maybe around fifty, stood in the doorway, dressed in a housekeeping uniform. Her hair was iron-gray, and beads of sweat glistened on the side of her tan, flushed face. With one hand, she held tightly to an enormous black bag; the other hand on the doorknob. She tilted her chin, surveyed the room, and fixed her eyes on me.

"You Mister Ezekiel Malone?" she asked. English was not her original language. There was a strong Spanish accent underneath.

Something about her pinched mouth and her intense stare made me uneasy. I felt my legs tense as I imagined her opening the leather purse and reaching in for a weapon or ...

I smiled. "It depends on who's asking?"

"Me. Esperanza Gonzales," she said firmly.

Standing, I gestured to the client chair across from me. "Won't you come in and take a seat? ... Most people call me Zeke, Mrs. Gonzales."

She said not another word as she entered. Her movements were deliberate and awkward as she shut the door. She sat and adjusted the bag in her lap like a shield. Stenciled above her breast was the name *Roosevelt Hotel.* She clutched the flier of the missing dog in one hand.

"Okay. You look warm, Mrs. Gonzales. I was about to have a Coke. " Not waiting for a response, I strode to the small dorm-sized refrigerator on the stand next to my gray filing cabinet. I grabbed two cans out, popped the tops, and extended one to her.

"Thank you." She chugged down a large swallow. "It's hot outside, and I transfer twice to get to your office. That sonofabitch driver let me off at the wrong stop."

"I'm sorry. Unfortunately, I'm not in the best location." I took my seat and sipped.

She drank again and eyed me over the top of her can.

I leaned forward and pointed towards the paper in her hand. "I see you have the flier about the lost dog—"

"Wally," she said.

"Oh, yes, Wally. I'm not sure why you are here, but I don't do missing dogs."

"No, no. Little girl handed me when I asked for directions to your office."

"Okay."

She lifted her chin. "Do you know me?" she asked, turning her head one way, then the other.

I squinted and studied her for a moment. Something was familiar about her features, but I couldn't put my finger on it. "Should I?"

Looking past me at the walls, at the cabinet, at the ceiling, she took another large swig. "No, I suppose not." She opened her purse, and I felt the hair on my neck stand up. She reached in and grabbed a wadded handkerchief with loud red flowers. After she finished wiping her face and neck, she stuffed it back into the bag, fixing her eyes on me. "You come with much recommendation."

I nodded.

"They said you were honest," she said.

"That's correct."

"They said you don't quit."

"Also true."

"And they say you could also be, how did he say, a real *son of a dick?*"

"Correct again." I gave a laugh. "What's the name of this person who recommended me with such glowing terms?"

"A thin black man with *grande* glasses." She formed binoculars with her hands in front of her eyes.

I leaned back in my chair, chuckling. "Only one man fits that description—Michael Jordan?"

"*Si,* Doctor Michael Jordan. He is doctor to dead people."

"Yes, that's him."

She nodded and finished her Coke before extending the empty can across the desk. I took it, crushed, and tossed it into the recycling by the filing cabinet. I tilted my head and asked, "When did you meet him?"

"A while back … " she said, snapping and unsnapping the clasp of the purse.

I didn't pursue it further but made a mental note to ask MJ how he met Mrs. Gonzales? And, where? And, why? But I'd find out later.

"I know about you," she told me. "I read about you in the paper."

"When was this?"

"Your wife died in an explosion two years ago."

A sudden cold lump formed in my stomach. My body tensed. I said nothing.

"That's you, right?" she added.

I nodded slowly. *Where the hell is this going?*

She said, "I knew it."

"Mrs. Gonzales—"

"Esperanza."

I squirmed uneasily in my chair. "Esperanza, how can I help you?"

"I want you investigate."

"Investigate?"

"I want to hire you!"

I hesitated and said in a measured voice, "Okay. You want to hire me to investigate? Go on."

She must have taken my *Okay* as a *Yes.* "Good," she said as she opened her purse and removed a fat, worn envelope bound with thick rubber bands. Dropping it on the desk between us, she said, "First things first. When I hire you, you promise no quit till you solve the case."

I shook my head. "That I cannot promise, Esperanza. Let me make it clear to you upfront: not every case can be solved."

Neither one of us spoke as she considered this. She sighed. "So long as you give it your best, I will be satisfied. No quit. No quit," she said, scooting forward again until she sat on the edge of her seat. "Promise?"

I was uncertain where this was going, but I nodded. *What was I getting into?* "I promise."

"*Bien,*" she said, nodding her head several times.

I opened a drawer and flopped a yellow legal pad on the desk. I jotted down today's date and her name. "Can you tell me what you want me to investigate, Esperanza?"

She exhaled slowly. "My son was murdered."

I put down the pen and looked into her eyes. They were brown, clear. Was she sincere? "I'm sorry about your loss. Did you go to the police?"

"The police," she snorted. "*Desgraciados!* Class-A-dicks!"

"That might not look good on their recruiting posters." I smiled. "What did they do?"

"*Nada.* Not a *goddamnit* thing. That why I come to you."

I picked up the pen. "What was your son's name?"

"Juan ... Juan Figueroa."

"Not Gonzales, like yours?"

"No, that *pendejo* abandoned us after our boy was born, when he see Juan was not all there." She motioned her hand towards her head. "He left."

I wrote the name *Juan Figueroa*. And my fingers froze. I jerked my eyes up at her. "I've heard this name before."

"You should," she said, leaning forward, eyes fastened on me.

My face tingled. My throat closed. "Why?"

"The explosion that killed your wife—also killed my son."

"Lady, I ... " My breath caught in my chest.

"I want you to find out who set up *mi hijo*—my son, Juan. I want you to find who murdered my boy."

CHAPTER 22

"I won't do that," I said, shaking my head.

"Why not?" she demanded.

My mind froze a moment as I grappled for a reason. This was relatively simple. I couldn't take this case. But all I blurted out was, "Well—because it's a terrible idea."

She looked at me. "It's a bad idea—because y*ou too close?*"

"Yes. That's precisely the reason," I said, relieved—she had provided me with the answer why I wouldn't touch this with a ten-foot pole. "I'm too close to this."

My legs and arms were tingling. I took a deep breath and placed my palms down on the desk to steady myself, hoping to look decisive rather than weak. I cleared my throat. "Understand me, Mrs. Gonzales, we both lost someone dear to us. That's normally *Rule Number One* in Police Work: don't become emotionally involved because it clouds your judgment. Things get overlooked. There's no way I might keep a distance between myself, your son, and—the death of my wife."

"So, you tell me you can't handle this?!"

I cut her off. "I never told you I *couldn't* handle it. I said, *I won't.*"

She sat back in her chair and folded her arms across her breasts. I lifted my hand off the desk and saw the wet imprint. I moved the yellow pad over it.

"The police investigated this. The case is officially closed." I wrote the word CLOSED in big letters and circled it. "They concluded your son was acting out of some crazy notion he'd get a million dollars just by strapping explosives on his chest. Remember, I was there? I *spoke* to your son."

"My boy wasn't capable of such thoughts. Someone put him up to it. My son was simple. He could not have planned such a thing—*como se dice*—how do you say, scheme? He was slow learner, but had good *corazon.* A good heart. "

"The case is closed. What do you expect me to do?"

"I want you to do what the police should have done," she said. "If they pull their asses out of their butt."

Pull their asses out of their butt. I chuckled. "I used to be one of them."

"Yes. That is why I want you. You one of them." She drew herself up straight. "You know police and what they do. I want to hire you. You have as much at stake here as I do."

I sighed. "I won't. It would be unethical."

We sat there in silence.

She sighed. "Did you ever see the report that the police filed on Juan?"

"Well, no," I admitted. "Not the actual report."

"So, how do you know what it uncovered about my son? *La verda?* The truth?"

"I read a summary report."

"Hmm, and what else?" she demanded.

"The head of Homicide gave me a full briefing ... " I stopped. Come to think of it, Jojo Turner was in charge. He was not forthcoming with information nor generous in giving me details. His reluctance to go into motives irritated me, but times were rough for me then. Besides, I thought he was attempting to spare me emotional pain. But none of that mattered. I spiraled down, like a BB going down a drain, hitting bottom. Only this time, the bottom was inside a bottle.

She glared at me. "You a P.I.?" She would not quit. She peeled the rubber bands off the envelope and dumped three, thick stacks of bills. "I pay you. Whatever you ask."

"It isn't the money," I said.

This seemed to set her off as her face reddened and her eyes blazed. "Don't turn up your nose at this money, *Mr. Detective Man*," she snapped, shoving the stacks across the desk. "For two years, I've clean hotels in the day, clean office buildings at night, people's houses on the weekend. I earn this money honest scrubbing out latrines, cleaning up other people's *shit!* I work while the police do nothing. *Jesus Cristo!* And now you say: *It's not the money!*"

'Look, Mrs. Gonzales. You want me to find a missing spouse that walked out on you? I'm your man. Investigate cheating husbands? I can handle that. Get evidence for a divorce? I'll swear in court based on the evidence I collect." I looked down at the flier about the lost dog. "If you want me to help find Wally, I'd scour the streets till we find his carcass."

She rolled her eyes."I'm not asking you to find a lost dog. I'm not asking you to find that shit-ass husband of mine. I need you to find who murdered my son. If you can't do that—just what the *hell* do you do then?"

I shoved the stacks of money back at her, stood, leaned forward, and put my fist down on the desk like a gorilla. I wanted to make sure she understood. "Save your money, Mrs. Gonzales. Maybe someone else can help you. I can't."

"Someone else? Who—another investigator?"

"The city is full of private investigation firms. Google them!" I moved to the door and opened it.

She gathered up the stacks of bills and stuffed them in the envelope. "All they want is the money," she mumbled, pushing it down into the black leather purse. She marched to the doorway, turned, and leaned in towards me.

I smelled the sweat coming off her and saw the veins in her neck pulsating. "I want you to investigate." She stepped across the threshold and faced me. "You have *everything* at stake here."

I stepped back. "Mrs. Gonzales, I don't investigate killers who murdered my wife," I sputtered and slammed the door in her face.

CHAPTER 23

And that was that. I never expected to see Mrs. Gonzales again. It was back to business and getting on with my life.

It's been five weeks since I had hired Fred LaForge. He sat on the opposite side of the desk, jumpy and nervous as a fish on a hook. He has been dressing more casually since he first came in asking for a job—an open-neck pullover with a light Saints' jacket. From my second-floor office, we could hear the chug of engines and boxcars clanking as they trundled to and from the wharf and warehouses along the river.

"Well, what do you have?" I asked.

"You're going to love these." He slipped open his newsboy bag and extracted a stack of eight-by-ten glossy photographs. "Take a look."

I picked them up and studied the first one. It looked like a black-and-white Rorschach test. "What is this? I can't make it out."

"Oh," he said, reaching and flipping it over.

Suddenly, the picture came into focus. It was a close-up of a male butt parked between two spread legs. "This is too close. You can't identify anybody."

"Keep looking," he encouraged.

The next picture was a close-up of the woman's face contorted in ecstasy ... Or was it pain? No doubt about it. It was the wife of the longshoreman. I shuffled through them. It was much like a deck of pornographic playing cards. There was even a shot of her new thongs hanging on the back of a chair.

"Where ... How did you get these?"

"It wasn't too hard. After our client left for the rig, she waved bye-bye and hot-tailed it over to meet her lover at *The Hot Pillow Motel,* off Airline Highway," he said.

The Hot Pillow Motel, off Airline Highway? I searched through my memory bank and recalled back in the day that Reverend Jimmy Swaggart got caught consorting with hookers in those motels around that area. His whole televangelism empire came crashing to the ground. But, like a bad penny, he kept turning up. Flipping through the cable channels, I stumbled across him, big and brassy as ever. Still charismatic, still praying to God for forgiveness, and still asking for money to keep his ministry going.

"They were so predictable," Fred said. "Rendezvous every Tuesday and Thursday. Even insisted they rent the same room. Sometimes he'd pay, sometimes she'd pay."

"That's only fair. Taking turns."

"It was a room on the backside of the motel, away from the street."

"So, how did you set up your cameras?"

"That was simple," Fred said. "The motel rents rooms by the hour. So, I rented the room for a few hours, installing my cameras and mics in the vents and light fixtures. Easy-peasey. When the lady in question drove there, I followed. I sat in my van, watching the entire thing on my monitor, recording it all. Boy, this guy had stamina." Fred handed me two DVDs marked Tape One and Tape Two, with dates and times stamped on them. "You want to watch them? That second tape has some real doozies. Screaming. Hollering in the valley."

"No, I don't think I'll watch these. Technically, they belong to the guy." I slide them into my desk drawer and locked it.

I looked up and said, "Good job, Fred." And I meant it.

Fred LaForge leaned back in his chair, beaming like a peacock. "Thanks, Boss."

Fred launched into his plans to catch the employees from the Pork and Chicken Shack. His enthusiasm was obvious. He sat upright in his chair, bobbing up and down as he talked in a high-pitched voice, head whipping around for emphasis.

He had done an excellent job. *Hey, I misjudged him.*

Of course, the big case was the fund manager who wanted his ex-partner, Rocky Stream, tracked down and the ten million dollars found.

"Nothing yet," Fred said. "But I've located some relatives of his in the Houston area. I notified a friend of mine to check them out." He got up from his chair, slung his messenger bag over his shoulder. "Gotta run!"

"Hold up a second," I said. He stopped halfway to the door. "Turn in a sheet of expenses for the motel and the electronic equipment. I'll reimburse you for out-of-pocket expenses."

"Right, Boss."

"And give me a tally of the hours you put in."

"You mean the five hours per week?"

"No, the *actual* hours you put in. We'll discuss a reasonable salary the next time you come in."

"Right, Boss," he said, slipping out and shutting the door.

Alone in my office, I studied the photographs. These were hardcore quality: some shots she was on her knees, others their bodies contorted like circus acrobats. I debated the wisdom of giving the oil rig worker these photos. No telling how he might react—no use pouring gasoline on the fire.

Men had murdered their wives and their lovers over less than that. Possible I could just give him a typewritten report with a shot or two of her leaving the motel room. Or maybe have those computerized-fuzzy patches over the delicate areas—like that *Naked Alive* show on the History Channel. I stuffed the photos back into the envelope, locked them and the DVDs into my wall safe behind the *Dogs Playing Cards* painting.

•   •   •

Dr. Lucy was decked-out in a gauzy Cinderella dress sparkling with sprinkles, wand with a star on the end, and a Queen Elizabeth crown on her head.

"What gives with the ... the costume party getup?" I asked, slumping into my familiar, over-padded armchair.

"Oh, this old thing?" Smiling, she turned a wheelie in a circle, the sun from the window gleaming like diamonds on her dress. "They selected me as Queen Mother for the Krewe of Little Rascals. You know, for special needs children? It's for a Mardi Gras ball tonight. Fundraiser! You want to come?"

"Uh, I've already got plans. How about I just send a check?" I said. "You're going to ride on a float?"

"*Hell no*, I'm my own float. I've got a motorized wheelchair at home—I'm leading the parade."

I laughed out loud, and this seemed to stop her.

She pulled up short, pivoted towards me with a quizzical look on her face. Then she wheeled towards me, till her chair bumped my leg. She leaned in. "Something's different about you."

"Is there?"

"Yeah." She backed up, observing me, hand to her chin. "You won the Louisiana Lottery? Quick Pick?"

"Nope."

"Wait, wait, don't tell me. I'm good at this! I used to be a fortune teller before I became a shrink."

"Why did you change professions?"

"More money in this. Less work." She squinted at me, her mouth in an O, thinking. Then she broke out in a grin. "You. Got. Laid. Didn't you?"

I blinked at her. I must have a tell that I'm unaware of because she began rolling her wheelchair back and forth hurriedly, grinning like the cat that just ate the canary.

"Oh, my God, Malone. Come on, the truth."

"Well. Yeah."

"And ... was it good?"

"What kind of question is that for a psychiatrist to be asking her patient?"

She wheeled over to the coffee table and poured herself a cup. "All pussy is good—or so I've been told," she said over her shoulder. "Want some?"

I shook my head.

She rolled back. "Well, come on, share. Who was she?"

"What about patient confidentiality?"

"She isn't my patient."

"She's a cop I met."

"Is she hot?"

"Sure. In a pretty sort of way," I said. "She's attractive but not beautiful."

"And ... ?"

"I met her just recently."

"Does she know Bull?"

"Yes, she's his partner. Or was. She just transferred to Special Victims." I took a deep breath and looked away.

She paused, then asked, "What?"

"Oh, nothing."

"Did you enjoy being with her? How was the sex?"

"Like I already told you! Now, leave me alone about it."

Dr. Lucy shook her head. "Well, at least you're not telling me it was boring."

"No, it wasn't that, for sure."

"Then why didn't you fully enjoy it?"

"Who said I didn't?"

She stared at me as if I were a schoolboy and said in a low voice, "Why didn't you fully enjoy it?"

"I don't know," I said.

"Were you comparing her to Jane?"

I took another deep breath and looked past Dr. Lucy to the window towards the river. The smokestack of a ship passed by. "No, I wasn't comparing her." I paused. "It was just ... different."

She shook her head again. "Look, your wife passed away. And I know you feel responsible for her death. But quit comparing every girl you meet to her. No one will ever measure up to Jane. What's it been—two years?"

"Over two."

"And whatever flaws she had—*and she had them*—we all do, you've glossed over them and built her up to some kind of goddamn goddess. A cross between the Virgin Mary and Irma La Douce."

I was silent.

"Look, I'm not saying forget her. No one will ever replace her. I know that."

She sipped her coffee and made a face. "Ugh. Bitter." She rolled over to the sink, poured it out, rinsed her cup and left it. "You feel guilty, don't you? Guilty cause you screwed another woman? And enjoyed it?" She wheeled towards me. "Even after Jane's been gone for years, you still feel guilty? Is it maybe because you're moving on?"

I stared down at the grooves worn in the carpet where her wheels had passed, leading from the door to the coffee urn, and back to a position across from the easy chair. *Am I forgetting Jane?* I asked myself.

"Good god, I've never met a man who felt so guilty about *everything*." She let out a huff. "You know, sometimes I feel like snatching you up and shaking you. Or grabbing you by your gonads and tossing your dumbass out that third-story window."

I laughed. "It's a good thing I can outrun your wheelchair."

"I wouldn't be so sure, sucker!"

. . .

Later that night, I drove over to visit Birdie Birdsong in her yellow Queen Anne apartment with its sky blue trim off Canal Boulevard. She answered the door in a pair of shorts and halter top. After the door closed, she kissed me hard and sank to her knees in front, saying, "Drop those pants, Mister." She unbuckled my belt and pulled them down to my knees.

We maneuvered over to the couch and after a few minutes, we switched places as she wiggled out of her shorts.

"Now, it's my turn," she said as I felt the pressure of her hands pushing my shoulders down.

What we did that night, well, I won't go into it. A cop, even an old ex-cop, never tells. Old habits die hard, we don't kiss and tell. I *can* say this, though: Birdie was a very sensual woman and her appetite for carnal knowledge was limitless. Based on the empirical evidence—*just the facts, ma'am*—I was lucky enough to taste her limits a few times.

CHAPTER 24

It had been some time since I started visiting Birdie. Okay, no reason to be coy about it. It was sex, unadulterated sex. But let's be fair about it—she had invested about as much as I did, which wasn't much. Still, it unsettled me and I needed to sort through the feelings underneath.

In the past, when I wanted to think things out, I took walks by the Mississippi River. Watching the ships and tankers glide by on the flat, fast-moving surface has always fascinated me. These ocean-bound behemoths weighed in at hundreds of thousands of tons, but cut against the current, moving in slow-motion, like the shuttle docking with the space station in *2001*. After walking for an hour, I came to no major conclusions, but I still felt better. The sun was going down behind the spires of the Cathedral as I headed back to my office.

Before I made it back, my cell phone began buzzing—a number I didn't recognize. I clicked the green button and waited in silence.

"Zeke Malone?" a woman's voice asked.

"Yes, who is this?"

After a lengthy pause, she said, "This is Kitty Fowler." A picture of her popped into my head, complete with a white dress and blonde hair under a yellow sunhat. Or was that Leslie Baronne?

I informed her, "Everybody's been looking for you. The police want to question you."

"So my husband told me. He said ... a man dressed like a woman died."

"Murdered, Mrs. Fowler. And not just any woman, either. A man dressed to look like you, with a blonde wig and high heels. Shot dead."

Neither of us spoke. The streetlights were coming on.

"Mrs. Fowler?"

"Yes."

"The police want to talk with you," I repeated. More silence. "Where are you?"

"I don't want to speak to the police now."

"You need to talk with an attorney ... then the police," I said.

"After I speak with you—" She hesitated. "Alone. Can you come speak with me? My husband said he hired you to follow me."

"True, he did."

"And he seems to trust you. He said you're honest."

"Also true. Where are you?"

"If I tell you, you must come alone. No police. I'll talk with you, only."

"Where are you?"

"In my home, near St. Charles Avenue."

The drive from my office was slow, and it was dark by the time I arrived. The sodium streetlights peeked through the tree branches overhanging the street. I pulled up in the driveway behind a very expensive red Maserati convertible. I assumed it belonged to Mrs. Fowler.

The lights were on in the front rooms. Before I reached the porch, the door opened. The glow from the interior lights silhouetted her body.

She greeted me, "Thank you for coming so promptly, Zeke. Can I call you Zeke?" She spoke with a light noticeable southern drawl. But also with noticeable slurring.

"Yes, that's okay."

"Fine, come in." She pivoted and led me in, trailing the fragrance of Maja soap in her wake, the same type Jane had used. Kitty Fowler must have just showered, her blonde hair still damp, swept straight back, swinging to mid-shoulder. The photograph didn't do her justice—she resembled a young Michelle Pfeiffer. She was in her mid-thirties, but plastic enhancement made her look as if she stepped out of Cosmopolitan. Her white shorts accentuated long legs, tanned all the way to turquoise painted toenails.

"This is terrible. Just terrible," she muttered, leading me through the house. We entered the living room with windows looking out to the lighted garden and fountains. I remembered it from when Bull and I entered, looking for the doctor. The white marble flooring still looked as if you could skate on it. The room smelled of whiskey and musk, not out of a bottle. She motioned for me to sit in a chair, and she collapsed onto a white-plush oversized leather couch. Leaning forward, she picked up a half-empty crystal tumbler of amber-colored liquid from the glass coffee table. Her pale blue silk shirt was half unbuttoned, revealing ample cleavage. "May I offer you anything to drink, Zeke?" she asked.

"No, thanks. It had been several years since I took my last drink." I felt my mouth watering, though, at the thought of it. "Where's your husband?" I scanned the hallway, thinking he might appear. Several large oil-paintings filled the interior walls.

"He's away. I told him to leave 'cause I wanted to talk with you alone." She downed the rest of her drink. "First of all, I had nothing to do with the death of this ... this person's death." The words tumbled from her lips like a drunk stumbling up a staircase.

"No one's accusing you," I said.

"Yes, true," She cocked her head to the side with a half smile. "No one has—yet."

"Is there a reason they might accuse you of killing him? Other than the fact you hired him to impersonate you?"

She stared at me in amazement for a ten-count, then broke into a half-laugh. "So, you know?" She got up and wobbled over to a liquor cabinet, stood with her back to me and poured herself another drink. I could hear the uncorking of a bottle and the clink of glass against glass as she poured. "You sure I can't get you anything?" She glanced over her shoulder.

"You were sloppy." I said. "The Spider Man mask at the costume ball was smart. And you're tall, as tall as an average man. But the fingerprints on the letter and the cash were pretty conclusive. You were the one who hired Leslie Baronne to impersonate you." The truth of the matter, the prints were still unidentified, but she didn't know that. I was playing a strong hunch.

She turned towards me, the amber-colored drink sloshing over the edge, leaning back against the bar, thrusting her hips forward. She observed me through narrow eyes for a moment, crossed her arms, balancing the glass with one hand. "I know you're lying," she said, taking a sip. "I wore rubber gloves."

"Spider Man doesn't wear rubber gloves," I said. "You hired the cross-dresser, Leslie Baronne, to create an alibi. Had him traipsing all over town so you could hide."

"Hide?"

"Hide what you were doing."

She waved her hand. "There's no law against that. I wanted to party and not call attention to myself."

"In other words, he was your alibi. His appearance fooled me. You were having an affair?"

"Perhaps. I'm not confirming or denying that." She returned to the couch, crossing her legs. "I'm denying it, of course." She giggled and took a sip.

"Okay, you were *not* having an affair. But it's been some time since you hired Leslie, so I assume there were more ... rendezvous ... you are *not* having."

She nursed her drink, swirling it around, staring down into it as if she might be reading her fortune in tea leaves. "You make a lot of assumptions." Every once in a while, she took a tiny sip.

"And the good doctor, what does he think about these meetings you're *not* having?"

"We have an agreement."

"*Have?* Or *had* an agreement? After all, he *hired* me to follow you."

"Yes, well, sometimes he gets jealous."

"Is that why you hired an impostor?"

"Now and then, my husband gets enough gumption to act outraged." She said with a small coy smile, eyeing her drink, swirling it around. But I detected an undertone of anger and bitterness in her voice. "I hired ... Leslie to *protect* the doctor."

"To protect him? Or you?"

"Him, of course." She slid her finger around the top rim of the glass. "Possibly ... both." Her voice low and throaty.

"Where were you that morning, Kitty?"

"I was with ... someone, " she said, leaning over and placing the glass on the tabletop. She looked up at me.

Tearing my gaze from her bosom, I examined her face.

That's when I recognized her eyes. They were deep blue, like Carla's, and I almost flinched. I hadn't noticed them in the photographs. My breath hitched in my chest. And I thought of Jane.

So much for thinking I could get past all the achy remembrances. My psychiatrist said, you're near the end of the grief period when there is *Acceptance.* But I felt no further along than when I had started. Past the sensation of Jane's presence, her scent, her embrace, the feel of her lips. I realized that time had stood still for me. Since that day.

I drop my gaze down to Kitty Fowler's mouth—full, exaggerated, pouty—not like Jane's at all. A hot jolt of anger bubbled up inside me, surprising me. I furrowed my brow and thought, *Here's this woman in front of me—alive, breathing, and telling me lies. While Jane was in her grave ...* I shut my eyes and inhaled.

When I open them again, I saw Kitty had lifted her chin and was staring at me.

"What?" Her eyes locked on mine.

"Nothing." I looked away, feeling her gaze on me. I surveyed the room again. My eyes drifted over her shoulder to a large nude portrait of a woman reclining on a bed with rumpled white sheets— an *Olympia* pose. The painting covered half the wall.

I suddenly realized the naked woman in the painting was Kitty Fowler. The artist had captured the same little coy smile that played on her lips now.

"That's a nice painting of you. Is it new?"

She turned and stared up at it with a frown. "Yes. The doctor mounted it a week ago. He simply adores it. I can't stand it."

"Mind if I take a closer look?"

She gave a bark of laughter. "No, no, of course. Be my guest. So, you're an art connoisseur? Or do you just like seeing me naked?"

"No, not a connoisseur. But I know what I like." I got up and inspected the painting. Kitty reclined on a bed with wrinkled satin sheets, propped up on two plump white pillows. Her only concession to modesty was a black shoe-string ribbon tied around her neck. A red magnolia flower adorned her hair. She lay on her side in the classic Manet *Olympia* pose, hand delicately draped over her pubic hair. It's the same pose you've seen in saloons above the bar in a thousand Western movies. Hell, even the Half Moon had one. I only knew the history of the *Olympia* painting because my wife had written a paper about Manet and French Realism.

She laughed. "My husband insisted I wear those high heels. Ha! High heels in bed," she snorted. "I guess to suggest a *streetwalker.*"

Behind her, the artist painted heavy shadowy-green drapes and a small open window. The view through it depicted the back of the St. Louis Cathedral, an homage to the fact he painted it in New Orleans and not Paris. At her feet, a black cat sat with two yellow spots above bold green eyes, staring out of the painting at me.

"Your cat?" I asked.

She turned again. "Oh no, it belongs to the artist."

I returned to my seat. "So, the artist was the one you were having an affair with?"

"My, my, you are perceptive, Zeke. And cute." She smiled. "*Was* having an affair, Zeke. *Was* is the keyword here. After the portrait was finished, I cut him off. Anyway, he was taking forever, and I was tired of lying there in the air-conditioning, doing nothing, catching cold." She batted her lashes. Then she laughed. "He got rather upset and didn't want to let me go ... but *c'est la vie.* " She finished draining her glass. Then she said, her voice sharp. "I can't stand to be held against my will, unless it's part of a game I have chosen."

I nodded. "And now?"

"Moved on. I have moseyed on down the road to greener pastures. I get bored easily." She got out of the low-slung couch with some effort, making her way over to the liquor cabinet with the gold counter top. "*Capiche?*"

"I got it. And what else?" I said.

"Huh?"

"You said you wanted to talk to me ... alone. What else did you want to say?"

She tipped the bottle and poured. "I wanted you to hear it from me, that's all. For you to understand, I didn't kill that poor—man. That's all."

"That you didn't kill Leslie Baronne?"

"You bet your ass I didn't, buster. I thought if you heard it directly from my lips, it would carry more weight."

I stood to leave. "Well, I think I've gotten what I came here for."

She cocked her head again. "You sure I can't get you something—*anything* before you leave?"

"I have to go. Another time, maybe."

A nod. "Oh, I see; you're still on duty, so to speak."

"I'm not a cop anymore. But, yes, something like that." I headed towards the door to let myself out.

"No, I don't think so. You're not the type." She said, smiling. "But if you change your mind, you have my phone number now."

Outside, the night had turned cool. I called Bull as I walked to my car.

"We lifted one print off the letter," he said. "It was the doctor's wife, Kitty Fowler, in the Spider Man mask."

I guess she was sloppy, even with rubber gloves.

CHAPTER 25

As I drove home to the Marigny, the aroma of Kitty Fowler's perfume and musky scent still intoxicated my nostrils. I needed to sort through the facts. So, I left the windows down and let the fresh night air clear my head.

The female impersonator, Leslie Baronne, died of a GSW while impersonating a wealthy doctor's wife. Kitty, the good Doctor's wife, liked multiple partners to break her boredom, so she hired Leslie Baronne, who bore an uncanny resemblance to her.

In the meantime, she's off making the beast with two humps with her new Romeo. Not a first, I'm sure. For whatever reason, Dr. Fowler grew suspicious—although they had an *understanding*—so she said. It might have been a unilateral agreement, though.

And that's where I come in. Dr. Fowler hired me to keep tabs on his wife. Only she pulled a switcheroo, and I ended up trailing the look-alike.

Meanwhile, she dumped her old lover, which makes him an ex-boyfriend. He isn't thrilled and doesn't go gentle into that good night. And Kitty, as all discrete wives should, refuses to name names.

That was it. The last piece of the puzzle just fell into place.

I was so excited I made a quick U-turn. The Magazine Street bus slammed into the rear-side fender of my ten-year-old patrol Bonneville cruiser, from a city auction. Not that badly damaged, but I had to wait two hours until the police accident unit arrived and wrote a report. Luckily, I had worked with one cop, and I told him I was working with Bull. He wrote me a ticket and let me go home.

I called Bull. "Meet me at St. Louis Cathedral in the morning."

"Why?"

"The answer is at the Cathedral."

It would be morning before we'd catch the killer.

•   •   •

The next day, an early morning breeze brought crisp sunshine and the oily scent of the Mississippi River into the Quarter. Needless to say, I didn't sleep well that night. This time, not because of the bad dreams, but in anticipation of the morning. Yet, by the time I arrived, street artists were hanging their paintings on the spiked fences around Jackson Square. The tarot card readers and face painters were unfolding their tables.

As I turned into Pirate's Alley, I located Detective Bull, reading by a rack of books on the cobblestones in front of *Faulkner House Books*. He spotted me out of the corner of his eye, but didn't bother looking up. Instead he waved me over with one hand, and continued reading for a few minutes. His powerful neck bulged against his collar.

He glanced at me and pointed up. "Did you know when William Faulkner lived upstairs on the third floor, he threw chicken bones at the pedestrians right where we're standing? That was back in the twenties when the Quarter was still a Bohemian gathering place." Bull shut the book, went in, paid for it at the counter, and asked them to hold it for him till he returned. He stepped outside. "Before the Quarter became a tourist trap."

"I didn't know you were a literary buff," I said as we joined the flow to Royal Street.

He shrugged.

A glance into the garden behind St. Louis Cathedral revealed no evidence of the death there. The white marble statue of Jesus remained unperturbed, standing on his pedestal with outstretched arms.

"Where are we going?" Bull asked.

"To get an art lesson." I led the way along the spiked fence and crossed Royal Street to Le Chat Noir Art Gallery.

We paused in front of the canvases in the window before entering, the bell tinkling above our heads. The owner/artist, Clive (*one name only)* looked up. With arms outspread, he held the edges of a canvas and didn't appear happy to see us. Today, he'd changed from a black turtleneck to a laborer's denim work shirt, speckled with little rainbow colored dots of paint, sleeves rolled up. A red and black spider web of tattooed words and images crept up his arms.

"Ah, Detectives. Visiting again? You've got more questions?" He adjusted the painting on an easel.

"Just a few," I said.

"Have you caught the killer yet?" He asked as he turned and placed his hands on his hips. "The news said the lady killed was not a lady at all, but a guy."

"Yeah, someone shot the wrong person."

The shop owner scraped his fingers through his hair, hurrying about, fidgeting with other paintings. "That's dreadful news. But how does that involve me?"

"We were hoping to see your art studio again." Bull motioned upward with his thumb.

"Didn't you see enough of it the first time you visited?"

"Yes, Clive. But I wanted to check out a theory I have."

He frowned. "A theory?"

We stood silent for a moment, playing face-off. See who would blink first.

I glanced up towards the ceiling, then back at him. I didn't consider a glance as a blink.

"Yes, my art studio. Sure." He cleared his throat, hesitating. "I'll need to lock the front door." He flipped the OPEN sign to CLOSED.

He led us into the cluttered backroom again. The black cat was still there, and it leapt off the window ledge to safety under the desk. The narrow staircase had gotten none less steep, and Bull was puffing by the time we reached the second-story studio. The aromatic odor of oil paints still permeated the air.

On our first visit, I was unsure what I was looking for. Now, I spotted what I wanted under a pile of drapes, pillows, and gowns: a couch with a high armrest at one end only. The satin pillows and white rumpled sheets reminded me of an unmade bed after sex. Beyond the sofa, a small window looked out to the back of St. Louis Cathedral, the garden, and the statue with the welcoming arms. The green shutters were open.

"That's an interesting couch." I tossed the pillows to the floor.

"It's actually called a divan," he said, rubbing his hands down his pants leg.

"Yes, a divan. That's funny, I saw one identical to it last night. The same size and shape." I squatted, my knees audible, ran my hand over the smooth, silk material. It was threadbare and tacky with grease. Not at all alluring as in the painting. I looked up at Clive. "Actually, I think it's the same one."

Bull gave me a *What Gives?* tilt of his head and motioned with his hand.

Clive looked away. "You did?"

"Yes. In a portrait, a nude portrait. You did an excellent job of capturing the essence of Kitty Fowler." I stood.

The artist flopped down on a chair, lowered his head, and stared at the floor. He took in a deep breath.

Bull, who was rubbing the back of his neck, turned towards Clive. "You painted Mrs. Fowler? When?"

Clive exhaled, all the fight ebbing out of him like air out of a balloon. "About a year ago. Her husband wanted a nude—like Manet's *Olympia*."

"Kitty Fowler is a beautiful woman, isn't she?"

He gave a small nod. "At first, it was purely physical. Kitty had a perfect shape, flawless skin, and long blonde hair. I'd done nudes before, but she was like a Venus. A goddess. Her face like a Madonna."

I thought it somewhat ironic that he described her using religious references, while the original model for the *Olympia* was a French hooker.

"She was beautiful, all right," he said. "We consummated it here, right on that couch. Soon, we were spending more time making love than I was painting. That's why it took so long—a full year. I can usually finish a full-length portrait in three months. Tops. I never wanted it to end."

"What happened to this idyllic love affair?" Bull wondered out loud, twisting one end of his mustache.

"When the portrait was finished, she dumped me," he mumbled in a flat, monotone voice. He stared up at me with a puffy face. He didn't look handsome anymore.

"You were just another one of her conquests," I said. "Another notch on *her* belt."

"I begged *that bitch* to stay." His nostrils flaring.

"She turned you down?" I asked.

"I'm not a rich artist, like Rodrigue or Picasso." The muscles in his jaw were visible as he spoke. "But I could have provided for her. I've got a home, this studio, and a good client list."

"But nowhere near the wealth of Dr. Fowler," Bull added.

I remember what Kitty Fowler had said. *I hate being held against my will.* But the money wasn't the issue. Clive could have been as rich as Creases, but he could never buy her faithfulness—or her love.

"So, you figured you'd dish out a little payback?"

"She agreed to visit one more time. She always entered the Cathedral in the front and exited to the alley. Then walked to the studio."

I thought it best not to correct his gender identification. I just wanted him to keep talking.

"How did she end up in the garden behind the church, instead of in the alleyway?"

"I guess she took the wrong door. So much the better, she wandered around tying to find an exit." He laughed with an edge. "That whiny, stupid *whore* was trapped."

Bull said, "So, you see her, open the shutters, and—*Bam!*" Bull made a trigger-finger motion, while holding an imaginary rifle.

"You should have seen her expression!" He said with a small, tight smile. "She was confused, not sure which way to turn. If she had gone out the side door, she would have walked down the alleyway. I might have missed. Now, it was too easy."

"Like shooting fish in a barrel?" Bull said.

"Yeah, you got a lucky shot in," I said.

"Clive, will you repeat this in a court of law?" Bull asked.

He said he would. He wanted to get it off his chest. But to me, it seemed more like a brag.

"Where's the rifle?" Bull asked.

Clive hesitated.

"Come on," Bull said, glaring. "Do we need a search warrant? Those CSI guys could tear this place to pieces. Paintings damaged, canvases ripped."

A look of terror crossed his face. His eyes darted around like a bird searching for a branch to hide under. Paintings were stacked and scattered around the room like books and posters in a college dorm. His shoulders slumped, and he motioned with his head towards the staircase. "It's in a space behind a loose board. I'll show you." He led us to the landing and removed a board. Bull reached in and pulled out a rifle.

"Now, don't you feel better?" Bull said, "Now tell me again." Clive repeated the entire story while Bull made notes in his flip-pad. After he finished, Bull read him his Miranda Rights.

Bull called it in, and within a half-an-hour, Le Chat Noir Art Gallery was crawling with dozens of police officers and crime scene investigators. The bell above the front door rang with a dissonant jangle, announcing their comings and goings. For the second time, the cops cordoned off the area behind the Cathedral with yellow police tape. It would not be a productive weekend for the artists. The lead technicians tagged the rifle and placed it in a large plastic evidence bag for prints and ballistics tests. The firearm was a .22 caliber Long Rifle with a silencer used as a prop by the artist. However it was in good working condition, it turned out.

A burly arresting officer again read him his Miranda Rights.

As they handcuffed his hands behind his back and led him out, he turned to us and blurted, "Be careful with the canvases. They'll be worth a fortune. Everyone will want to buy a *Clive*."

As it turned out, he was right.

The value of a *Clive* painting doubled, then quadrupled. As the headlines grew, so did the prices for a *Clive* oil on canvas. Hard to believe, but even his small charcoals and watercolors skyrocketed in price, selling for thousands. Go figure.

Dr. Fowler's nude of Kitty Fowler in her ersatz French-Manet-*Olympia* pose with satin sheets was estimated to be worth a cool million. Hang that above your bar.

Before I left the *Chat Noir*, I searched the backrooms for the black cat with the two yellow dots. Nevertheless, it was nowhere to be found.

CHAPTER 26

Detective Bull and I sat slouched against the dark oak bar in our usual haunt, the Half Moon. It was the long weekend before the Fourth of July and five months since Clive's arrest for the murder of the female impersonator, Leslie Baronne. The sun had set, and the air-conditioning blew a bit of respite from the sweltering summer heat.

I stared up above the big steamy bar mirror, and above the rows of whiskey bottles at the cheap reproduction of a smiling, naked girl reclining on a couch—in the Manet-*Olympia* pose. In a Kitty Fowler pose. Her hand draped delicately over her pubic hair. I thought of Kitty Fowler and blew on my piping hot cappuccino in a chipped cup. Someone had pumped some money into the jukebox and played Little Richard, followed by the Top Cats, a local group. As I gazed up, I had a feeling of breathlessness because I had achieved the Holy Grail of detective work—finding the murderer and bringing them to justice. And I'm not even a cop anymore.

Bull sipped his beer and said, "The couch, *excuse me*, the divan, really gave it away, huh?" Bull half-turned towards me, propping his chin in his hand, grinning, elbows on the bar.

"Yeah, the divan," I said, sipping my coffee from the heavy white ceramic mug. I placed the cup on cracked blue Dutchware. "The divan was only part of it, though," I said.

He waved for another round at Yolanda, the barmaid. "What do you mean?"

"A couple reasons. Well, three, actually. First, the divan, as you pointed out. Second, the view from the window."

His bushy eyebrow arched. "The window at the art studio?"

"Yes and no. The window in the nude of Kitty Fowler at the doctor's home. The artist, Clive, painted a window and captured the exact likeness of the rear of St. Louis Cathedral and its garden."

"So?"

"The details were so perfectly matched that it could only have been painted from that studio window. He went through great pains to get every detail right."

"Yeah, it took him a year while he banged the model," Bull snorted.

"And yet, she refused to name the lover. But it was obvious, put two and two together, and Clive had to be the guy, her lover. Or should I say, ex-lover? Who else would have a motive? My hunch was all circumstantial, though, but, I had nothing to lose just by walking in and pretending to know."

Bull nodded. "Yeah, you're lucky. You always had uncanny instincts. The sign of a good cop. And the third reason?"

"The clue that sealed the deal was the *chat noir.*"

He looked puzzled. "The name of the Clive's art gallery?"

"*Chat noir* means black cat in French. The black cat at Kitty Fowler's feet in the painting. It was the same black cat we saw in Clive's office: green eyes, bold stare with two distinctive yellow spots on its forehead."

Bull laughed and shook his head. "The cat, huh?" He took a handful of cashews and tossed them into his mouth, crunching them.

Silence. Except for the clack of the pool balls rattling around the tables. Somewhere outside, a car screeched by in the night.

"Teenagers on their way to an early grave," Bull said.

Bull sat his glass on the bar and asked, "Ever thought of coming back to the force, un-retiring?"

Over two and a half years had passed since I quit the force. Images of Jane disintegrating into nothingness continued to creep into my consciousness when I least expected. She haunted my daytime, woke me from sleep, kept me tossing and turning. Dreams. Nightmares. Hopes. Wishes. Blown to bits. Tomorrows and tomorrows. I often woke from my sleep in a cold sweat.

"No, I don't think so." I clenched and unclenched my jaw muscles, grimaced, and finished my coffee. Dreams. Nightmares ...

We sat for a couple of minutes, watching Yolanda waiting tables, her hips swaying to the music from the jukebox. Eventually, Bull turned to me and said, "You know, I never thought to ask?"

"Yeah?"

"Your name, Zeke? Who were you named after, an uncle or someone like that?" Bull asked.

"Zeke? My mother named me Ezekiel from the Bible. It got shortened to Zeke. She left us when I was about twelve. My old man said she was a Bible freak. Always nagging and preaching at him about his drinking. About failing at his jobs. He said he wasn't that sorry to see her leave."

"Bummer," Bull said.

"Before she left, she used to tell me stories from the Bible," I said. "The one about my namesake still sticks in my mind. This guy, this prophet Ezekiel, stood in a valley full of dried bones. A tornado comes and stirred them up till all the bones got up and started dancing, and skin grew on them."

"Did she tell you that to scare you?"

"Nah. As a lesson. She said the valley of dried bones was *this* city, New Orleans. And with that, I must leave."

I slid off my stool and left. The night was stifling hot. The light from the neon sign of the Half Moon cast an eerie orange glow over the sidewalk and over St. Mary Street. I tried to take a deep breath, but the heat in the air tasted like cotton in my mouth. The feeling of satisfaction I had earlier evaporated like water droplets on hot pavement.

PART II

CHAPTER 27

From the back of Judge Melvin Thompson's courtroom, I scanned the rows of benches and spectators till I found a bear of a man with a head of curly black hair and broad back, on the fifth row. Sensational media coverage had drawn an overflowing crowd for the opening day of the trial of *The State of Louisiana vs. Clive Bronsky* for the murder of Leslie Baronne. This was a day I had been waiting on for six months, and I felt calm. The death of Leslie Baronne would be vindicated.

Judge Thompson's courtroom was a cramped boxy room with a hip-high banister railing that separated the rows of spectator benches from the tables for the lawyers, the jury box, and the elevated bench where the judge sat. American and Louisiana flags adorned the podium, and everything felt crammed together. The walls were of paneled pine with paintings of past Presidents of the United States hanging next to current governors and judges.

I made my way towards Bull. Normally, it was first come, first serve in getting seats in Judge Thompson's court, but Bull took up two seats and he scooted over to allow me to sit. He'd dressed for the occasion in a blue suit, pressed shirt and dark tie. Even his Pancho Villa mustache was trimmed and neat.

"It's a slam-dunk case," I said in hushed tones as I slid in beside him.

Bull frowned. "If you say so."

I hadn't expected that answer. "You've got doubts?"

Bull looking around, puckered his mouth as if he had sucked on a lemon. "There's a negative energy in the courtroom."

I looked around. Whatever Bull was seeing, I didn't recognize. Of course, he was a better detective than I had ever been. "Why? What's up?"

Bull motioned with his ham-sized hands towards the front. "His attorney is Zip Romero."

"Zip?" I did a double take and straightened up, searching the front. Sure enough, Emilio Zapata Romero, our old nemesis from the interrogation room, emerged from a crouched position after speaking with his client. Today, he did not look like an oversized lemon, but rather a huge pink pomegranate. As was his custom, he wore his trademark white linen suit, but today, he wore an outlandish pink silk shirt with a green bow tie. His hair was jet black, swept away from a widow's peak, like a silent movie star. Rudolph Valentino handsome. Two gold earrings gleamed in the gristle part of his ear.

I muttered under my breath. "Where did that loser get the money to hire Zip?"

"Over there," Bull nodded towards the side of the courtroom.

Four men stood lined up one after the other against the wall. One I recognized immediately.

"Theodore Onyx?" I said. He was short with plenty of fat covering a small frame that his expensive suit, like a tent, did not cover. He had florid chipmunk-bloated cheeks and soft plump lips, and no neck. But don't let his chubby Pillsbury Doughboy appearance fool you. He was mean as a rattlesnake underneath. "I busted him five years ago," I whispered. "He was supposed to be serving a twenty-year stretch. How did he get out?"

"Ask Zip," Bull said. "He never served a day. Political dollars greased the wheels on the freedom train. He got a pardon from the governor."

Standing behind Onyx were two guys, like sentries, one big, one short. Both wore black coats, black sweaters underneath, arms crossed.

The tall one in the back looked taller than Bull, maybe six-five, six-six. Possibly outweighed Bull by twenty pounds. Under his coat, his shoulders looked as if he had a rack of bowling balls. His head was shaved, as if he were trying to channel The Rock Dwayne Johnson or Bruce Willis. His enormous round shoulders wouldn't allow him to button his coat. I knew his type. In a fair fight, I would never win. Usually I shot them in the knee rather than get into a fight—usually.

The other bodyguard was the polar opposite of the big guy: short, like a fireplug with muscle that looked pumped-up on steroids and gym weight machines. Beneath his fat forehead, he had two squinty pig's eyes. Hair cut close. He reminded me of the German guards in *Schindler's List.*

"Who are the muscles?" I asked.

"Some new out-of-town guys, brought in by Onyx. I nicknamed the big one: *Bowling Ball.*"

"Sounds about right. And the short one?"

"The Nazi."

In front, the fourth member of the gang was a neat, short man in a dark suit, white shirt and conservative tie. He was only a few inches taller than Theodore Onyx, but had a compact body and a guarded expression behind wire-rimmed glasses. Or rather, a lack of expression. He looked like a professional person. Maybe an attorney? Maybe an accountant? But more than that. If I had to describe him, I would say he looks like an agent for the FBI. Unobtrusive. Maybe the CIA.

"Who's the *Tom Hagen* in front?"

"His name is Goldenstein. He's not a licensed lawyer. But he's always hanging around. He gets things done for Onyx."

I scanned the rest of the spectators. Suddenly, out of the corner of my eye, I noticed a person entering the court. Straight away, a coldness hit my core. Jojo Turner walked in. He wore his Class-A Police Blue Uniform, black tie and silver bars on his epaulets. I tilted my chin up. "What's that turd doing here?"

Bull turned and cranked his thick neck. He lowered his brow and shook his head. "I don't know. Something's been going down all morning, but I can't put my finger on it."

Jojo Turner stood at the back and surveyed the rows of seats until his eyes locked on Bull and me. His thin lips turned into a crooked smile. This appeared to satisfy him, for he turned and left the courtroom. Jojo Turner was my old commanding officer and, as much as I tried to respect my superiors, he was one guy I flat-out despised.

What's going on? Jojo was here. And so was fat Onyx with his consigliere and two bodyguards. Lurch and Fester. Bowling Ball and Nazi. Whatever you called them, they were all the same: *goons*. Well-paid goons. There's no such thing as a coincidence. I believe that.

Goldenstein, the compact smart guy with the wire-rimmed glasses, slipped over to Zip Romero and whispered in his ear. Zip nodded, and Goldenstein returned to Onyx. The four of them pivoted like a drill team and filed out of the courtroom. I believed Bull: something *was* going down today.

Clerks and officers of the court scurried back and forth in the front, attorneys chit-chatting with clients, flirting with court secretaries—the usual noise and commotion of a courtroom.

However, when Judge Melvin Thompson entered, voices quieted with all eyes on him. He carried himself with self-importance. He had a sour look on his face, stopping at the desks of several young court clerks, loudly reaming one out for some infraction. The court fell totally silent. Listening.

Judge Thompson finished his say with the clerk and nodded curtly at the bailiff.

The bailiff was an old-timer that I had gotten to know during my visits to the court. He stood up straight and adjusted his shoulders back, as if he were a train conductor about to call out the next arrival. His voice was very crisp and carried the length of the court. "Ladies and gentlemen, please rise for the Honorable Judge Thompson." Everyone stood.

The judge hiked his robe like a skirt and took his seat on the podium, shuffling papers on his desk and looked up, a frown on his face. "Mr. Romero, are you ready?"

Zip called out, "Certainly, Your Honor. We can hardly wait."

The judge then addressed the prosecuting attorney for the State of Louisiana. "Are *you* ready, Mr. Voltarian?" The prosecutor was a career public servant by the name of Phillip Voltarian, a nervous type with a bald spot that covered nearly his entire head, which he tried to hide with the most god-awful comb-over. No matter how new his suit and shirt, he looked rumpled and his tie never hung straight down.

Mr. Voltarian said, "Yes, Your Honor."

Judge Thompson already looked tired. "Okay, Mr. Romero. Why don't you call your first witness?"

Zip called out in a loud dramatic voice, "We call Detective Hugh Bulardeaux."

Bull got up and worked his way to the front. He placed his hand, as large as a grocery store fryer, on the Bible, which covered it entirely. The bailiff asked, "Swear to tell the truth and only the truth?"

"I do."

"Have a seat."

Bull adjusted himself in the seat which seemed a bit too snug for him. He straightened his jacket and quickly smoothed out his Pancho Villa mustache with his thick fingers.

Zip strode to stand in front of Bull, reaching one hand into his coat pocket, extracting a pink, silk handkerchief and tucking it into his white suit breast pocket.

"Good morning, Mr. Bulardeaux. My name is Zip Romero." He fiddled with the handkerchief till two pointed ends stuck up. Gazed up and smiled. "I've been hired by the defendant, Clive Bronsky. Would you state your name for the record?"

"Hugh Bulardeaux. Detective in Homicide for the New Orleans Police Department."

"You've been on the force how long?"

"Sixteen years."

"How many years as a detective?"

"Ten."

"So, you *should* know police procedure?"

Voltarian jumped to his feet. "Objection. Detective Bulardeaux's length of service and conditionals speak for themselves. He *knows* police procedures."

Zip smiled and turned to the jury. "Of course. After *sixteen* years, ten of those as a detective, Mr. Bulardeaux *should* know police procedures."

"Move along, Mr. Romero," Judge Thompson said, a hint of weariness in his voice.

Bull shifted in his seat.

Zip Romero turned from the jury back to Bull. "Detective Bulardeaux, on the morning of February twenty-second, you entered the premises of Le Chat Noir Art Gallery. Is that right?"

"Yes."

"What prompted you to enter that morning?"

"I wanted to speak with him, Clive."

"This was not the first time you spoke with Clive. Didn't you talk with him on the day of the murder?"

"I did."

"At the time of this first meeting, was anything *suspicious?*"

Bull wrinkled his brow. "What do you mean by suspicious?"

"You know. Bloody knives, dead corpses, bodies handing from the rafters?"

A titter of laughter swept through the courtroom.

"No, nothing suspicious like that."

"Okay. No smoking gun. Good. So what changed your mind that caused you to *revisit* my client?"

"I ... I got a call from Zeke Malone."

"Zeke Malone!" he said as if it was the most extraordinary name in the world. "And what did this Zeke Malone say?"

"He told me to meet him behind the garden at St. Louis Cathedral."

"Off Royal Street? Across from my client's place of business?"

"Yes."

Zip Romero strolled over in front of the jurors, staring them in the face, speaking without looking back, "And what did Zeke Malone say that would cause you to meet him? ... At ... What time was this?"

"Nine A.M."

"At nine in the morning. Did he invite you for a cup of coffee? Some *café au lait* and *beignets*?"

A suppressed smattering of laughter came from the spectators in the courtroom.

"Objection, Your Honor." Voltarian stood up at his desk. "Can we get past these cute remarks?"

Judge Thompson sighed, "Stick to the questions, Mr. Romero."

"Of course, Your Honor." He turned towards Bull. "What did Zeke Malone say to convince you to meet him?"

"He ... he said that he knew the identity of the murderer."

"So, Zeke Malone told you to meet him behind the Cathedral because he discovered who the killer was? The murderer of Kitty Fowler? AKA Leslie Baronne?"

"Yes."

"Enlighten us, Detective Bulardeaux. You met the next morning, and what happened? Did you go get a cup of coffee?"

Judge Thompson said, "Mr. Romero."

"What happened, Detective? After you met up with Zeke Malone? Did he give you the name of the murderer?"

"Not initially, no. He repeated he could identify the murderer, and he asked me to go with him to the Chat Noir Art Gallery."

"You entered with the expectation of apprehending a murderer—even though you did not know his name? Was that your thinking?"

"Yes."

"You entered *not* to appreciate a piece of art? Nor buy a painting? Or to get a cup of coffee?"

"Objection!"

Zip ignored the objection and plowed ahead. "You entered to arrest a killer?"

Bull nodded.

"That's a yes?"

"Yes."

Zip Romero walked to the defense table and examined paperwork on his desk. He pivoted back to Bull. "I'll put it to you again, Detective—with sixteen years of service and eight years as a detective—"

"Ten," said Bull.

"Excuse me. Ten. Ten years as a detective." He paused as if for a theatrical effect. "Were all police procedures followed?"

"Yes."

Zip turned with a dramatic flair, as if he'd just won the lottery. "*Excuse me?* Did you say: *Yes*?"

Voltarian was on his feet, his face red. "Objection, Your Honor. Mr. Romero is badgering this witness. How much longer must we cover the same ground? Again, Detective Bulardeaux's credentials and—"

Judge Thompson: "Move along, Mr. Romero."

"Well, Detective Bulardeaux—" he paused and took a small red-covered booklet from the table. It looked worn and dog-eared. Zip walked in front of Bull and held it up. "Do you recognize this?"

"It looks like a police procedural manual for the New Orleans Police Department."

"Very good, Detective. It *is, indeed,* a police procedural manual for the NOPD, as it says on the cover," he said, as if complimenting a child. "I've marked a section in this manual and highlighted a passage. Would you turn to it?"

Voltarian rushed over to Zip and snatched the booklet, turning it over, examining the front and back. "Objection, Your Honor. We keep plowing the same ground, over and over."

Zip turned towards Judge Thompson. "Your Honor, Detective Bulardeaux has sixteen years of service which should make him an expert on procedures, as observed by our esteemed prosecuting attorney. The detective testified that he followed police procedure." Zip reached out and lifted the booklet with two fingers from Voltarian's hand. "If that is so, his testimony and the police guidelines—should be identical."

Judge Thompson placed his hands together into a steeple, peering over the top of his fingers at the two attorneys, lips pressed together. He rubbed his thumbs together for a minute. "I'm going to allow this, Mr. Voltarian. Detective Bulardeaux, you may read from the manual."

Bull wet his lips before taking the manual and flipping it open to the marker. He ran his finger down the page and appeared to read it to himself.

"Oh, my good Lord." Zip placed his hands on his hips, legs apart, staring at the jury. "Out loud, please, Detective."

Bull looked up at Judge Thompson, who nodded.

Bull cleared his throat and took a deep breath. "When a person becomes a suspect, then his Miranda Rights must be read to him—"

Zip cut in. "Hold it right there. Did you just say *his Miranda Rights must be read to him?*"

Bull nodded.

Then Zip positioned himself in front of Bull. "When you entered the defendant's shop, did you read him his rights?"

"No."

"Why not, Detective? Wasn't he a suspect when you entered?"

"No."

"NO? Didn't you testify that Zeke Malone told you to meet him behind the Cathedral because the killer was there? When you set foot in the Chat Noir, what did you expect to find? A line-up of ten felons?"

Voltarian: "Objection."

"No, you expected to see only one person—him, Clive, the owner—he was your only suspect?"

Bull hesitated. "Yes, I suppose so."

"So again, I ask you, did you read him his Miranda Rights *when you entered the shop?"*

"No, I did not."

"Even though he was a suspect?"

Bull did not answer.

Zip turned to Judge Thompson, arms spread like Christ on a cross. "Judge—"

Bull cut in. "He was a person of interest."

"Your Honor, I've had enough!" Zip shouted, sprinting across the court to the jury, gripping the railing as if he might leap over it. "Detective Bulardeaux keeps changing his testimony. First, he is a suspect. Now, he's a person of interest. Which is it, Detective?"

"Objections, Your Honor!" screamed Voltarian, leaping to his feet, his comb-over flopping to the side. "Badgering."

"I withdraw the question, Your Honor. It's obvious the detective was following the advice of Zeke Malone. This Malone character was behind all this. I have no further need to question Detective Bulardeaux. Instead I'd like to call Zeke Malone to the stand."

Voltarian said, "Objection, Your Honor. We haven't deposed Mr. Malone."

"Neither have I, Judge Thompson. Your client opened that can of worms. And I want to see what crawls out. I only call Zeke Malone because Detective Bulardeaux brought out his name. Maybe Mr. Malone can shed some light on this case."

"Okay, Mr. Romero, I'll allow this. Detective Bulardeaux, you may step down." He turned to the gallery. "Is Mr. Malone in the courtroom?"

The bailiff stood up and began shouting out my name in full voice. "Is Mr. Zeke Malone in the courtroom?" People started craning their necks, looking around. I hesitated but realized I couldn't get out of this. I entertained leaping up, sprinting out of the courtroom, past gasping spectators, past security, and escaping down the flight of marble stairs in the courthouse's front.

Instead, I raised my hand as if I were in a classroom. "Here, Your Honor," I said, making my way as deliberately as I could to the front, passing Bull on his way back to his seat. After the bailiff swore me in, I took my seat, trying not to squirm.

I waited while Zip Romero thumbed through some papers on the defense table. He took an inordinate amount of time until Judge Thompson coughed. "Mr. Romero?"

Zip looked up and smiled. "Good morning, Mr. Malone."

I nodded. He strolled over to me, smiling, hands on his hips as if he discovered a plate of sugar-coated donuts. And for the second time today, I didn't feel good about this—since I appeared to be the cream-filled eclair.

"So, Mr. Zeke Malone. It comes out you are the one behind all of this. The one who was certain my client was guilty."

Voltarian said, without getting up, "Is there a question in there?"

The judge let out a slow breath. "Mr. Romero, questions, please."

"Very well. Mr. Malone, you are a police officer?"

"No. I used to be."

"Really?" His brow wrinkled. "You left?"

"Over two years ago."

"You left because of … ?"

I shifted in my seat. "Personal reasons."

"It wasn't because they fired you?"

"No."

"Then, you resigned because of incompetence?"

Voltarian jumped up, sputtering. "Objection. Relevance? Why Mr. Malone left the police force has no relevance to this case."

Zip turned to the judge. "*No relevance?* My client's life is on the line. If Mr. Malone was fired because of bad conduct, the court has a right to know."

Judge Thompson paused, rubbing the side of his face as if he had a migraine, grimacing. "I think I'll let Mr. Malone answer this one. Please answer the question."

I took a deep breath. "No, I was not asked or forced to leave. I was injured and left for personal reasons."

"I see. Personal reasons?" Zip tugged at his lower lip as if in deep concentration. "Okay. What have you done since then?"

"I run a small private investigation agency."

"And that is how you become involved in this case?"

"Correct. I was hired to follow Mrs. Fowler."

Zip paused before asking his next question. "It was a while before you met the *real* Mrs. Fowler. You went to see her, is that right?"

"Yes."

"Where?"

"At her residence."

"And while you were in her home, what did you see to convince you that—" Zip turned and pointed. "—*he*—Clive, was the killer?"

"There was a large nude painting of Mrs. Fowler on the wall."

"A nude painting of Kitty Fowler?" Zip arched his brow. "I'm sure that caught your attention."

A small chuckle of laughter ran through the courtroom.

"Yes."

"During this visit with Mr. Fowler, what made you certain my client, Clive ... was guilty?"

"I saw her cat in the nude painting," I said.

Zip's mouth fell open, and he turned to the jury as if he were in a stage production of *A Streetcar Named Desire.* And he was Blanche. "Are you telling me, telling this court that you saw Kitty

Fowler's cat? Her pussy? And from that, knew my client was the gunman?"

The courtroom burst out in laughter.

"Objection, Your Honor," Voltarian jumped to his feet, throwing his arms in the air. "Is this a courtroom or the Comedy Improv?"

"Mr. Romero, would you please rephrase?" I could tell even the judge was stifling a laugh.

"Of course, Your Honor. I'll rephrase my question. Mr. Malone, are you saying you set your eyes on Mrs. Fowler's vagina?"

"*No*," I said louder than intended.

Even the jurors were laughing.

"I noticed a cat, a house cat in the corner of the painting," I added.

"A *pussy* cat?"

Loud laughter filled the courtroom. The judge brought down his gavel. "Mr. Romero, please."

"I'm sorry, Your Honor, I couldn't resist … You observed a domestic cat, a *Felis catus*, in the portrait?"

"Yes."

"And what about this Felis catus was so unusual?"

"The cat had two yellow spots over its eyes. And this was the same cat I had seen during my previous visit to the Chat Noir Art Gallery. Clive had painted the cat into the picture."

Zip's mouth fell open. "Wow." He stared wide-eyed at the jury. "Wow. Wow. WOW. That's quite a leap—from a house cat to a killer?"

Voltarian said, "Your Honor."

"Withdrawn. So, Mr. Malone, after viewing this painting, it convinced you my client was the guilty party? That he was the man responsible for killing Mrs. Fowler? AKA Leslie Baronne, who was a stand-in for her?"

"I suppose you could say so."

"So, you called your friend Detective Bulardeaux to meet you the next day, because A, you were no longer a policeman? And B, there was no doubt my client was the murderer?"

I sat silently.

Judge Thompson said, "You may answer, Mr. Malone."

"I suppose—yes."

Zip Romero turned to the judge. "Your Honor, without overstating the obvious, Detective Bulardeaux and Zeke Malone entered the Chat Noir with their minds already made up. My client was, indeed, a suspect in the murder of Leslie Baronne. And his rights, Mr. Clive Bronsky's rights—should have been read to him."

Voltarian, already on his feet, waved his arms in the air. "Your Honor, what is clear here is attorney Zip Romero has no defense for his client and is attempting to throw out the evidence on a technicality. When Detective Bulardeaux entered the premises, nothing conclusive was clear at that time. But his statement and the evidence leave no doubt as to the guilt of Clive Bronsky."

Emboldened, Zip jumped in. "Why or on what pretext Detective Bulardeaux entered the Chat Noir is indeed the question! My client was already under suspicion for murder. Mr. Malone was certain after seeing a nude portrait of Mrs. Fowler. He was so certain, he called his old friend Detective Bulardeaux to meet him—*because the killer is there behind the Cathedral.*" Zip made the quote, unquote motion with his hands. "If you want, I'll have the court stenographer read it back to us ... "

Judge Thompson said, "No need. We heard."

"*Indeed,* we heard," Zip continued. "Detective Bulardeaux entered the shop, not for a cup of coffee or to browse the paintings—but to apprehend a killer. They did not read him his Miranda Rights: therefore, all statements my client may have said, and all evidence found, must be thrown out!"

"That's ridiculous, Your Honor," shouted Voltarian. "Detective Bulardeaux was investigating a crime and had every right to enter the Chat Noir."

"Which *gave* him the right to ignore police procedure? *I don't think so.*" Zip turned towards the jury, hands on hips. "Your Honor, do we now live in a *police state* where the police can harass and trample our civil liberties with impunity?"

Voltarian: "Your Honor, we are—"

Judge Thompson cut him off. "Enough!" Held up his hand.

You could hear a pin drop. Judge Thompson narrowed his eyes, tilted his head back and inhaled a long breath, before lowering his gaze. He said, "Okay, I've heard both sides of this. We will take a thirty minute recess while I take this under advisement. I'll expect everyone back here in half-an-hour."

"All rise."

After he left through a side door, the room exploded with voices.

What just happened? I searched for Bull among the shuffling audience. His Pancho Villa mustache exaggerated his frown, looking as if he were a pallbearer at a funeral.

CHAPTER 28

I followed Bull into the corridor. He stopped after a few steps, unable to move forward through the crowd. People packed the hallway, more than I've seen before for a court case. With only a thirty minute pause in the proceedings, we couldn't really go anywhere except stand in the hall.

"Surely they can't toss this case?" I said to his back.

"I wouldn't be too sure of that," Bull said over his shoulder. Though he appeared calm on the outside, I had worked with Bull long enough to know he was seething.

"Why? What makes you say that?" I said.

"Nothing. And everything," he said. Typical Bull. Things never were what they seem. Something sinister always lurked beneath the surface. Here, though, he might be right.

"The evidence is overwhelming." I said. "The confession. The gun. Even the bullets matched, for God's sake."

He hunched his shoulder in a shrug, either trying to relax the tension in his back or in an *I don't know* gesture.

"The judge would be nuts to dismiss this case," I told him.

Voltarian, the prosecuting attorney, comb-over back in place, was speaking with his assistant. He did not appear to be happy. He glanced up at Bull and me, frowned, and turned away, rubbing the back of his neck, trying to straighten his tie which looked as if the wind had blown it over his shoulder.

Up ahead, a clot of reporters surrounded Zip Romero, who was entertaining them with a story. He spread his arms wide, his expensive coat flopping open, revealing the very pink, very shiny silk shirt. He held his hands apart as if measuring the size of a fish. The spectators and the reporters burst into laughter.

Bull and I edged over to three marble pillars along the walls lined with dour-looking portraits of past judges and mayors. The crowd stared at us and moved to the side. We stood silent for a minute before I spotted a knot of blue-uniformed policemen moving towards us, spectators stepping aside. Leading was the new police chief, a tall man with a bulldog visage. An entourage of officers followed him, one of them trailing at his elbow was Jojo Turner, a grin on his face. They entered through the main corridor and halted at a door marked DO NOT ENTER. One of his subordinates opened the door, and they marched in.

Turner approached us. "The police chief wants to see you, Bull."

"What about?"

"You'll find out."

Bull started down the corridor and Jojo turned to me. "You too."

I cocked my head. "The police chief wants to talk to me?"

"Yeah. Both of you."

I followed Jojo into the room that was used as a jury deliberation room. A long wooden table took up most of the center, surrounded by a dozen straight-backed chairs. Tall windows faced into an inner courtyard. A water cooler and a coffee machine sat in the corner.

Chief Washington stood facing out the window. He was a stout-built man with silver-gray hair and broad shoulders. A transplant from the Detroit Police Department, he had a reputation of being an efficient director. I recognized several other officers in the room with him, men and women I had worked with in the past. He turned and eyed us both.

The police chief walked around the table and stood in front of Bull, hands on hips. "Detective Bulardeaux."

"Chief Washington." Neither extended their hand. Neither looked as though he were going to back off. No smiles.

"Detective, I'm following this case closely. I read your reports and have received updates from Jojo about the progress."

Bull nodded. "My reports are thorough."

"Yes, they are," the police chief said, scratching the side of his chin. He sighed. "I just hope you didn't screw up this case."

"I stand by my reports. And my police tactics," Bull said. "It was a clean arrest."

"Not according to the questions raised by that flamboyant defense attorney," Chief Washington pointed out.

"Zip Romero," Jojo whispered.

"Yes, Mr. Romero. I just hope this case doesn't get thrown out on a technicality."

"That's Zip's job," Bull said. "Try to trip up the law. Get his clients off."

"That may be so. But our job is to do clean police busts," he said, stepping back a foot. "In the meantime, I'm reassigning the case to someone else."

Bull blinked once and clenched his jaw muscles. "Any reason for that?"

"Upon the recommendation of your department head, Jojo Turner here. He says you're an excellent detective, Bulardeaux. But—"

Jojo interjected. "Bull's good, but a little headstrong. A little bullish, if you will." he said with one of his trademark sneers.

Bull kept his gaze on the chief. "I hope this is temporary, Chief. No one knows this case better than I do."

"We'll see," he said.

Both men glared at each other. *Easy, Big guy. Easy.* Eventually, the chief sighed and broke eye contact. Jojo took this opportunity to lean in and whisper, nodding his head towards me.

Chief Washington turned towards me. "Zeke Malone?"

"Yes."

He took two steps and stood before me. His eyes were chocolate brown. "My understanding is you were a detective with us a couple of years ago."

"That's right."

"I read your reports and evals—Your work was outstanding, top-notch. In addition, you wrote some of the best reports I've ever read. You were a credit to the department."

"Thank you," I said.

His eyes narrowed, as if he were trying to get a read on me. He said, "It's unfortunate what happened before you left the force. Nonetheless, you no longer have any standing with the police."

I knew what was coming.

"I'm giving your *fair* warning, Malone. You're no longer a cop. You're to keep out of police business or I'll have you arrested for obstructing a police investigation. Is that understood?"

I nodded. He appeared to be biting the inside of his cheek, mulling something over. But whatever it was, he didn't say it out loud. Then he turned and stormed out of the room, followed by his officers. Before he left, Jojo Turner glanced over his shoulder, smiling smugly, and shook his head. No one shut the door, and the babble of voices from the hall filled the chamber.

Bull emitted a long-drawn-out breath. "*Shit,*" he said.

CHAPTER 29

Now what? I thought.

Outside in the corridor, the volume of the voices lowered as the crowd shuffled back into the courtroom.

A tight ball of fear gripped my stomach as I followed Bull into the hall, neither of us saying anything. Most of the lobby was empty by the time we entered the double doors. Jojo Turner stood off to the rear, arms crossed.

Bull appeared sunk into his own thoughts. He rubbed his knuckles, the size of walnuts, into the palm of his other hand. All the seats were taken, so we stood in the back.

After a few minutes, the bailiff emerged from the side door, positioning himself by the elevated judge's podium. "Ladies and Gentlemen, please rise for the Honorable Thompson."

The sounds of knees creaking and feet shuffling came as people stood. I took a deep breath and held it until Judge Thompson entered and sat down. He didn't look happy. The room rumbled as people sat back down.

He adjusted the microphone close to his face and sighed into it. "This is an untenable situation." He cleared his throat. "It appeared this case was open and shut—on the surface," he said in a deep voice that echoed off the back wall. "But despite the preponderance of evidence and statements, certain procedures were not followed."

A low murmur rippled across the courtroom.

"Therefore, this defendant was not afforded the protection of the law so that individuals or institutions can not trample on his rights—and I might add, ours as well." He cleared his throat again. "For that reason, all statements after the detective entered the premises are not admissible. So, in the *State of Louisiana versus Clive Bronsky*, I am dismissing the case."

Zip Romero looked ready to leap to his feet in celebration. He turned to Clive and patted him on the back.

The judge continued, "Furthermore, all physical evidence gathered after that point cannot be used."

I whispered to Bull. "Shit, the confession and rifle are out."

"Mr. Romero, would you have your client stand?"

Zip leaped up. Clive stood, appearing unsure of what was happening.

"Because of these procedural errors, I am granting the defense's request that these legal proceedings be terminated." Judge Thompson banged his gavel down twice, sounding like two gunshots. "Case dismissed!" He rose and hurried from the podium.

Zip turned to Clive, whispering in his ear while shaking his hand. Clive's face broke into a wide grin. He spun to two women on the front row, and they hugged across the railing. The tall blonde giggled and squealed as if she'd been selected for a game show.

"That motherfucker did it," Bull mumbled. "He got him off."

I could hardly believe it.

In the hallway, Jojo Turner made a beeline towards me and blocked my way.

"Take it easy, Jojo," Bull said.

I didn't back off as he inched closer to me till we were nearly nose-to-nose. "Something I can do for you?" I said.

"Yeah. Take the advice of the chief. Stay out of police business. You queered this case for law enforcement."

"Says you," I snapped back.

"Says, everybody. You're a *fuck-up* and always have been. Your inability to follow orders screwed up that hostage situation."

My fists clenched at my side.

"Back off, Jojo." Bull tried to step between us.

"Your blunders got your wife killed," he said.

"That's not fair, Jojo. Some things just happen." Bull grabbed Jojo's arm hard. Jojo's eyes flickered at Bull and then down at his arm. Bull did not release his grip.

Jojo stepped back and shook off the hand. "You did the department a favor when you quit, Malone."

I felt like a kettle about to boil. But I restrained myself.

He faced Bull. "And you, you follow orders. You're off the case."

Jojo eyed me one more time, snorted, then strode away, rubbing his arm where Bull had grabbed him.

CHAPTER 30

"Don't pay attention to that *prick*," Bull said.

I didn't answer. People filed hurriedly out of the courtroom. Clive and the giggling girls brushed past us. He turned. "Tough luck, assholes." The ladies burst into giggles. There was a sinking feeling in my gut.

"Don't pay attention to *any* of them. You know Jojo was a prick back then. Well, he hasn't changed. No one blames you for what happened with that bomber and Jane."

"You mean, *I'm Innocent* on paper."

Bull said, "That crap is nothing but gossip. Internal Affairs cleared you. They did a thorough job, and no one holds you responsible."

I turned to him. "I hold myself responsible."

"Bullshit. You handled yourself right. What did anyone expect you to do?—Turn around and abandon your wife? Nine out of ten cops would have done the same thing. The only exception might be Jojo—he'd sacrifice his own mother if he thought it would get him a promotion or impress his bosses. Zeke, things turned out badly. Nothing more. Let it go."

The hallway emptied. I stared up at Bull's brown eyes and tried to smile. "Thanks, Bull," I said. But, inside, I didn't believe him. I turned to leave out the side exit to avoid the front steps. I'd gone over it in my mind a thousand times. *Did I do the right thing? What if? Did my actions cause Jane's death? What if?*

I shook off the thoughts as I made my way down the ramp to the parking lot. The brilliant sunlight reflected off the walls of the whitewashed jailhouse across the street, blinding me for a second. "Mr. Malone. Mr. Malone," a voice called out to me.

Up ahead, I made out a clump of people. I cut to my right to avoid them, but to my surprise, the group started hurrying towards me.

"Mr. Malone. Mr. Malone," one of them called out. I recognized the voice. It belonged to a sleaze-hound reporter from the independent news station—Dan Milwaukee—EYE ON THE CITY. I felt a ball of anger welling up in me. *What a joke!* He sensationalized and specialized in pure gossip and innuendo. He was the equivalent of an ambulance-chaser. The biggest farce, though, was the logo in the corner of the TV screen, screaming out NEWS. But he had a following; his show had the highest ratings for the time slot.

"Mr. Malone? We want to speak to you," he shouted, running towards me, thrusting his microphone in front of him like a gun. He was running so fast, the wind lifted his expensive suit coat with silver buttons that sparkled in the sunlight. The only thing that glittered more were the dazzling, white crowns of his teeth. His cameraman ran to keep up with him, a video camera protruding out of his head, like a fat cyborg in a T-shirt and cargo pants.

Veering to my right would take me farther away from my car, and I wasn't about to run to escape him. Footsteps came flapping up behind me. A moment later, he was in front of me, and a microphone stuck inches from my face. I blinked and gave him a menacing stare.

"Mr. Malone? It's Dan Milwaukee with EYE ON THE CITY." He kept pace with me, step for step, backwards like we were dancing. "Mr. Malone, the big question of the day—*What do you think of the verdict?*"

I ignored him and made a beeline for my car. He sped up. I had to tell myself: *Don't react. Don't protest. Say nothing.*

Suddenly, half-a-dozen people stood in my way: other news reporters, tourists, and curious onlookers.

"Mr. Malone." Dan Milwaukee planted himself in my path, microphone extended into my face.

I came to a stop. "You're blocking me from my car."

"Zeke, how does it feel?" He broke off to allow his cameraman to maneuver around behind him to catch my expression. "How does it feel … ?" He paused for dramatic effect. I tried sidestepping him, but he two-stepped with me. "How do you endure knowing you *allowed* another woman to die under your watch?"

I pulled up short. "What *did* you say?"

"Wasn't this the second time?" He flashed his white teeth in a reptilian smile. "Your wife was the first."

I couldn't help myself. I slugged him.

He fell back onto his butt, the microphone still extended outward. I held back on the punch. But I shouldn't have.

He was stunned, a look of surprise on his face, but that was replaced with a look of recognition. I had made a big mistake and he would not let it get away. He leaped to his feet, trying to hide the glee and show mock outrage. And at what a great opportunity was staring him in the face.

"Did you get that?!" he screamed at his cameraman. "He punched me in front of my thousands of viewers. An innocent reporter just trying to do his job!"

"Get out of my way," I shouted, forcing myself around him and two old ladies dressed in shorts and sunhats. I unlocked my car and jammed myself into my seat, slamming the door.

Had I just slugged a reporter in front of cameras? My hands trembled as I fumbled and stuffed the key into the ignition. *How did all of this shit happen?*

Dan Milwaukee stood inches outside of my driver's window, addressing his cameraman. Before I could start my car, I heard him say, "Once again, Zeke Malone caused the death of an innocent person through his mistakes. Or is he just plain incompetent?"

The motor turned over, and I threw it into gear, shooting forward away from the reporters and spectators. In my rearview mirror, I saw the crowd swarming around him as if he were a rock star. Accelerating too fast, I missed the exit to South Broad Street. I exited and cut across to Tulane Avenue, but not the way I wanted to go. My heart pounded in my chest.

Why does it have to be this way?

I drove unsure of where I was going. Nothing had changed. The memory of Jane's death flooded back to me. I shook so hard, I almost rear-ended the car in front of me. I pulled over and put my forehead on the steering wheel. Visions of the blast filled my head.

Let it go. Let it go, Dr. Lucy in the Sky said. But I couldn't.

CHAPTER 31

My hands shook as I pulled up in front of Mark and Doris' ranch-style suburban home in River Ridge.

Doris stood among her daisies in the well-manicured yard with a garden hose in hand, watering the flowers. She looked up and shaded her eyes. She frowned when she recognized me, but only for a second, before smiling. Slender and pretty, Doris is the girl-next-door type, with her blonde hair tucked up under an Astros baseball cap. She is married and devoted to Mark Billingham, my brother-in-law. I have always found him hostile and cold. Doris makes up for that—and she loves Carla.

The courts awarded them custody of Carla after the explosion that killed Jane and sent me to the hospital in a coma.

She twisted off the water faucet by the house, dropped it, and gave a small wave as she crossed the lawn. I nodded, shutting off the engine, and wondered if this was such a good idea, showing up at their home unannounced.

She leaned in the car window. "Zeke, what a pleasant surprise," she said brightly.

I smelled the warmth of the sun on her body. "Hello, Doris. I'm sorry to drop in unannounced—Is Mark home?"

She glanced over her shoulder. "Yep. He's probably in his study watching golf or the Astros."

Her brow wrinkled. "Caught you on TV today. That news guy—*asshole* Milwaukee—sure laid into you pretty good. Never understood what's so appealing about that *sack of shit*. You shouldn't have punched him, even though he deserved it. But it sure made his newscast go viral."

I only nodded. "Doris, I know I didn't call, but I wondered if I might see Carla?"

She studied me for a minute, wiping her hands off on the pants legs.

"I really need to visit with her," I said, trying not to sound as if I were begging.

"Zeke, you look peaked. Tired, agitated. And with that crap in the courtroom, I don't blame you for needing to see Carla." She let out a small breath. "I'm sure it will be okay."

"What about Mark?"

"Most likely asleep, like always. Carla's in her playroom. Let's find out," she said, stepping back from the car.

"Thanks, Doris, this means a lot to me." I said, stepping out of the car.

I followed her into the open garage and through an inner door to a hallway. She washed off her hands in a sink, grabbed a towel, and motioned me to follow her while she dried them off. We didn't speak as we made our down a hall towards the back of the house. Pictures of family members lined the hallway.

The next thing I knew, Mark stepped out of a doorway and blocked our path. His hands hung at his side, balled into fists. "What are you doing here?"

Doris stepped up to him. "Take it easy, Mark. He's only here to visit Carla."

"I got that." He stepped forward.

"I know I didn't call ahead. But I only wanted to see her for a few minutes."

He turned to Doris. "And you let him in the house?"

"It can't hurt. Besides, it's my house, too."

He crossed his arms. "You know the rules. The court said you can only visit on appointed dates."

"I realize that."

He tried to step around Doris. "And with prior approval."

"Not with prior approval. With *proper notice.*"

"Exactly. Did you call?"

Doris cut in. "He called me. I forgot to tell you, Mark."

Mark stared at Doris and then back at me. "It's not scheduled. Why should we make an exception now?" he said.

Doris put her hand on his arm. "Mark, it can't matter that much. Carla is playing. It isn't unusual for a father to want to see his daughter."

Mark snorted. "Only he isn't the actual father."

"That's a technicality, Mark. I'm the only father she's ever known."

"Some father," he laughed.

"What does that mean?" I demanded. The bad blood between Mark and myself had been going on ever since I courted and married Jane.

"I watched you on TV today. Up to your same old foul-ups again and—"

Doris interjected, "You can't blame Zeke for what those jerks on TV said."

"I can defend myself, Doris. They're just looking to get attention. The more outrageous, the better the ratings."

"Unless it's the truth. You screwed up again," Mark said. He was building up a head of steam.

"I came here to see Carla. Not get into an argument with you. I was hoping you'd be cooperative."

"Your antics got Jane killed. If it hadn't been for you—she'd still be alive."

Doris got up in his face. "Mark, that's not true."

"Isn't it?"

I clenched my fists open and closed. Many times, I had said these same words to myself. And said them to Lucy in the Sky. Blame felt like a knife in my heart. Over the past year, I had withdrawn the blade an inch at a time. To hear Mark utter these words, it shoved the dagger back in, twisting it. My mouth felt dry as cotton balls. "Mark, I want to see Carla."

"And if I say no?" He stepped forward, breathing hard. It was all I could do to stand my ground. He took his fist, brought it up, and shook it in my face. "The day Jane met you turned out to be the worst thing that ever happened to her. Right next to you getting her blown up! Try punching me! If you got the guts!"

Doris wedged herself between us and grabbed his hand. "That's enough, Mark." Her eyes blazing.

"I only want to see Carla," I repeated.

"Zeke wants to visit his daughter." She said. "And it's okay with me. I own half this house, and he can visit on my side. Don't be such an asswipe, Mark."

His eyes broke with mine and dropped to hers. She would not let his hand go. At length, he lowered his fist. She shoved hard against him like pushing a car until he backed up a step. "Go on, Mark. Go back to your shop, watch TV, or work on that birdhouse you've been building for six weeks. Or, whatever it is you do back there. Just go!"

Mark stormed off down the hall.

"And don't come out! Go on," she shouted after him. "I'm fixing supper, and I'll call you when it's ready."

He slammed the door with a bang. Breathing hard, she turned to me, shaking her head. She rubbed the side of her face and sighed. "Come along, Zeke. Take as long as you like. I'll control Mark." She led me to a closed door at the rear of the hallway, muttering curses under her breath.

"Carla's in there." Doris retreated to the kitchen.

I took a deep breath and knocked once before entering …

•　•　•

Light from a large curtained window illuminated the playroom. Blue-flowered wallpaper with Disney Princesses decorated the walls.

Carla knelt before a three-story miniature dollhouse set on a short table. The front was cut away like a tiny movie set so you could see every room. Her hands were inside the dollhouse, moving plastic people around from room to room like God or a puppet master. She hummed. I felt a fluttering in my stomach. She wore yellow shorts and a light blue T-shirt with a Lego Yoda on the back. I was always amused by that, since Carla didn't select her clothes, it was Doris, the picture of motherhood, with no children of her own.

"Carla," I whispered.

She continued to hum and never slowed the movement of her hands.

"Carla, it's Daddy," I said.

I know she heard me. I crossed the room and knelt beside her. Our daughter, Jane's daughter, was autistic, and never spoke. But she was aware of others around her.

I leaned in and kissed the top of her head. She never missed a beat. The rhythmic humming streamed out of some part of her brain I could not fathom. She often stayed like this for hours on end, moving objects back and forth, a compulsive activity.

Tossed on the floor next to the dollhouse were several finger puppets, a rag doll, and some stuffed animals. I selected a furry dog and placed it on the sidewalk. With my hand, I made the floppy-eared dog leap and knock against the front door of the dollhouse. It pawed at the door.

"Wolf, wolf."

She did not respond.

"Wolf. Wolf. Let me in." In my best dog imitation.

She paused her movement of the dolls. Then she took the mother doll and walked her down the stairs to the front door. She opened it.

Rover continued to bark as he bounded into the miniature house.

After half-an-hour of playing in the dollhouse with her, I had the dog wave bye-bye and bolt out the front door. I placed it on the floor and stood, my knees cracking, and I kissed her on the top of the head again. Reluctantly, I left the room. And left her behind.

I heard Doris in the kitchen and smelled the aroma of baked chicken.

I stuck my head in the kitchen. "I'm going now, Doris."

"Oh, Zeke, I'm sorry Mark behaved the way he did." She came around the counter.

I just shrugged.

"Here." She shoved a Saran-Wrapped plate towards me. "Cookies. I baked them myself."

"Thanks, Doris." I let myself out the door silently through the garage, feeling a dull ache in my chest.

CHAPTER 33

"Drinks for everybody!" Clive shouted to the guy behind the bar.

Tonight, Clive Bronsky had a good buzz going. Today, he had gotten a Get Out Of Jail Free card, and he wasn't about to waste it. He had dodged a bullet in the courtroom, and he felt on top of the world tonight. "Drinks for all of my friends—especially my beautiful friend here, Maggie!" He had just met Maggie, a curvy, big bomb with shoulder-length hair, and candy apple lips that matched the color of her dress.

There was a friend with her, but Clive focused on Maggie. She was his type—that tight, clingy dress—while her friend was okay, but not in the same class. He was already figuring out how he could separate the two.

"What you celebrating?" Maggie asked with those smoldering smoky eyes. The two girls started giggling.

"Oh, didn't you hear?"

They shook their heads, laughing. "What? What?"

"Well, I just had the best of luck!"

"Did you strike it rich?"

The bartender slid three fresh drinks in front of them, eyeing Clive.

"Yeah, you could sort of say that." *I'm a free man. The sweet aroma of being freedom from the charges of murdering that drag queen, Leslie Baronne,* he thought, but said out loud, "I'm lucky, I just met you." He could smell her perfume. Smell her female sweetness. He was on a roll now.

This morning, he'd exited the courtroom after they dropped the charges with a hard-on. He wanted some pussy. After the congratulations in the courthouse, he'd sped to his apartment and took a long, hot shower to wash off the funk of the trial. *Free on a technicality! What luck.*

"Damn, you're *some* fine," he told her.

She smiled coyly. "I bet you say that to all the girls." By her accent, he knew she wasn't from New Orleans.

"Where you girls from?"

"Chicago." They squealed.

They came to the Big Easy to spend a long weekend with a gang of friends, a *Big Easy Get Away.* Three nights, four days at the Royal Orleans, just down the street from his art studio. Clive never had trouble picking up girls at bars. Mostly tourists. Down to have a good time. *Fuck. Las Vegas had nothing on New Orleans. The Crescent City. The Town that Care Forgot.*

"Drink up," he encouraged the girls.

They giggled.

Clive straightened his tie and adjusted his suit jacket. He knew he looked sharp. It cost a fortune. too. He deliberately dressed like a wealthy businessman. That drew in the chicks. For a moment, he imagined Maggie in the nude. Lying on a couch. He could paint her—capture the curves of her body, that come-hither look. Blood-red lips. *Damn!* But right now, he didn't want to paint, he wanted to get into bed with her and screw. Too bad, he had to shell out so much cash to get them drunk.

Gazing across at his image in the mirror behind the bar, he saw himself staring back at himself. What was wrong with him? Through half-closed eyes, he knew he was handsome. No, correction, more than attractive—he was glamour-magazine gorgeous. So why didn't he feel that way? For a second, he suppressed a flinch as he remembered the fists and blows from his father. He shook it off and took a gulp of his drink.

He turned his thoughts to that *hard-ass* Detective Bull, reminding him of an oversized circus gorilla. And the other little shit, Zeke Something-Or-Other, the retired cop. Served them both right. *Their fuck-ups got me off the hook. Thank God.* And that flaming attorney, Zip Romero, definitely gay, but definitely sharp. Had the court eating out of his hand.

But right now, he forced his attention back on Maggie. This was her fourth or fifth shot, and they were having their intended effect. *She's pressing her two Congo bongos against my arm. Damn. She's hot.*

He signaled the barman to set up another round. He was about to say—*Why don't we get out of here?*—when his phone vibrated. *Damn!* No one knew this number—except for Onyx's man, that tight-ass Goldenstein. *What in hell does he want?* Not now! He fumbled it out of his pocket. It wasn't a call, it was a text message:

BRING THE STATUES NOW.

Motherfucker! This wasn't supposed to happen until tomorrow. *What is this shit?*

He texted back:

CAN'T NOW. TOMORROW.

He leaned in to whisper into Maggie's ear. *Damn, she is definitely fine!* Her perfume intoxicating. His phone vibrated again.

NOW. HE WANTS TO SEE THEM IN AN HOUR.

DON'T KEEP HIM WAITING.

What the ...? This was a load of crap. All his plans were being blown to hell. *Leave Maggie?!*

Since leaving the courthouse, he had the eerie feeling he was being watched, followed. And what if he was being tailed? But by whom? The only man he could imagine would be that Big Foot, that cop.

His impulse was to ignore the text. But the truth was, he owed Onyx. He's the one that hired—and paid—Zip Romero, the best attorney you could buy. Onyx knew he was guilty as hell. *Why the shit did I ever confess? Dumb. Dumb.* But that was in the past.

When you got down to it, he owed Onyx his freedom. But nothing in life is free. Clive was a survivor, and he wasn't stupid. But, he had to admit, the trio of carvings proved to be his ticket out of jail. After they threw him in the clink, Clive refused to reveal where he had hidden the wooden container. Forcing Onyx to get him out of jail. "Or no statues," Clive told him.

Maggie was pressing up against him. He could feel the heat of her body, smell her.

Clive decided: He had to go. Damn! As much as it hurt, business came first; he couldn't mess around with Onyx. He'd heard what happened to people that crossed him—they wound up in the swamp.

After promising Maggie he'd return and exacting a promise from her to wait, he made his way towards the back hallway as if he were going to the loo, and slipped out the rear exit. Within seconds, Clive was on the sidewalk, mingling with the Quarter crowds making their way to Bourbon Street. Glancing over his shoulder, he saw no one trailing him.

He hated sneaking like this, but he couldn't be too cautious. He fell in with another group of revelers, shouting and hollering, their hurricane glasses held high in the air. After a block, he veered onto Chartres and made his way to Royal towards his shop. Suddenly, he stepped into an alleyway and faded into the shadows, remaining motionless, watching for a tail. After a full two minutes—he saw no one and left.

• • •

Clive climbed into the dented blue van he used for delivering paintings. His destination was Lucky Storage in New Orleans East, near the Almonaster Industrial Parkway.

He drove a zigzag route across town for half-an-hour before arriving at his destination, parking a block away, and cutting his engine. His hands were sweating, and he rubbed his palms on his thighs, as he watched for headlights or movement in the rear-view mirror. No one. He drove to the gate, punched in his pass code, and watched the gate swing open. Row after row of low slung, cinder block units filled Lucky Storage behind ten-foot-high hurricane fences.

He unlocked the padlock on a corrugated-metal door and rolled it up. Inside, the interior was as he had left it. Used chairs stacked on tables, a broken box fan, and large cardboard boxes filled with clothes and books he'd purchased at Goodwill, as a cover. If anyone looked in, it would look like an average storage unit filled with household junk.

Underneath an old mattress was a wooden crate draped with packing blankets. Nothing changed. Months ago, he had pried off the lid, though, of course, he had been warned: *Don't fuck with the merchandise.*

Inside were three wooden statues—each one about three feet tall, chiseled from blocks of wood. They appeared to be Inca warriors with hand-painted red headdresses, reminding Clive of a trio of redheaded Woody Woodpeckers. On the internet, he searched for like-images and found similar ones from long-forgotten Inca tribes from South America and Mexico. Each figure looked like a small garden gnome, with a stylized square-flat face, hooked nose, and spears in their hands. Above all, the most outstanding feature was the red headdress.

Clive knew the value was not in the carvings themselves, but what was hidden inside. He had looked inside each statue. *Three Little Indians,* as he called them, were filled with cocaine in vacuum-sealed bags, worth millions on the streets of New Orleans. He had been tempted to cut open a bag and sample the goodies, but that would have been his death sentence. You only screw around with Onyx so much. He had taken a risk just opening the crate.

Good thing I took the precaution of hiding them. Just before the shit came down about shooting that fruitcake-queen Leslie Baronne instead of the doctor's wife, Kitty Fowler. What a fool she made of me! Goldenstein had pressured him for the location of the crate full of blow while he sat in jail, but Clive knew the only way out was to keep his mouth shut. It was his Ace-in-the-Hole, his Get Out Of Jail Free Ticket. And it had worked! Onyx had hired the best attorney to defend him, and Clive had walked out a free man. Now he had to deliver the *Three Little Indians* and get back to that hot tourist waiting for him at the bar.

He slid the lid back, nailed it shut, and loaded the crate into the back of his van, checking his watch. *Shit, only five minutes to get across town.* He texted:

ON MY WAY.

• • •

As Clive pulled into the driveway to Onyx's luxurious mansion off Lakeshore Drive, his headlights illuminated two bodyguards at the gate. He'd seen them before, Mutt and Jeff, who never smiled and seldom spoke. They scared the shit out of him. Both wore identical black coats and black T-shirts underneath. The tall one had a lumpy round head, shaped like a bowling ball. The short one looked as wide as he was tall, close-cropped blonde hair, and narrow eyes, like some Germanic version of an evil Leprechaun.

Clive steered up to the gate and rolled down his window. "Hi," he said, smiling. "I'm here to see—"

But they didn't wait for him to complete his sentence. The Big One waved to the other to open the gate. After Clive pulled through, the short one motioned him out of the van.

As Clive was exiting his van, the guy muscled past him, climbed into the driver's seat and put it in gear.

"The brakes are spongy!" Clive warned, barely stepping out of the way. The new driver swung the van around the corner of the house, screeching to a stop, then backed up to a set of garage doors.

Bowling Ball motioned for Clive to follow him inside, down a dimly lit hall to a small paneled room, no windows, no pictures on the wall, two straight-backed chairs faced each other at a metal table. A single lightbulb hung down from the ceiling, like a police interrogation room. He shuddered at the memory. The big henchman put his enormous hand on Clive's shoulder, pushing him into the chair, and stood behind him. Clive wiped the sweat off his face with his sleeve.

The room was silent, and the giant standing behind him had a slight nasal whistle when he breathed, possibly from a broken nose in the past. But Clive wasn't about to ask. After half-an-hour, a concealed door opened in the far corner. A neat, compact man in a well-tailored suit and tie stepped into the room: Goldenstein.

"Mr. Goldenstein," Clive said, getting up, "Boy, am I glad to see you!" The heavy hands pushed him back into his chair. Goldenstein said nothing but stepped aside to allow a short, round man shaped like a doughnut to enter. Theodore Onyx. Dressed in a suit-tent made of expensive fabric, Onyx waddled towards the table. His round face was *not* jolly and his eyes, feral cunning.

Clive got up. "I'm sorry I was late—" Again, hands that felt like a twenty-pound weight knocked him down.

"Late. Early. It doesn't matter. You *fucked* up," Onyx growled, taking the seat across from Clive. His voice was raspy as if he'd had an injury to his throat. Clive would not ask about that either. Clive wasn't sure what to expect. His heart sank as he tried to read Onyx's expression. A fleeting thought crossed his mind—*I may not get back to fuck that girl, Maggie, in her red dress.*

Goldenstein positioned himself off to the side of his boss. Onyx placed both elbows on the metal table and interlocked his fat fingers. His face was like a happy-face turned upside down with an unfriendly scowl, eyebrows forming a V that came together between his eyes.

Not good.

"You nearly queered the whole deal with this shooting." Onyx said, his lower lip stuck out. "What the hell did you think you were doing shooting that *Lady-Boy*?"

"I thought it was Kitty Fowler," Clive mumbled.

Onyx twisted in his seat to Goldenstein. "What do you do with someone this stupid?"

Goldenstein, unsmiling, shook his head. "Shoot him?"

Onyx barked out a laugh, then turned back to Clive. The V between his eyes deepened. "Why in the hell would you want to shoot her from your balcony?"

"I—you didn't say where."

Onyx laughed again, short, with a rattle in his chest. "I ought to have you taken outside and put a bullet through your thick skull."

Goldenstein did not laugh.

Clive's palms were as sweaty as his face now, and little beads of perspiration trickled down his ribs. For a moment, he imagined the thug jerking him out of his chair, dragging him outside in the dark, and ... The picture of his brains splattering onto the well-manicured lawn made him cringe.

"It ... It was dumb of me. I agree. But she led me on. She got what she deserved."

"You mean, *he* got what *she* deserved, don't you?"

"Well, yeah. I didn't expect that she'd switch—"

"*Shut up,* you moron." Onyx shoved his chair back and stood, the chair legs scraping on the concrete. "The only reason I didn't kill you back then is you hid the statues and my shipment from me. That saved your ass. That lawyer, Zip Romero, cost a fortune."

"I'll pay you back," Clive intoned like a chastised schoolboy.

"You're damn right, you will. And the only reason you're not dead now is there's a new shipment coming." Onyx turned towards Goldenstein. "We got what we want out of the three statues, right?"

Goldenstein nodded.

Onyx turned back to Clive. "We're putting the crate with the three empty statues back in your van now. You get rid of them." And, without another word, Onyx wobbled towards the door.

For the first time, Clive gave a sigh of relief. Maybe he'd get to fuck that Maggie after all.

Goldenstein nodded at the guy behind Clive.

Clive felt himself being jerked up, and his body slammed on the metal table, face first. He turned his head at the last second to avoid smashing his nose. The big one behind him twisted Clive's arm in a way it wasn't supposed to go—up the middle of his spine till it touched the back of his head. An electric bolt of pain shot up his shoulder into his skull as if he'd brushed against a live-wire. Clive screamed, his eyes clamped shut in agony.

"Clive." It was the clipped voice of Goldenstein. "Clive, open your eyes."

He let out an involuntary moan but obeyed. The face across from him was blurry. Goldenstein's narrow face came into focus inches from his, turned sideways, so they were eye-to-eye.

"Listen up, dick-wad," Goldenstein said. "You take care of the empty statues. You screw-up again and I'll cut your dick off and then it's *no more* pussy. Do you understand?"

Despite the pain, Clive shook his head up and down, his face sticking to the metal.

"I can't hear you, Lover Boy!"

Clive gasped to get his breath. "Yes," he blurted out. "Please..."

The next thing Clive knew, his arm was released, and he flopped onto the hard concrete floor like a wet fish. Black spots danced in front of his face, and he felt as if he might pass out. He couldn't move his arm or feel his fingers.

After a few minutes, the pain subsided enough to allow him to prop himself up on an elbow. The room was empty. Feeling faint and dizzy, he struggled to his feet and stumbled outside to the empty driveway, puked on the lawn, and then crawled into his van. The wooden crate sat in the back with the three empty statues. The gate open. He careened out into the night, steering with one hand, swerving to miss the gate post. The crate slammed against the side panel. *There would be no Maggie tonight.*

After he was gone, the short crew-cut Nazi came out, hit a button, and the gate shut. He paused and looked into the dark for a minute before disappearing back inside.

CHAPTER 32

At that moment, across town, the night was just warming up for the Oasis Club. Presley Baronne straightened his winged-bow tie, black tux with tails, white shirt, and gloves, looking like Joel Grey from *Cabaret.* A diamond-encrusted rosary dangled on his chest. The crowd at the Oasis Club was loud, almost to the point of not being able to hear yourself think. The club smelled of beer, sweat, spilled drinks, and a dozen distinct scents of perfume and cologne; a perfect mixture for making money, something that would typically have made Presley Baronne happy. But there was uneasiness in his heart. He pasted a giant grin on his face and hop-stepped onto the small stage beneath the fixed spotlights.

Tap-tap-tapping his cane on the wooden stage, he tipped his top hat and leaned into the mic, "*Guten Tag, meine Herren und Damen, und Nicht-Binar Folk.*" The crowd went nuts, whistling, and stomping their feet. Two red rouge dots on his cheeks contrasted against the white-face makeup that glistened with layers of sweat.

"Welcome, Ladies and Gentle-*mans, and non-binary folk!*" he announced again in a faux-German accent, scanning the room. "And I use the term loosely!" Hoots of laughter, and fists pounding the tabletops. It was a good crowd. "How *Goot* of you coming tonight. Ve appreciate your business." He twirled his cane. "And in appreciation, ve only poured half-the-*wasser* ve regularly add to the drinks." Another chorus of laughs and whistles. A trickle of sweat dropped off his chin.

"Enough of this frivolity!" he shouted, followed by a soft-shoe. Presley Baronne glanced off to the side of the stage and saw the two young men dressed in black fishnet stockings, garter belts, padded bras, and Liza Minnelli black wigs. They were good. Both of them dressed like Sally Bowles, her character from the movie *Cabaret*. All afternoon, the two had been arguing, bickering over—*over who knows what*—but they were professionals and would put on a good show. They were his main headline act, ever since Leslie died—*shot in the chest between his silicone breasts*—he shook off the image. Today marks the six month anniversary.

But business must go on. Presley knew the more ridiculous, the better, for this crowd anyway. The queens had to straddle the delicate line between funny, naughty, raunchy, all while not taking themselves too seriously.

"Please give a big *Willkommen* to ... " he pointed with his gloved hand and cane towards the edge of the stage,"—TO THE LIZA SISTERS!"

The two Liza Minnellis sashayed onto the stage in tiny steps with exaggerated hip movements, puckered lips, and hand waves. The crowd whistled, laughed, and cheered. Batting their enormous black eyelashes, the Lizas blew kisses, reacted with fake blushes, and gave naughty-naughty finger waves at the crowd.

Presley Baronne hurried off-stage and watched from the shadows. The two were on target tonight—worth every penny he paid them. They straddled chairs, like cowboys, as the music started. He took a sip of vodka from a Dixie cup he hid inside the fire-hose box to calm the burning in his stomach.

The queens broke into "*Life Is A Cabaret, Old Friend*"—Fast. Fun. The crowd ate it up. At the end of the song, both hooked a leg over the back of their chairs.

These two are good, Presley thought. *But not the best. Leslie. Now, she was the best.* Suddenly, he wanted to be away from the Oasis Club. It reminded him too much of her. He remembered his lover lying dead in her tomb. Her life gone, her future snuffed out.

And they knew who did it: that maniac playboy, Clive. The son-of-a-bitch got off on a technicality.

The acid gurgled up into his throat. He emptied the paper cup of vodka and crumpled it in his fist. When the Minelli's went into another medley of songs, he slipped away to check the bar.

"Not a bad night," Felix said.

Presley nodded at his bartender, a thick-built, leathery guy, his white apron covering a hard belly. Felix had been with the Oasis Club for over ten years. Honest. Knew his drinks. And, as needed, Felix served as a bouncer whenever a patron got too drunk or too rowdy.

"Pour me another," Presley said.

Felix gave him the eye, but pulled out his favorite brand, splashed in half-a-glass.

"All the way," Presley demanded.

Wandering from the bar, Presley's next check-in was with Delilah, the lead waitress, returning with a tray from the tables. Delilah was tall and lean and spoke in a deep bass voice that Isaac Hayes would have envied. She had been with the club almost as long as the barman. She served as head wrangler, kept the other servers in-line, recruited new ones, and trained the inexperienced.

"How's tips?"

"Not bad. A good crowd tonight," she said in a gruff voice.

"How's the newest addition?"

"She's okay," Delilah said, refilling her tray. "A little slow, but she picks up fast." She scurried back into the crowd, the tray balance on fingertips above her head.

Presley watched the two Lizas on the stage, even laughing at the corny jokes though he'd heard them a million times. Circulating about the club, he mingled and chatted with regular customers.

Back on stage, he introduced a couple of more acts: Dorothy from *The Wizard of Oz* with a magnificent voice and a short schoolgirl-dress barely covering her frilly-panties. His rendition of "*Somewhere Over the Rainbow*" always brought tears to customers' eyes. Needed to work on his stage presentation, though, still a bit stiff.

After the last act ended about two in the morning, half the patrons had already left, and the Oasis Club started shutting down.

Presley stood at the door. "Thanks for coming." Presley shook hands and patted regulars on the back. He escorted an unsteady one to the door and poured him into a cab. "Hope you enjoyed the show."

After locking the doors and saying goodbye to the crew, Presley walked through the club, assessing the night. It was good. The cleaning crew would not arrive until six the next morning. He threw the switch shutting down the flickering *Oasis Club* neon sign, checked the backdoor and side entrances before shuffling to his office. He nursed a Dixie cup of Jack Daniels while checking the inventory sheets. At his makeup table, he stared at the clownish image gazing back at him. *Ugh, I look grotesque.* He peeled off his eyelashes and removed his hoop earrings. He slathered and scrubbed his face with Neutrogena cream before rubbing it off with a towel.

Since Leslie's death, the lines on his face had grown into deep crevices. Especially around his eyes, sunken like that of a skeleton. The feeling of heaviness would not lift and it made breathing difficult. Nothing seemed right since then. He wasn't sure if he was having a heart attack because his heart actually ached in his chest. An image of his lover bubbled to the surface.

Dear God, he thought, *what can I do?*

Staring into his own brown eyes, tears glistened on the rims, then ran down his cheeks.

The voice said, *You know what you need to do.*

Presley shook his head. "No, I can't."

End the pain.

Presley gulped the rest of the drink and dropped the cup to the floor. Then, with an overwhelming compulsion, he opened the side drawer of the makeup table. The revolver hid under a stack of scarfs. As if someone were inside his skin moving his hands, he lifted the small Bodyguard Smith and Wesson—not a big gun, but enough to do the job.

His hands shook so much, he could barely hold it.

Suck it.

He brought the gun up to his lips and stared at his reflection in the mirror.

Suck it.

I can't.

Do it.

He shoved the barrel into his mouth and felt the terror, hot as boiling water.

End the fucking pain!

But he couldn't. The gun slipped from his hand, clattering to the floor.

His shoulders convulsed, and he dissolved into tears.

"I'm sorry. I'm sorry."

Later, he stumbled into the bar, uncorked a bottle of his best vodka, and drank until there was no more pain. When the cleaning crew came in at six the next morning, they found him on the floor between the bar stools, passed out.

CHAPTER 33

It had been a week since the footage of me slugging the reporter had been shown on every local, national, and cable news network from here to Timbuktu. *The Punch*, as it was being called, went viral on Facebook, Twitter, and TikTok. At least a thousand kids shared the meme, "The Punch," with songs like "Kung Fu Fighting" or the "Rocky Theme" song. They debated it endlessly on the talk shows. Even though he was a sleazeball, the news community closed ranks around Dan Milwaukee because he was one of their own. His ratings doubled overnight.

After I clicked the off button on the sixteen-inch flat screen I kept in my office, I settled into a funk. Which lasted all of two minutes before I heard footsteps on the landing. These were not timid steps either. With that racket announcing the approach, I didn't need to pull my gun from the desk drawer, but—better safe than sorry—I slid the drawer open six inches, just in case I needed to make a quick draw. *Yeah, like Wyatt Earp, huh?* I picked up a folder and pretended to read.

The knock on the door was forceful—at least he didn't kick it in. "Come in. It's unlocked."

The door swung open Presley Baronne stood there, red slacks, beige shirt, and a defiant look on his face. "Zeke Malone," he said.

I hadn't seen him since the trial.

"Mr. Baronne. Come in, please," I said, standing. I was about two feet taller, and that seemed to slow him down. He hesitated.

Obviously, he'd come in as angry as a hornet. But confrontation didn't appear to be part of his nature. I would let him punch himself out.

"Come in," I repeated, sitting down.

He stepped in and stood there.

"Shut the door, please, Mr. Baronne?" I gestured towards the chair opposite me. He didn't sit down. I suppose doing so would have taken away even more of his resolve.

"Now, what brings you to see me?"

"I want to know," he said, "What *you've* done?"

I knew what he meant. "About what?" I wanted him to say it out loud, so there was no mistake.

"About ... about the death of Leslie."

I let out a slow breath. "Mr. Baronne, you were there in the courtroom. The judge ruled."

He plopped down in the chair like a balloon deflating after a pin prick. "But it wasn't fair," he said, the starch leaching out of him by the second.

"Fair or not, the wheels of justice did turn, and they rendered a judgment. Like it or not. There is nothing I can do." I told him in my most kind and sincere voice. I felt for the guy, I really did.

"But he killed Leslie," he said in a shaky voice, his shoulders drooping.

I felt sorry for him, afraid he might break into tears. "I'm sorry, Mr. Baronne. But my hands are truly tied."

With downcast eyes, he said, "Please call me Presley. My father was Mr. Baronne." The last of his determination was circling the drain. "It's been six months since Leslie died. And not so long since the court date. And you've done nothing."

"Presley, let me remind you, I'm not a policeman any more. Neither am I a lawyer." I didn't go into the fact that I'd been warned to not get involved by none other than the Chief of Police. And how that asshole, Jojo Turner, dressed me down—keep my mouth shut and nose out. He'd like nothing better than to come down on me like a ton of bricks.

"But you've got to do something. I've talked to the police, and they just ignore me. Detective Bull is off the case."

I shook my head and rubbed my nose. "Don't you think I would do something if I could?" I looked away, a guilt-ball knotted my stomach, and I crossed my arms. Besides, the case had put Bull's job in jeopardy. The muscles of my legs tightened. "I wish I could help you," I said.

Presley Baronne fixed me with his big brown eyes. He'd come in like a bulldog determined to get action, but now, he sat in front of me like a wet poodle.

"You don't know how hard it is," he said, his voice cracking. "Every night, I ... I ... " He didn't finish the sentence.

My thoughts rolled back to Jane. *Didn't I know?* The sleepless nights. The heartbreaking images of her head exploding. I stopped myself. I wasn't sliding back into that rabbit hole of pain and self-pity. After years, I was climbing out of the black pit I'd spiraled into. I was seeing Birdie. Well, once in a while. Fred LaForge had taken charge of the agency and had put his clown's life behind him. I could do the same thing. The agency was working as it should and finally making a profit.

Presley Baronne closed his eyes.

It wasn't fair to expect me to put my life back out there. I had done the best I could. All I wanted now was to be left alone. I felt for him, but ... "I'm sorry, Mr. Baronne—uh, Presley. But I can't help you."

He stood up. "Yes, of course. I understand. Thank you." He forced a laugh. "I shouldn't have taken your valuable time. I thought it was worth a shot. But I see now I shouldn't have come."

"Don't apologize, Presley. I'm glad you stopped by." I stood and extended my hand, but he ignored it and made his way out of my office, leaving the door open. His heavy-footed walk dragging on the landing, down the wooden stairs, and fading away on the slate alleyway.

I lowered my empty hand. *Could it get any worse?* First, Mrs. Gonzales with her fucking crazy request I track down her son's killers. And now this.

In the distance, I heard the whine of engines and blaring horns of the sea-going freighters chugging up the Mississippi River. The aroma of the city drifted in, a mixture of heat, bananas, bougainvilleas, and—was I imagining it?—pixie sticks. I went and shut the door.

I thought of Carla, standing in front of the dollhouse, her hands moving the little people from room to room. Suddenly, the temperature in the room seemed to fall ten degrees.

I needed to see her—now.

CHAPTER 34

Today was Tuesday, and I knew where Doris took Carla on that day—the Audubon Park Playground.

I slumped into my car and made my way across the city. I hoped I wasn't too late.

Audubon's Day, Doris called it. Regular as clockwork, Doris brought Carla to play on the swings and monkey bars near the zoo. Mark, my brother-in-law, normally worked out of town during the week, supervising at the oil refinery upriver—whatever it is engineers supervise. After Carla tired herself out on the swings and seesaws, Doris usually took her to the zoo to watch the elephants and feed the animals in the petting zoo.

If it rained, Doris took Carla directly to McDonald's for chicken nuggets and the indoor gym. Today, dark clouds swirled in from the Gulf but not enough to cancel her date at the playground.

I hurried uptown to beat the rain, taking St. Charles Avenue past the green streetcars swaying on the tracks down the neutral ground. When I was a kid, I rode the streetcars just for the fun of it and thought it was the height of transportation. And I could hardly wait till I grew up so I could ride the car to and from work—whenever I wanted.

By the time I arrived at the playground, fat drops were splashing on my windshield. Doris and Carla weren't that hard to spot. Dressed in a men's blue work-shirt, Doris sat on a bench, watching Carla run back and forth between the slides and the swings.

I steered in next to her car and parked. When she heard the door slam, Doris turned and looked at me. She was smoking a cigarette. *When had she taken up the habit again?* She didn't smile, and I could tell she wasn't thrilled to see me. She exhaled a long draft of smoke.

I waved, and she nodded.

Carla, in shorts and a sagging Star Wars T-shirt, hadn't seen me yet, concentrating on trying to swing herself. She had mastered the trick of extending her legs on the upstroke and bending her knees on the down, but not with a lot of luck. As I approached, she caught me out of the corner of her eye. She turned her head, but her expression did not change. Dragging her tennis shoes on the ground, little lights blinking on the heels, she leapt off before it stopped and ran towards me. I scooped her up, and she hugged my neck.

As usual, she didn't say a word, her face not registering any reaction. Whatever hard-wiring in the brain that prevented her from expressing her feelings or speaking, it did not keep her emotions on lockdown.

It all felt as if everything was alright. I could forget about the pain. Forget about Presley Baronne's visit. Forget about Mrs. Gonzales. Forget about how much I missed Carla. How much I missed Jane. Wishing I could work things out with Mark and get my little girl back.

Her arms circled my neck, and I could smell that faint fragrance that was always with her—cinnamon sticks and Dove soap—a combination that tickled my nose and enticed my heart. I kissed the top of her head.

After a minute, she released her grip and pointed her index finger at the swings. No words, only her finger, and I understood. I hoisted her and piggy-backed her back to the swings—pushing her higher and higher—into the cloudy Louisiana sky, her blue and white tennis pointed towards the heavens.

Doris took a long last drag on her coffin-nail, dropped it into the dirt, and rubbed it out under the sole of her shoe. Walking towards me, she dug her hand in her pocket, face upturned towards the sky, until she stood by me.

I never missed a beat on pushing the swing. My hands felt her bony back through the T-shirt. "I thought you went through a smoking-cessation program at Ochsner?"

"I did." She fished a pack of gum from her pocket, offering me one. I shook my head. She unwrapped a stick and shoved it in her mouth.

"Guess who visited me today?" I said.

"Who?"

"Presley Baronne, the owner of the Oasis Club."

She thought a second. "The husband of the drag queen killed by mistake?" She asked.

"Yeah, that's the one."

"What did he want?"

Carla looked behind her as I slowed. I gave an extra effort on the seat and shoved her higher. "He wanted to know why I hadn't done enough about bringing the killer to justice."

Doris stared at me, a puzzled look on her face.

"I told him that the murderer was arrested and brought to trial. He got off on a technicality. Presley wanted to know why I had done nothing to rectify the injustice."

"What did you tell him?"

"I told him I had done all I could. The court ruled. My hands were tied."

"Did you throw the little fucker out?" she said.

I didn't answer.

She sighed and popped another stick of gum in her mouth. "Mark's on a tear."

I said nothing, just kept the rhythmic pushing of the swing.

"He still holds you responsible."

"I know," I said.

"I think I should warn you, he's trying to get a restraining order against you."

"For what?" I turned towards her. Carla swung back and bumped into me.

"He thinks you're not safe. Doesn't want you to see Carla at all."

"That's crazy, Doris. And you know it! Can't you reason with him?

"He won't listen. He's hired a lawyer to file the petition."

" Which means he hasn't filed it yet?"

"Not yet," she said.

"When was he going to present me with the restraining order?"

"He's trying to get it before our next custody hearing."

I took a deep breath. "That doesn't leave me much time." I started letting the swing slow down and Carla looked back at me. "Do you think he has a chance?"

She nodded and took a pack of cigarettes out of her pocket, spitting out the wad of gum. Lighting one up, she took a deep drag, held it for a second before letting it out.

"Those things will kill you," I said.

"Thank God," she said. "I was afraid I would die of old age."

CHAPTER 35

Goldenstein felt he was back in control. Onyx had gotten his shipment from the three Inca statues, and the mistrial had taken the heat off of the operation. Now it was back to normal business.

After returning from breakfast, he hung his coat on one of those shoulder-fitting coat hangers in his closet. He never prepared meals at home—always out—or he had meals prepared by a chef that brought them in twice a week. The chef never met Goldenstein. The food was wrapped and placed in a large refrigerator with glass doors. Each one labeled and dated. In the bathroom, he brushed his teeth with an electric toothbrush, washed his face, and stared at his reflection with satisfaction.

He removed his tie and hung it next to a dozen identical ones before he flipped on the local news. When he heard the voice of Dan Milwaukee on EYE ON THE CITY, he was about to change channels. He hated talk shows. On the surface, Goldenstein appeared to be a patient man, but deep down, he lacked tolerance for others. Calculating and hard, he was not a man to be taken lightly.

He stopped and listened to the jabbering for a moment and realized he needed to absorb what was being said. He disliked talking on the phone, so he sent a text to Onyx:

WATCH CHANNEL WGNO 26

He knew he would get a call back, since Onyx did not like sending texts, fingers too chubby to hunt and peck the keyboard.

As predicted, within a few minutes, Theodore Onyx called. "What am I looking for?"

"Did you watch?"

"Nah, just got it on. What's that loud-mouth Dan What's-his-name saying?"

The face of Dan Milwaukee filled the screen, his hair swept up and back, in a stiff pompadour, grinning so widely you could see his molars. Then a cut away to a full screen with trumpets blaring: COMMENT OF THE DAY. When it came back to him, he was staring solemnly into the camera.

Dan: "Today, I look at one of the greatest injustices of all time."

Cut to grainy photo of Zeke Malone. Photoshop had darkened his beard, so he looked as if he hadn't shaved for the better part of a week.

Dan: "Did this ex-cop, with his actions, cause another miscarriage of justice?"

Cut to video of Malone slugging the reporter, in an endless loop. Punch, Dan's head jerked back. Punch, Dan's head jerked back.

Dan: "But I can understand his frustration, his guilt, at causing another death. But to strike at those around him is unacceptable. And I've forgiven him and reached out to him. But he hasn't returned my calls."

Cut back to Dan. "Zeke Malone, I know it's been two weeks but I implore you: if you are watching this, please call me so we can talk." Dan turns to face the camera to his right. "And what of the victims and their families?"

Cut to video of Presley Baronne, with a gold crucifix dangling around his neck, appearing tired and defeated. He stood in front of the Oasis Club with a mic stuck in his face.

Dan: "How has it been since the death of your husband?"

Presley Baronne: "It's been *horrible*. I miss my wife every day." (Presley begins to cry on camera) "There isn't a day that goes by that I don't think of her beautiful smile. And her murderer is out free!"

Baronne says between sobs, "Walking free. I won't rest until we bring him to justice."

Cut to Dan in the studio. Dan: "And what of the man who is accused of shooting Leslie Baronne? *Allegedly* shooting the victim, I might add."

Cut to footage of a very drunk Clive stumbling about, propped up by a brick wall, being interviewed by Dan.

Clive: (Slurring his words) "I'm innocent. (wobbling on his feet) They couldn't prove anything. It was a fair trial!" (stumbling off down Royal Street).

Dan: (turning to camera) "Did Clive Bronsky kill Leslie Baronne as the prosecution attempted, but failed to prove? Did he get away with murder? Because of this man ... ?"

Cut to footage of Zeke slugging Dan Milwaukee on a continuous loop again.

"Enough! Enough!" screamed Theodore Onyx over the phone.

Goldenstein held it away from his ear.

Onyx sputtered. "I've seen enough! That idiot Clive will sink us all. He's going to say something that will implicate me. Implicate us all. What in the world possessed him to speak to that reporter?"

"He was drunk," Goldenstein said calmly, not given to histrionics or displays of emotions.

"He can't keep his mouth shut."

There was silence. Goldenstein could hear Onyx's asthmatic wheezing on the other end, under the layers of fat. "What do you want to do?" Goldenstein asked.

"Shut his mouth for him! Permanently. And that little fag, Presley! He will not stop either. Do them both."

CHAPTER 36

It had been a week since Onyx issued orders to Goldenstein: *Do Them Both.*

At the Oasis Club, it was early, but not yet open, and Baronne sat hunched in front of his makeup mirror preparing for the day. He frowned and then washed his face with a wet towel. He started on his forehead and worked his way down, making small, discrete circles. He tried smiling by lifting his cheeks and baring his teeth. But it was even more hideous—like the Joker.

As a young man, Presley saw himself as a freak—that's what his father called him. Presley enjoyed putting on his mother's clothes when his parents went out to the movies and left him alone. The feel of the silk skirts against his skin thrilled him. It became an obsession he could not suppress. But he also remembered the blows he endured after his father caught him, still felt the sting of the belt and punches. Presley remembered wearing his mother's gold earrings, dressing in his mother's white slip while he painted his lips with her blood-red lipstick.

"You fucking pervert!" his father shouted, punching him with his fists. "No son of mine is going to be a *freak!*"

After that, Presley was more careful, but he never got over the feeling of arousal dressing in a frilly blouse, a padded bra, high heels, and silk panties.

You're a Freak!

After applying a white base, Presley pasted on the fake eyelashes and reddened his lips into a bee sting. He puckered his lips. It reminded him of Leslie, his wife—the most beautiful person in his life. He shook his head; it was no good thinking about her. Leslie would never return from that cold mausoleum. She was gone.

The thoughts of suicide were under control now, or at least he hadn't put the barrel into his mouth since the last time. In fact, he tossed the gun, standing on the concrete steps leading down to Lake Pontchartrain. He slung it with all his might, saw but didn't hear the splash.

There, nearly done, he thought, admiring himself, turning his head to get a profile view in the mirror. One final touch: a pair of gold earrings. An anniversary present from Leslie—on their second wedding anniversary. Bliss.

He completed his transformation by putting on a silvery silk shirt, open to his chest. Done.

He had read that most people hated their jobs, or at least only tolerated them. But not Presley. He loved the Oasis Club. It gave him all he ever wanted. It gave him legitimacy and introduced him to a world that accepted him. No longer feeling like an outsider, he had made friends. Met lovers. Met the love of his life: Leslie.

You're a freak!

The daily grind of opening the nightclub and managing the talent and bar staff was completely fulfilling, more than he could ask for. The Oasis Club was his life.

That morning, his first job was liquor inventory. He stopped by to chat with Felix who was restocking bottles on the shelves in front of the mirrored wall. The barman handed him a list of items to order. Presley stuffed it into his shirt pocket and intended to contact the liquor company after the Oasis opened.

Second, he inspected the stockroom, checked the bathrooms and the freezers, and checked the exit doors to ensure they were unlocked. No use getting a citation if the health department showed up unexpectedly.

"Okay, Felix, let's open," he called to the barman as he unlocked the front door. He stepped outside and saw three vehicles in the parking lot. He recognized two—a gray Lexus and a gold Caddy—belonging to regulars. When they saw him, the car doors opened, and three men climbed out of the Cadillac and two from the Lexus. They waved as they walked over.

Presley greeted them at the door, shook their hands, and said, "Tell Felix, the first round of drinks are on the house." This was a practice Presley had done for years. First customers in the door got their initial drinks *gratis. Good PR builds goodwill.*

Scanning the rest of the parking lot, he saw a light-blue panel van parked off to the side. It didn't belong to any of his regulars. A man sat in the driver's seat. The van had a little wear and tear, two dents on the side.

A guy got out of the cab, and started walking towards the front door where Presley stood—good-looking in a Hollywood-sort of way, a snappy dresser, wearing casual slacks, expensive shoes, and an open-neck shirt. At first, Presley didn't recognize him, and then, suddenly, Presley gasped as if someone had punched him in the gut. He couldn't believe his eyes.

Strolling towards the Oasis Club, as if he didn't have a care in the world, was Clive Bronsky, the guy who shot his wife. Presley's first impulse was to smash his face in with his fist. Or run back inside to his office and retrieve the gun and put a bullet through Clive's head. Then he remembered he'd thrown it into Lake Pontchartrain.

Clive stopped in front of him. "Did anyone ask for me?"

Presley's mouth fell open. Had he heard him right? "What?!"

"Someone called and left a message."

Is this guy for real? Presley clenched his fists, resisting the impulse to slug the creep. *The cojones on this guy!* "What the *hell* are you doing here?"

"Take it easy, old man. Like I said, somebody left me a message and said to be here when the club opened. You're open, right?"

Presley glared at him.

"Okay, well, I'll let myself in," Clive said, walking around him into the cool darkness of the club.

Following Clive into the bar, Presley let the door bang shut behind him, hard. Clive stood, legs apart, hands-on-hips, viewing the room. He nodded at the five regulars. They eyed him suspiciously.

Clive concluded none of them was the one that had called. He went to the bar and spoke with Felix who was putting cashew nuts into the little bar cups. Felix shook his head, then went and drew a draft for Clive. Presley assumed it was the same question—who had called and told him to meet at the Oasis Club.

Clive glanced at the others before making his way to a table, sitting to wait alone, sipping his beer.

From behind the bar, Felix finished dumping a bucket of ice into the bin before noticing Presley, red-faced, breathing heavily and staring hard at Clive. Felix made eye contact with Presley and gave him a *What's happening?* look, lifting his chin.

Presley's heart tripped in his chest.

Drying his hands on a towel, Felix came out from behind the bar. "Boss, you okay?"

Presley couldn't answer, unable to break his gaze from Clive.

"You know him?"

Presley said, "He's ... he's the asshole who shot Leslie."

"He what?" Felix turned abruptly and put his hands on his hip. "You sure?"

"Yes."

"Oh, no, he's out of here," said Felix, tucking his bar rag into his belt, weaving between the tables like the full-back he played in college—till he stood over Clive.

Clive looked up, a puzzled *What?* look on his face.

The burly barman reached down and grabbed Clive by the collar. "You the motherfucker that killed Leslie?"

The regulars at their table, stopped their conversation, and twisted in their seats.

A split-second later, the front door slammed open with a bang, letting in the sun's glare, and the hot humid air. A man in an overcoat barged in and stood still, surveying the interior. All eyes turned towards him. He was a large man, and his frame filled the doorway.

Though Presley was focused on his barman getting ready to toss Clive out on his ear, the sight of the intruder alarmed him—muscular, massive, with a bald head. Something was not right, and it was more than the fact that the man was wearing a knee-length overcoat. Something was menacing in his stance and expression. Presley tasted copper on his tongue.

Felix looked up, still clutching the back of Clive's collar. "Who the *fuck* are you?"

The man in the overcoat didn't answer. Instead, he threw aside the front of his coat. The bar lights reflected off shiny, black metal of the automatic rifle that suddenly appeared in his hand as if by magic. He clutched the rifle with two hands and hitched it against his waist.

Presley nearly jumped backward when the loud cracking noise, the RATA-TA-TAT! began, as flashes of light jumped from the muzzle. Mirrors and glasses exploded and crashed to the floor. It seemed to happen in a millisecond.

The slugs buckled Clive and the barman as they twisted and pitched backwards under the force of the rounds.

"What the shit?!" one patron shouted as he leaped under a table for protection. Two tried to duck behind the bar and another simply tried to outrun the bullets. Screams filled the air.

Now, Presley, in a panic, understood he was next, and he pivoted to escape down the only exit available—the hallway to his office. But it was like a cattle chute, trapping him between its paneled walls. He never made it to his office. The gunman sprayed the corridor with bullets and Presley stumbled a few steps before collapsing to the floor.

The gunfire stopped.

Presley's last thoughts were of Leslie. *Oh, to be together at last, my love.*

A layer of dense smoke hung a few feet above the floor like a gray, lazy cloud.

The gunman sniffed the air—sulfur and cordite.

"It's the sweetest smell in the world," he murmured, as he left out the front door as quickly as he entered.

CHAPTER 37

It had been thirty minutes since the gunman left the Oasis Club. The security firm had gotten no answer by phone, so they sent an SUV to check out the alarm.

Detective Bull, who knew nothing about the shooting, was the first NOPD officer on the scene, purely by accident. He had stopped in to ask Presley Baronne a few questions. He slowed his LTD to a crawl and pulled in behind a white SUV with the name of the security firm on the side door panels. Two men in black pants and white shirts were on the scene. On their sleeves were gold shields identical to the logos on the car doors. One stood by the car, looking shaken and pale. The other guy stood with his back pressed to the exterior wall, by the entrance.

Bull's heart rate kicked up. His pulse always quickened when he arrived on a scene, when he did not know what was happening. *It serves as protection, makes me more vigilant. Less chance of a mistake.* Bull got out and asked the one behind the cruiser, "What happened?"

"It's a bloodbath in there. The place is shot to pieces, along with everyone inside. Fucking war zone, man," the security guard said breathless, shaky. "Bullet holes everywhere."

Bull needed to calm him down. He was young. "What's your name?"

"John Patos." He pointed to the other guard. "His, Oswald."

"Okay, John. Anyone alive in there?"

"I don't think so. I called out. Got no answer. And then I got out as fast as I could and called my office. I've never seen nothing like it."

"What brought you here?" Bull asked.

"The alarms. The office said the alarms were going crazy. We get dozens of these calls a week, all false alarms, you know. I just thought it was a routine check. Didn't expect to see this."

"Just you and your partner, so far?"

"Yeah. How did you get here so fast?" John Patos asked.

"I was in the area," Bull said, flipping back his coat, revealing his shoulder holster. "Okay, let me see if there's anyone who needs an ambulance." *And see if the gunman's still around.* He didn't say *that* out loud.

Bull held his pistol, the muzzle up, in the ready position, and took a deep breath. It wasn't so much a matter of fear, as hesitating to allow police training to take hold. Go on auto-pilot.

Just do the job, he told himself. Bull made eye contact with the security guards, one at a time. "You guys stay out here, okay?" They both nodded.

His heart rate clicked up another notch. He shoved the door open with his foot and stepped inside, sidestepping to the right to make himself less of a target. The interior was dark, and it took several seconds for his eyes to adjust.

Music still pulsated from the speakers, distorted with static— Prince belting out *Purple Rain*. The inside, as Patos had said was a *fucking war zone*. On the back wall, a lopsided red sign hanging by a wire, blinking and flickering. The room smelled of burning electric wires. Cracked mirrors scattered light like a disco ball; bottles, and glasses in little pieces on the floor and on the bar counter.

Bull shouted out, "If you can hear me, call out!" No answer.

He edged further along the wall, saw bodies sprawled between the overturned tables and chairs, a shoe-less foot protruded into the air held up by an overturned table. Bull scanned the shadows along the wall, the doorways, and searched behind the bar. The shooter was probably long gone. The knot in his shoulders loosened, but not much. Until the place was swept completely, he reminded himself, you can't be too careful.

Bull stepped around the bodies, checking for pulses while scanning for clues. Bull examined a large, burly man. He looked like a bartender with a dirty apron. He didn't even have to feel for a pulse; a jagged hole in the neck told all he needed to know.

Lying next to him was a man Bull recognized—his handsome face turned up to the ceiling, mouth open in the death *O*. It was Clive, the artist. The Clive Bronsky that dodged a murder charge. On a technicality. *What the actual fuck?*

Bull stood and surveyed the scene. He counted, seven. *What the hell happened?* He could hear the howl of sirens approaching in the distance.

Stepping over the bodies, Bull made his way to the hall and saw a man lying halfway in an open doorway. He knelt beside the body. Presley Baronne.

"That makes eight," he mumbled.

Bull was trying to understand the sequence of events when he heard the screech of brakes and slamming car doors. Making his way back to the lounge area, to his surprise, he heard the voice of Jojo Turner. *What the hell is he doing here? The investigation hasn't even started yet, and he's here already?* A bubble of rage welled up in him but he suppressed it.

In the front, about a dozen police officers fanned out around the edge of the room. Jojo Turner entered through the front door and walked straight down the middle of the room, barking orders.

"Hey, you're contaminating my crime scene!" Bull yelled.

Jojo stopped. "Bull? What are you doing here?"

"I was the first detective to arrive. This is my case, and I've done a walk-through already. What are *you* doing here?"

The two locked eyes.

"I am *Captain of the Homicide Department*. I go wherever I please. To any crime scene."

"Not if you're tromping on my evidence," Bull replied.

"You're not supposed to be here," Jojo said.

"What? I'm first on the scene. My case."

"You're to keep out of anything to do with the look-alike murders."

"What's that got to do with it?"

"This is the Oasis Club where Leslie Baronne once worked."

"This doesn't deal with Leslie Baronne."

"But it does if Presley Baronne is dead."

"How do you know that?"

Jojo paused and slightly shifted his feet. "I don't. I know he was the manager, and I assumed—" He straightened up, face stony. "You need to leave, Detective Bulardeaux."

Bull could feel the blood pulsating in his neck. *What's going on here?*

Jojo took a step towards Bull. "I'm reassigning this case. You can compile your notes and submit it to me later."

Bull stepped towards Jojo till they were nearly nose to nose. "*You're* a *dick*, Jojo."

"And you're bordering on insubordination, Bulardeaux. Now get the *hell* out of here before I have you thrown out and take your badge."

CHAPTER 38

By the end of the day, the media had dubbed it the *Oasis Club Massacre,* and the police had squat. No motive. And no identity of the murderer or murderers.

The news coverage was overwhelming. The headlines compared the shooting at the Oasis Club to the gay bar killings at The Pulse in Orlando, Florida. In that mass killing, the killer was a lone white guy who held off police and was killed by a police sniper after a three-hour standoff. In the *Oasis Club Massacre,* they had nothing.

The local television, newspapers, and radio stations all scrambled for details. The news coverage went nationwide. Worldwide attention had been brought to the Crescent City for all the wrong reasons.

Standing at the back of the news conference room, Detective Bull watched the menagerie of reporters with cameras, lights, and banks of microphones, scrambling for position close to the rostrum. Soon the Chief of Police would deliver his speech from the Information room at police headquarters. Throngs of reporters crowded in, jockeying for the best seats near the front, notepads, and tape recorders in hand.

Bull shifted back and forth on his feet with relief that he was not part of this circus. However, he also felt resentful. He'd been told in no uncertain terms to keep out. It was a double-edged sword, he realized.

Close to him, an announcer spoke into a camera: "Another hate-crime terrorist? Like the killer in Orlando? Hopefully, the mayor and police chief will soon shed some light on this. We'll cut back in when the press conference starts."

In his mind, Bull ran over the similarities between the Orlando shooting and the Oasis Club. And the lack of similarities. The Pulse was a popular nightspot frequented by the LGBTQ community. On the other hand, the Oasis Club was not only a haven for the LGBTQ community, it was a club with drag shows and other entertainment. Mixed couples attended: businessmen, wives, and college kids. They all came for the fun of the shows and the drinks.

The timing was all wrong, as well. The Pulse shooter walked in at two A.M. when the club was packed. His intention? To cause maximum causalities and destruction. Whereas, the Oasis Club had just opened with only a few unlucky patrons. The civilians were businessmen, not members of the LGBTQ community.

The murmuring crowd told Bull that the mayor would soon enter and address the media. The press secretary for the mayor's office, an ex-news guy with manicured hair and a serious expression, entered first with a leather-bound folder under his arm. Stationing himself behind the podium, the PR guy read a few prepared notes and introduced the mayor. She entered through a rear door, followed by the police chief and other city officials.

The mayor began, "Ladies and gentlemen, thank you for coming." A hard-nosed politician, she had been in office only a year. Bull thought she had done a good job. She compared the deaths in the Orlando nightclub to the Oasis Club Massacre. However, she labeled it a terrorist attack.

"It was a hate-crime, no doubt," she said. "We're saddened by the perpetrator or perpetrators taking out their hatred on innocent people. We will catch those responsible for this heinous crime and bring them to justice."

As the mayor spoke, Detective Bull continued comparing the two crimes. Usually, terrorists are making a statement. Usually.

They hang around for the police and media to arrive, so that they can publicize their cause. If they're killed, they leave notes. They want the world to know. If they escape, they call it in. Why carry out the attack, if no one knows? At the Oasis Club, the gunman disappeared. No phone calls so far.

After the mayor finished, the new chief of police, dressed in his dress blues, took over the microphone. "All available personnel are on the case. Be assured, the New Orleans Police Department will not rest until this crime is solved and the person or persons are brought to justice. Mark my words."

After the chief concluded his speech, the mayor departed, surrounded by her entourage. The police chief continued to take questions, then he left.

One of the reporters for The Advocate spotted Bull and came over. "Bull, you're not part of the press conference? What can you tell me?"

Bull shook his head. "Nothing. Maybe next time."

The reporter left.

A familiar voice came behind him. "Still hanging around?"

He turned.

Jojo Turner said, "Did you write your report yet?"

"Yeah."

"Then, why are you still here?"

Bull didn't answer. He just turned and left through the back door.

As he walked back to his car, he pictured a giant 1,000-piece puzzle on a table. Only the edges were in place. The middle—still empty. Tapping his fingers on the steering wheel, he sped out of the parking lot onto South Broad and headed uptown. Despite the objections of Jojo Turner, this was still his case, and Bull wasn't about to let it go.

CHAPTER 39

On Magazine Street, the large letter H, in the neon sign, flickered on and off over the Half Moon Bar. It was a constant problem, maybe caused by the damp south Louisiana weather. Every six months or so, a letter in the sign blinked off. The proprietor tried to fix it by calling out electricians, but to no avail. Tonight, the letter H burned out, and now the sign read in large neon letters: ALF-MOON.

Zeke slid into his old familiar booth by the oval window that looked at the wedge of grass below the statue of Lottie Moon, the inventor of night school for adults in the U.S. The city of New Orleans was filled with metal, and marble statues, tucked away on lawns, grassy parks, and lining driveways. The statues commemorating Confederate generals had all been removed.

Yolanda, the waitress, came to his booth and pressed her hips into the tabletop. "What are you having, Zeke?"

"Just some coffee. I'm waiting for Bull."

She smiled. "Haven't seen the big guy for a while. What's up with him?"

"Busy, I guess."

She brought him his coffee in a chipped Disneyland mug with a picture of Mickey Mouse on the side, and Zeke stirred it slowly. After only a minute, Bull strode into the bar, waved at Yolanda, and flopped down in the booth opposite Zeke. He looked to be in a hurry.

"Sorry I'm late." Bull grabbing a handful of cashew nuts, popping them into his mouth. "You finished that coffee?"

"A couple of sips."

Bull took the coffee cup and washed down the nuts.

"Thanks," Zeke said. "I've had enough."

"Well, good, 'cause we gotta go," Bull said, getting up.

"Where to?" Zeke threw a couple of bills on the table. He shouted at Yolanda, "I'll see you next time!"

In the parking lot, Bull pointed at Zeke's car. "Let's go in yours."

"Yours broken?" Zeke asked.

"Incognito. You'll see," Bull said. He directed him to the river near the docks along Tchoupitoulas Street. There was the old joke about cops finding a dead mule on this street. They dragged it over a block to Front Street because they didn't know how to spell Tchoupitoulas.

"Turn in here," Bull said. The building was red brick and may have been a church at one time. They wheeled along a driveway that took them around back. They parked near a green metal door, and Zeke killed the engine.

"What place is this?" Zeke asked.

"Since you left, the *old* tech lab moved into this *new* tech lab, a state-of-the-art facility." He fumbled with his cell phone, typed in a text message, then hit Send.

After a few minutes, the metal door opened. A short, bald man appeared: MJ.

Zeke was happy to see his old friend. MJ waved them in. They exchanged whispered greetings in the hall.

"You sure no one saw you?" MJ asked.

"Nobody."

MJ led them down a corridor. They passed rooms, lights out, doors closed.

"Why all the secrecy?" Zeke asked.

"You're not supposed to be here," MJ replied.

"Why not?"

Bull said, "You heard Jojo Turner and the new chief. I'm *persona non gratis*."

MJ escorted them into a small studio set up with rows of keyboards, monitors, DVD players, and control panels. He said he'd be back before leaving them alone.

They flopped down on swivel chairs in front of the screens. Bull said, "As you know, I was first at the Oasis Club shooting yesterday." He let out a long breath as he settled in.

"What was *that* like?"

"Gruesome and messy. You know. You've been to those scenes before."

Zeke had indeed been on those types of scenes. They were bloody and ghastly. The images stuck in his mind for years, no matter how hard he tried to block them out.

"Eight people killed. Shot dead." Bull sighed. "Our little man, Presley Baronne, was one of them." Bull's jaw muscles tightening. "He must have been the last one killed. He tried to escape down the hall. Shot in the back."

Zeke's imagination filled in the blanks. He could imagine the bullets slamming into Presley, the force knocking him off his feet. The shock of realizing you've been shot. The shock of knowing you are about to die.

His heart went out to the man. Not only for how he died, but for the pain he suffered in losing Leslie, his wife. He tried not to compare it to the loss of Jane, but he could not help himself. It wasn't the same—but it *was* the same—lost love was lost love.

Bull said. "You know who else was there?"

"No, who?"

"Clive."

"You mean, the same prick that shot Leslie?"

"The one and the same."

Zeke scratched his jaw. "Doesn't that strike you as peculiar?" Coincidences don't work well in police investigations.

Bull said, "The official word is: it was a hate crime." Then with a raised voice. "Bullshit. By the time I arrived, the shooter was gone.

Unlike the Orlando nightclub shootings, there were no witnesses. No statements. No declarations issued by terrorists."

"Then what happened in that press conference? What the chief and mayor said about hate-crimes? About terrorists?"

"I'm not totally sure. That's why I'm here—to see the closed circuit tapes."

MJ entered the studio with a small plastic case in hand. "Now, as far as anybody is concerned, you never saw this. I never saw you." He shoved a small DVD into the player. After typing a few instructions into the computer, the screen lit up. He pointed at the console. "Here's the start, stop, rewind. You've got a couple of hours." And with that, MJ left.

The screen was subdivided into quadrants. All four were grainy, black-and-white security videos. "Here we are, CCTV footage of the club," Bull said. The image on the upper right was the exterior parking lot. On the upper left, an interior shot of the main lounge area with tables, chairs, a bar at one end, and mirrors along the wall. On the lower left, the hallway leading to the office where Presley's body was found. Down on the lower right was the back of the building, a dumpster, and the edge of the seawall overlooking Lake Pontchartrain. A time code sped numbers in a little rectangular black box in the extreme right-hand bottom corner.

"All the crap went down after opening time." Bull typed into the controls, hit a button, and the tape sped up, figures speeding by. Then slowed down. Stopped and played at regular speed, with no audio. In Screen Number One, they saw Presley opening the front door and the patrons getting out of their cars. They spoke with Presley before entering the building.

"Those five: wrong place, wrong time," Bull said. "They were regulars."

Next, a man exited a panel van.

"That's Clive," Bull said. "What the shit is he doing there at opening time? Watch Presley's reaction. He seems stunned to see that bastard at the Oasis."

They watched Clive enter, followed by an agitated Presley.

Within a few minutes, a black sedan pulls into the handicapped parking space—late-model Buick. The license plate was not visible. The time code indicated the driver sat there for forty-two seconds before getting out. He was big, wore a baseball cap, and gray overcoat, and paused to adjust something underneath his coat. As he approached the front door, he ducked his head and fooled with the bill of his cap.

Bull pointed. "He knows where the cameras are located."

Next, he entered the premises, the flare of the exterior light blotting out his figure until the door closed. He stood in the doorway for a second. All faces turned towards him.

In the next couple of seconds, the gunman pulled his automatic weapon from beneath his coat. The white flashes of the muzzle darken the screen with the autocorrect.

Moments later, on Screen Number Three, Presley Baronne fled down the hallway towards his office only to be cut down by a hail of bullets.

Bull allowed the DVD to play. The shooter exited the building, taking care not to let the CCTV get a clear view of his face.

The two men played the DVD again and again until MJ stuck his head in the studio.

"Well, y'all had enough?" he asked. "Or you want to watch it again?"

"No, that's enough," said Bull. "Thanks, MJ. I owe you, man."

MJ ejected the DVD. "Let me check to see if it's clear for you to leave." He walked out of the room.

"All these deaths are connected." Bull said, rubbing his chin. "Leslie, the cross-dresser. Clive and Presley Baronne. But I don't get the thing that connects them all together."

"It was a professional hit," Zeke said.

"It was." Bull agreed. "All that crap in the press conference about hate-crimes and terrorists was ... was bullshit. But the big question is—why would the police join in on the cover-up?"

MJ stuck his head in the door and waved them out.

"A cover-up? What are they trying to conceal?" Zeke asked as they drove off.

"I don't know," Bull said. "That's where you come in, Zeke."

"Remember? I'm off the force."

"Yeah, how could I forget? And I'm on shaky ground."

Zeke pulled over to the side of the street and sighed. "I was told to keep out of it."

Bull said, "And if I investigate, it will be too obvious."

Zeke was ready to say he didn't want to get involved. The agency was beginning to turn a healthy profit. And he was finally putting the past behind him. All his sensibilities told him to walk—no—run away from this case.

Before he could protest, Bull interjected, "If I'm suspended and kicked off the force, we'll never find the truth." He turned to Zeke. "Besides, you owe me."

Suddenly, all of Zeke's resolve dropped away. He did owe Bull. For a thousand reasons, he couldn't even begin to list.

"What do we do?" Zeke asked.

"Wait for my call. Give me till tomorrow."

CHAPTER 40

Zeke waited for Bull's call the next morning and couldn't sit still in his apartment. He went to his office, but it was no better as he sat, stood, sat again, before making up his mind to get out and walk. Coffee would be good. Pocketing his cell phone, he walked to Café du Monde across from Jackson Square, ordered a café au lait and *beignets* and sat where he could view the comings and goings in the Square.

How ironic, he thought, *this case started when I followed the Kitty Fowler look-alike into the Cathedral.* Now, he sat here calmly drinking coffee and wondering if he should get involved with solving the murders of Presley Baronne and Clive at the Oasis Cub. His reverie was interrupted by the vibration of his cell phone.

It was Bull. "Meet me tonight behind the Cathedral. At ten." He hung up before Zeke could ask why.

That night, when Zeke arrived, Bull was eating popcorn from a red-and-white striped bag, watching the tourists. He leaned against a lamppost by the entrance of the alleyway.

Zeke asked, "Why'd you want to meet here?"

"We're going to get an art lesson." Bull wiped his lips on a paper napkin and tossed the half-eaten bag into one of the green metal garbage cans scattered throughout the Quarter.

Zeke held off asking questions because he knew Bull always had a plan, even if he didn't announce it ahead of time. After circling for several blocks, they made their way to the back of Le Chat Noir Art

Gallery. Bull stopped in front of a wooden door, painted blue, flush against the sidewalk. He glanced both ways, then stepped up the one step, produced a flat metal bar from beneath his coat. In one clean forceful move, he stuck it into the jam, and the door flew open. Zeke stepped in behind him, and shut the door.

Only the lights from the Quarter illuminated the back office. Zeke's heartbeat quickened, as they stood silently, listening for sounds. "No alarms?"

"Not back here. Only the front door is wired."

"This is breaking and entering, you know." Malone said.

"I'll tell them I found the door open while I was walking by and I just entered to investigate."

"With a burglar bar in your hand?"

Bull tossed the bar on a table cluttered with paintbrushes and disassembled frames.

Zeke tried to relax, took a couple of deep breaths, and willed his heart rate to slow down.

"Come on," Bull said, flipping on a flashlight.

"What are we looking for?"

Bull said, "I'm not sure."

"So we're breaking into Clive's art studio, and we don't know what we're searching for?" Zeke said.

"He won't mind."

After picking through the storeroom, they moved to the hallway.

Zeke's heart rate was almost back to normal when a furry black animal leapt from the dark. "What the hell?"

A rat! He stumbled back. But it was only the cat with two yellow dots above its eyes. It scooted through the open door into the supply room. His heart rate was up again.

"You afraid of a cat?" Bull said.

"Just jumpy."

"Relax. We're cops, remember?"

"Yeah. One ex-cop and one cop about to get suspended."

They made their way upstairs to the prop storage room where Clive had confessed, and where he had painted Kitty Fowler in the nude. The room looked like a garage sale. The CSI crew had piled clothes in heaps on chairs, emptied boxes on the floor, and moved furniture around.

After they searched the room thoroughly, Malone said, "Nothing here."

Bull grunted, and they started downstairs. They avoided the front of the art store—too easy to be seen from the street.

They stood at the bottom of the stairs, listening to each other breathing.

"It all looks the same," Zeke Malone said.

"Yeah, I guess you're right. Let's go," Bull said.

They exited the backdoor unto the street and started their circular walk back to the front of the Cathedral. The two parted company, and Zeke went home to his apartment. He could not fall asleep, staring at the light patterns on the ceiling. *Another dead end.*

CHAPTER 41

Zeke had just dozed off when his phone rang. "Wasn't there a closet under the staircase?" Bull asked.

Zeke's eyes burned, and he shook his head to get the cobwebs out. "What time is it?"

"It's two o'clock. Meet me at the Chat Noir in thirty minutes," Bull said and hung up.

Dressing hurriedly, Zeke met Bull at the same location as earlier, and they retraced their steps, entering the art studio from the rear. The closet was under the staircase, the door cut at a triangle to fit, with just a notch to work your finger in. Zeke tugged on it, but it was locked. Bull pulled a Swiss Army knife from his pocket, unhinged the blade, and after a minute, popped the door open.

Malone shone the light into the dark. A wooden crate had been shoved into the space.

They exchanged looks. "That wasn't here when Clive was arrested. CSI would have found it." Bull said. "Clive must have stored it here. After he got out of jail. Obviously, before he was murdered."

The crate was about three feet wide and four feet long, much worn, with indentations where straps had cut notches on the top and bottom edges and had been nailed shut.

"What's inside, you think?" Malone ran his hand over the rough wood.

Bull shrugged. "Could be anything. Old newspapers. Dishes." He thumped it with his foot.

They dragged it into the hall. Bull said, "Whatever is inside, is heavy."

"One way to find out." Malone went to the storeroom and returned with the flatiron. After a minute, they had pried up the nails, lifted the lid, to reveal ...

"Garden gnomes?" Bull said.

If they were gnomes, they weren't the regular garden variety. Carved out of wood, and on top of their heads were headdresses that resembled feathers—painted red.

"They're like three little *indians*," said Bull.

"They're called *indigenous people* now," Malone said.

Zeke and Bull lifted the middle one out and set it on the floor between them. "Looks Aztec or Mayan," Malone said.

Bull shrugged and started examining the figure. Each warrior wore a loincloth, held a spear in their right hand, and a knife in their left.

What they had in common were the elaborate carved wooden headdresses made to look like red feathers. The red had faded, but was still vivid enough to make out its color.

"Is that what all this is about?" mumbled Bull.

"What?"

"Stolen antiquities?" Bull picked up the statue. "I know big bucks are spent by art dealers for these things to resell to collectors. Black market statues. Tomb robbers stuff. Nazi stealing from the Jews in the Second World War."

"I hope not," said Malone. "So far, it's cost the lives of seven people."

"It's hard to believe they were murdered over three old statues."

"Why was Clive storing them here?" Zeke asked.

"I'm not sure," Bull said. "But it definitely was recent."

They continued to examine the two other figures inside the crate. At the bottom, beneath musty straw, they found crumpled papers—shipping documents. Malone read through them. "It says these statues are going to the New Orleans Art Museum."

Bull looked puzzled. "These statues were going to a *museum?* But what was Clive doing with them? He's just a two-bit painter. "

"That's what it looks like." Malone turned the pages, scanning quickly. "It says here, the statues arrived on a Panamanian freighter."

"Mean anything to you?" Bull asked.

"No. It makes little sense," said Malone. "Stolen statues aren't addressed to museums. They go to private collectors with dummy addresses. Or are labeled PRINTERS or COPY MACHINES and shipped to a warehouse somewhere. But Clive? He didn't strike me as being into primitive art."

Bull scratched the side of his face. "Unless there were other reasons? Something more valuable than pilfered artwork?"

"Like what?"

"I don't know. Maybe they're hollow?"

The two stared at each other, thinking the same thing. "Damn!"

They both jumped up, and Bull lifted the first red-headed statue and flipped it upside down.

"Damn right," he said. At the bottom of the wooden statue was a barely discernible, perfectly round circle etched into the base. Bull tried to insert his fingernail with no success. After struggling with it for a few minutes, Bull pulled out his Swiss Army knife again and slipped the blade into the narrow crack. Bull pried on one side, then the opposite, until the round wooden plug began to lift out.

Bull paused. "Here it comes."

The lid popped off and bounced to the floor.

Empty.

Malone reached his bulky hand in and felt around, like a kid trying to get the last cookie. Even flipping it upside down and shaking it like a piggy bank didn't help. They removed the second and the third statues. All three were hollow.

Both men were on their haunches, squatting over the statues. Suddenly, Bull knees popped, and he plopped down on the floor with his back against the wall. He began massaging his left knee. "I forgot how that knee locks up."

Malone sat down beside him.

Their uneven breathing began to slow down as they sat studying the statues with the red-headdresses.

Malone sighed. "What would we have done with a million dollars' worth of diamonds?"

"I can't think of a thing," Bull said. "Can you?"

Malone laughed. "Yeah. A few. Well, what do we do now?"

After a few minutes, Bull said, "We've broken and entered and found three hollow wooden Indians—I mean, *indigenous people*."

Malone stroked the scar on his chin. "Why didn't Clive deliver them to the museum?"

"Maybe death got in the way over at the Oasis Club." said Bull.

Both men sat quiet for a minute. "What's our plan now?" asked Malone.

"We put the crate back where we found it."

"Okay. Then what?"

Bull thought about it for a minute. "Zeke, you go to the art museum and find out *why* this shipment was going to them. Was it stolen or legitimate art? And if so—why?"

Malone nodded. "And the freighter?"

Bull held up the papers and read aloud: "*Santa Maria II*, the freighter from Panama. I still can't expose myself just yet. What's that clown's name who works for you?"

"Fred. Fred LaForge."

"How's he working out for you?"

"Pretty good, actually."

"Have him find out as much as he can on the freighter. And report back."

Malone took out his cell phone and took photos of the three statues.

Bull stood up and groaned. "Let's get out of here."

They replaced the statues and shoved the crate back under the staircase.

At the back door, Bull opened it just a crack. A crowd of dozen drunken revelers staggered by on the sidewalk. Bull and Malone exited, quietly shutting the door behind them, falling in with the group. They began singing with them for the next two blocks till they were well away from Royal Street and Le Chat Noir Art Gallery.

CHAPTER 42

It was early morning when I parked in City Park beneath a sprawling oak tree with moss hanging down, like the scraggly gray hair of an old hag. From my vantage point, I watched two long-neck white swans gliding silently on the placid waters of Bayou St. John as if they were skating on ice—two swans-a-swimming.

The morning sun streamed between the trees on Esplanade Avenue and splashed on the six marble Doric columns at the top of the steps of the New Orleans Art Museum. The building could have passed as a look-alike of the U.S. Supreme Court Building in Washington, D.C.

Two workmen on twenty-foot ladders were hanging banners between the fluted columns. The banners read:

TOMBS OF THE INCAS

Well, the three red-feathered statues we found certainly fit in. I wasn't sure of the link, but I knew there was one. Bull was even more sure than I was. Now, all I had to do was find the tie-in. The trick was how to get into the museum? I couldn't quite barge in and demand answers. Or could I?

Putting my car in gear, I drove down the driveway leading to the stone steps of the museum, circled the complex, and parked behind the building under more oaks. I hoped this would not be a dead end.

The doors didn't open till ten A.M. and I needed to get in before they opened for business.

About four years ago, after Jane and I met, we attended a reception for the unveiling of a new still-life painting by a Dutch artist, whose name I forgot. The painting depicted a banquet table overflowing with fruits and a dead quail. Jane made me go with her. It was a very elegant affair with champagne, caviar, and wealthy guys in tuxedos.

I remembered Jane, absolutely stunning in a sleek black dress, skin as smooth as silk, and dangling diamond earrings. I remembered her laugh, light, almost tingling—almost hear it still.

I got out of my car and started walking towards the back of the museum. I strode up to the back entrance—a sunken ramp for trucks, and concrete steps leading to an elevated back entrance.

From above, a voice called out, "Zeke!"

I looked up. "Zeke Malone," the voice called out again.

A fat security guard in a blue uniform was waving down at me. It was an old ex-cop I recognized, gray hair, sloping shoulders, and a wide grin.

"Zeke Malone, it's me, John Benzatti!" He was one of my mentors when I was a rookie. He motioned me up.

We greeted each other as if we hadn't seen each other in years, which indeed was true. John Benzatti had taught me to be a better policeman. He was one of the good guys. I saw he had grown softer in retirement. Soft in the middle, and needing suspenders to hold up his pants.

"Good to see you," he said. "What brings you to the museum, Zeke?"

"I need to see the ... the guy in charge of the Inca Exhibit."

"They call them curators here," he said, glancing around. "I assume it's not official police business. I was sorry to hear about your wife."

I nodded and thanked him.

"I won't pry into your business, though, Zeke. So I'll just tell him an *investigator* is here."

"Tell him it's about smuggled artwork."

He picked up a telephone next to the desk and punched in a few numbers. He held for a minute, then smiled. "Pardon me, Mr. Spinoza. I hate to disturb you, but an inspector is here and would like to speak with you," He paused. "Uh-huh. Something about stolen art. That's right." After a brief conversation, he hung up. He turned to me. "I told him you work *with* the police department. I didn't tell him you were no longer with them."

We chatted a few more minutes. He asked about Bull and other old friends on the force. I updated him as best I could.

The curator, Spinoza, strolled through a pair of banged-up double doors and made a beeline towards us. He was a slender man, very handsome, nattily dressed in an expensive, dark tailored suit, Italian leather shoes, and a silk tie. Hair slicked back. His looks were more like a well-dressed Wall Street executive rather than someone who worked as a museum curator.

Extending his hand, he identified himself as Lukas Spinoza. I introduced myself without showing a badge. He looked me straight in the eye as he gave me a firm handshake. His fingers were soft and well-manicured. "You have some information about illegal artwork?" His voice had a refined quality to it, an undertone of Castillion Spanish.

"Possibly illegal art," I said. "What I really need is to ask questions about smuggled artwork."

He studied me for a moment. "Okay, why don't we talk in my office? It's better than out here on the loading platform."

I thanked Benzatti and followed Spinoza. We passed through a holding area full of packages, and wooden crates, similar to the one Bull and I found. I felt a sense of accomplishment having gotten this far.

Since it was before opening, the museum was empty and our footsteps echoed on the marble floor and glass display cases. Spinoza chatted about the upcoming Inca exhibit, pointing out displays still being installed. We passed two workmen mounting a plastic shield over a case of crude-looking hatchets and spears.

We entered a door marked EMPLOYEES ONLY, headed down a flight of stairs into a narrow hallway. A mixture of turpentine, musty books, and furniture polish filled the air. He ushered me into his office which was cluttered-to-overflowing with books, piles of paintings propped against filing cabinets, and a large stuffed condor with outstretched wings.

"I'm always delighted to cooperate if it means stopping the import of illegal artwork," he said, making his way between cabinets and the wall, ducking under the condor's wing. The desk was stacked with folders and a small wooden carving of King Tut.

Lukas Spinoza invited me to sit down.

I thanked him and said, "I need your expert opinion. We recently came across a shipment of what appears to be Inca or Mayan art— three wooden statues."

Spinoza did not react, except for a flicker of his eyebrow.

"Initially, we thought they had been smuggled into the country," I said. "But paperwork from the shipping crate said they were legally imported, destined for this museum."

"Can you describe these three statues?"

I indicated their height with my hands. "About three feet tall, carved out of wood. Nearly identical, but a great deal of detail was given to the faces. So there was no mistaking they were different individuals."

I brought out my cell phone. "But the most distinguishing feature are the headdresses. Red. Hand-carved to resemble feathers."

I scrolled through to find photos of the three statues I had taken and handed it to him. Spinoza studied the photos.

His brow wrinkled. "I'm familiar with these statues. They are *Los Tres Jefes*. Ceremonial statues from the Yucatan Peninsula."

I sat back a little surprised.

He handed back my phone. "These were to be delivered to the museum about six months ago. But they vanished. We've been looking for them ever since." He got up and went to a filing cabinet behind several cardboard shipping tubes, shoved them aside, and opened a drawer. He removed a file and placed it on the desk.

"Here they are," he said, handing me the eight-by-ten photographs. "They are called *Los Tres Jefes,* or The Three Chiefs, or The Three Bosses."

Those were the ones, all right.

"Where did you say they were located, Mr. Malone?" He sat back in his chair.

"They are still in their shipping crate under the stairs at the Chat Noir Art Gallery."

He took a *Mountbatten* pen from his inside coat pocket and jotted the name down on vellum stationary.

I gave him the address on Royal Street. "I should tell you, the studio and its content are still under police tape."

He looked up at me. "Are they part of a police investigation?"

I nodded. "The owner of the studio was one of the men killed in the Oasis Club Massacre."

"Okay, I'll notify our attorney to query the police as to when we can retrieve the artwork."

I said, "It might be best if you didn't tell them where you got the information."

He nodded. "I understand."

"The shipping papers we uncovered in the crate indicated they were to be delivered to this museum. Do you know how they ended up in the Chat Noir Art Gallery?"

"No, not really," he said. "You see, those three antiquities were a donation. It came to us from an anonymous donor in Latin America."

"Anonymous? Any ideas who?"

"No. Only that he was very wealthy. It was really all rather mysterious. But the museum didn't see any reason to refuse the gift."

"Estimated value?" I asked.

"Needless to say, the objects were priceless. One of a kind. But we did insure the pieces for a third of a million dollars each. These were some of the best examples of pre-Columbian era artwork. In remarkable condition, I may add."

"I see." But I didn't see how this tied in with the murders.

"The black market for stolen antiquities is a billion-dollar business," he said. "Its tentacles reach worldwide. As the demand for Primitive and Indigenous Art grows, so does the looting of ancient burial grounds. It's nearly unstoppable. With many sites in jungles and rural areas, criminals pay local officials to look the other way, then strip the sites bare."

He described how Interpol and the FBI intercepted only a fraction of the pilfered artworks.

It appeared as if I had gotten all the background information I could get from him. He was forthcoming, and I had no grounds to suspect otherwise. How the smuggling and the murders fit together was still a mystery. I stood and thanked him for meeting with me.

"Anything to help the police," he said, shaking my hand with his soft, firm fingers. "Even if the person isn't with the police any longer. I know you have your reasons."

"You know me?"

"Let's just say, I know your situation."

I turned to leave. What he said next, though, stopped me cold in my tracks.

"I knew your wife." he said flatly.

I spun around, trying hiding the surprise in my voice. *"What?"*

"Jane. I knew her."

I stared at him, unsure of where he was going with this. "How?"

"Jane brought us deals."

This was the first I had heard of this.

Spinoza rubbed a smooth hairless hand over the side of his face, as if unsure of himself. *Was he going to tell me more?* And then he said, "In fact, this whole Inca-Mayan exhibit was her baby."

"*Her* baby?" *None of this made sense.* "I'm not sure what you mean."

"Jane was the go-between, the liaison, between the museum and the anonymous wealthy donor." I guess the curator saw the puzzled expression on my face. "You didn't know?"

"No."

"Jane was the conduit that funneled millions of dollars into the museum. It was all very hush-hush. In fact, maybe I shouldn't be telling you this at all."

My legs no longer supporting me, I sagged back into the chair, trying to listen. I just couldn't believe Jane had lived a double-life that I was oblivious to. Was this what she meant when she warned me: *If you love me, you will not ask?* When she said this, I thought she was only hiding her past. Now I learned she had hidden a secret life.

Her secrets swirled around me like a whirlwind.

CHAPTER 43

I stumbled from the museum after Spinoza's bombshell about Jane. Nothing fit. Jane, a smuggler of antiquities? *What the hell? And I knew nothing ... and never suspected a damn thing.*

What had the curator said? *"She was the conduit for millions of dollars."*

How could that be? Before I retired, I earned a policeman detective's salary. She made more than I did as a freelance art dealer—but *millions?!*

Something didn't make sense. My heart was in a gallop—*millions from an anonymous donor?* I felt numb as I slid into the front seat of my car.

The two swans that had been peacefully gliding over the water were now in mortal combat on the bank of Bayou St. John. The pair bobbed their heads back and forth on their long necks, then charged each other in battle, hissing like cobras.

Slow down, I told myself. *Think this through.* First, there was the murder of Leslie Baronne, body sprawled between the rose bushes behind the Cathedral.

Then, the massacre at the Oasis Club. Who was the target? Clive Bronsky in his expensive silk shirt? Or Presley Baronne, gunned down in his own club? Surely not the five customers. A terrorist hate crime? As the police called it. The gunman still unknown. I thought of the five innocent bystanders that didn't seem connected. I also added Felix, the barman.

Bull said otherwise. "It has all the earmarks of a professional hit with a police cover-up."

Second: How did this tie into the smuggling? There were the three statues—*Los Tres Jeffes.* The shipment entered the country, legally, bound for the New Orleans Art Museum. But ended up in a small gallery run by a small-time hood. If it was a smuggling operation, why was Clive killed? He was low man on the totem pole.

I pulled out the shipping invoice to check—*deliver to the New Orleans Art Museum.* No question about that.

I rubbed my hands over my face. Another piece of the picture that I couldn't make fit. Were the deaths connected? Or just a series of coincidences?

I put the key in the ignition, cranked the engine and drove over the Esplanade Avenue Bridge and headed towards the lake. The two geese were still fighting. They looked like a married couple. They were on their feet, wings outspread, flapping.

I rolled down the window to get some fresh air to clear my thinking.

And the Big Number Three, which had just been lobbed on me like a hand grenade.

Jane was involved. My reptilian brain kicked in and a ball of fear knotted my stomach. Was she *really* part of this? And if so, how? No, that can't be. My rational brain fought back, and I took several deep breaths. Think it through, I warned myself.

The curator, Spinoza, appeared to be impartial. He knew about me. He knew about Jane.

Jane was involved. My heart began to sink.

As I drove along Lakeshore Drive, an image of her face, grass-green eyes, leapt into my mind. My hands began to shake, my heart raced. No, not again. Her face just before the explosion. Fear soaked into my body. *"Slow it down,"* Lucy in the Sky told me. *"Don't fight it."* I clenched and unclenched my jaw.

Jane's face. Her lips mouthing. *"I love you."*

I felt sick, as though I were going to vomit. I screeched to a halt on the side of the road and stumbled out to the seawall overlooking Lake Pontchartrain. The flat, gray lake stretched to the horizon, dark clouds hugging the dividing line between water and sky.

Take control, the psych doctor said. *Take control. You can't change the outcome. Change yourself.*

This is sheer madness. I thought.

And suddenly, I allowed the memory of Jane's death to come to me instead of fighting against it. I was back in the lobby of the Whitney Museum, and I could see the boy with the explosives in sharp detail. This was new. Previously, in my dreams, he was a shadowy figure, like a ghost.

I allowed the images to return. *Don't fight it.*

Now, his features were crystal clear. Dark hair, ruddy complexion. Perspiring. His voice tinged with fear. "*You're not supposed to be here,*" he said.

What did he say? I slowed the image down to hear and see exactly what was happening.

" *...you're not supposed to be here.*" Sweat poured down his face. But he had said something else that came before that. Words I had forgotten until now. *"They said—you're not supposed to be here."*

"They said ... ?"

I wasn't supposed to be there—*they* said? My body was tense, heart pounding.

And for the first time, an unfamiliar emotion boiled up inside of me. Instead of panic and pain and fear—I felt rage. Who were *they?*

Was her death more than a random act of lunacy? Were there others involved? Was Bomber Boy a fall guy? But for whom?

I got out of my car and stumbled along the shores of Lake Pontchartrain. An old man was throwing bits of bread to the seagulls. Shrieks filled the air. The flock circled the old man, plucking pieces out of the air before even hitting the ground.

The bitterness I had felt minutes before started to vanish. My heart rate began to slow. If I was right, Jane was involved. And her death was not a random act. She'd been set up. *But why?*

It's odd, but the list of dead had grown: Leslie and Presley Baronne, Clive Bronsky, the barman, Felix, and the five unlucky patrons of the Oasis Club.

To that list, I added the name of Jane. The list had grown from eight to nine. I then included the Bomber Boy.

Ten.

Jane was involved. But who murdered her? And for what reason? What bastard had blown her to bits?

PART III

CHAPTER 44

Where do you start to find who killed your wife after two years?

I returned to my office and sat down, trying to work this through. I decided that this was something I had to follow myself—don't call Bull or anyone else. I had to follow it on my own.

So, where do I start? Mrs. Gonzales came to mind. I had initially dismissed the idea that her son was murdered. Because I didn't want to get involved. But based on what I've just learned, I needed to reevaluate her visit. What does she know that I don't? Apparently, a lot, since I never suspected Jane's death was anything but bad timing. Esperanza's son, who she admitted was not very bright, was Bomber Boy. Had Jane stumbled into a crazy scenario?—A lunatic had strapped explosives to himself in an attempt to collect a million dollars? Or was it as Mrs. Gonzales said—her son was murdered? It still didn't make sense.

But where would I track down Mrs. Gonzales? I concentrated, trying to picture her. Short, sweating from the heat and a strong Spanish accent. Dressed like a housekeeper. She cleaned houses to save the money for a private investigator. And she wore a hotel maid's outfit. The tag on her dress said ... *The Roosevelt Hotel.* That's it.

The Roosevelt Hotel is one of the oldest and most historic landmarks in a city filled with history. As they said, if those walls could talk. The Roosevelt had played host to celebrities, the wealthy, Hollywood stars, politicians. Back in the day, Governor Huey P.

Long kept a suite on permanent standby to entertain his mistress, Blaze Starr. Or did she entertain him? Whichever way it went, he was notorious for holding raucous, drunken parties whenever he slipped into town.

Hotels are pretty reluctant to give out that information to anyone. The only person I knew with any connections to the Roosevelt was Moshe *"Hit Man"* Enos. Moshe had been my connection to the underworld when I was a cop. He only spoke to me, and he ran an underground racket buying stolen goods, flipping them for a handsome profit. He owed me. One of the favors I did for him was getting his nephew out of jail and a job at the Roosevelt Hotel.

The problem was I hadn't spoken to Moshe in over two years. I found I still had his number on my speed dial and punched it.

"Zeke, my man," he greeted me. "How's it hanging? Long time no hear from you since ... " He fell silent, then said in a soft voice, "Sorry to hear about your lady."

"Thanks," I said, "Moshe, I need some information."

"Shit, man, I *am* a legitimate businessman now, Zeke. I gave up fencing purloined material brought to me my associates. My wife said that if I didn't stop messing with that line of work, she was gonna leave me."

"It's not like that. Does your nephew still work at the Roosevelt?"

"No. But what do you need? Is in trouble again?"

"No. Nothing like that. I need information on a lady that works there. A housekeeper by the name of Esperanza Gonzales. Middle-aged. Speaks with heavy Spanish accent. I need her address, phone number and anything else you can dig up on her."

"I'll call you back." He hung up.

One hour later. "Yo, she doesn't work there anymore. But I got her address. No phone."

I thanked him and said, "I owe you."

"Shit, man, as much as you did for me, I'm glad to give a little back."

. . .

The address he gave for Mrs. Gonzales was off Euterpe Street in the Irish Channel. An old section along the river, it is full of rundown apartment buildings, neighborhood dive bars, and boarding houses. Euterpe, from Greek mythology—*the muse of music.*

The two-story building was unpainted clapboard, and her apartment was on the second floor with wooden steps leading to her door from a narrow alleyway. A mailbox stuffed full of circulars told me she didn't live there anymore. I knocked anyway and leaned over the railing, balancing on one foot, peering in a window. The empty room had worn linoleum floors with a plastic bag of trash by the door.

I walked down the stairs and knocked on the door of the downstairs apartment.

After a minute, I heard clicking, unlocking, and a bolt thrown. The door opened about six inches; the chain preventing it from opening farther, and an old man stuck his frowning face in the gap. He was maybe ninety, with pale skin that looked like it never saw the light of day. Maybe he had something to hide? Or maybe he was just not sociable?

"Excuse me," I said, "but I was wondering about the lady upstairs."

"Did you knock?"

"Yes."

"And?"

"And there was no answer," I said. "The apartment is empty."

"You a cop?"

"No."

"A relative?"

"No."

"Then get the *hell* off my porch!" He slammed the door in my face. The bolt slammed back into place.

Well, that didn't help. There were no answers to my knocks at the houses on either side. I walked the neighborhood and came across a Creole Cottage in the middle of the block. On the front porch, two elderly ladies sat in wicker chairs, watching me. Both wore flower-print housecoats, once called moo-moos. The one on the right had bunny slippers, the one on the left, shower tongs. They smiled at me, and I thought, what the heck? And made my way past the creaking metal gate and a sidewalk lined with elephant ears and ferns. A small patio table sat between them with tall tea glasses and a pitcher. The one on the right had bleached blonde hair as fine as cotton candy, which matched her bunny slippers. The one on the left had Shirley Temple sausage curls the color of a blue sky.

I stood with one foot on the bottom step. "Good morning, ladies," I said. Both of them smiled at me. "I was wondering if you can help me? I'm looking for a lady that lived down the street in that big, unpainted house."

"The Spanish lady?" the blue-haired woman asked.

"Yeah, that's the one. A Mrs. Gonzales." I was elated. At last, I might get some answers.

"She wasn't Spanish. She was German," the blonde one piped in.

"No, Millie, you're thinking of the lady over by the streetcar line."

"Am I?" Blondie looked down. "Yes, I guess so. My memory is getting so bad."

"You're telling me. I correct you all the time."

"No, you don't," Blondie huffed. "Just once in a while."

I sighed. "Mrs. Gonzales doesn't live there anymore, and—"

"That's tragic. Just tragic," Blue said. "The way her son died."

"What happened to her son?" The white cotton candy lady asked.

Blue shook her head. "You know. He blew himself up."

"Suicide? I thought it was her daughter," Blondie said.

"No, Millie, it was her son. She claims he didn't do it."

"No?" Blondie looked surprised, turning towards her. "She never said that to me."

"Well, she said it to me," Blue said, nodding her head, blue curls bouncing up and down. "Said he was murdered. Murdered! Can you imagine that?"

"Oh, she was from Honduras," Blondie said, sipping some tea.

"No, she wasn't. It was Cuba," Blue insisted.

"Was not! It was Honduras, alright. She had that blue-and-white flag with the stars, hanging in her window."

I interjected, "Was it or wasn't Honduras?"

Blondie slammed her iced tea onto the plastic top, spilling it. "Honduras."

I interrupted their conversation. "Do either of you know where she might have moved? A forwarding address, or something?"

The two looked at each other, frowning.

I took another step up. They turned towards me. "Is she still in the city?"

"Yes, she's still here," Blue said.

"Good," I said. "Do you know where?"

"Yes. She's in the cemetery. She died."

My heart sank.

"I didn't know that," Blondie said.

"Sure, I showed you the article in the Picayune. Of course, you don't remember."

Blondie shook her head sadly.

"How?" I felt a hitch in my chest.

"Shot dead in the street one night. Somebody came up behind her while she was walking from the bus stop."

"Poor soul."

"The funny thing," Blue said. "They didn't steal anything. She had just cashed her payroll check and had a purse full of money."

Blondie tsk-tsked with her tongue, and shook her head. "Gangland like, huh?"

"Yep. They popped a cap in her. Just like in *The Godfather*." Blue said.

"One or Two?" asked Blondie.

"The Godfather One," said Blue.

• • •

My phone buzzed.

"Hello," he said. "Mr. Malone." It was the refined and cultured voice with the Spanish accent of Lukas Spinoza, the curator of the New Orleans Art Museum.

"Yes?"

"First of all, I want to thank you for helping us recover the three Inca statues—*Los Tres Jeffes,*" he said.

I pictured Lukas Spinoza in his expensive, well-tailored Vanquish suit, with a James Bond snug fit.

"They are unloading them at the museum as we speak."

"You have them already?" I said. "That was quick."

"Oh, yes. We have special contacts with the police. They were very cooperative."

"Okay."

"The reason I'm calling is: there is a special unveiling of the three statues. *Invitation only.* Needless to say, *Los Tres Jeffes* will be our prized possession for the Inca exhibit. They are unique, photograph well, and the press loves them."

Mixing with a bunch of elite museum donors? Not my idea of a good time. I hesitated, and maybe he sensed that I was going to brush him off.

"Oh, please, do come, Mr. Malone? You are responsible for recovering these valuable artifacts. I want to thank you personally." He interjected quickly. "Besides, I already have a limo scheduled to come and deliver you to the museum."

What could I say? I said yes.

"Very good, Mr. Malone. An invitation is already waiting for you at your office." He hung up.

. . .

The cream-colored envelope with an invitation to the New Orleans Art Museum was waiting under my door when I arrived. My name was handwritten on the front in an elegant John Hancock flourish you might see in the *Declaration of Independence*. The card was of heavy, expensive stock with embossed letters. I ran my fingertips over the raised letters and logo.

It was for the early unveiling of *Los Tres Jeffes*, the most prized possession of the Inca/Mayan exhibit opening in two days. I could picture the three wooden sculptures with their carrot tops enclosed in a Plexiglas case with gold plaques on all four sides. I could imagine the wealthy patrons in tuxedos, accompanied by women in beautiful evening gowns, posing for photos in front of the statues.

A note was attached: *Please do come, Mr. Malone,* signed *Lukas Spinoza.* I think I could almost smell the expensive cologne impregnated on the card.

CHAPTER 45

Seventeen-year-old Iggy was suspended from high school for fighting. It didn't matter that much to Ignatius T. Rossis, nicknamed Iggy, because he never intended to go back anyway. He hated school and those know-it-all teachers and that wise-ass principal.

As usual, his dad raised holy hell with him for brawling at school and punched him a few times for good measure. But *that* didn't matter either. Iggy stole his father's mint-condition 1999 blue Cadillac, a Coupe DeVille, with a black ragtop, a grille that passed for a grin, and smelled of Armor All Leather Care, his father's pride and joy.

He left the house in a Saint's T-shirt, torn jeans and motorcycle boots and vowed never to return, drove by and picked up a couple of his loser buddies, goofy Lee and Midget Joe, and they drove around drinking beers, telling jokes, farting, and smoking a joint or two. Later, he picked up an eager Jennifer Bienville, in too-tight white shorts and smelling of lilacs; she told her mother she was spending the night with friends.

After she ran and jumped in, Iggy asked, "How old are you, girl?" popping open a Bud, guzzling half of it down. He pressed down on the accelerator, and the Caddy shot forward.

"I'm old enough. Gimme some of that beer!" she squealed, reaching for the can.

He held it away from her and said in mock surprise. "You too young," he grinned at her.

"'I'm old enough," she repeated, snatching the beer from his hand. Iggy knew she was only fifteen, which made it even more exciting. Tonight, he was out for a good time. *To hell with my father,* Iggy thought.

His two buddies in the back seat fished out two Red Bulls from the Igloo cooler that sat on the floor between them. They all giggled when Lee burped and threw the can out the back window. "Hee-Yaa!" he yelled.

"Where we going?" Jennifer snuggled up against him.

"Just you watch," he said.

Iggy gunned the Caddy into the hushed darkness on the two-lane River Road in St. John's Parish, upriver from New Orleans. On one side was the sloping grassy, forty-foot-high levee, dotted with NO VEHICLES signs. As they whizzed by, it looked like the side of mountains holding back the Mississippi River. On the opposite side of the two-lane blacktop were trees and thickets, broken only by the entrances to working-class subdivisions and the occasional convenience store. Deer were known to jump out in front of cars, but Iggy didn't mind if he bagged an eighteen-pointer on his dad's grille.

"Can't you go any faster?" shouted Jennifer.

Then Iggy got a brilliant idea. "Hold on!" he hollered, suddenly jerking the steering wheel to the left, crossing the empty lane, jumping the curve, roaring up the steep incline of the levee.

"What the … ?!" Jennifer screamed, mouth open.

From the back, Lee and Joe howled with laughter, "Yaaahooo!"

The tires dug into the grassy turf, pitching divots of dirt as huge as basketballs into the air. At the top, they screeched to a stop, straddling the walking track and sat there, engine idling in a loud rumble, shaking like a train locomotive. The whole car smelled of spilt beer. From the ridge of the levee, they could see the dark silent waters of the Mississippi River, flat, broad, and so black it reflected the moonlight.

"Ain't that the most beautiful sight in the world?" Iggy said softly.

Lee got out of the backseat and took a leak on the walking track. After he got back in, Iggy revved up the engine, foot on the brake, revved it up again and again until the engine shrieked like a nitro drag-racer on the Nevada Salt Flats. *Damn, those fools can hear it on the other side of the river,* he thought. Jennifer clamped her hands over her ears.

"Hold on!" Iggy lifted his foot off the brake and accelerated down the grassy embankment. Before he reached the bottom, though, he reversed directions and started climbing back up, the tires tearing out grass and digging twin trenches. He repeated the maneuver, so the side of the levee looked as if someone had carved a giant, wavy S in the grass.

"I think I'm gonna be sick," Jennifer wailed.

"Uh-oh!" Lee called from the back seat, pounding on Iggy's back to get his attention.

"What?"

"The cops." Blue and red flashing-lights reflected in the rearview mirror.

"Oh, shit!" Iggy raced to the top of the levee again and bumped along the walking trail. He turned his head to look back.

"Watch out!" Jennifer shrieked.

The Caddy ran over a NO VEHICLES sign. They could hear the scraping sound of the metal pole digging into the undercarriage. Iggy slammed on the breaks too late—the damage had been done.

The muffler took on a thump-thump-thump sound, followed by the engine starting a metallic kerplunking noise. "My dad's going to kill me," Iggy muttered. He put his head down on the steering wheel.

Jennifer said, "I think I peed myself," before sticking her head out the window and puking. He stared at her heaving shoulders. The dread he felt was replaced by a giddy sensation of lightness. Excitement thumped in his chest, and he felt as if he didn't care. *Damn his father.* He began laughing because this was the most fun he had in his life. Even the police lights flashing on River Road below was funny. The Caddy was coiled like the giant black panther he saw at Audubon Zoo—its motor idling, kerplunking, thumping, and growling, ready to leap.

They heard the police loudspeaker: "Turn off the engine! Get out of the car." That was the funniest thing ever, and Iggy hooted with laughter.

"Are you stupid?" screamed the girl, wiping spit off her chin. But soon everyone in the car was laughing hysterically. The police car started up the side of the levee towards them. Iggy waited till the cop car was halfway up before punching the gas pedal.

"Grab tight!" He shouted, barreling down the embankment. The Caddy's grille bounced off the asphalt road, smashing in the front fenders, fishtailing, then straightened up and streaked away on River Road. When Iggy pumped the brakes at the curve, his foot went all the way to the floorboard. *Shit! No brakes.*

•   •   •

The caretaker at the St. John's Cemetery had forgotten to close the gate that night after he trucked in a load of sod to cover new graves. As he was hanging a shovel and rake onto pegs in the workman's shed, he heard the screech of tires, indicating a vehicle was careening into the cemetery at a high rate of speed.

Crap! It's those damn kids again, he thought. *No respect for the sanctity of the dead!* This wasn't the first time he'd caught shitheads sneaking onto the property, spraying graffiti on the sides of the mausoleums.

But before he could exit the shed, he heard the thump of tires bouncing off the drive into the grassy area with the graves. Followed by a loud KABAM! of metal on a headstone.

The caretaker ran out of the shed and saw a statue of an angel broken into pieces on the grass. He looked up just as the car slammed into the side of the Heavenly Grace Mausoleum, an above-ground, all-white marble building, twelve-tiered, and twenty crypts wide. Later, he would describe it as if the Jolly Green Giant had taken a toy car and jammed it into a miniature dollhouse. Only the red taillights stuck out.

Just then, he heard the wail of police sirens and saw cars swerving into the driveway. A second later, he saw the flicker of flames shooting out the side of the mausoleum like red tongues. "Oh, my God!"

He bolted back inside, grabbed the fire extinguisher, and raced towards the fire. By the time he reached the car, two boys were scrambling out of the back window and sprinting towards the fence. A third boy crawled out next, dragging the limp body of a young girl after him. He flopped her on the ground and knelt beside her. The caretaker ran to them. She looked as if someone had poured a bucket of red paint on her: blood matted her hair, soaked her face and chest.

"What the hell happened?" the caretaker shouted.

"The brakes … " the boy mumbled, a dazed look on his face. Iggy's nose was bleeding, and his eyes were wide in panic.

A cop ran up, grabbed the girl under the arms, and dragged her away from the intense heat. The extinguisher was useless against the flames that engulfed the interior of the car like a crematorium and the caretaker scrambled back from the heat.

That fool kid had driven the car smack dab into the middle of two crypts on the bottom row—A-3 and A-4. The force of the crash wedged the front end upward into the B level, pushing into the vaults above, and popped a casket from the second-level out, much like a spit-out watermelon seed. Hitting the ground, the casket rolled away about a dozen feet, landing lid down in the grass. The flames and black smoke shot out of the back window.

•   •   •

The next morning, after the Diamond Towing Service had wrenched out the burnt metal frame, the caretaker saw it had once been a Cadillac. The coffin still lay face-down in the grass.

In a greasy jumpsuit and dirty white lobster boots, the tow truck driver stepped around the flat-bed, writing on his clipboard. "Who's going to pay for this?" he grumbled.

"Insurance," the caretaker responded without looking up. He stood by the coffin that had once been an expensive Bronze-Deluxe with a purple metal sheen. But now, it was scorched black, and the faux-gold metal handles had melted from their hinges.

"What are you going to do about that?" The driver nodded at the casket, wiping the grease off his hands with a rag.

The caretaker shook his head. "Help me turn it over?"

The driver frowned, but squatted by the caretaker's side, as if they were going to roll a log.

"One, two, three," the caretaker said. They grunted, and rolled the casket over onto its side. The lid popped off, and the contents tumbled out onto the scorched grass.

"Oh, *shit!*" said the caretaker.

"Oh, shit!" said the tow-truck driver.

•   •   •

Later that night, the limo picked me up but did not go towards the museum as expected, instead headed to the lake.

"Hey, Pal," I leaned forward, speaking to the driver. "You sure you're driving me to the right place? The museum is back that way."

"Yes, sir," he said over his shoulder. "The affair is on a yacht, on the lake."

A *yacht?* It was odd to be holding *the affair* there. But maybe a large donor was showing off his new toy. I was about to tell the driver to turn around when he pulled up to the harbor gate. Then he left me there, looking stupid in my rented tuxedo until a small man in a white jacket approached me. "You, Mr. Malone?"

"Uh, yeah, that's me."

"Would you come this way? We have a small skiff to transport you to the yacht." His idea of a small skiff and mine were different—

it was a thirty-footer with cushioned seats. But it was small in comparison to the three-hundred-foot yacht anchored out in middle of Lake Pontchartrain. It loomed large as a freighter when we tied up to a loading platform, with stairs leading up the side. I could see lighted portholes, people walking on the upper decks, and heard music. An attractive young lady in a blue uniform extended her hand to steady me. "Mr. Malone, Lukas Spinoza is expecting you. Watch your step."

At the top of the stairs, a waiter in a white coat tried to hand me a drink. I declined, asked for a Coke, and walked through French doors to a lighted ballroom. A small string quartet played Bach's *Brandenburg Concerto*, or something like that.

At once, Lukas Spinoza spotted me and hurried towards me. He wore a well-fitted black tuxedo, unlike mine, a red carnation in his lapel. "Ah, Zeke. Thank you for coming," he said, diamond cuff links sparkling as he shook my hand.

"Well, it was hard to refuse since you sent a limo."

"It was the least I could do. After all, if it wasn't for you," he said, in his cultured English, with the Castilian undertone, "Our most prized displays would have missed the exhibit."

"You would have eventually gotten them."

"But in time for the exhibit?" He took my arm and led me to a bullet-proof Plexiglas case. And there they were—*Los Tres Jeffes*—The Three Chiefs with red-feathered headdresses glowing. "Well, what do you think? *Magnifico*, yes?"

"Yes, they are quite beautiful," I said.

But then, he spotted an elderly man in a tux with a young wife in a sleek gown entering the room. "Please excuse me for a minute," he said, turning and leaving me hurriedly.

The waiter brought me a Coke. Since I knew no one there, I stood, studying the three warriors. In this light, I made out the expressions on their carved faces. They appeared about as unhappy as I was. But then, after a few minutes, a woman, in a plunging neckline that nearly reached her belly-button, came and stood beside me. *Close.* "You rich?" Slurring her words, she was unsteady on her feet.

She laughed and possessed a low charm that passed for beauty with some men. I stared at her. "Nope, just a poor guy here for free food and to admire the three statues."

She nodded. "You're funny. Me too. And get laid." She giggled and pointed at The Three Chiefs. "They're great, huh?"

"Yes, they are."

"What do you think of this boat?" she said, making a wide gesture with her glass.

"What?"

"This boat? This yacht?" She leaned against me and ran her hands over my biceps. "My, what a muscular guy you are. You work out, don't you? What's your name?"

I looked around, not sure how to exit, so I played along. "It's Zeke Malone."

"Well, Zeke, how much do you think this yacht cost?"

"It's a little out of my class. I wouldn't know where to start. I never owned more than a flat-bottom fishing boat with an outboard motor."

She started laughing as if this were the funniest thing she ever heard. "When I tell you how much it really costs, you won't believe me."

"Lady, you could tell me it cost ten million bucks, and—"

"Call me Sweetie," she said.

"Sweetie, I couldn't argue with you, one way or the other. Why? Is this your yacht?"

"Me?" She broke out in a high cackle. "You got to be kidding!"

About that time, Lukas Spinoza had finished playing host and returned. He ran his manicured fingernails through his thick black hair and frowned at her. "I see you met Sweetie. I hope she hasn't been a nuisance, Mr. Malone."

"No, not at all," I said. "We were just chatting about the exhibit. And the price of boats."

Sweetie turned towards Spinoza. "Go ahead, tell Zeke how much. He'd be interested."

Lukas did not answer.

She smiled, but I didn't think it held any warmth. "Now, he's being modest. It starts with a six, followed by seven zeroes."

Sixty million dollars!

"That's enough, *Sweetie,*" Lukas said, grabbing her arm. She winced. "Don't you think it's time to freshen up?"

"Of course," she said, pulling away from his grasp. "Whatever His Majesty wants, He gets." She stumbled unsteadily across the dance floor and out the door.

Lukas said, "I'm sorry, sometimes she gets ... "

"Look, Lukas, I appreciate the invite." I decided the best exit was to be direct. "But I've got to get up early tomorrow, work, you know, and ... "

He stared at me hard, but with a smile on his face. "You sure you can't stay a little longer?"

"No, thanks. Like I said, I've got things to do."

As I walked down the gangplank to board the *small skiff,* I glanced in a porthole. I paused. Even though I couldn't hear the words, I could see Lukas Spinoza shouting and cursing at Sweetie. I looked away and made my escape. By the time we made land, I couldn't help but think, *Where does anyone get the money to own such an expensive yacht like this?*

CHAPTER 46

When Dr. Fowler heard that he had stage IV liver cancer, he thought of his wife, Kitty. From where he sat on the examination table, in the hospital gown, black socks with his legs dangling over the edge, he felt like a child. The paper sheet crinkled under him.

The news was delivered by his old friend, Dr. Willam Gallbrith, a general practitioner Dr. Fowler had known since medical school. They often golfed together and lunched at the Boston Club or Commander's Palace.

"I'm sorry," Will said, placing his hand on Dr. Fowler's shoulder.

"You sure?" he asked, a little hope beneath his voice, even though he knew that his death sentence was final.

"Yes, there's no doubt. It's spread from a tumor in your pancreas, and metastasized to the liver. Stage IV."

Stage IV liver cancer. A death knell. He thought once again of his wife Katrina Fowler, though he never called her Katrina—it was Kitty. It had always been Kitty. On the morning of his appointment to learn the results of his lab tests, Dr. Fowler asked her to accompany him.

She refused, telling him she had a date with a hairdresser, she just couldn't break. "Oh, you don't need me, do you? It's only some silly test I wouldn't understand." She slipped on a pair of slingback high heels, primping in front of the full-length mirror. She was the most beautiful woman he had ever known. "Besides, it took forever to get this appointment with this *delicious* hairdresser. He's fabulous. I was lucky he could fit me in."

And so he went alone. He already suspected the results would be bad.

Now, Dr. Fowler took a deep breath of resignation and said to his old friend, "Well, I guess that's it."

"Not totally. We can try chemotherapy. New stuff is being developed all the time."

"Don't shit me," he said with a hard smile. "We've known each other too long. Besides, I've sat on that side of the table more than I'd care to remember. How much time do you think I have? The truth, please?"

"Three. Maybe six months. Of course, there's no way to be absolutely certain. Possibly a year with chemo."

"No, *thank you*, no chemo," he said, sliding off the table and shedding his hospital gown. He stood in the middle of the exam room in his underwear and socks, staring at his friend. He grabbed his shirt, put it on, and began buttoning it, staring out the window. Dr. Fowler could see the tops of trees, brick walls, and the windows of Touro Hospital.

Suddenly, he felt the need to be with Kitty, to speak with her, and hold her close—even though they had grown further and further apart over the years.

He thought it ironic that as he grew older, the age difference between them seemed to have grown wider. She didn't appear to age at all. She still looked like the voluptuous blonde he had met a dozen years ago. In public, he felt like her father instead of her husband, her lover.

"I know it may be too soon for this stuff," Dr. Gallbrith interrupted his thoughts. "And I know you could write your own prescriptions." He tore out a page from his prescription pad and handed it to him. "But when the pain starts getting worse—"

"And it will."

"Right, of course. Don't hesitate to use them."

Dr. Fowler stared down at the prescription, oxycodone. "Isn't that stuff addictive?" he asked. They both laughed.

After he dressed, Dr. Fowler said goodbye to his old friend, rode the elevator down, and found himself on the street in front of Touro Hospital, in the heat and the noise.

His thoughts turned once again to Kitty. With a pang of desire, he fumbled in his pocket and dug out his phone.

His hands trembled. He hit Kitty on speed dial. It rang three times before going to voicemail. "Kitty," he said, trying to keep a calm voice, the tightness in his throat, to keep the pleading tone out. "Kitty, I need to see you. Call me. I just came from Dr..." he couldn't complete the sentence. This wasn't the way he wanted to tell her. He needed to see her and talk face-to-face.

He sat in his car with the A/C on full, waiting, hoping she'd call back. After ten minutes, he tried again. He left another message asking her to call him. Their relationship had been on rocky ground for years now, coming to a head with the death of the female impersonator, Leslie Barrone. That's when the truth came out. The affairs. With that artist creep—Clive. How many others were there?

Dr. Fowler pounded his fists on the steering wheel. "*God,* I still love her," he moaned. "How did I let this happen?"

Though small waves of hurt and humiliation swirled inside him, he still could not bring himself to hate her. He needed to move, so he put his car in gear and wheeled out of the parking garage. Without realizing it, he found himself following a familiar route to Canal Street and North Rampart Street to St. Louis Cemetery Number One.

It was a ritualistic visit he made every few months to this historic old cemetery, the oldest in New Orleans. It was surrounded by ten-foot brick walls, plastered over in whitewash, with small ferns growing out of chinks of exposed brick in the crumbling walls.

He waved off the tour guides that greeted him at the gate and entered alone into the eerie City of the Dead, with its narrow streets between the mausoleum and crypt. It always reminded him of a miniature white brick city built by Lilliputians that giants strode in—a place where regular-sized people went to bury the dead among dwarfs.

He passed a tour guide chattering away, followed by a gaggle of tourists near the tomb of Marie Laveau, the Voodoo Queen. Dr. Fowler knew she existed, alright. She was a real person a hundred years ago. But the legend had overtaken facts and now bore little connection to reality.

Not like the grave of his son.

He made his way to the rear of the cemetery, near a back wall. Here, the crypts and mausoleum were less well-kept with broken plaster and ivy growing out of the cracks. His family had owned this tomb since before the Civil War. Scores of Fowlers were buried here.

A pang of bitterness and ache clutched at his heart standing before his son's burial crypt.

Benjamin A. Fowler

Beloved son of ...

Fowler stopped reading. He knew it all by heart. Remembered the day Ben was placed in the vault as if it were yesterday, watched them brick up the entrance, sealing his boy inside. The same pain he felt back then, bubbled up anew.

The police had killed him.

He clenched his fists at his side.

Three years ago, he vowed revenge, but ended up letting it go. Nothing he could do was going to bring his son back. *Nothing.*

The official report cleared the police of any wrongdoing. His son had been high on crack and ran screaming towards them, cell phone in hand.

It looked like a gun, they said.

He could taste the bile in his throat.

Now, he knew his time was running short. The Cancer Death Clock was ticking and it would not be long before he joined his son.

His thoughts were interrupted by laughter behind him.

"Hey, is this Marie Laveau's grave?" A pretty young coed approached with three other girls, all college age. They all wore shorts and LSU T-shirts. She had long tapered legs and a smooth face. His son would be that age now.

"No, her mausoleum is over that way," he said, pointing.

"Oh, okay. Who's tomb is that?" she asked.

One of the others jumped in. "Another voodoo queen?" They all joined in, laughing.

"No, it's the grave of my son," he replied.

"Oh. Sorry, we ... " she paused, motioning to her friends. "Well, I didn't know ... Come on." They ran off, giggling and elbowing each other.

CHAPTER 47

Dr. Fowler watched the girls running away between the white-washed tombs. He left his son's tomb and headed back to his car. Once again, his thoughts turned to his wife, Kitty. The girl reminded him of her—the giggling, the pouty lips, and blue eyes.

His imagination took over. He thought he smelled her fragrance and could picture the smoothness of her skin beneath his fingertips. The sound of moans when they made love. Twenty years his junior—the only way he could satisfy her now was with his mouth. But he didn't mind. His erections were useless, even with the pills.

He pulled the cell phone from his pocket and dialed her number. Her cell phone rang and rang before going to voicemail. He had already left a dozen messages—but he tried again, hoping against hope she'd answer. Though he didn't want to, he left another message. *Don't sound desperate. Don't be desperate.* Before he could gather his thoughts, he hung up.

Returning to his car, he drove to his home off St. Charles Avenue in the Garden District. To his astonishment, her Thunderbird was in the circular brick driveway in front of their two-story mansion.

He let out a huge breath. At last, he would see her. He brushed away thoughts of shame—was that any way for a man to behave? *I'm not pussy-whipped!* he told himself.

As he walked into the house, he heard the tinkling of ice cubes in a glass. He rubbed the back of his neck. If she's been drinking, that wouldn't be good. She was on the phone, her voice slurred, laughing in that high-pitched peel.

He called out to her. Her voice dropping into a whisper. He could almost imagine what she might be saying.

As he entered the kitchen, she said, "I gotta go." She punched out with one hand and slid the phone into the pocket of her white shorts. In her other hand, she held a glass tumbler with amber-colored whiskey. She leaned against the counter.

"Well, look what the cat dragged in." she slurred.

"You're drunk." He tried to keep a controlled tone in his voice.

"Ha! Nice assessment, Doctor." She motioned with her glass. "Want one?"

He shook his head.

She turned her back and placed the empty glass on the counter.

"Where have you been all day?" he asked.

"Nowhere." She took a fresh glass. She turned and squinted at him. "And where have *you* been?"

"To the graveside of my son."

"Oh." She staggered over to the refrigerator and plopped in a few ice cubes that tinkled like marbles.

"Do you want to know where else I've been?" He asked, stepping in close.

She reached out for the liquor bottle on the counter. "Where?" she said, as if bored with the whole conversation.

As she put her hand around the bottle, he covered her hand so she couldn't move. She tugged at the bottle, but he wouldn't release it. She didn't feel like fighting.

"Okay, tell me," she said, relaxing her grip.

"I was at Dr. Gallbrith." He released her hand and the bottle.

"That's funny." She turned. "Doctors needing to go see doctors," she giggled, pouring the whiskey over the ice. It popped and cracked. She took a swallow. "What happened to *physician heal thyself?* Or something like that."

He felt like slapping her, but instead clenched his fists at his side.

She stepped away from him. "What did he say? What's the diagnosis?"

"He said I have liver cancer."

She paused and stared at him. "Liver cancer?"

"That's right."

She blinked several times. "Isn't that serious?"

"Yes."

She put the glass on the counter, her brow wrinkling. "How bad?"

"Fatal."

"Fatal? You mean ... ?" She stepped to him.

"Yes."

"Oh, my dear. I didn't know." She took him in her arms.

He held her tight and put his head on her shoulders. Tears came to his eyes.

"There, there, Mommy's going to take care of it," she said in a soft voice, stroking his back, pressing herself against him.

How long they stood there, he wasn't sure. She took his face in her hands, turned his face to hers and kissed him several times, stroking the back of his neck. Finally, she leaned back and stared into his face. "Oh, baby, I'm so sorry."

She kissed him again and whispered, "Go wash up, and we'll make love."

He kissed her. "I'm not sure I can."

"Yes, you can. I'll let you do me. Go on. I'll even suck you," she said, groping him.

Though he did not want to, he felt his blood begin to throb. She was unzipping his pants. "I don't think I can," he protested.

She slapped him hard with one hand and grasped his cock in the other. "Yes, you can."

Suddenly, all his pain and misery lifted. The hurt of losing his son, the diagnosis of cancer, all seemed to fall away. He felt a lightness he hadn't felt in several years. *God, I love her.* Only she could do this.

"Go on." She pressed her body against him. "Take a warm bath. I'll be with you shortly." She stroked him.

He stumbled up the stairs to the spacious bathroom. Turning on the gold-handled faucets, he cranked up the hot water.

This was what he needed. Wash away the depression. The pain. He stripped off his clothes, and he stared at his erection with something like pride. How long had it been? He stepped into the marble tub and settled under the warm embrace of the water.

On the table by the tub sat a line of bottles. He selected one. Sprinkling in the bubbly stuff she liked, he slid down and submerged his head. It was like a healing embrace. When he came up, he heard movement in the bedroom and called out, "Kitty?" She did not answer.

After a few minutes, he climbed out and toweled himself off as he entered the bedroom. She was not there. He dropped the towel and tried to decide if he should slip into a pair of silky blue pajamas she had bought him—or put on nothing—when he heard a car door slam.

Oh, no. No visitors now, please. He stepped over to the window and peered through the blinds.

His heart stopped. From the upstairs window, he saw her throwing a suitcase into the back of her Thunderbird and getting in.

He ran down the stairs, stumbling out the front door just as she backed out to the street.

"Kitty!" He shouted, leaping off the porch.

She glanced at him once, before slamming the car into gear and speeding off, tires squealing on the pavement at the corner.

He ran out into the middle of the street, shouting her name, "Kitty! Kitty!"

On the sidewalk across the street, eighty-two-year-old Mrs. Pakentsky, who lived next door and walked her toy schnauzer on a leash every day at the same time, stood by the magnolia tree at the corner while her fluffy white dog peed. Her mouth fell open, and she shouted, "DR. FOWLER! PUT SOME CLOTHES ON!"

Dr. Fowler staggered back into the house. Kitty had left a half-empty glass of whiskey on the glass table.

He took it into his hand. There was lipstick on the rim. He stared up at the large nude painting of Kitty reclining in her *Olympia* pose, the coy smile on her face.

"Fucking *bitch*!" He flung the glass towards it as hard as he could. The glass missed the painting and smashed into the mantle beneath and shattered into a thousand pieces on the cold, white marble floor.

CHAPTER 48

Zeke went on stakeout, watching the warehouse where Theodore Onyx kept his headquarters. His offices were located on Desire Street, in the Lower Ninth Ward, and only blocks from the Mississippi River. Yes, *that* Desire made famous by Tennessee Williams' post-WWII stage play and later into a movie with Marlon Brando. However, in the 1960s, the streetcars, old-fashioned, clanging, were replaced by diesel buses, belching smoke. The streetcar tracks were either pulled up or paved over. But not all the rails were removed, though, they played peek-a-boo along the routes.

From where Zeke sat, he saw a twenty-foot section of iron tracks exposed. He also saw the entrance to the three-story warehouse. Delivery trucks jammed the side entrance and backed up to the elevated loading dock. Nothing out of the ordinary: heavy cardboard boxes unloaded on handcarts by workers, wooden pallets lifted out with a forklift.

Malone was questioning what he was doing here. What did he expect to find? The warehouse was probably filled with household goods, furniture, import-export stuff, like boxes of Mardi Gras beads from Hong Kong—all legal merchandise. Besides, Onyx couldn't be that stupid to run an illegal operation in the heart of an old section in town.

What would Zeke expect to find? *I just can't walk up to the front entrance and knock to gain entry. Hi, I'm Zeke Malone, here to check out Onyx and his warehouse full of ...* What? Stolen goods? Carnival beads?

Zeke was about to abandon his stakeout, and start back to the office, when a convoy of black limousines came speeding around the corner. The lead limo screeched to a halt in front of the mechanical security gate and the driver's side window slid down, and a thick, burly arm poked out and swiped a card.

The barrier went up like a drawbridge, and the three limos barreled through the gate, pulling to a stop in front of the loading dock. Doors flew open, and a gang of men jumped out, all with black suits and dark glasses. Zeke recognized two of them: the tall one and the short one, Bowling Ball and the Nazi. They seemed to be scouting the parking area. Nazi opened the back door as if for a Hollywood celebrity.

Out stepped Theodore Onyx.

Zeke recognized him immediately. He hadn't seen him since the day of the trial. Short and fat, a distinguished looking butterball in a gray pin-striped suit, silver hair slicked back, like a fashionable Italian film director. He laughed and whispered something to the Nazi, who was holding the door. They shared a laugh.

Malone wasn't sure what to do. What could he do? Onyx arrived at his *own* warehouse, surrounded by bodyguards. So what? No crime in that.

There was bad blood between them—that went without saying. Malone had busted Onyx five, maybe six years ago, but Onyx walked free.

Suddenly, Zeke sat up straight. Who was getting out to the other side of the limo—but Jojo Turner?

What the hell is he doing here? Malone opened his car door. His blood began to boil. Without thinking, Malone found himself crossing the narrow street, slipping under the barrier arm, and making a beeline towards Jojo Turner.

He approached so quickly, the bodyguards failed to react. They all turned their heads at the same time. The blonde Nazi-looking bodyguard finally unfroze and headed to intercept Malone.

"Hey! Who are you?" he shouted.

Jojo Turner turned, and his eyes grew huge.

The short bodyguard stepped in front of Malone and put his hand out towards his chest. Instinctively, Malone grabbed his hand and bent the fingers up. So unexpected was the move, that the bodyguard fell to his knees. He tried to reach under his jacket to grab his gun with his left hand. Malone yanked up hard and chopped the bodyguard's other hand. The gun went bouncing to the pavement away from them. Zeke shoved the bodyguard so hard he landed on his butt.

Within seconds, Malone found himself surrounded by a ring of five men, all pointing their weapons at him. He heard the multiple cocking of hammers.

"Wait!" cried a voice.

All heads turned towards the loading dock, including Malone.

It was Onyx, on the stairs, one polished shoe on the upper deck, body half-turned, looking back at the activity below. "Wait, it's only my old friend," he said, a smile curling his lips. "Officer Malone, well should I say, former officer? He's come to pay us a visit."

"It wasn't you, Onyx, I came to visit." Malone stepped around the flange of men. "It's him." Zeke walked up into the face of Jojo Turner, saw the surprise on his face. "What the *hell* are you doing here, Jojo?" Malone demanded.

Jojo's surprise turned into a snarl. "I don't have to answer to *you,* Malone."

"That's right, you don't. You're just hanging out with the worst scum on the earth."

"I don't think you're in any position to be lecturing me."

"No? Then, what are you doing here? Soliciting for the Policeman's Retirement Fund?"

"Malone, get out of my face."

"Jojo, the stink coming off this place is enough to make the rats under the wharf gag."

"Malone, you were told to keep out of police business."

"Go ahead, report me—if you can explain what you're doing here!"

Jojo gave him a dismissive grunt and started to walk away. Malone called out after him, "You're so corrupt, Jojo, you smell like shit walking!"

Jojo stopped, fire burning in his eyes. "Why, you *lousy* motherfucker!" he shouted, charging at him.

Malone was getting ready for the rush when several strong hands caught him under the arms and held him back. A bulky body stepped in between. The next thing Zeke knew, punches were coming at him from several directions. He ducked as best he could, but couldn't avoid getting hit on the side of his head. Flashes of light. He swung back and caught someone on the jaw. One punch caught Zeke in the gut, and he went down. He covered his head. The next thing he knew, someone was kicking him in the ribs.

"Enough!" shouted a voice. It was Onyx. The kicking stopped. The side of his face felt as if someone had used it for a workout bag. He fought to get his breath and saw spots in front of his eyes.

"Stand him up." A moment later, Zeke found himself on his feet, feeling faint and dizzy. Onyx was speaking to Jojo. "It's not such a good idea to punch a policeman, even an ex-cop. Not here on my property. Might draw too much attention."

Onyx turned to Malone. "You've had your say, Zeke. You are trespassing on private property and you can leave now under your own volition—or my men can throw you out on Desire Street!"

Zeke felt blood trickling out of his nose. "Sure. Just a friendly chat between old pals." Taking deep breaths, he straightened his jacket and stumbled towards the security gate. He may have ducked under the arm of the security gate coming in, but not now. Zeke turned and looked back at Onyx, who was mounting the steps. Onyx signaled to the goons, and the barrier arm lifted. Though he may have acted cool in his retreat, he was cursing himself inside. He had let his emotions and hatred of Jojo get the better of him.

He'd blown his cover on the warehouse surveillance. And now, they'd be on guard against him. Any element of surprise was gone.

He swore as he got back into his car. Still no closer to finding out who killed his wife. Or the connection to the Oasis Club murders. The headlines would continue to read *A Hate Crime,* instead of what it was—a cover-up.

Zeke could kick himself.

CHAPTER 49

I hurried to my apartment to wash off the blood and change out of torn clothes. The bloody nose the bodyguards had given me had stopped, but my head still ached from the punches. This court hearing about Carla couldn't happen at a worst time. If Doris were correct, my brother-in-law would be asking for a restraining order because I was *an unsafe parent*. Unsafe to be with Carla? What a crock. I questioned whether I should have hired an attorney. Too late now. I had to clean up so I would not walk into the hearing room looking like a drunken bum.

I gulped two Tylenol for my headache and as the stream from the hot shower washed over me, it eased some of the aches in my body. The cut inside my mouth wasn't too bad. My ribs ached. I could have stayed under the shower all morning, but I had to hurry.

I toweled off, dressed in my best suit and tie, needing to make the best appearance. My body ached so much, I had to sit on the edge of the bed to put on my socks and shoes when my cell phone started buzzing—the number was unfamiliar—and I debated not answering. But I answered, anyway.

"Hello, Mr. Malone, this is John Fowler."

I was in no mood to speak with him and nearly hung up on the good Doctor, trying to keep an even tone in my voice. "Look, Dr. Fowler, no offense, but I'm too busy right now to speak to you."

"*Please* don't hang up." He blurted out. "I'm desperate."

Against my better judgment, I said, "Okay, make it quick."

"My wife is missing! You've got to find Kitty."

I wanted no part of this business. The reason I was stuck in this mess was because of her. "Dr. Fowler," I said, feeling a tooth loose with my finger. "I can sympathize with you, but it isn't my concern that your spoiled, self-centered wife ran off." My anger got the best of me. I took a deep breath to calm down. "In most cases, the wife gets tired, or bored, or hungry and returns—if not within twenty-four hours, within a week. Besides, I've got more important things to deal with right now." *Like getting to the courthouse on time.*

There was silence on the line. I wasn't sure if he had hung up. I was about to hang up myself.

"Malone," the doctor said. The tone of his voice had changed. It had a dark undertone.

I answered cautiously. "Yes?"

"Did you know that my wife, Kitty, knew your wife?"

I fought to get on my other shoe. "They did? Jane never mentioned—"

"I mean, they knew each other a long time ago."

"What?" A small wave of fear fluttered across my heart. "What are you talking about?"

"Kitty and Jane were old, *old* close friends."

Where was this going? "You're lying."

"Am I? Your wife told you her name was Jane Alberato," Dr. Fowler said. "She never mentioned anything about her parents, correct? Or where she came from, right?"

"So?" My muscle were tensing up.

"Doesn't that seem off? Odd? A person with no background, no history?"

I felt a wave of coldness came over me. "What's your point? Many people don't talk about their past, and—"

He interrupted me. "Why do you think I called you in the first place? I learned about you from Kitty—who knew you from Jane. She said you were an honest cop."

"You're crazy," I said. "When you hired me, you said you got my name off the internet. I don't believe you. Your wife and Jane never ... " but the words dried up in my mouth as I remembered her involvement with the museum. The words of the museum curator, Spinoza, came back to me, *"Your wife brought us deals worth millions of dollars."* Indeed, there were things I did not know about Jane.

I stared at the clock above the fake fireplace. I was supposed to walk into the courthouse in ten minutes.

"I ... I don't believe you," I said.

"Then find my wife," said the doctor. "And she'll tell you the truth. The truth about your wife."

My hand was shaking.

"And two more pieces of information for you to digest. Her brother, this Mark Billingham that you're in a custody battle over Carla—is not her *real* brother."

I stood up from the bed, still holding my shoe in my hand.

"The second piece of information: the little girl you are fighting over is named Carla, right?"

I was dreading what was coming next. I couldn't speak.

Dr. Fowler continued, "Her birth certificate—which I presume you've never seen?—lists her name as Katrina, like the hurricane. Her name has been shortened to Carla, which is what you call her. She was named after my wife."

Suddenly, the resemblance to Kitty became apparent. Kitty's blonde hair, like Carla. While Jane's hair was more reddish-brown. Carla had blue eyes. I tried to remember Kitty's eyes—sparkling blue, the same as Carla. While Jane's were grass-green with flakes of gold. And Carla had a lighter complexion, nearly pale. Kitty, the same. Whereas Jane always seemed to have a natural tan. How could I have missed the similarities between Kitty and my daughter? And the differences between Carla and Jane?

The doctor's voice cut through to my consciousness. "Try tracking down my wife by her real name—Katrina Broussard, not

Kitty. How does the old saying go, Mr. Malone?—*Find the truth, and it will set you free?* Start at the *beginning,* Malone. The beginning."

He hung up.

It can't be true. I did not believe what Dr. Fowler had just told me. How could I have lived for years with my wife and not known *who* she really was?

The questions came at me fast, one after the other. Was she tied up in all this drug smuggling bullshit? She loved art, of that I was sure. But had she turned her love of art and her affiliation with the New Orleans Art Museum into—what?—an illegal art smuggling operation?

The closer I got to uncovering the smuggling ring, the less I liked what it revealed about Jane. Like peeling away the layers of an onion to get at the heart, I thought I knew my wife. But was she someone else entirely? Someone I never knew?

The clock above the mantel began to chime.

Shit, I'm late.

CHAPTER 50

Driving like a madman, I barreled through several red lights and cut over on back streets before skidding into the courthouse parking lot. I still had my old policeman parking pass, and I hooked it on the mirror. I hadn't thrown it away for an occasion such as this. And was glad now.

I bound up the worn marble steps, three at a time, scattering a flock of pigeons feeding on bread crumbs, and through the front entrance. As soon as I made it past security, I burst into the double doors of courtroom number 107 E. In this courtroom the fate of my relationship with my daughter would be decided. The doors banged against the wall. The judge looked up and frowned. "You're late, Mr. Malone," he said.

I was out of breath. "Yes, my apologies, Your Honor."

It didn't look like a courtroom in the movies, but a small paneled room with three tables. The judge sat at the center table with his assistants hovering at his left, a stenographer to his right. On my right, seated was my brother-in-law, Mark, and his wife, Doris. A gray-haired guy, in a neat pin-striped suit, who I assumed was their attorney, sat at the end. Seated between them, dwarfed in an oversized chair, was Carla, her head barely visible above the back.

I took a seat at the table on the left.

In one swift action, before anyone could react, Carla bolted out of her chair and hurried to me. She hugged my neck and buried her face in my chest. I closed my eyes and kissed the top of her head, which smelled of soap and pixie sticks. The courtroom was silent except for the scrape of chairs and I knew they were standing, staring at us.

Finally, the judge cleared his throat and shuffled his papers. I opened my eyes and saw Doris patiently standing only a few feet away. "Zeke?" she asked. "What happened to your face?"

I shook my head—not now. "Honey, you need to go and sit with Doris." I whispered into Carla's neck. Slowly, she unwrapped her arms, and I handed her off to Doris, who eyed me uneasily, before leading my daughter back to their table.

"Is there a compelling reason you delayed these procedures, Mr. Malone?" the judge asked.

I exhaled. "Sorry, Your Honor. I was caught up in traffic." I lied because I certainly couldn't tell the truth about the twists and turns this case has taken.

He looked at me, frowning. "It looks like you were in a fight, is that right?"

Damn it. "Yes, Your Honor."

"Would you care to enlighten us?" he asked.

It was apparent I couldn't reveal my conversation with Dr. Fowler, nor my altercation with Theodore Onyx and Jojo Turner.

"Well?"

I cleared my throat. "No, I can't go into details, Your Honor. As you know, I am a private investigator." I adjusted my tie. "And due to the nature of the work, this means sometimes I am drawn into unavoidable conflict. I'm truly sorry for the delay."

"I see," he said, leaning back, viewing me over the top of his spectacles. He seemed to be weighing my excuse for its validity. "I hope the other guy is okay."

I did not respond.

"Very well, let's proceed. First up is a partition filed by Mark Billingham, who currently has protective custody of Carla. He's requesting a permanent restraining order ... " he looked up, "against you, Mr. Malone."

For the next thirty minutes, the judge asked Mark why he felt it necessary to keep me away from Carla. And then he asked me why I had not brought an attorney with me.

"I only recently learned of the petition. I haven't had time to hire one."

"Hmm." The judge flipped through several pages. "I see that you have missed many of your court-mandated counseling sessions. Why is that, Mr. Malone?"

"I … I was busy, Your Honor. I got my dates mixed up. It won't happen again," I said, kicking myself mentally.

The rest of the hearing seemed to go downhill after that.

Finally, the judge raised the palm of his hand, and we all fell silent. He read to himself, flipping pages, while I fidgeted in my seat. He slammed the file closed. "In your defense, Mr. Malone, you and your daughter have—"

"Stepdaughter," Mark interjected.

The judge shot him a stern look. "Are you correcting me?"

Doris gave her husband a killer look. Mark stuttered, "Uh, no, sir. Sorry."

The judge continued, "Mr. Malone, you and your daughter have a close bond—which is evident in what I have read and seen. However, I am putting off a decision until I get more information from your counselor. As for the restraining order—that I will *not* okay. But I must warn you, Mr. Malone, no unofficial visits and only if Doris Billingham is present. Is that understood?"

"Yes, Your Honor."

"And no more fights. Understood?"

"Yes, Your Honor, I understand."

Then, he stood, gathering folders under his arm, and said, "We'll meet here in thirty days." And with that, he left the room, his assistants and the court stenographer trailing behind him.

The chairs at the other table began pushing back. I sat, nearly numb, trying to gather my thoughts. So much had happened in the past twenty-four hours. A surveillance operation against drug smugglers had gone horribly wrong. Slugged and kicked. The unnerving phone call from Dr. Fowler, looking for his wife. His request soon turned nasty with unwanted revelations about Jane and raised questions about her past. And Carla's parentage.

And now this. The possibility that I might lose the right to visit Carla. A restraining order that wasn't executed, but still hung poised over my head like a guillotine.

Doris walked over with Carla, who threw her arms around my neck, and I told her I loved her. I smelled the fragrance of soap and shampoo in her hair.

Doris said, "Time to go, Honey." To me, she said, "For god's sake, Zeke, you look like shit."

Finally, Carla let go of my neck, took Doris' hand, and followed her to the exit.

Mark lingered at the table, chatting with his attorney. He waited till they were out the door before storming over to me.

"You think this is over?" he said. "But it's just getting started, dickhead."

CHAPTER 51

After I left the courthouse, I felt as if I'd been given a reprieve—thirty days to prove I was a worthy father. And thirty days to find Kitty Fowler. The words of Dr. Fowler still ringing in my ears. "Find my wife, and she'll tell you the truth about Jane."

The Truth? What truth? And the beginning? The beginning of what?

If there was one thing I learned from my years on the force—be thorough, turn over every stone, examine what's hidden underneath. Bull had said, *"Sometimes, the missing piece to your puzzle is waiting to be found if you only looked further."*

Had Kitty Fowler disappeared of her own volition? Or was she part of a mystery I wasn't aware of? My mind whirled in circles with too many questions and emotions to sort. And somehow, it seemed as if all these problems were my fault, even though I knew that was the guilt speaking. Where was the truth behind the Oasis killings? Behind my wife's involvement? Kitty Fowler's disappearance? Somehow they were all related, but I couldn't tie them together.

And why was Dr. Fowler so certain that I cared about *his* wife?

The doctor said, "Start at the beginning." So I did.

For the next several days, I started beating the bushes to find the doctor's wife. I had no idea if that was folly, or whether he was just blowing smoke up my ass to get me to locate his runaway spouse. Or if something else might have happened? For all I knew, she had left the city. Or maybe hiding with friends? Or maybe fell into the river?

Who knew?

Then, I thought of Moshe Enos, my contact in the underworld. He knew everything. Well, everything that was going on illegal. He seemed to have his finger on the pulse of the city and had located Mrs. Gonzales, even though that led to nothing.

I called Moshe.

"Zeke. What can I do for you?"

I explained how I was looking for Kitty Fowler and that I had exhausted all of my leads.

He was silent for a minute.

I thought he had hung up. "Moshe?"

"Hold on a moment. I'm texting someone."

Finally, he said. "Be at the corner of Royal and Elysian Fields at eight tonight." And hung up.

That night, I arrived fifteen minutes early and stood on the corner, chewing the inside of my cheek, trying to remain calm. I dressed as inconspicuously as I could, with a Saints baseball cap pulled low. A blue Chevy pulled up to the curb, and the window went down.

"Hi, you looking for some action?" a muscular, young man in a black wife-beater shirt said.

"Who sent you?" I asked.

"Why, nobody sent me. I thought ... "

"I'm a cop," I said.

He sped off.

At eight o'clock sharp, a black limo with dark windows slowed down and stopped, idling by the curb. I could feel the eyes examining me through the no-see windows. Finally, a tall, fierce-looking black man got out.

"You Malone?" he asked.

"Yes."

"Get in the back seat."

"Where are we going?" I asked.

He didn't reply, but got back in, slammed the door, and began pulling away without me.

"Hey, wait," I shouted, ran to rap on the driver's window. It stopped. The window buzzed down a couple of inches.

"Get in."

I got in.

The inside of the limo had one of those black partitions that separated passengers from the driver. I rapped on the glass. It did not go down, so I just sat back. My tooth had not gotten any looser, and I could drink my hot coffee in the morning. Was I on a fool's errand trying to find the doctor's wife? Dr. Fowler had more money than I ever had and could have hired a whole team of detectives to track down his wife. So, why call me? I thought of Carla. She would probably be getting ready for bed now. Doris would be reading her a book.

The limo slowed and stopped in front of a faded brick building in the old Warehouse District. Plywood sheets had been neatly cut to fit where there had once been windows. In the past, this building might have housed a thriving business, maybe a hundred-fifty years ago. Now it just sat, boarded up.

The partition buzzed down an inch. "Get out," the driver said. A man of few words. This time I didn't ask any questions. I walked straight ahead towards an open doorway. I stepped into an entrance totally without light. I stopped.

"Zeke." It was the voice of Moshe. "Follow me."

"I can't see," I said.

He flipped on a penlight and led me up the rickety wooden staircase. The wood smelled of coffee. Moshe said, "This used to be a coffee roasting plant years ago." We stepped into a dimly lit corridor with rows of doors on either side. He stopped at the second one, a green reinforced, solid metal door. Moshe rapped. The door opened and two rough-looking guys holding automatic weapons appeared.

Moshe said, "Farrell's expecting me."

They gave me the once over.

"He's with me," Moshe said.

No words were spoken as they led us down a narrow hall to another metal door. This one had super heroes and *Star Wars* posters taped to it. The two gunmen disappeared back down the hall.

We stood there quietly for what seemed a minute. "Aren't you going to knock?" I asked.

Moshe remained silent. Then a speaker above our head said, "Come in, Moshe, and bring your friend." The door sprung open.

A young teenager sat in an elevated captain's chair in front of a wall of monitors and half-a-dozen keyboards curving around him like the keyboards of giant pipe organs. He wore a stretched Tupac T-shirt, wrinkled cargo shorts, and unlaced tennis shoes. He had on a backward NY baseball hat. The room smelled of peppermint. And funky electronic music thumped off the walls.

The music faded and Moshe said, "Hi, Farrell."

Farrell greeted him back and then turned to me. "I know what type of toothpaste you brush your teeth with."

I glanced at Moshe, who was smiling.

"You use Pepsodent," he said and sang, "Wonder where the yellow went."

I said, "So does a third of the population of the city."

"And then you rinse with Act, Dentist Recommended, for a cleaner, brighter smile—Alcohol-free."

"So does—" He cut me off.

"Three percent of the population. Lot of ex-alcoholics use it, too, for obvious reasons." He looked me up and down as he pointed at a swivel chair next to him.

"Okay, where do I get my hair cut?"

"At David's Hair Salon by a girl named Sarah. You tip her well."

"I think I may be impressed."

"Mr. Malone, I know more about you than you know about yourself. I even know how much money you got in the bank." Then he proceeded to tell me.

"Okay, I am impressed." And I was. Even though I was embarrassed by the meager amount. "How do you know these things?"

"You really should reset your passwords more often. You've used the same one for years. And forty-four percent of the population uses the name of their first pet dog."

Moshe laughed. I laughed, too.

"Okay," he said, still smiling, turning back to his keyboards. "Now tell me who we looking for?"

"Kitty ... Kitty Fowler." Farrell's fingers were already dancing across the keyboard like the organist in St. Louis Cathedral. "Her birth name was Katrina Broussard. She's the wife of—" He completed my sentence.

Farrell said, "The wife of a Dr ... Fowler. Retired neurosurgeon. Born and raised here in New Orleans. Graduated Tulane. His current wife is Kitty ... Katrina ... " A long list of names scrolled down the screen in front of him. "There are over three thousand people in New Orleans with the name Katrina."

Farrell flipped from one screen to another so fast, the images that popped up barely registered. There were multiple photos of Kitty Fowler on the Society Page, at carnival balls, fund raisers. She was beautiful, always smiling, almost always with a drink in her hand, in diamonds and thrills.

"That's odd," Farrell said.

"What?"

"Prior to ten years ago, there is no mention of Kitty Fowler. Nor a Katrina Broussard. *Nada*. She didn't seem to exist. Just materialized out of thin air."

"Maybe widen the search?" I suggested.

He gave me a sideways glance. "Way ahead of you. There are four—nope, three Kitty Fowlers in North America—an eighty year old, just died. One thirteen year old in Toronto. Another one, sixty, California. The last Kitty Fowler is—seventy. None of them seem to qualify."

"How about under Katrina Broussard?"

"Uh-huh. One is married to a minister. She's Oriental. The other is three years old." He gave a brief snort through his nose, and tapped the space bar, as if tapping his fingers on a tabletop. "Wider didn't help. Let me go deeper."

"Deeper?"

"Back in time," he said, leaning forward, eyes jumping back and forth between screens. Then he sat back and smiled. "Aha! Pay dirt."

There it was. Katrina Broussard. A birth certificate filled out in Iberville Parish.

"Nothing came up until I searched the old birth records in Louisiana," Farrell said triumphantly.

The year was right, which would have made her about the same age as Jane.

Farrell dug further back and found another reference to Katrina Broussard in a small rural newspaper.

"It says that a Katrina Broussard disappeared from an orphanage."

"Where?"

"Just outside of Carville, Louisiana."

"Carville? The town with the leper colony?"

"The date … " Farrell said, calculating. "Katrina would have been a teenager when she disappeared. And then reappeared a decade later as Kitty Fowler in the Times-Picayune Society Pages."

"Are we assuming this is the same person?" I asked.

"Not necessarily. It's a question I can't answer yet," said Farrell. He continued his search in silence for the next several minutes. "There doesn't seem to be more information."

"Now what?" Moshe asked.

"I'll keep searching," Farrell said. "If I come up with anything, I'll pass word back through Moshe."

I stood up. "Thank you, Farrell."

"No, thank you, Mr. Malone. You don't remember me, but I'm Moshe's nephew. You helped me avoid juvie. I've got myself straight. If I can be of further help, let me know."

As I made my way down the dark stairs led by Moshe, I was elated as this was the first positive news I'd heard. At the same time, I dreaded what I might find. What if Dr. Fowler was right? What secrets hid in Jane's past?

·   ·   ·

For several more days, I kept calling and tapping my contacts for more information with no results. Kitty Fowler had gone underground.

I sat in my office, listening to the sound of the river barges chugging on by and the echoes of the calliope off the Natchez. *Where do I go from here?*

Doctor Lucy in the Sky had said, "The journey starts with the first turn of the wheel."

Start at the beginning. Okay, one step at a time.

So I did. And that would be Carville, Louisiana, the little town upriver from New Orleans, nestled on the banks of the Mississippi River.

It seemed as good a place to start as any.

CHAPTER 52

WELCOME TO CARVILLE, LOUISIANA
HOME OF THE OLDEST LEPER COLONY IN THE UNITED
STATES
... read the sign as I drove into town.

Carville, Louisiana, was once known for its leper colony that started in 1906, set up by the federal government to treat and house the poor unfortunate. The reports of the disease dated back over thousands of years. Back then, lepers were outcasts, chased away from homes and villages. If a leper tried to leave, they ran the risk of being stoned to death.

In the twentieth century, lepers were treated more humanely. But still shunned by society and confined to Carville to live in a leper colony managed by the Sisters of Charity. According to the Bible, only Christ was able to heal the lepers. That is until the 1940s when Dr. Guy Fage discovered that sulfone therapy could cure the disease.

The last Carville resident with leprosy, also known as Hansen's Disease, was a Hubert Thitler, who died in 1988. After his death, the facility was shut down a year later. It's been used by the state as a museum. Since then, the communities around Carville have dwindled by more than half since its heyday. When I rolled into town, I stopped at a Circle K convenience store to gas up and ask directions.

"Is there a local paper?" I asked the clerk as I paid for my gas and bought a Coke. He was skinny, with ten or more ear piercings. Purple hair in a mohawk. And had never heard of the orphanage.

"Just a throwaway." He reached under the counter and handed me a rumpled tabloid printed on cheap newsprint. It consisted mostly of ads for babysitting services, yard work, tree trimming, and trash hauling.

He pointed me towards the edge of town, by way of giving directions, to the publication office in a two-story building. "It's the only skyscraper in the area. You can't miss it."

The building had once been a movie theater. The round ticket booth had been sealed off with bricks. I parked at a broken parking meter in front and entered the building. The publisher was a tall, angular woman, fortyish-looking, dressed in a man's shirt, worn jeans, with her hair shorn short. She looked busy and rushed. "You here to ask about the leper colony? That's why most out-of-town folk ask for me." She gave me a suspicious eye. "You a reporter or something?"

"No, I'm not."

"You're not what? Not looking for the leper colony? Or not a reporter?"

"Neither. I'm searching for the Carville Orphanage."

"Ha, that's a new one." She chuckled. "You're the first person asking about that orphanage in nearly ten years. You're not a reporter. Come on in and have a sit-down. I bet you're a ... " She ran her eyes over me. "You don't seem like one of those genealogy-freaks, tracking down your long-lost uncle."

"That's right."

"Ah, thought so. You're a private eye." We sat at her desk, cluttered with stacks of papers, each about a foot deep. "Well, what can I tell you?—That orphanage has been closed for years—at least fifteen. I was a young looker back then." She batted her eyelashes. "You woulda been impressed."

"I'm sure I would have been," I said, smiling. "Do you know if there are any records of who was there?"

"You mean like the employees?"

"No, the orphans."

"No records at the courthouse, if that's what you mean. All the files were kept at the orphanage, and they went up in smoke when it burned down."

This was a setback. Maybe my trip to Carville was a dead end, after all. But I had learned through years of investigations that you should examine all details. The reason I had come had not changed—I was not going to give up so easily.

"Can you tell me how to get out to the orphanage? Or what's left of it?" I asked.

"You going out there? Nothing there now but wild 'possums and feral hogs."

I told her I just wanted to satisfy my curiosity.

"Okay, Mr. Private Detective, I'll draw you a map. You stop at the Circle-K 'cause you'll need mosquito spray." She flipped open a yellow pad and plotted out my directions.

CHAPTER 53

She was right on two counts: I needed the bug spray; and the grounds were nothing but overgrown bushes and stubby trees, good for *possums and feral hogs.* The main structure appeared to have burned to the ground. The roof collapsed onto itself, and the timbers were now a heap of blackened boards overgrown by vines and scrub elms growing between the rotting beams. A sign hung by one side with the words barely readable: *Carville Orphanage.*

Now, viewing the remains of the orphanage, I truly felt the trip here had been a dead end, and I resigned myself to return home, empty-handed. Erring on the side of caution, I drove through the tall grass to make sure I hadn't missed anything. A fallen tree stopped me. I could see other derelict buildings half-hidden among the new growth and scattered long-leaf pines. All in the same state of disintegration—caved in roofs, walls, and a tilted porch post.

I was about to put the car in reverse and leave when I caught a glimpse of something dark moving under the canopy of trees. It vanished as quickly as it appeared. An icy chill ran from my butt up to my neck. Was I seeing things that weren't there? Then it reappeared, a person dressed in a black cloak wearing a big white sombrero. But as they got closer, I realized—it was a nun. And the sombrero was an old-fashioned habit with wings like sails on an outrigger canoe.

I don't think she realized I was there because she kept approaching and didn't stop until she was only ten feet from my car. Her mouth fell open, and she backed up a few steps.

I got out of the car and said, "Excuse me, ma'am. I didn't mean to scare you, but I wondered if you might be able to help me?"

Her surprised look turned into a friendly smile. "I'm not sure how I could be of service. But if you promise not to be a serial killer?"

"I hated *Silence of the Lambs*," I said.

"If you are one, I'm sure that's in God's plan."

Her name was Sister Ella, and she lived on the property in a small cabin near the rear of the estate. Though she was elderly, she seemed fit with a hurried stride. She led me along a narrow path, worn down to the dirt, winding between the tall grass and the trees. Her nose was hooked like a hawk, and there was a white line down the side of her face that she unconsciously rubbed when she spoke.

I asked her if there were any old records and where they might be kept.

"Oh, they vanished in the fire when the big dormitory burned to the ground. My goodness, years ago." She spoke in a refined, Southern accent. Direct and without hesitation.

"Sister Ella, do you remember the orphanage?" I asked.

She laughed. "Of course, I was the headmistress for over forty years."

"I'm searching for someone you might remember. A young girl by the name of Katrina Broussard? Katrina, like the hurricane."

Sister Ella frowned and stroked her scar. "I'm not so good at remembering names anymore."

I reached into my wallet and pulled out Kitty Fowler's picture, the one I snitched from her mantle. I handed it to her.

"Oh, of course, that's Kat. She had a *sassy* mouth." Her face clouded over. "How could I ever have forgotten her?" The smile had dropped away, and in its place her face grown taut. She unconsciously rubbed her fingers several times over the white line that ran down her cheek until it turned red.

"I take it you did not like this Kat, Katrina Broussard?"

She continued to stare at the picture. "I can still remember the night she was brought to us by the authorities. She was four or five then, I think—a skinny, frail-looking little girl, dressed in rags. She was from an abusive family—mother, a drug addict. Her sadistic father abandoned them. Both died in prison. Kat had that look of pain and rage so familiar to children from *white trash homes*."

We continued to walk the path until we came to a clearing of short trees and scrubs.

She continued to speak, turning back to me. "There was something different about Katrina. There was an icy fire inside her that made her different from other children in the orphanage," she said. "She was a beautiful child, but her anger with the world made her the most stubborn … " She trailed off, fingering a cross dangling from her waist. She paused. "You say you are trying to track her down?"

"Yes."

"You a cop?"

"Used to be. I was hired to locate her. She's missing."

"So, she's gone missing again? I'm not surprised. And what about her friend?"

"What friend?"

"Why, *her* friend, her *only* friend! They both came in about the same time." Her fingers rubbed furiously at the cross, as if that would help her remember. She continued, "What was her name? They were inseparable. Where one went, the other stuck with her. But her friend was different from Kat."

Something clicked in my head, as if someone had snapped his fingers by my ear. I pulled out my wallet and snatched out a photo, shoving it into her hand.

Sister Ella took it in her bony fingers and studied Jane's photo for only a second. "No, no. That's not Katrina. That's not Kat."

I asked, "Then, who is it?"

"Why, that is the friend I was telling you about, Carlotta. They called her Carla. Who could forget those grass-green eyes and that defiant stare?"

My heart skipped several beats. *Carlotta. Carla,* like my daughter? So, what the doctor said was true! Some of the pieces began to fall into place. Jane had grown up in this orphanage with her friend Katrina—Kat—Kitty. But why didn't she just tell me? There was no reason to keep it a secret.

"Well, you know, come to think of it, they were both sullen girls, never with a smile on their faces. Unless they were in a corner somewhere, hatching some devilish plan." The sister said.

My hands were shaking. I put the photo back into my wallet. "And what was Carlotta's last name?"

"She was left at the orphanage with only her first name, Carlotta, penned to her blouse. She was old enough to speak, but she said little at all. So, we listed her as *Carlotta Jane Doe.* "

Jane Doe! So, that's where she took her name—*Jane.* So, Carlotta *Jane* Doe became *Jane* Alberato. I shook my head. This was becoming curiouser and curiouser.

We walked a little farther to her cabin. Several benches sat in front of a neat, small building that looked fifty years old, but well-kept, with a metal tin roof, a flower bed, and a picket fence. But the most unusual thing about it were the rainbow colors of the outer walls, each panel painted alternate colors: brilliant red, yellows, blues, greens. It reminded me of a gingerbread house. We sat on the wooden bench.

"What happened to them in the orphanage?"

"Well, as I said, you couldn't keep the two apart. Whenever we were fortunate enough to place Carlotta in a home, she'd refuse to go unless the couple took both of them." She sighed. "But inevitably, Kat would cause trouble, and she would be kicked out. Carlotta wouldn't stay if her friend were not there with her. She'd ask to return or simply run away back to the orphanage to join her friend. Placing them in separate foster homes didn't work either. Both ran away again and again. No one could get through to Carlotta. I tried locking them in separate rooms for their own good. But it never worked. Discipline one. Discipline both. It was no good and just never worked."

She sighed. "They were as different as night and day."

"How so?"

"Kat was wild. Carlotta was level-headed. And the older Kat grew, the wilder she became. She was beautiful, though. Those blonde curls and the piercing blue eyes. The boys were like dogs, attracted to the scent of *a bitch* in heat."

I was a bit surprised by the way she phrased that. Sister Ella got up and motioned for me to follow her. She led me along a path that led into the woods.

She continued to speak. "At the age of fifteen, Kat became pregnant. She never named the boy responsible. She lied and said a priest raped her. *Nonsense.* But I suppose God had had enough of her fornication and lies. She lost the child. And soon after that, they both ran away. I tried to stop them."

She turned to me. "Do you see this?" she said, pointing at the scar on the side of her face. "Guess which one gave me this?"

I shook my head.

"You would have thought it would have been Kat, the wild one. But it was Carlotta Jane Doe. She turned out to be the *truly* ruthless one. She slashed me with a razor when they ran away together," Sister Ella said, her lips curling down. "Come see this." She rushed forward, almost running on the narrow path between trees forming a narrow passage.

I ran to catch up with her. Suddenly, we broke into a small clearing, and she stopped at a rusting, sagging, iron spike fence that bordered a small square plot of ground, overgrown with weeds and bushes. "Jesus loves the little children," she said, extending out her hand.

I realized I was looking at a children's cemetery.

"Here. Here is where Kat's baby is buried," she said, her eyes overly bright, grasping the spikes in her hand. A worn path ran along its edge as if someone walked it many times. The tops of a few white marble markers peered above the tall grass.

"There was a tombstone for her baby ... once. I used to have the new girls keep the grounds clean and well-kept. Trim. But after the orphanage burned, there was no one. I tried to do it myself for a few years, but it was a losing battle. I couldn't keep tending to the cemetery alone. Eventually, the markers fell over, swallowed up by the earth, like wild baboons, eating their own babies ... " Her voice trailed off, her face sagging.

After a minute, I asked, "Do you know what happened to them? To Kat and Carla?"

She turned towards me. "No. After they ran away together, I never saw them again."

I thanked her.

Sister Ella walked along the path that circled the wrought-iron fence until she came back towards me, but she did not look at me, appearing lost in the memories of her past. She walked right by me as if I didn't exist, vanishing into the trees and brush.

I stood at the edge of the cemetery, wondering about Katrina Broussard and Carlotta Jane Doe. How had they survived? Where did they go after they left? Dr. Fowler had told me that Kitty would reveal the truth. But what did that *really* mean? So, they were orphans together. There had to be more.

There was a rustle of the leaves in the wind—like a rain squall coming. I looked up. Clouds blackened the sky, and I felt an icy chill on my neck. I looked down, and I'm sure it was an illusion brought on by the old nun. But the unkempt weeds began undulating like waves on a beach, exposing the tops of whitewashed tombstones. One bleached headstone would rise for a moment before sinking back down. Followed by another one, like white skulls of little babies playing peek-a-boo. I jerked away from the metal fence spikes as if they were electrified. Then a few large drops splashed on my shoulders, and I rushed back to my car.

I made it back to my car just before the downpour started. And I sat there. *Who was my wife? How had Carlotta Jane Doe morphed into Jane Alberator?*

CHAPTER 54

At the Half Moon Bar the next evening, the sound of billiard balls clicking off each other filled the air, while Irma Thomas sang from the jukebox: *"It's raining teardrops."* Progress had been made: The neon letters had been fixed, no more ALF-MOON, so the full name cast an eerie orange glow over the parking lot.

Bull slumped his massive body into the back booth with the cracked red vinyl covering and pulled the bowl of nuts over to him.

Yolanda, the waitress, sauntered over and asked, "You okay?"

"Me? Always," Bull said, cracking a few peanuts open and popping them into his mouth.

"You want anything?" she smiled, and leaned her hips against the table.

Bull smiled back. "What you got?"

"Oh, I can think of a lot of things," she said with a flirtatious smile.

Bull knew she had a soft spot for him. As he had for her. They dated a while back when he first signed on as a cop. But he broke it off, never certain why.

"Well, just a beer for the moment. I'm expecting Zeke in a few minutes."

She looked disappointed. "Okay, maybe next time."

"Yeah, next time," he said, admiring her walk as she left to get his beer.

Bull was waiting for Malone, eating peanuts and sipping beer, when a tall, skinny guy with a goofy expression and loose gait walked in. He stood there, absently staring around. *Must be the clown, Fred LaForge,* Bull thought. A minute later, Zeke entered, greeted Fred, and spotted Bull in the booth. Holding up two fingers at Yolanda, he pointed towards Bull.

"This is Fred LaForge," Zeke said, sliding into the booth opposite Bull.

"Glad to meet you, Fred." he said, extending his hand.

"Yeah, that's me," Fred said, pumping his hand vigorously before scooting in next to Zeke.

They exchanged pleasantries until Yolanda brought a beer for Fred and a coffee for Zeke.

After a few minutes, Fred told them about the Panamanian ship and the three statues, *Los Tres Jefes.* Apparently, Fred had managed to meet the steward and invite him out for a night of drinking. At first the steward was closed lips, but after a few rounds, told Fred all he wanted to know. The captain and crew knew the ship was carrying something illegal. The steward said things were very hush-hush, and no one was allowed down into hole number three.

"What about the three statues?" Bull asked.

"The steward really didn't know anything about that. But he did say a wooden crate was picked up by just one guy. He loaded it into the back of a panel van and disappeared."

Bull and Zeke exchanged glances. "Any markings on the van? Or a plate number?"

"Nope. Just an unmarked panel van. Light blue with a few dents."

"Like the one Clive drove?" Bull said to Zeke.

"Could be," Zeke agreed.

All three took sips of their drinks. Bull turned and waved at Yolanda and motioned for repeats. "Anything else?" Bull asked.

"Not really," Fred said.

Bull took a deep breath and let it out slowly. "You know what that means? This vessel is tied into some larger operation."

"Like organized crime," Zeke said.

Yolanda brought them two more beers. The guys remained silent with all eyes following her walk across the room.

"What's next?" asked Zeke.

Bull said, "Under no circumstances can we let this information leak to the New Orleans Police."

"Why not?" asked Fred.

"Bull's been called off the case. He can't be seen actively investigating *Los Tres Jefes,* or the Oasis Club Massacre."

Fred nodded.

Bull added. "There's more going on here than small-time smuggling. Somebody's trying to cover up something bigger." He finished his beer and put it gently down on the table. "Good work, Fred."

Fred beamed and lowered his voice. "Just doing my job, chief. Oh yeah, I nearly forgot." He slid a piece of paper across the table to Bull. "That's the owner of the freighter—*Atlas Line Vessels.* And the other name is the previous captain, Olivera. He disappeared mysteriously three months ago. The current captain took over after Olivera vanished."

Bull rubbed the side of his face with his ham-like hand while studying the names. "I've got a friend who is with the DEA in Washington. We worked together several years ago."

The jukebox started playing The Allman Brothers, "Ramblin' Man."

"He owes me a couple of favors," Bull said, taking out his cell phone. "You guys wait here."

Bull lifted his bulk out of the booth, taking the paper. He disappeared out the front door. Zeke and Fred watched him as he paced back and forth outside, cell phone to his ear.

After fifteen minutes, Bull returned. "We've got help. But keep it under wraps. We can't afford any leaks."

Zeke's phone started vibrating. It was a Louisiana number he didn't recognize.

The voice was deep. Authoritative. "Hello, Zeke Malone?"

"Yes. Who is this?" Zeke answered.

"This is Sheriff Andrew Taylor." He broke his last name into two parts, as in Tay-Lor, as if to make sure Zeke understood it.

His stomach clenched into a knot, and his first thought was of Carla. "Did something happen?"

Sheriff Taylor seemed to ignore his question. "Have you ever been to Edgard, Louisiana, Mr. Malone?" The sheriff seemed to break proper names into two parts.

"Uh. Sure, I've been to Edgard, passing through."

"I need you to come visit me."

Zeke hesitated for a moment.

The sheriff said, "Can you come in the morning?"

"May I ask what this is about?"

"About ten-o'clock." He replied.

This guy, whoever he was, didn't seem overly eager to reply to any of my questions.

"I'm kind of busy tomorrow. I've got to meet someone—"

"This won't take long."

And he didn't appear as if he were going to take *No* for an answer either. "Look, Sheriff—"

"Sheriff Tay-lor."

"Sheriff Taylor, is there a problem? I don't know anyone in Edgard and unless you can clue me in on what—"

"I'll answer all of your questions when you arrive."

"Am I in trouble?" I asked.

"I don't think so, unless you've broken the law. We got some … some things we need you to help us on." He hesitated a count. "Please, Mr. Malone. This is very important."

Zeke remained silent, mulling it over before saying, "Okay."

"Good," the sheriff said. "See you at ten. Come to the sheriff's office and introduce yourself."

Then, he hung up.

CHAPTER 55

The town of Edgard is about thirty miles upriver from New Orleans. Edgard was once notorious for its racist policies, tamping down the black community. Until the Federal Government intervened and sent in federal troops in the 1960s to integrate the schools.

It was, and still is, the parish seat of St. John the Baptist Parish. The sheriff's office was on Tenth Street, which I took to mean, was ten blocks from the river. I pulled in and parked in the visitor's space in front of a one-story modern building. Twin statues of alligators lay prostate by the entrances where normally you might see replicas of the MGM bronze lions. There was a flagpole in front with the American flag, and a side parking lot with St. John Parish Sheriff vehicles parked along the building.

This morning, Sheriff Taylor sent me a text message:

IMPORTANT YOU KEEP APPOINTMENT, 10 AM.

He signed it: *A. Taylor.*

I know I'm innocent, but an uneasy feeling arises when called in to be questioned by the police—*Sheriff,* in this case—*Did I do something wrong?* A twinge of uncertainty tightened my chest. I've seen it before. Perfectly innocent people become tongue-tied, stumbling on their answers. It's like the question, "Do you still beat your wife?" No matter how you answer, you're still guilty. That was the way I felt, even though I had been on the other side a hundred times.

The sun blazed down as I sat with the A/C blasting. Trying to stall for time. What was this all about? No way to tell unless I got off my butt and went in.

I turned off the ignition and made my way to the door. Beyond the double door glass entrance was a small lobby with pictures on the wall, a counter, a Plexiglas partition, and a row of plastic-scoop chairs. All police buildings seem to have the same smell—a mixture of sweat and gun belt leather. Behind the counter, a matronly-looking woman in her mid-fifties sat clicking away at her computer.

"Hi." I said.

"Hi," she said, looking up and giving me a motherly smile. "Can I help you?"

"Yes, I'm here to see Sheriff Taylor."

"Do you have an appointment?"

"Yes, I'm Zeke Malone."

Her smile fell a little, but didn't make it all the way down. "Oh, yes. I'll let him know you're here." She picked up the phone on her desk and punched in a number, then turned her head so I couldn't hear. "Uh-huh. Okay." She hung up. "Mr. Malone, would you please have a seat? He'll see you in a minute." She returned to her computer.

I didn't feel like sitting, so I looked at the pictures on the lobby wall. They were old black-and-white photographs, like those shot by news photographers. At first, I couldn't figure out what they were depicting. Some sort of demonstration with black citizens, mostly teenagers, confronting white cops in khaki uniforms, firearms strapped on their hips.

"Mr. Malone." The voice of the secretary interrupted me. "Follow me."

I followed her down a long corridor with small offices on either side. Before we reached the end, a door flew open and a young black man, a teenager, maybe seventeen, eighteen, came storming out and brushed past us. He was tall, broad shouldered, and dressed in an oversized football jersey, a scowl fixed on his face. He stormed into the parking lot up to an old Chevy and stood with his hands on hips.

A tall black man in gym shorts and T-shirt stepped out of the office, a frown on his face. He stood with his back to us, watching the young man. He had the look and size of an inside linebacker. Suddenly, the young man kicked the door panel of the car, jumped in, and peeled rubber out of the lot.

The secretary said, "Sheriff, this is Mr. Malone."

He turned and stared at me. "Thanks, Mildred. Hold my calls." His expression did not change, but he extended his hand.

He had a powerful grip, calloused, as if he did hard labor.

He gestured with his head for me to enter.

"What's his problem?" I asked.

"He's my son."

I didn't say anything.

He pointed at a chair opposite his desk. "Well, what did you expect? Sheriff Andy Taylor and his son, Opie?"

"I didn't know what to expect," I said, "Since I have no idea why you called me." I sat. "What can I do for you, Sheriff Taylor?"

He stationed himself in a large office chair, wiggling to make himself comfortable, and pulled over a file, and flopped it open. He flipped through, scanning down the pages. Above his head was another of the oversized black-and-white photos from the lobby. This one had a young man facing off against a line of armed cops.

I figured I'd wait him out till he got ready to speak.

He looked at me, still frowning. "Mr. Malone, you're a cop, right?"

"Was," I corrected. "What's this about?" I asked, yet again.

Sheriff Taylor looked down. "A detective. And a good one. Decorated."

I glanced at the file. It was thick. "You've got a file on me?"

He ignored my question. "You resigned—what? Two years ago?

"That's right. Can you tell me what this is about?" I was getting annoyed with this Sheriff *Tay-Lor.*

"We're getting to that," he said.

The temperature of the room seemed to go up a degree, and I wished he'd get to the point. "Do I need a lawyer?"

He looked up. "I don't know. Do you have something to hide?"

"You asked me that last night. The answer is still *no.*"

"Good. That's fine."

"Good?" I crossed my arms. "Look, I'm not going to answer any more questions till you tell me what this is about."

He leaned back in his chair. The springs groaned. "We're trying to clear up a mystery."

"Involving me?"

"Of course, do you think I asked you to come here to chit-chat and swap police stories?"

I didn't know how to answer that, so I said nothing.

"Good," he said, flipping another page. "You resigned after your wife died."

I felt a cold icicle forming in my stomach.

He looked up at me. "She was … killed by a suicide bomber who held her as a hostage."

"That's public knowledge."

"Now, about her funeral?" he continued.

I was lost. I didn't know where this was going. "What about it?"

"Did you attend your wife's funeral?"

"No, I was in a coma. My brother-in-law handled it."

"So, you didn't see her body?"

"I *said,* I was in a coma." I could feel the tension forming in my neck. "They told me because of … it was a closed casket."

He seemed to contemplate that, rubbing the side of his face. "You know they buried her here in St. John's Parish, right? Not in New Orleans. Why was that?"

"You'll have to speak to my brother-in-law. I didn't make the arrangements."

"Have you been to see ... to, uh, visit her grave?"

How could I explain the pain was too great? That I just couldn't go? That I had repeatedly lied when asked? Lucy in the Sky said that I should go. *It would help with closure*, she said.

"No, I've never been," I murmured.

He sat back, watching me with an intense gaze. "It must be strange," he said.

I looked at him. "What do you mean?"

"Here you are answering questions. Normally, you'd be on the other end of the shovel, digging into people's lives, questioning people. Now it's changed." He swiveled in his chair and pointed up at the black-and-white photo of a teenager confronting the line of policemen. "You see that picture? It's from the 1960s when the black youth of Edgard protested the lack of integration in schools. That's me. I was sixteen and got busted on the head a few times by *cops.* Now, I'm the *cop.*" He paused, with an unfocused gaze on his face.

Then he turned back to me. "My son, who you just met, is the same age as I was then. All he cares about are cars, hanging with his friends, and getting laid. Times are different." He shook his head.

I took a deep breath. "Sheriff Taylor, I've been cooperative. I've answered your questions. Suppose you tell me what happened and why you called me in to review my wife's death?"

He closed the file, drumming his fingers on his desk. "Three days ago, a drunken teenager rammed his car into the side of a mausoleum over at St. John's Cemetery."

"Where my wife is buried?" I was getting a sick feeling in the pit of my stomach.

"Yes."

"Anyone injured?"

"A couple. It's a wonder they lived. But that's not the important part here. The crash, however, dislodged contents of some crypts." He picked up his phone, pushed a button, and after a pause, said, "Mildred? Could you have Jeff join me?" He hung up the receiver and stood. "I want you to follow me."

"Where to?"

"Just across the hall. I want you to see something."

He took his keys and unlocked a room that looked like a conference room with large monitors, bookshelves, and a map of St. John Parish that covered half the wall. Next to the conference table, mounted on wooden sawhorses, was a casket. The casket had obviously been in a fire. Its surface was tarnished with soot, the finished metal scarred and scorched. And the air stank of singed metal.

"What's this?" I murmured. My mind shut down, my fingertips tingling.

"Do you recognize it?" he asked.

"No. Am I supposed to?"

There was a quiet knock on the door, and a young policeman with blonde hair entered. He was tall, serious. Sheriff Taylor nodded, and they positioned themselves at both ends of the casket. They lifted the lid off and set it on the floor.

He turned towards me. "Go ahead. Take a look."

I stepped forward, my heart pounding in my chest. I leaned forward and looked in.

It was full of rocks.

"Whose casket is this?" I managed to get out.

"It's your wife's."

"*What?!*"

"The marker said Jane Malone."

"Jane?"

"Yes, your wife. She was supposed to be in this coffin."

I suddenly felt light-headed.

CHAPTER 56

"Would you look at this?" mumbled Bendix Montague to Jojo Turner, who had come into his office to pick up a report. Montague's office, located in the basement of the NOPD headquarters, stank of sweaty bodies and chocolate. Jojo hated coming down here. *It's like a dungeon. A stinky dungeon.*

"Look at what?" Jojo said sharply, not looking up from a report he held in his hand. *Mo, that's what they called Montague. Fat, sloppy, Mo.* "What, Mo?"

Bendix Montague had been a policeman clerk for five years, monitoring reports from other police departments throughout the state of Louisiana. A dead end job if there ever was one. During that half-decade, his appetite had grown for chocolate bars: Hershey's Milk Chocolate, Butterfingers, Crunch Bars, Oreos. He kept a drawer full of them.

"Says here," Mo said, reading off a printed report. "They found a coffin full of rocks."

Jojo looked up. "Rocks?"

"Yeah. Happened over in St. John's Parish."

Jojo remembered a girlfriend he once dated from Edgard, Louisiana. She was pretty. Curly black hair, not kinky. A smooth, dark complexion—*Mahogany, I think they call it now.* They dated while he was on military leave from ...

Jojo watched with disgust as Mo inserted his finger into his ear, screwing it around and around. *God, it's deep as his second knuckle.*

"Anything else of interest—besides rocks?" Jojo said, turning to leave.

"No." Mo removed his finger from his ear, inspecting it.

"Okay, I've got a meeting with the chief. Be sure to—"

"What was the name of that woman?" Mo asked, reaching into his drawer for a snack.

Jojo was nearly out the door. "What woman?"

"The detective's wife. The one that got herself blown up."

That got Jojo's attention. "Malone. Jane Malone."

"Yeah, that's her," Mo said, peeling the wrapper off a Babe Ruth. "Says here it was the coffin of—"

"Let me see that." He jerked the report out of Mo's hand.

St. John's Sheriff's Department reported that a coffin was opened resulting from an auto accident ...

An auto accident?

The coffin contains rocks of assorted sizes, wrapped in bubble wrap. Weight of the coffin: 110 pounds. An investigation by the Sheriff's Department has turned up no answers about the missing body, identified as Jane Malone.

Jojo flinched back slightly. The report was dated yesterday. *What the hell!?*

He hurried into his office and lifted the phone. He told the police operator to connect him to the Sheriff's office in St. John's Parish.

After a minute, a lively, warm voice answered. "St. John's Sheriff's office. This is Mildred. How may I direct your call?"

"Mildred, this is Captain Jojo Turner, head of Homicide in New Orleans." That always got their attention.

She seemed unimpressed. "Yes, Captain Turner. How can we help you?"

"The report. The one about the rocks in the casket. Can I speak with Sheriff ... ? I forgot his name, sorry."

"Sheriff Taylor," she offered.

"Yes, we met a few times. Can you put me through to him?"

"Unfortunately, he's off today. Gone to LSU to enroll his son."

"Would you have him call me when he returns?"

After Jojo hung up, he sat staring at the phone, rubbing the side of his face unconsciously. She was dead, he was sure of that. He had seen the pieces of her body in the morgue, or what was left of her. It was a woman's torso, alright. A ghastly sight, half her head missing, an arm ripped off, mutilated chest. It couldn't be—but …

He slipped his cell phone out, not wanting to use the police systems. He hit the name—*Precious Metal.*

Half-a-dozen rings later, a deep voice answered. He recognized the voice of Bowling Ball. "You ain't supposed to call unless it's an emergency."

"I know. I need to talk with Goldenstein."

There was silence. "Hold on."

After what seemed like five minutes, Bowling Ball came back on. "He'll meet you in an hour at the usual place."

The line disconnected.

Damn! Jojo had promised to pick up his wife and take her to her mother's house for lunch. A meal he wouldn't mind missing. His mother-in-law was a pain in the ass. He'd think of an excuse, anything, because this couldn't wait.

CHAPTER 57

By the time Sheriff Taylor had finished questioning Zeke about the coffin, it was after twelve noon. The sheriff concluded the incident was bizarre, but nothing illegal had occurred. And Zeke seemed to know nothing about it. Sheriff Taylor let him go, and Zeke charged back to New Orleans, flying over the Luling Bridge, zipping in and around slower traffic. The sunlight sparkled off the choppy waters of the Mississippi River like broken glass.

While he drove, he punched in Doris' number. At first, there was no answer. The calls kept going to voicemail. Finally, after the fourth call, she answered.

She said, "Hi, Zeke. Sorry, I was outside with Carla. What's up? Is everything okay?"

He could not contain himself. "Doris. What the *hell* is going on?"

She did not answer for a beat, caught off-guard. "Why? What's the matter?"

"I just came from Edgard." Anger bubbled up in his throat. "Jane's coffin—"

"What about it?"

"They opened it ... "

She was silent. He thought she had hung up. "Doris?"

"Yes, Zeke," she said quietly.

"The coffin was filled with rocks."

She was silent again.

"Jane's body is missing."

She made a small noise. It came out as, "Oh."

"Did you know about this?" he demanded.

"Zeke, I'm sure there is an explanation," she said rapidly.

"Oh, yeah? What kind of explanation? That someone stole her body and exchanged it for a bunch of rocks?!"

"Now, calm down, Zeke. I'm sure there's a logical reason for all of this."

"How can I be calm? There can be no logical reason for Jane's missing body!" He pressed down on his horn at the cars in front of him. He said, "You need to tell me what's going on. *Now.* Are you at home?" Zeke shouted into the phone.

She said nothing. He waited, but there was no response.

"Doris?"

Nothing.

"I'm coming over there."

"Zeke, don't. Mark isn't here." Then she paused and asked, "*Where* are you?"

Zeke saw lines of cars stacked like dominoes with red taillights. "I'm stuck behind a pile-up. It looks like an accident up ahead and—" It was then that he realized she had hung up.

•   •   •

Traffic was indeed slow, so it took Zeke nearly thirty minutes to arrive at her home near the lakefront. His front tires jumped the curb, and he leapt out, sprinting towards the front door. The garage door was rolled up. He pounded on the entrance with the stained glass oval. No lights were on inside the house. He pressed the doorbell repeatedly.

He was fuming inside. *I told her I was coming. What a mistake.* After half-a-minute, he pounded harder on the wooden door, fishing out his cell phone, he hit redial. It went straight to voicemail.

"Doris!" He increased his pounding. "It's me. Open the door!" He edged over to the plate-glass window in the front and put his hands up to the side of his face to block the reflective light. The living room was picturesque neat—beige couch, magazines stacked neatly on a coffee table, a picture of a plantation over the fireplace. But no people, no Doris.

Circling the house, he found the side gate secured with a padlock, remembered Doris always chained it to keep Carla from wandering off.

He pulled over a garbage can and jumped over the fence. An elaborate ten-foot-high, redwood, children's playhouse stood in the center of the yard. A blue ball, a miniature dollhouse, and a tea set lay scattered next to the sliding patio door. No answers to his rapping.

He realized Doris had taken Carla and fled during the time it took him to get here.

When he returned to the front, an elderly couple stood in the driveway. She wore a flowered housecoat; he, a white T-shirt and baggy khaki shorts. A look of concern on both their faces.

"I've seen you here before," the man said. "So, I didn't call the police."

"Have you seen Doris?" Zeke asked.

The elderly lady said, "She and Carla left here about twenty or thirty minutes ago. We were weeding the flower bed."

"Did she say where they were going?"

"Not to me." She turned to her husband.

"Wherever she was going," he said, frowning. "She drove off as if the devil were after her."

CHAPTER 58

Jojo Turner sat in his car, talking into his cell phone, making excuses to his wife for missing lunch, when a long, black sedan pulled up to the fence about thirty yards away. The windows were impenetrable, black-tinted. It swung in and parked by the ten-foot-high wire fence that surrounded the Audubon Horse Stables, right near the Audubon Zoo. Jojo could hear the roar of lions echoing through the trees. It was midday. The rendezvous was beneath the shade of a hundred year old oak. The spot was their usual meeting place.

"Got to go, Honey," he said abruptly and hung up before she could protest.

An uneasy feeling consumed Jojo. The man, Goldenstein, always gave him the chills. Goldenstein was compact and always dressed the same every time Jojo met him—pressed dark suit, tie, and collar.

The limo sat idling for a minute before the driver's door opened and the big guy, the one they called Bowling Ball, got out. His massive shoulders stretched the fabric of his coat, and his bald head reflected the sunlight filtering through the tree limbs. He stood by the back car door and stared at Jojo's car.

Jojo sighed. No use waiting. He got out and walked to the door that Bowling Ball held open. He got in and slumped into the plush leather seat facing the neat little man. The giant shut the door. The interior of the limo smelled of sandalwood and expensive liquor.

"Hello, Mr. Goldenstein. How are you?" he said.

Goldenstein ignored his comment. "What's so important that we had to meet now?"

"It's the woman."

Goldenstein studied Jojo for a moment. "What woman?" he asked, a bit impatiently.

"The one that died in the explosion."

Goldenstein realized who he meant. Either through habit or carefulness, specific names were seldom used, even though the limo and the mansion were scanned daily for electronic bugs and spying devices. He could picture her in his mind—a beautiful woman, Jane Malone—though he'd only met her a few times while she was alive and saw her body afterwards. "What about her?"

"There's been a complication."

"What type?"

Jojo cleared his throat. He wanted a sip of the expensive brandy, but none was offered. Besides, it was better to keep a clear head while dealing with Goldenstein. "She was supposed to have died in the ... accident."

Goldenstein called on his excellent memory of images. He pictured Jane Malone on the autopsy table—head nearly decapitated from the upper torso, breasts and arm shredded as if placed in a meat grinder. Goldenstein sighed. "She was dead. I saw the body. What's the problem?"

"Her body is missing," said Jojo.

"I don't understand."

Jojo leaned forward, eager to relate the story. "I'll tell you what happened and you tell me what you think." And with that, Jojo began the tale about the kids stealing his old man's car, crashing in the St. John's Cemetery, and the discovery of rocks in her coffin. He concluded. "This sheriff, Andy Taylor, put out inquiries."

Goldenstein had listened, scrutinizing Turner. "What did this sheriff find?"

"Nothing, yet."

"Does her spouse, the ex-cop, know?"

"I think so."

Goldenstein continued to study the other man in the limo. He picked up a faint odor of sweat and—fear? *What is he not telling me?*

"I need more information," Goldenstein said. "This may mean nothing."

"I'll keep digging," Jojo said.

"Monitor the husband as well. Do whatever it takes to find out what happened." Goldenstein rapped on the window. Bowling Ball opened the door.

"You mean, *do whatever* it takes?" He asked as he got out of the limo.

"Yes. That's what I said. Verbatim." *Jesus, do none of these morons around here listen?*

Bowling Ball shut the door and got back in. Jojo stepped away, and the limo reversed and drove off. As he walked back to his car, Jojo was overwhelmed with a sense of relief: *I live to see another day.*

Inside the limo, Goldenstein thought, *Damn, I'll have to tell Onyx.*

•   •   •

Zeke sat in his car in front of Doris and Mark's house, wondering what to do next, when his cell phone began chirping.

Zeke answered without looking at the screen. "Doris?"

"No, Zeke, not Doris." It was the deep voice of Mark, her husband. "She asked me to call you."

Oh, shit! Zeke's blood pressure shot up before another word was uttered. "Mark, where is Doris? And what the *hell* is going on?"

"I'm not sure where she is, but she is afraid of someone—of *you.*"

"I'm just trying to get some answers," I said.

"So, she said. She wants you to know the truth."

There it was again: that word, the *truth.* Zeke wasn't sure of what anyone told him anymore. "The truth about *what?*"

"*Give* me a minute, will you? I'm only speaking to you because she is in a panic. Did you threaten her?"

"Are you crazy? I would never threaten her."

"No? Well, whatever you said caused her to run for her life. *And* Carla's, I might add."

"What are you talking about?" Zeke said. "I would never harm her. Or Carla."

"Sure, just like you punched that reporter."

"Listen, Mark, I just came from seeing Jane's coffin." He continued. "It was full of river rocks. What did you two do?"

Mark hesitated for a long count, then proceeded with a measured, even tone. "It was for your own good."

Zeke's cool evaporated. "My own ... my *own* good!? What in hell's name have you done, Mark? Are you out of your mind?"

"It was Doris' idea."

Zeke was silent, trying to assimilate what Mark had said. Doris' idea? Rocks in a coffin? Jane's body: missing! But, why?!

Mark said, "Listen to me. After Jane's death, you were in a coma for weeks. Doris had to decide."

"Decide what?"

"Jane's funeral. Cremation or burial. You guys had no written wills."

A sudden chill came over Zeke as he imagined her cremation. It was true. They had written nothing concerning the possibility of death. After all, they were both in good health, neither expecting anything to happen. He said nothing.

"Doris thought since Jane's body ... " he cleared his throat "was so ... so ... well, you know. Doris decided cremation was best. But she was only ever thinking of you. And how you might feel when you woke up. *If* you ever woke up. The doctors were unsure if you would even regain consciousness."

"Okay, cremation, I understand. But why the rocks?"

"Doris thought if you ever woke up, you'd like a place to mourn. A place where you could sit and be with her ... So, we bought a crypt in the St. John's Cemetery Mausoleum." Mark cleared his throat again. His voice took on a hard edge. "But you never visited, *did you?*"

Zeke's cheeks burned, and he muttered, "No, I—"

"No big conspiracy here, Zeke. Just people trying to look after you and your lack of appreciation. I don't understand what Jane saw in you to begin with. She died because of your negligence. And this is how you repay the memory of her death? You never even once visited her grave ... Shame on you."

Zeke could say nothing.

"And why Doris still thinks you're worth a shit is beyond me. As far as I'm concerned, you're still a piece of garbage." And he hung up.

CHAPTER 59

Goldenstein was on the phone with Onyx. "Our contact reported the coffin was opened by accident. It was full of rocks. Her body's missing."

Onyx did not answer, the only sound his raspy breathing.

Goldenstein continued, "I told our contact we didn't have enough information. Possibly there was a mistake."

"Wasn't there a funeral with a casket?" Onyx asked.

"Yes, there was. I saw her body," Goldenstein said. "Her body was so badly mutilated in the explosion, it was closed casket."

"What about the rocks, then?" Onyx asked.

"I haven't cleared that one up yet," Goldenstein said. "The death certificate omitted the mention of a cremation."

Onyx was quiet.

"Should we do anything?" Goldenstein asked. "Or just sit on the sidelines and let it clear up on its own?"

"Too risky. Things get uncovered," Onyx said. "Things leak when you don't take the initiative."

"I agree," said Goldenstein.

"Better to get on top of it. If there's a problem, we can control it."

There is always the risk that we might stir things up, Goldenstein was thinking.

"How much should we … ?"

"Do whatever it takes. Use your discretion. Sniff out what is behind this."

"Okay," said Goldenstein.

"But keep it quiet. We don't want to raise *any* attention."

•   •   •

MJ stood over the autopsy table, scalpel in hand. He had just made the first incision on a woman who died of cancer, starting the incision at the notch of the sternum, slicing between the breasts, to the pubic bone. "Now, take it easy, Zeke," MJ said into the phone.

"Take it *easy*?" Zeke said brusquely.

"There's has to be a simple explanation," MJ said, playing for time. He placed the sharp blade down on the metal table with a clink.

"What simple explanation?" Zeke shouted. "They said, they burned her body and stuffed her coffin full of rocks so I'd have a place to sit and meditate?"

MJ said nothing.

"I'm not buying it, MJ. There's something else going on ... I can feel it."

MJ sighed. The cat was about to claw its way out of the bag. *I have to tell him the truth.* "You're right, Zeke. There *is* something else at play here."

Zeke listened, waiting for MJ to continue.

MJ hesitated. *I need to make a call before I tell him the truth.*

MJ said, "I can't tell you over the phone. And I'm in the middle of an autopsy. We need to be face-to-face."

"When?"

"After I complete this autopsy. Later at my apartment."

"What time?"

"About five. You know where I live. Go there and wait for me. There's a key under the Hide-Away-Rock by the back door."

Zeke hated waiting that long, but he said, "Okay."

Zeke hung up.

MJ stared down at the corpse. She had tattoos on her arm and right breast. The tats on her arm looked like spider webs. On her breasts, two half-moons curved on the underside of her nipples, like smiles. The nipple, the nose.

MJ made the call. "Hey, Google," MJ said. "Call *École de France* on the North Shore."

"Sure," said the voice of Google.

CHAPTER 60

Across the lake, on the playground of *École de France*, Alice Potterfield was listening to the nun complain.

"Alice, correct her," the nun said. The nuns had long ago given up the sailboat hats, exchanging them for the dark bandannas that resembled black mullets. Behind them, the sun-baked playground was full of shouting and screaming children.

A small, dark-haired girl with a grim face, eyes downcast, stood before them.

"What did she do?" Alice asked in an even voice.

"She hit another child again."

Alice Potterfield knelt down, so she was at eye level with the young child. She could almost feel the little girl's pain, the loneliness, and angry defiance—a loner. They dressed the girl in hand-me-downs: a button missing on the front, a worn collar. Alice had seen this type before. More than that—she had been one long ago. She reached out and placed her hand on the girl's shoulder, felt the bony protrusions beneath.

The girl flinched. Eyes on the ground.

Alice said in a soft voice, "Mandy, I know you didn't mean to hit the other girl, did you?"

The girl's eyes jerked up, and she squinched up her face into an angry frown. Alice knew she had intended to hit her classmate.

The nun looked off towards the playground. Children were taking advantage of the lack of supervision. The boys were chasing the girls, who were screaming like wild animals.

"Take care of it," the nun said. "I had to send the other child to see the school nurse. Again, because of her actions." She hurried back to the playground, shouting, "You boys! Stop that!"

It was then, on impulse, Alice reached out and hugged the little girl. At first, she resisted, but when Alice would not release her, she relaxed. Alice felt her body begin the small convulsions of crying. She smelled of dust, sweat, and bubble-gum. Alice kissed her on the top of her head and whispered, "That's alright. We still love you."

After a minute, the crying stopped and little Mandy wiped her tears and nose on her blouse. Then, holding her at arm's length, Alice said, "Now, that's better. Don't let the other girls get your goat."

Mandy looked confused. "But I don't have a goat."

Alice laughed, out of embarrassment for using such an old term, and because the girl looked so innocent. "No, you don't. What I meant to say was, don't let them get under your skin." Then she continued to laugh because Mandy didn't understand that phrase either.

Alice sighed. "Go on back. And no more fighting. Do you know *sticks and stones?*"

The girl's face brightened. "I know that one. Sticks and stones may break my bones, but words will never hurt me."

"Good girl," Alice said, standing up and sending Mandy back across the playground. A pain clutched her heart as she remembered her own daughter whom she saw infrequently.

"Alice ... Alice Potterfield!" a voice cut into her thoughts. The school secretary stood in the breezeway, calling her name. She was a short, plump woman who always looked harried, but with an air of efficiency. "Alice, you have a phone call," she said before disappearing back into the school.

Alice frowned. She was always on the alert for anything out of the ordinary. A call in the middle of the day qualified as *out of the ordinary.* Her heart rate upped a notch.

She followed the secretary into the building. The secretary stationed herself back behind her desk and began pecking away at her keyboard.

Alice asked, "Did they say who was calling?"

"No. Some guy," she said without looking up. Then she paused. "He said to tell you *basketball.* Said you'd know."

Alice's heart skipped a beat. "I know this is an unusual request … " she said to the secretary. "But is there a place I could take this call in private?"

The secretary looked up, squinted, and adjusted her glasses. "Well, the principal is gone today. I suppose you could take the call in his office."

"Thanks, I'll just be a few minutes."

She tried not to hyperventilate as she walked to take the call. This was not the way it was supposed to be. The agreed procedure was broken. He was supposed to call on the fifth of each month. Near midnight. No words were to be spoken. She would count to ten. If he said nothing, she was to hang up. The silence meant all was well.

But now, a call in the middle of the month, in the middle of the day, meant something was not right. Her mouth was as dry as dust as she fought to steady her breathing. She lifted the receiver and looked up at the giant clock on the wall between the plaques and framed photographs. She started counting, using the second hand as her guide: One-Two-Three-

"The coffin," MJ said.

Jane Doe Alberato Malone—AKA Alice Potterfield—was stunned. Her breath caught in her throat and she sat down in the principal's heavy leather chair. She took a deep breath. "Go ahead."

"Jane's coffin was opened," MJ said. "Some freak accident."

Her heart sank. "Okay." Was all she could muster.

"They found the stones."

Had she expected it to last forever? "Okay, tell me what happened."

Michael Jordan told her the entire story about the boy stealing his father's car, the crash into the mausoleum at St. John's, and the dislodging of the coffin.

"Does Zeke know?"

"He sure does. He called me mad as a hornet and wanted to know what was going on."

"What did you tell him?"

"Well ... I put him off until I had a chance to speak with you."

The secretary stuck her head in the door, and Jane waved her away. She shut the door.

"When will you talk to him? What will you say?"

"This evening. The truth. I told him to meet me after work and I'd explain it all. He believes you're dead, died in the explosion. What he doesn't know is why everyone is lying to him."

That sounds like Zeke, all right. "Explain."

"He thinks Doris and Mark are lying," MJ said. "He doesn't buy the story about your cremation and burial."

She shook her head. What did she expect? That the convoluted knot of lies could go on forever?

There was a long silence. MJ asked, "Jane, what are you going to do?"

She was tired of hiding. Tired of visiting her daughter just once a month in the middle of the night. Tired of it all. *It may be time*, she said to herself. *Time to collect my daughter and husband and bring this to an end.*

She checked the time on the big round school clock on the wall of the principal's office. The school bell sounded at the top of the hour.

"It's one o'clock now," Jane said. "I'm leaving and I'll be in New Orleans in two hours."

CHAPTER 61

Goldenstein took his wire-rimmed glasses from an inside coat pocket and put them on. A clean, neat, dark suit, same as before, with a starched white shirt but different tie. It was easy to imagine him as an accountant or a tight-lipped bank executive. He might even be mistaken for an FBI agent—compact, contained, unremarkable. Untraceable.

He sat on an exercise bench in a small private gym attached to his office as he thought about the missing body and the rocks in the coffin. Goldenstein studied his companion, the giant built like a bulldozer, in his ill-fitting exercise t-shirt. Bowling-Ball, that was what Goldenstein called him. Heck, that's what everybody called him. In fact, no one even knew his real name.

"Are you sure?" asked Bowling Ball, before bench pressing three hundred fifty pounds.

"Yes, the coffin contained only rocks," said Goldenstein, astonished at the sheer strength of this brute.

After ten reps, Bowling Ball sat up, wiped his face with a towel, asked breathlessly, "Rocks? What kind of rocks?"

Goldenstein sighed. "How would I know? Rocks are rocks."

"Hey, maybe they were precious rocks?" Bowling Ball said.

"What?"

"You know, like diamonds. The coffin was a perfect hiding place. They was going to dig it up later."

"The rocks aren't important here," Goldenstein said. His face remained expressionless. "It's the body. The body was missing."

Bowling Ball chug-a-lugged a bottle of Gatorade. "Where did it go?"

"Possibly it didn't go anywhere."

Bowling Ball thought about that a minute, "Maybe it was a mistake."

"No, Jojo Turner said the coffin was empty."

Bowling Ball stood before the rack of dumbbells, trying to decide which to use. "What does it mean?" he asked.

"Let me think. If the body was missing, a couple of things may have happened."

"Such as ... ?"

"The body was cremated, and the coffin was a ...?" He stared at his goon. "The coffin was ... a diversion?"

"Like to hide something? The precious rocks?" the goon asked.

"No! You idiot! She died in the explosion."

"So, she's dead?"

"Yes." Goldenstein said. Then he stopped speaking, and the spooky tightness in his stomach expanded, like an icy-crystal dagger digging at his insides. *Of course, she was dead,* he told himself. *But what am I missing?* Goldenstein said, "Everybody said she was dead. Nobody could have lived through that explosion."

Bowling Ball selected two weights and started doing arm curls in the mirror. "Who identified the body?"

"The coroner."

"The one with that funny name? The little black shrimp with the bald head?"

Goldenstein removed a small leather-bound notebook from his coat pocket and flipped through it. He knew he had made a note of it. *The coroner that identified her body.* His eyes ran down a list. There it was. "Why, yes, Michael Jordan," he said out loud.

"Michael Jordan, like the basketball player?"

"Yeah. Like the basketball player."

"Yeah, that's it. Big name for such a tiny guy. But she was in pieces. Maybe *he* made a mistake."

Goldenstein looked up, "A mistake?"

"Yeah, you know," Bowling Ball said, straining. "The body was so tore up, maybe he mistook it for somebody else."

"Then she'd still be dead," Goldenstein said, slowly. "Unless ... "

"Unless what?"

"Unless ... the body *wasn't* hers." Goldenstein said as images of the living Jane flashed through his mind.

Bowling Ball grunted through the last few reps and then clanged the weights back on the rack. "Did anyone else see the body?"

"Yeah."

"Who?"

"Me." Goldenstein saw an image of her body mangled. No face. "I think we need to visit the coroner. This Michael Jordan."

CHAPTER 62

The drive across Lake Pontchartrain from *École de France* to New Orleans took less than two hours. This was the first time Jane Malone, AKA Alice Potterfield, had been back to New Orleans during the daylight hours. She thought of herself as a vampire sometimes, like one of Anne Rice's vampires, never showing herself in the daylight, avoiding sunlight. Would she burn if she walked outside now? She saw the sun trying to penetrate into the motel room through the window slats.

The motel she checked into was called the Happiness Inn with a lighted sign out front: Free Wi-Fi, Rentals by the week, night, or hour. This sad motel was one Jane Malone would never give a second glance. It was sandwiched between a tire shop and a car wash, the air full with the roar of the dryers and the smell of soap. None of her former friends would ever check-in here. It was a low, two-story 1950s-style motel with a metal frame carport in the rear with a corrugated roof. The other inhabitants of the motel were truckers and migrant workers and people passing through on a budget—a very strict budget. A pickup truck sat on blocks in the parking lot.

This was close to the morgue in New Orleans East and offered her cover from being identified by anyone she knew.

After a quick shower, she sat in a white terry-cloth robe, staring at herself in the mirror. The contact lens had done their job, changing her grass-green eyes to dark, chocolate brown. She removed them and blinked away the tears. The dye job had also done its job. For the past two years, she had colored her hair a mousy brown. No more French braids. Loose now, and longer to hide her face when she thought someone was staring at her.

It was risky coming back, and she understood the stakes. What if someone recognized her, despite her precautions? But she had no choice, now that the rocks had tumbled out of the casket. It would only be a matter of time.

Her fingers shook as she ran the plastic brush through her hair.

How long could she keep in hiding? She removed her fake ID from off the dresser and inspected the photo. Yes, it was her, but not her. The name beneath her photo was Alice Potterfield.

Now, she had been Alice Potterfield for over two years. *Alice Potterfield?* Where had that name come from? Oh, yes, MJ had created it, taken it off a dead woman that nobody claimed and was to be buried in Potter's Field out in New Orleans East. *"You are nearly the same everything: age, height, general description,"* MJ said.

She was filled with uncertainty. Maybe this was a mistake coming back. But things always change, of that she was certain. She felt powerless to stop what was happening. Once a body starts in motion, it stays in motion—until you hit a brick wall. She had hit her brick wall. Returning was her only option.

She picked up the phone and dialed MJ's number. He answered after the second ring. She said, "I'm in town."

"Where?"

"Close. At the Happiness Inn, off Chef Highway."

MJ hesitated a moment. "Why that rat trap?"

"Nobody will recognize me here." She fidgeted with the phone cord. "So ... when can we get together?"

"After I meet with Zeke. He and I will meet at my place."

She took a deep breath. "And *what* are you going to tell him?"

"I think ... maybe the truth. The whole truth. Things are about to blow up in our faces. It's better that he hears it from us before he finds out from someone else. Eventually, Onyx and the crime mob will find out." He paused. "Do you agree?"

"I suppose so. It's like we're back at square one. What do you want me to do?"

"Wait until I call you. You know Zeke. When I tell him you are alive, he'll break down any doors that get in his way."

Outside the motel room, a loud BANG! sounded like a gunshot. She jumped. "Hold on." She rushed to the window. A dark swarthy man in a wife-beater leaned over the open engine of the beat-up green pickup. He looked as if he were being eaten by the hood. Another man sat by the open door, one leg outside the cab. Shouting something in Spanish, the man inside the cab started the truck. It shook and backfired again.

She shuddered. The noise brought back memories of the Whitney Museum. She could still feel the boy's arm around her neck. The odor of sweat, so powerful, she could taste salt on her tongue. And there was Zeke standing in front of them, trying to talk the boy out of it, attempting to stay calm, attempting to save her life. Followed by gunfire and being dragged to the staircase. All so sudden, all such a blur. She thought she was going to die then, and out of desperation, she grabbed his hand, trying to force it away from the button. His skin was so slick with perspiration, she couldn't hold him. Then, to her horror, he clamped his thumb down on the button. But nothing happened. He did it again. And again. His thumb jumping up and down on the detonator button. With no explosion.

No explosion!

That's when she realized the detonator was not connected. She shoved him as hard as she could and he tumbled down the staircase. He grunted with each bounce, step by step, even did a cartwheel.

She ran in the opposite direction—up the stairs, three at a time, running for her life. She heard shouts. Heard the bang of more gunshots. And made it to the top, opening the door, just as the terrible explosion echoed, thundering in the stairwell, knocking her off her feet.

She shook off the image. She had replayed it a thousand times. What if she had been a step slower? What if she had frozen and not acted? The thought gave her nightmares.

She returned to the phone and MJ was still on the other end.

"What was that noise?" he asked.

"Nothing," she said. Her hands were still shaking. She glimpsed her pale face in the mirror.

"How long do I need to wait after you meet with him?" she asked.

"Not long. Wait for my call," he said.

"Okay, I'll wait. I'll be here." Jane gave MJ her room information so he could call the motel.

It was going to be one of the longest waits of her life.

CHAPTER 63

Goldenstein and Bowling Ball turned into the gravel parking lot of the morgue, the tires emitting a crunch like rolling over Rice Krispies. Bowling Ball steered to the side of the first building and parked next to a white SUV with a New Orleans Coroner's Office decal on the side doors.

They sat idling for a minute, the engine purring like a cat, tensing-down, crouching, waiting. "Is he still in, you think?" asked Bowling Ball.

"I don't see why not."

"What do we do if he's in?" Bowling Ball shut off the engine.

Goldenstein stared at Bowling Ball with a look that would chill most men. "We find out the truth."

Bowling Ball smiled, as if he had given him permission to take the biggest piece of pie. He took out a .45 snub-nose from his shoulder holster and checked the chamber with a soft clank.

"We won't use that," said Goldenstein. "Unless we have to. Let's do it like Grandpa used to."

Both men got out and walked around to the front, adjusting their coats as if going for a walk. The front door was locked, but it didn't stand up to Bowling Ball's massive frame. The lobby was silent. There were mismatched red and green plastic chairs and an empty reception desk. One of the overhead fluorescent lamps flickered and hummed.

Goldenstein nodded and Bowling Ball locked the front door and turned off the lights. They crept down the hall beyond the double doors, searching each room. Satisfied that no one else was on the premises, they arrived at the back rooms. Goldenstein recalled the time he came to the morgue to verify the body of Jane Malone. It was at the request of Theodore Onyx. He demanded that one of his men, Goldenstein, see the corpse. "Not only see it," Onyx had said. "Touch it with your own two hands," Goldenstein recalled the stink of disinfectant and the funky smell of green and yellow fluids oozing out of the body. Her mangled body lay on the table in pieces. He had lied to Onyx. He had assured him he had touched her body. "She's dead," he told him. "Cold stone dead." He never touched the body, however.

And now, here he was two and a half years later to see if he had made a mistake.

The two men approached a set of double doors with round windows. They stationed themselves on either side and peeked in. A short, skinny man dressed in green scrubs was leaning over a dead body.

It was Michael Jordan, all right. He was moving around the tilted metal table like a billiard pro. On the table, lay the naked body of a woman, legs splayed, arms at her side. Goldenstein heard running water, and he could have sworn it sounded as if the little man was humming or singing a song to himself. Because of Michael Jordan's size, Goldenstein remembered the scene from Walt Disney's *Snow White,* where the seven dwarfs were singing and dancing. Any second now, he expected Michael Jordan to start with "Whistle While You Work."

"He sure does like his work," Bowling Ball whispered.

CHAPTER 64

MJ reached up and repositioned the large round overhead light above the body on the metal autopsy table.

It had been a long time since MJ thought about Jane Malone's death and his part in the deception. He had put it firmly out of his mind, and it only bubbled up to the surface now and then. But it was always there, just beneath the surface, like a nagging toothache that never healed, ready to jolt him awake in the middle of the night.

Over two years. It had been over two and a half years, *long years*, since Jane Malone, AKA Alice Potterfield, was declared dead.

The deception had been complete. Zeke Malone had accepted that his wife was dead, as did everyone else. No one questioned the final report. So why bring it up now? At the start of the duplicity, all he had wanted was to unburden himself of the lie, but that would only bring disaster. He figured he'd either burn that bridge or cross it when he came to it.

Her fake death was water under the bridge, so to speak. But he knew this day would come, and that he'd have to deal with it. Well, it was here. The levees were about to break and send the waters flooding the streets, just like Hurricane Katrina. He was trapped in the middle of the deluge, and the only way to safety was to tell the truth and paddle like hell.

MJ took metal shears that looked like two-handled garden clippers and snapped through the sternum and rib cage, much like snipping roses in his garden.

He wondered, *Is there another way out?* How would he explain her survival? But not her death. A miraculous escape? Amnesia? Nope, no one would believe that. These thoughts started the day of the explosion and had returned every day since.

Jane Malone was his friend—just like Zeke and Bull. After all, who but those three would tolerate his Death Games? His quirky fascination with the dead and his quizzes of death statistics and oddities? Who, indeed?

MJ fitted metal clamps to pry the two halves of the ribs apart, exposing the heart and the lungs. His mind drifted back to that day when Jane had called from the Whitney. Her voice, a controlled hysteria, "MJ, you've got to help me."

"Jane? What's the matter?"

Then she said something he would never forget, her exact words etched in the stone tablet of his mind. "MJ, someone is trying to kill me."

"Did you call the police?"

"Yes, I did. But *they're* the ones trying to kill me."

"What? Where are you?"

"I'm hiding on the top floor of the Whitney museum. There's been an explosion, and I think Zeke is dead." Quickly, she told him about the Bomber Boy, dynamite strapped to his chest. How Zeke had confronted him. The gunshots. And how the boy tumbled down the stairs while she made her escape.

Then her voice dropped to a whisper. "I can't talk anymore. I'm hiding inside the Japanese exhibit, behind the Samurai armor. You've got to get me out of here. *Please?*" She clicked off.

Through some miracle, Michael Jordan got her out of there and escaped detection.

In the morgue, MJ tagged the toe of a homeless woman no one would miss. They were about the same size and coloration. His coroner's skill came through as he mutilated her body to look as if it had been in an explosion. That was the body that Goldenstein saw. Zeke, in a coma for weeks, would never have to identify the body.

MJ turned on the circular bone saw used to cut through skulls. The high whine of the saw reverberated off the tile walls. He took pleasure in the spinning, buzzing sound.

After he completed the autopsy, he washed off the body, sewed the chest in the Y-pattern, transferred it to a stretcher, and rolled it into the refrigerated cabinet. He finished his notes, speaking into the microphone suspended above the table, and cut off the mic.

The clock by the double doors read five o'clock, finished on time. He dreaded telling Zeke the truth, but the time had arrived to confess his deceptions. After shutting off the water, he stripped off his gloves, tossing them in the hazardous waste, and threw his lab coat in the dirty clothes hamper.

He clicked off the lights and stepped through the double doors, with the porthole windows, and found himself face-to-face with two men.

One was huge, like a weightlifter with gigantic shoulders. The other was smaller. A neat man in a suit, white shirt, and tie. For a long count, he stared at the strangers.

"Who are you?" MJ asked. But before the words left his lips, he knew who they were. And what they wanted.

The Giant stepped forward, and before MJ could react, slammed his fist in MJ's solar plexus. MJ doubled over. It was a pain like he'd never felt before and he fell to his knees and hands, retching. He couldn't breathe, his diaphragm in spasms.

The next thing MJ perceived was being dragged back through the double doors, lifted, and slammed down on the metal autopsy table. The Giant pressed down on his windpipe, cutting off his air. MJ clawed at the man's hands. Finally, the shorter stranger signaled for him to release his neck. MJ sucked in air like a drowning man coming out of water.

The short man's face appeared over him.

"Now, Michael Jordan," he said, "tell us all about Jane Malone. We know you know."

The Giant's fingers dug into his abdomen, beneath his ribs, until he was digging into his liver like a claw.

"Is she alive? Or is she dead?" asked the neat man.

CHAPTER 65

As I approached the French Quarter apartment where MJ lived, I asked myself for the hundred time. *Why had they lied to me?*

And it was lies, multiple lies, multiple times about her death. They lied. And lied.

I tried to dismiss what they had told me, searched for excuses. Cremated? Not buried?

Why didn't they just tell me? For my own good? What a crock!

Jane had never lied to me. She just didn't tell me everything. Is the omission of facts lying? She said, "If you love me, don't ask about my past." I loved her and I never asked. Are omissions of truth just as bad as straight-out lies? In fairness, she was doing both. And in fairness, I had no answer about what was up with Jane. Truth is, I loved her. Would always love her. Nothing would change that.

And Doris, my sister-in-law, whom I entrusted with the safety of Carla—had to be in on it. Trusted. Until she disappeared with Carla. But why lie, though?

I parked on a side street half-a-block from his apartment and crossed over to Esplanade Avenue. MJ's apartment had once been a small Seafarers' church that gave shelter to sailors who shipped in and out of the port of New Orleans.

MJ had bought the building at auction, kept the cross, and rebuilt the entire interior. I passed through the front metal gate and around back, down a narrow alleyway to an elaborate Japanese rock garden. The courtyard garden had a small tinkling water fountain, dwarf cherry blossom trees, and a ten-foot stone fence. The key was where he said it would be, inside a fake rock.

I let myself in and ran into a large six-foot African death mask carved out of wood with feathers and emerald eyes. The apartment was filled with assorted Death objects, like a *museum de los muertos*: Etruscan funerary items, a painting of Death of Marat, Greek Gorgons. Even a death mask of Rescue Annie, the famous nineteenth century drowned woman's face that was the model for thousands of CPR dummies. Ah, MJ! Where did your fascination with death come from? He was in the right profession.

I took a deep breath to steady myself and slumped down on a beige couch across from a coat hanger, a tall replica of a French guillotine. The place might have given some people the heebie-jeebies, but I had been here before for Christmas parties, Saints games, and cards with the guys. On the wall was a photograph of the three of us, during happier times, at the Half Moon. It was getting to be after five o'clock. *Come on. Where are you?* I mumbled to the clock-skull sitting on the coffee table. Its eyes tick-tocked from side to side. No answer. I was growing as nervous as a worm on a hook.

I checked my watch. Any time now.

Come on. Come on, MJ, I'm waiting.

CHAPTER 66

The Truth.

It isn't hard to get to the truth. The real Truth. When you'll stop at nothing to get it, Goldenstein thought. And Bowling Ball was an expert at extracting the truth.

At first, the little coroner had screamed and fought back on the metal dissecting table. But he was no match for Bowling Ball, who had fingers like steel claws and outweighed him by over a hundred pounds.

After it was all over, Goldenstein watched with fascination as Bowling Ball washed his hands at one of the deep sinks. Goldenstein had never seen anyone with such strength and dexterity. He dried his hands with a green surgical towel. And just like a real surgeon, Bowling Ball was an expert on the human anatomy. Goldenstein marveled at the way the oversized man knew exactly where to dig under a person's diaphragm, to grip and squeeze the liver, or crush a kidney, delivering agonizing pain. Pain so powerful that you would do anything to make it stop.

In the middle of the room, the coroner, Michael Jordan, lay on the stainless steel table, vacant eyes staring at the bright bank of lights. It had taken an hour. Very few men lasted more than a few minutes beneath the probing fingers of the goon. Goldenstein did not remember anyone lasting so long. At first, he had lied. But in the end, MJ had talked—telling the truth—before he died.

So, Jane Malone was *not* dead. Had *not* died in the explosion and had been in hiding for over two years.

And the husband, the ex-cop, Zeke Malone, did not know she was alive.

And the cherry on top was that Goldenstein knew where she was waiting, in some run-down little motel off Chef Menteur Highway. The Happiness Inn. Waiting for MJ's call to come join them. *Well, we'll save her the trouble. We'll go see her.*

Bowling Ball finished drying his hands and was about to toss the towel on the floor.

"Don't," Goldstein said. "Might be traces of DNA." He was all brawn and no brains. *I have to do the all thinking.*

Bowling Ball nodded and tucked the towel into his back pocket just as a phone started vibrating on a side table, like an alarm clock. It continued to buzz. Goldenstein walked over and peered at the screen.

Zeke Malone.

He exchanged looks with Bowling Ball and, on an impulse, picked it up.

The voice on the other end was loud and angry. "MJ, where the *hell* are you?!"

·   ·   ·

It had been over an hour, and I had grown tired of waiting in MJ's apartment, being stared down by the death mask and knives and swords on the wall. I had run out of patience, and so I called.

It rang about a dozen times before it was answered.

"MJ, where the *hell* are you?!" I said, a bit more rough than I had intended.

There was no answer.

Maybe I had come on too strongly. In a calmer voice, I said, "I've been waiting for over an hour. At least you could have called."

There was an eerie silence on the other end. The empty feeling in my gut ratcheted up a notch. Something was not right. Whoever had answered, it wasn't MJ. "Hello?"

A low voice came on. "What's going on?"

I swallowed and tried to keep my voice even. "Where's MJ?"

"I must apologize. He can't come to the phone right now ... *Zeke.*"

By the way he said my name, he knew me. My hands were sweating. "Who is this?"

"You don't know me. But I know you."

"You have me at a disadvantage, then. Why don't you introduce yourself?"

"My name is unimportant."

I was up and headed for the door. "Then, what is important?"

"That's for you to find out."

I subdued my fear and tried to replace it with anger. "Where's MJ?"

"He's here. At the morgue."

"What have you done to him?"

"He's not important anymore."

My heart sank. I sprinted down the alleyway. "Let me speak to him."

"As I said, he's indisposed and can't come to the phone." He spoke with a tone that I can only describe as creepy and cruel, as if it were some kind of inside joke. "But he's waiting for you, Zeke. Why don't you come visit him?"

"Will you be there?" I said.

"No, unfortunately, I have urgent business elsewhere. There's someone else I must see. *Can't wait,* you know? But I am sure we will meet in the future." Then he hung up.

· · ·

While Bowling Ball sped away from the morgue, Goldenstein dialed a number. It was answered after two rings.

"I know where she is. We're on our way there now."

"Good."

"I thought you should know: Zeke Malone is on his way to the coroner's office."

"And, that's important because?"

"If you hurry, Turner, you'll probably catch him. Catch him red-handed. Red meaning blood ... and still fresh. In a position *indelicato*. Do you understand?"

"Yes."

They both hung up.

CHAPTER 67

When I arrived at the coroner's offices, the ten-foot chain-link gate was open, and all the parking lot lights were off.

Gravel crunched under my tires as I gunned it into the lot and skidded in next to MJ's white SUV. I pressed on the horn twice before bounding out. No response. The lights in the building were off.

What the hell is going on?

I ran around to the front of the building. The door stood open and behind it; the interior was dark. With my cell phone for light, I stepped into the waiting room and stood motionless until my eyes grew accustomed to the darkness. At the end of a long hall, leading to the back of the building, I saw a dim light. Behind the reception desk, I flipped the light switches. The fluorescent lights flickered on with a buzz.

"MJ," I called.

No answer.

He was here. I could feel it. I punched in his cell phone number, and a faint ringing echoed down the empty hallway. I clicked off. And the ringing stopped.

I made my way down the hall, sneaking quick peeks into the empty rooms. I called out his name once again.

The hall ended at the autopsy suite, and the sinking feeling in my stomach deepened. The lights were on, and I stuck my head close to the porthole windows looking inside. My heart started jack-hammering as if it wanted to bang out of my chest.

MJ lay on the dissecting table and was lit up like a display mannequin.

"Oh, god! No!" I burst through the double doors, rushing to the table. My legs felt like rubber.

"MJ!" I felt for a carotid pulse.

His eyes were open wide, his mouth open. I've seen it all before. Skin pasty and pale, like one of the death masks in his apartment. His body was icy and the blood from his mouth was dry to my touch. I jerked my hand away and staggered away until I felt cold ceramic tile on my back. The next thing I knew, I was in a chair, staring at the lifeless body of my friend.

I should have called 911, but I just sat there. That's when I heard the heavy footsteps clattering down the hall. I stood up. A blue uniformed policeman burst through the double doors, pistol pointed ahead of him.

He was followed by Jojo Turner with his revolver drawn. A gold police medallion bounced off on his chest from a chain around his neck. When he saw me, he jerked his gun up and pointed the muzzle at my chest.

"Put your hands up, MOTHERFUCKER!" he shouted.

CHAPTER 68

Jane paced back and forth in Room 202 at the Happiness Inn, walking to the window and peering around the curtains into the parking lot. The two men working on the pickup truck were gone. The truck had not moved. Maybe they gave up. The street lights were on, at least one was casting a yellow, gloomy light onto the parking lot.

Had MJ called, and she hadn't received it? She picked up the phone. It had a dial tone, still working. And she banged it down. *Damn, where are you guys? How long does it take to tell Zeke that I'm still alive?* It was after six, well past the time when MJ was supposed to call.

This was so stupid. How did she think he would react? Did she think Zeke would accept the news with, "Well, what do you know?"

Tears sprung to eyes as she imagined Zeke's face. The pain he must be going through. It was all so bizarre. The amazement in his voice when he found out she was not dead. How could she have ever thought this crazy plan could work? She splashed water on her face in the bathroom and looked at herself in the mirror. She was in a cold sweat and her face was ashen. Why hadn't they called?—Had something gone wrong?

"That's it! I can't wait," she said, hurrying and grabbing her jacket and bag, water still dripping from her face. *I can't sit here.*

She let herself out the door, locking it behind her, and hurried the length of the balcony to the staircase. She slipped past the ice dispenser and exited out the back, near the office. *The key. Might as well turn it in, I'm not coming back here.* She shoved open the glass door but no one appeared to be inside.

"Hello?" she called.

No answer. She realized what a dumb idea this was. She was in a hurry, stopping by to drop off a door key.

"Hello? I'm turning in my keys." Still no response.

Ah, to hell with it. She stepped forward, leaned over the counter to drop the key, when she looked down. Two legs stuck out from under the counter, next to an overturned chair.

"You all right?"

The man did not move. And then she realized he would never move.

Oh, Jesus! They've found me! Even though she did not know who *they* were. The hair on the back of her neck stood up. She spun around, expecting someone to be behind her. But there was no one. She bolted out the glass door and started running, past the broken truck, towards her car, fumbling to get her car keys out of her bag.

• • •

Not a hundred feet away, while Jane sprinted to her car, Goldenstein and Bowling Bowl were creeping up the staircase. They had just shot the night manager and were on their way to complete the job. Bowling Ball reached inside his coat to release the hook of his gun from the shoulder holster. Both men moved to either side of the door at Room 202.

"Now is the time to earn your pay," Goldenstein said.

Bowling Ball smiled, withdrew his pistol, and squared up to the door and with a crash of splintered wood and metal hinges, the door exploded inward from the force of his boot.

Got to act fast, Goldenstein thought, *before she screams.* But there were no screams. No woman sitting on the bed. No face with surprise and horror. No one. Goldenstein pointed towards the bathroom. Bowling Ball kicked it open. *Empty.*

"She's gone," Bowling Ball said.

"Yeah, no *shit*," Goldenstein replied. That's when they heard the grinding of a car engine trying to start in the parking lot. They ran to the balcony. "That's her," said Goldenstein.

Bowling Ball pointed his pistol.

Goldenstein grabbed his arm. "No," he said and began running towards the stairs.

• • •

While Jane was fumbling her key into the ignition, she heard the crash of wood and looked up as two men burst into her room. She turned the key. The starter put out a high-pitched, grinding noise as the engine strained to catch on. *Damn! Damn!* The car wouldn't start. *"Come on! Come on!"* Jane pleaded. Why hadn't she taken care of that when it began giving her trouble? The problem always resolved by waiting five minutes and trying again.

But she didn't have five minutes.

The engine shuddered, but did not start. She glanced up at the second floor. Her heart leapt out of her chest. The two men stood on the balcony, staring down at her. What was he pointing at her? A gun?

And the engine finally started.

She threw it into drive and stomped the gas pedal to the floorboard. The car shot forward and bounced off the broken truck, knocking it off the blocks. The car fishtailed, but she gained control and aimed it towards Chef Menteur like a shot from a cannon. In the rearview mirror, she saw the two men as they reached the bottom of the stairs.

She swerved into traffic. "Oh, God, help me!" she cried, cutting in front of a city bus to avoid rear-ending a slower car. The bus driver slammed on his brakes and the bus skidded across two lanes of traffic, and clipped an oncoming delivery truck. Jane jumped the curb, barreled through the car wash, and exited onto the back service road. To her horror, she was driving the wrong way, headlights swerving from her path. She jerked the wheel and made a U-turn onto the up-ramp leading to the I-10, headed towards the French Quarter. A dozen cars honked at her. She glanced at her rearview mirror. Relief flooded her: she had made it.

By the time Goldenstein and Bowling Ball swerved onto Chef Menteur Highway, the bus had blocked all the lanes coming and going. Bowling Ball leaned on the horn.

"Save it," Goldenstein said. "She's gone." They had lost her.

"I'll be goddamned," Bowling Ball growled. "That bitch has nine lives."

CHAPTER 69

The cop, who entered with Jojo Turner, had me turned around with my hands flat against the cold tile wall of the autopsy room. He kicked my feet outwards, so I was spread-eagle, leaning forward.

"Be sure and pat him down good," Jojo said.

I turned my head and saw him go to the cadaver table and stare down at the lifeless body of MJ. The cop shoved my face back towards the wall. His hands felt under my arms, down my waist, between my legs and down towards my ankles. It was a procedure I knew well. Rule number one when being arrested: *Don't resist, if you know what's good for you. Fighting can lead to disaster.*

Jojo said behind me, "My god, look what you did to that poor bastard."

"What's that?" The cop turned his head and looked.

They thought I killed MJ. *This is ridiculous.* The man on the phone, who refused to give his name, killed him—no, murdered him, not me.

What the shit is happening? "I didn't kill MJ," I protested, trying to turn.

The cop shoved me hard in the back, slamming me against the wall.

"Keep your *fucking* mouth *shut!*" Jojo barreled towards me, screaming, pointing his finger in my face. "Didn't I say, 'You're a fuck-up, Malone'," he shouted, as spittle hit my face. "Now I got you! And you're not getting away from me."

At the sound of his voice, I remember the same voice in my ear two years ago as I stood facing Bomber Boy and Jane: "Take your shot, asshole. TAKE YOUR SHOT!"

MJ was going to tell me the truth. But it had gotten him killed.

The truth that connected them together was that it was all a cover-up. How could I have been so stupid to miss it?

Jojo turned and walked back to the table. "You're going away a long time for this. And you know what they do to cops in prison." He shook his head. "He must have just killed him. The body is still warm. Look at those marks."

Jojo had made a point. I would go to jail for this. Something I could never do! Ex-cops often wind up with a shiv between the ribs. And there was no way I could unravel this mess sitting in jail.

The cop who frisked me made a mistake. After you pat down a suspect, you cuff 'em. Instead, he turned to see what Jojo was talking about. He hesitated.

That was his undoing. And all I needed.

Next to me on an instrument table was a metal bedpan.

The cop was about my height, clean-cut, broad shoulders and looked as if he worked out in the gym. He could beat the shit out of me in a fair fight.

But I wasn't thinking: *fair fight.* I had to get out of there. And now. My hand shot out and locked onto the lip of the bedpan and I spun like a kick-boxer. The spin gave me momentum, and I slammed the edge on the side of his head. Sounded like a game show gong.

And that sucker fell like a sack of bricks.

Jojo jerked his head around and stared wide-eyed at me, mouth open. His lips moved, but he never finished because I launched myself, catching him in the chest, dead center, with my shoulder, like an NFL lineman throwing a perfect block. He made an "UUFF!" sound, tumbled back onto the autopsy table, flipped over MJ's body before landing on the other side.

In two steps, I was around the table.

Turner was getting up on his knees. "You, crazy fuck! I'll—"

That was all he said before I cracked him on the head with the bedpan—for the second note of the Gong Show.

The adrenaline was pumping through my veins. I paused a moment, looking back and forth between the two cops on the floor and MJ's lifeless body. *What the hell have I done? Too late now.*

As I rushed into the hall, I heard the crunching of gravel as another police cruiser drove in, lights flashing. I had to get control of myself if I expected to get out of here alive. *Just do your job*, I told myself. I exited the building and stood, leaning against the doorjamb, as if I were waiting for them—It took all of my energy to be still. The cruiser screeched to a stop, the two cops flying from both sides, weapons drawn.

I recognized one of them, Stewart Ortiz. He was a good cop, and I stood in his wedding. I smiled and waved.

He lowered his gun. "Zeke, what the hell's happening?"

"It's nothing. A false alarm." I nodded a greeting to his partner. "Jojo's inside waiting for both of you."

"Aw, crap, we was in the middle of our lunch." Ortiz holstered his pistol. "Why don't they get their shit straight?" He reached into his cruiser and gave a code into his two-way.

They walked to the entrance. Ortiz hung back for a second, turned to me. "You coming?"

"Jojo said for me to wait outside."

His brow came together, but he nodded and entered.

I could see the flashing lights of approaching cop cars a mile away.

I sprinted to my car, threw it in gear, and sped out of the morgue parking lot, spitting loose pieces of gravel behind me like buckshot from a shotgun. As I drove away, an approaching police cruiser, lights flashing, siren wailing, passed me going in the opposite direction. It was only a matter of minutes before they would turn and start hunting me.

Where the hell do I go?

Then my cell phone buzzed. What the ... ? Thank God, who else? "Moshe!" I shouted, never so happy to hear his voice.

"Zeke," he said. "I may have found Kitty Fowler for you."

"Moshe, I can't go into that now. *The police are after me!*"

He paused for a beat. "Where the hell are you, man?

"On Almonaster Avenue."

"Go till you dead end at the Lake. Someone will pick you up.

PART IV

CHAPTER 70

While this was going on, across town at Police Headquarters, Detective Bull waited in the hallway on a hard wooden bench outside the Disciplinary Committee Hearing Room.

He'd been there over half-an-hour, suffocating in his dark-blue suit and tie, the one he wore to weddings and funerals. The door had a frosted-glass window with the words INTERVIEW ROOM.

From behind the door, he heard mumbling and raised voices, but couldn't make out what they were saying. Finally, the door opened, and a secretary stepped out—pretty, but not a police officer. He had met her before, maybe a year ago. *Louise ... Something?*—he searched his memory bank for her name. She had been friendly then, but now she was unsmiling. She didn't say hello either.

"Detective Bulardeaux," she said, "they're ready for you now."

He followed her into the room. Two tables—one large, one small. Louise, if that was her name, took her seat at the smaller one with a laptop and a small microphone. He assumed the back of her Apple computer was recording video, as well.

Behind the other table, the larger one, the mahogany one, sat three Internal Affairs officers, all upper-level brass. Since all three had worked with Bull, they exchanged reserved nods. Lieutenant McConnel, the one on the end he'd known since the academy. At least one of them was a familiar face. McConnel had worked Homicide with Bull before being transferred to IA.

"Hi, Bull, how have you doing?" McConnel asked. He'd grown soft in the middle since his move.

"Good. How's the old knee?" Bull said.

"Same old, same old. Aches sometimes." His transfer was because of an arthritic knee. Too young to retire. He couldn't work the streets anymore.

Off to the side, a man in a dark suit stood with his arms crossed. Bull did not know him, but assumed some politician had sent him.

Bull said, "I know you three." He walked past the table and stood in front of the man in the dark suit. "But *you*, I don't know."

McConnel offered from the table, "His name is Lester Knotts."

Bull eyed him. "And you are here because ... ?"

He smiled—or was it a smirk? "Just an observer."

"For what purpose?" Bull asked.

"Report to the mayor's office."`

"How is the mayor?"

"As good as expected, considering you cops still don't have shit on the Oasis Club murders."

Something about the man struck Bull as unsavory. A hail-fellow-well-met type. A hanger-on, ingratiating himself to those in power—Bull had met them before—always ready with a match to light up your smoke. But those accommodating rat finks always seemed to have their other hand in your pocket.

"Shall we get started?" McConnel called from the table.

Bull took his seat in front. The first IA guy opened a blue folder with a dozen type-written sheets stapled together. He read the charges. "This is a disciplinary committee meeting," he announced in a serious voice. "Detective Bulardeaux, you have been accused of defying direct orders not to become involved in a delicate investigation."

Bull had appeared before a few committees in his work life and never felt vulnerable. But now he did.

After the IA officer read the accusations, he paused and stared at Bull. "Do you have questions so far?"

"Yes. Who brought these charges?"

There was a pause as the two IA officers on the left exchanged glances. They had been cordial before, but now he felt the strain in the air.

Bull fixed his eyes on his former colleague. "Well?"

McConnel glanced at the others before answering, "It was the Captain of Homicide Division, Jojo Turner."

"Is he here?"

"No, he isn't required to be at this hearing," the IA officer on the left said.

Bull pursed his lips and nodded. "Go ahead," he said, as if he were giving them permission, his way of gaining some control of the interview.

He continued to read, a meandering litany of charges with lots of legalese thrown in, which took a full fifteen minutes. Afterwards, the IA officer put the folder down on the mahogany tabletop and looked up.

"Captain Turner wrote he gave you a direct order not to interfere, and he—"

"In what case?" Bull interrupted.

"The ... the ... " He flipped the pages on the report. "In the Oasis Club Massacre."

"I didn't interfere in that investigation," Bull said.

Silence again fell on the room.

"He said that your investigation brought you back to the Oasis Club. At that point, you should have reported your findings to your superiors and stood down."

Bull knew that this hearing was a losing proposition, but he wanted it down on record. "Look," he said leaning forward. "I'm a detective, and my job is to uphold the law and investigate crimes. It's the oath I swore to when I joined the force. It's the oath I took when I became a detective."

"No one is questioning that, Detective Bulardeaux, but a direct—"

"Let me finish," he said. "If I'm pursing a crime, I pursue it wherever it leads."

"Not if you were told to back off," the middle IA suit said.

Bull turned his focus on him. "Does the report say why I was told to back off?"

"That isn't the question here."

"I think it is. Have any of you questioned why I was ordered to back off?"

Inspector Number One closed the file. "I think this has gone on long enough. We didn't convene to answer your questions." He glanced at the inspector next to him, who nodded.

Inspector Number Two cleared his throat and spoke in an official voice. "Detective Bulardeaux, you are hereby suspended from the force. Turn in your badge and service weapon before you leave the room."

"Anything else?" Bull asked.

All three of the IA officers exchanged glances, and McConnel said, "No."

Bull stood up and removed his badge from his inside coat pocket. He lifted his revolver from his shoulder holster and unloaded the clip. He racked it to unload the bullet from the chamber and placed them all on the mahogany table.

"Anything else?" he repeated.

"No," Inspector Number One said, placing the badge, gun, and clip into a wide, yellow evidence envelope, before sliding a clipboard forward for Bull to sign.

Bull signed and left the room. In the hall, he realized he was breathing hard. He took a deep breath, letting it out, until he felt his heart rate slow. He had just started down the stairs, towards the exit, when McConnel caught up with him.

"I'm sorry, Bull," he said, stepping down beside him. "It's unfair, and I was against it from the beginning. But I was outranked."

Bull took another step, eager to get fresh air.

McConnel said, "I don't who you pissed off, but the higher-ups have it in for you. You've stepped on some toes and they don't like it."

Bull said, "Something is going on. Not sure what. I want to know why I was pulled off the case. That's where your focus should be."

"Wait ... " McConnel said.

Bull looked back at him.

"Your friend, Zeke Malone. They've issued a warrant for his arrest."

Bull blinked. "What reason?"

"For murder."

"Murder?" Bull felt a knot of bile rise in his stomach but he forced it back down.

"The report came in just before we went into session," McConnel said.

"Who was he supposed to have killed?"

"The coroner, Dr. Michael Jordan."

Bull went completely still, mouth open. "MJ?" Bull felt as if he might sink into the ground right there on the staircase. What came to mind was the image of light reflecting off MJ's glasses as he asked one of his Death Quiz questions. And he thought of his ex-partner, Zeke Malone. *This can't be.* His eyebrows furrowed as he tried to absorb the news.

"Bull? Bull?" McConnel broke through his thoughts and asked if he'd knew where Zeke could be found.

"No, I haven't spoken with Zeke since he disappeared," Bull said, hurrying down the stairs. "If I see him, I'll let him know."

Later, as Bull drove away from Police HQ, still numb with the news of his friend's death, his cell phone buzzed. It was his old contact at the D.E.A.

"Bull, you were right," he said. "We're walking in an investigation team. It's critical that we not tip our hands to the locals at NOPD."

CHAPTER 73

Almonaster Avenue ended at the levee, with a grassy rise leading to concrete steps overlooking the of Lake Pontchartrain. I parked along the cul-de-sac and waited, as Moshe had instructed. I killed the engine and slumped down to wait. In less than a minute, a black limousine approached and parked a block away, engine idling. The limo was familiar; the windows were dark, and I saw no movement. Then it crept towards me, stopped beside the driver's side. Its window buzzed six inches down. A face appeared. It was the same man who had picked me up before, when we visited the computer whiz kid, Moshe's nephew "Get in."

"My car?" I said.

"Leave it."

I got in. The last time I questioned his orders, he nearly drove off without me. I couldn't afford that now.

The limo drove us to a deserted street lined with abandoned houses. New Orleans had blocks of such derelict homes, abandoned since Hurricane Katrina. The families moved out, resettled in other parts of the country, never to return. Black plastic bags of garbage spilled into the yards beside wet mattresses, broken chairs, and bureaus, next to piles of dead trees. The smell of burning trash seeped through the windows. The car slowed and turned into a weed-covered driveway and eased between two clapboard houses. It stopped midway and my door opened. It was Moshe. The building to the right had a side entrance with just enough clearance for me to squeeze out.

"Boy, I don't know what you did," Moshe said. "But the police radios are burning up the airwaves trying to find you. They've already located your car. Another five minutes and you'd be in cuffs right now."

Moshe led me through a couple of rooms, the walls collapsing, sheetrock with punched holes. I realized I was still in shock over the death of my friend. But I shook it off because of more pressing needs, such as my need to escape the police. *Grieving comes later,* I told myself. *Right now, I have to survive.*

Moshe led me to a door and unlocked it. In contrast to the rest of the house, this room was like a luxury hotel with lamps, couches, 50-inch TV on the wall, and a large double-door refrigerator next to a minibar.

"You look like you could use a drink," he said, motioning for me to sit while he went to the refrigerator.

"No liquor," I said, flopping down on the soft leather couch. He brought me a large bottle of fruit juice. I unscrewed the top and drank deeply. I must have been more thirsty than I thought because by the time I set it down, the bottle was empty.

I never felt so exhausted. My eyelids were heavy and my legs rubbery.

Moshe sat in an easy chair opposite me and said, "You going to tell me what happened?"

"You sure you want to hear?"

"Look, Zeke, I may have cleaned up for my wife, but I still have my fingers in several pies, not all of them *Mom's apple pies*. I could go to jail for a long time for any of them. Aiding and abetting your escape is the least of them."

He got up and went to the fridge and returned with a large bottle of juice and two glasses. "Besides," he said, filling each glass. "I earned your story. You owe me."

I couldn't argue with that. So I began the story with the explosion that killed my wife and went on to tell about the death of MJ. And I concluded my tale with cold-cocking Jojo on the head with the bedpan. He smiled at that one.

"You wait here. Help yourself to whatever you find. I'll be back." And with that, he left me alone in the room. The next thing I knew, I was asleep.

How long I slept, I didn't know. But when I woke up, a blanket covered me. Moshe had entered the room.

"Zeke, wake up," he said, shaking me.

I sat up, fuzzy-brained.

"I located her."

"Who?"

"You know the doctor's wife. Kitty Fowler, the blonde."

"Where, Moshe?"

"I'm going to tell you. But don't rush me. I don't want you screwing it up and blaming me if I'm wrong."

"Okay. No rushing in. Go ahead." *But hurry, dammit.*

"If I'm right, *and I know I am*, the five grand is mine."

The five thousand dollars was Dr. Fowler's money. I told him it would speed up locating his wife. "What about Kitty Fowler? Where is she?" I asked.

He described the house on Elysian Fields Avenue. It was an old house just two blocks from the Edgar Degas House, where the artist stayed during his visit to New Orleans. The area was full of century-old homes with high fences and banana trees crowding backyards, and worn red-brick walkways between the houses. Rather than the stately homes on St. Charles Avenue, the Elysian Fields' homes were filled with bohemian artists, writers, and musicians. He concluded by saying, "One of my snitches led me to her."

Moshe seemed to have an endless string of *Baker Street Irregulars* spread out across the city. He was my best and most reliable source of information for action on the street. He continued, "I did a little more checking myself and found a good-looking blonde holed up in one of the houses."

"There's lots of good-looking blondes in New Orleans, Moshe. How do you know it's her?"

"I saw her myself. My snitch told me she goes swimming at the same time every day. I pretended to be a telephone repair man, working under the raised house re-stapling loose cables. That's when I heard footsteps out on the patio by the pool."

"A woman?"

"Not just any woman—a nude blonde with a beach towel thrown over her shoulder. *She's gorgeous.* Little patch of blonde hair on her … uh, privates. Pink nipples and onion butt."

"Onion butt?"

"Yeah. Brings tears to your eyes. It was her. No mistaking."

"What was she doing?"

"Going swimming. She dove in the pool."

"What did you do then?"

"I got out of there."

"Thanks, Moshe."

"Hey, man, don't forget the five thousand."

"It'll be here."

CHAPTER 71

There was someone hiding out at the Elysian Fields' house. But if Moshe had seen Kitty bathing in the nude, she did not come out for me. My surveillance revealed nothing. Had Moshe scared her off? His handy work included installing tiny, remote CCTV cameras. I sat in a car Moshe provided, watching the cameras overlooking the patio and the pool.

As I've said before, I hate waiting. But now that I was close, it didn't matter. Could Moshe be wrong? No doubt, he saw a naked woman. My only concern is that the sight of her *pint nipples and onion butt* overwhelmed him and he didn't pay attention to her face.

After sunset, I could see the glow of interior lights along the edge of the drawn drapes. At eight, they dimmed.

I was growing more impatient. I wanted—no, scratch that—*needed* to see Kitty Fowler.

The Truth, Dr. Fowler had said, *is with Kitty.*

I wasn't waiting any longer. As I walked to the wrap-around front porch, I checked the revolver Moshe gave me. My heart rate went up. I took some deep breaths until I calmed down. Reminding myself, just do the job you came to do. After all this time, I couldn't be sure what was worse: continuing in ignorance? Or learning the truth? Did I really want to know?

I stood in front of the door and jimmied it open with a credit card as quietly as I could. The lower levels were dark. Could she have left without me seeing? Then I heard a noise upstairs. Stepping with care, I climbed the carpeted stairs to the second level, to a hallway with several doors. The noise was louder now, and coming from a room with the door ajar. I tiptoed and peeped in. A small lamp on the nightstand illuminated two figures in bed—a man and a woman—caught up having sex, missionary style. She was moaning, and he was grunting. From the sound of their love-making, it sounded like they were nearing the finish line for a grand finale.

I debated, should I should let them finish?

Or get on with the job?

They settled the question for me as the guy let out a loud, moose-like groan. "Oh, fuck yeah!" he shouted. "Oh, fuck."

Enough. I stepped into the room and smacked him on the temple with my gun. He fell to the side, flopping on the floor.

She screamed.

"Shut up!" I shouted, pointing the gun at her face, while putting a knee on the bed. She quit screaming and grabbed the sheet, pulling it up to her neck. Her eyes were wide with fright. And then they narrowed.

"Zeke?"

"Hello, Kitty. Surprised to see me?" I said, lowering the gun.

The guy on the floor groaned. She glanced at him. "No, I always expect to be interrupted when I'm fucking."

I nodded towards him. "Another one of your conquests?"

She laughed. "Him? He's just a hot dildo to pass the time. Breaks the monotony."

I got off the bed. I took the belt from his pants that had been thrown on the floor, rolled him over, and tied his arms behind him with the belt. Then I hog-tied his legs using his trouser legs.

Kitty watched all this and got up, put on her robe and lit a cigarette. She poured herself a drink and sat down in a chair to watch me finish. "You playing the role of the jealous husband?"

"Nope, not my job."

She blew a stream of smoke and adjusted her robe. "Then why all the rough stuff?"

"I didn't like waiting while you and Someone-to-pass-the-time whispered sweet nothings in each other's ears."

"Uh-huh," was all she could muster. She took a sip.

I finished gagging him, threw a cover over him, and with my gun motioned her into the next room. She finished her drink and put the glass down on the bedside table.

The second-story living area was rather large, with expensive furniture and plush carpets. We walked through a den with a sofa and a large flat-screen TV on the wall. This opened into the kitchen, where we sat on opposite sides of a counter that held the remains of a half-eaten pizza, an open wine bottle and leftovers of a salad.

This was the moment I'd been waiting for. The reason I had traveled to Carville, to her past, was to find the truth. And here she sat, in front of me. Clearly, now was the time to fill in the gaps of the story. My heartbeat was increasing, and I took a breath and exhaled.

"What I want are some answers," I said.

She just stared at me. "About what?"

"I want the truth about—Jane."

Her mouth opened. Then closed, and she took a long drag before exhaling. "Who is Jane?"

"Oh, *don't* lie to me. You know—*Jane Doe*." I said. "Carlotta Jane Doe. I know about you, *Katrina*. And the orphanage."

"I don't know what you're talking about," she said.

My blood boiled, and I leapt up and came around the counter and shoved the barrel against her temple. She flinched. "You want to die?" I asked her.

Her voice was even. "No."

"Then tell me the truth!" I released the pressure.

She rubbed the side of her temple where the gun had pressed against her. She stared at me. "If you kill me, you'll never learn the truth."

I stepped back. "No shit. I won't know the truth. But *you*, you won't know life."

She crossed and uncrossed her legs. "Okay, fine. Put that *fucking* thing away and I'll tell you the truth about your wife."

I stuck the pistol back into the holster, and I sat down to hear the truth about Jane Doe.

CHAPTER 72

This time, Kitty fixed her drink and sat back down at the kitchen counter.

"So, you know about the orphanage?" she said.

"Yes, I spoke with Sister Ella."

"That bitch! Is she still alive?" She broke out laughing but there was a visible tightening of her jaw. "*God*, I hated that *whore*. What else did she tell you?"

I related the story that the nun told me: their stay in the orphanage, the pregnancy, the baby's death, and the night they ran away. I concluded by telling her about the slash to the nun's cheek. "It's still a long white scar down the side of her face."

Kitty smiled. "Good. Something to remember us by." Then she looked at me and gave a half-shrug. "Well, it's about time I told someone the truth about Jane Doe and Katrina.

"When Jane and I escaped that night, we made it to the river where we encountered the priest. The one who raped me and made me pregnant. He was drunk and attacked us. In the struggle, we all fell into the river. The current grabbed Jane, and I thought she had drowned."

"Drowned?"

"I won't go into that. Just know that after Jane and I were separated, I thought the river had swept her away. I was brokenhearted. My best friend—gone. We were like sisters from the day we met. I loved her. And she was the only one who loved me."

She stroked her glass with a faraway look in her eyes. "I felt guilty. If I hadn't convinced her to run away with me, she'd still be alive. There was nothing for me to do. I couldn't go back to the orphanage and had to keep moving to escape that hellscape."

"How old were you then?"

"Fifteen, but I had the body and the looks of a twenty-year-old."

"And Jane didn't drown," I said.

"No, she did not drown. But I didn't know that." She let out a small chuckle. "Jane thought I *had* drowned."

"So, neither of you knew the other had survived?"

She shook her head. "If only we had known, we might have found each other sooner. But believing the other was dead, we went our separate ways." Her eyes had an empty stare.

Then she looked away. "Well, I won't bore you with the details of my life. I survived on my smile—and my body. Men paid for me. And the Crescent City had just the right mix of local wealth and out-of-town fat-cats willing to pay top dollar. Rich old boys who had a sweet tooth for young, southern bells with honey suckle accents, especially virgins. Someone had deflowered me twenty or more times. Of all the men I met, only one was different. He was a doctor, and he knew I was lying about the virgin thing. He'd been through two marriages and, bless his poor heart, he fell head over heels in love with me. It was Dr. Fowler." She chuckled. "I had grown tired of the fast life anyway. How many times can you get away with screaming in pain when your hymen is broken? He proposed marriage—and I accepted. It was easy."

"What made it turn sour?"

"I didn't realize I was going to get bored." She laughed and drained her glass. "Can you get me another drink?"

I looked around the kitchen.

"Over there in the cabinet."

I poured her a drink. "That's when you started playing around?"

She took a tiny sip. "Whoa, you're getting ahead of me. You want to learn about Jane, right?"

I nodded.

"I thought Jane was just a memory," she said. "A happy memory out of my past—one I seldom visited. And then it happened." She took a full sip.

"What happened?"

"I was walking out of Canal Place. You know, the place with the Neiman Marcus and other high-end stores? That's when I saw a ghost."

"Jane?"

"Yes, my old friend from the orphanage. She was older, of course, not the skinny girl I once knew. Beautiful Jane, in the flesh. But still beautiful, as ever."

"Did she see you?"

"No, not at first. For a minute, I thought I might have been mistaken. A look-alike. It happens, you know."

"So, what did you do?"

"I followed her—she was delivering a painting to a shop in the building. I waited outside on the concourse while she conducted business. My heart was beating as if it might jump out of my chest. I watched her through the picture window. It was her, all right.

"I waited until she came out and walked right up to her. 'Jane. It's me.' And she said, 'Kat!' a name no one had called me since I left the orphanage.

"We both broke down in tears and hugged each other right there on the mezzanine in front of Neiman Marcus. We spent the next two days together, telling what had happened since we last saw each other at the river's edge. Because we thought the other had drowned, we never searched. We just wanted to get away that night."

Kitty got up and walked to the window, parted the drapes an inch, and peered out. The streetlight silhouetted her face. She had a short, pert nose. She looked as if she were trying to decide about something. Turning, she made her way back to the armchair. She said, "You might ask how we could both be living in the same city and never knew it?"

I nodded.

"For starters, we ran in different circles. She changed her name from Jane Doe to Jane Alberato. Where she got her last name, I never asked."

"And your original name was Katrina," I said.

"You know. Then you must know they shortened it to Kat in the orphanage. On my own, in The City That Care Forgot, I changed it to Kitty Lègére, more in line with my profession. I never thought to search for her. After all, the Jane I knew had died that night in the Mississippi River."

I rubbed my face. "So, just to make sure I've got this right: Jane Doe became Jane Alberato. And you became Kitty Lègére."

"Yes, Plus, you need to remember, I wasn't in the most noteworthy profession. And when I met Jane, I was Kitty Fowler, Mrs. Doctor Kitty Fowler."

"Why didn't she ever tell me she had been in an orphanage? Why the big secret?"

She looked at me hard and sighed. "I vowed never to tell anyone what happened that night. When we escaped, we did pretty drastic things."

"You mean the slash on Sister Ella's face?" I asked.

She chuckled. "Even worse. We killed the fucking priest that raped me."

I sat in silent contemplation on what I'd just been told. From the bedroom, the moans of the guy drifted out. "Just a moment," I said, getting up and leaving.

"Don't hurt him," she hollered after me.

I knocked him over the head again and returned. "Just checking his bonds." I sat down and crossed my arms, staring at her.

"What?" she asked.

"That explains why she didn't tell me about her background." I rubbed the back of my neck.

"What else?" she asked.

"There's a bigger question I need answered."

"Such as?"

I stared into Kitty's eyes. "Was Jane involved in the drug operations?"

She did not evade my stare. "You know about that also?"

I nodded. "I want the truth."

"Yes, Jane was involved," Kitty said.

CHAPTER 73

I couldn't believe it. "You're lying."

"Am I?"

I took out my revolver and placed it on the table in front of her. "That can't be. I told you I wanted the truth."

Kitty laughed. "You think that scares me? Zeke, you're a pussy compared to some men I've known. Can you accept the truth?"

I nodded, unable to say the words.

"Then put that away and I'll finish the story. The truth."

I left it there on the table.

"The fact of the matter is that I'm the one to blame for her involvement with the drug operations. I had gotten involved myself with a crook by the name of Theodore Onyx. I think you know him. He sure as hell knows you. And *hates* you."

I nodded.

"As Jane and I reestablished our friendship, I found Jane was quite the art expert. She was intelligent and was an outright authority in all things art."

"Yes, she sure was."

"I introduced her to Onyx. But not in that way. Onyx explained that he wanted to invest in the import of art objects. I didn't realize what he was up to. He wanted her to advise him on what pieces to buy and bring into the country. It was of the utmost importance that he remained anonymous. She acted as the go-between for funneling money to the art museum and other art institutions. The money was actually drug money from the drug cartel. He used dummy corporations to set it up. Art was an excellent cover. And it made her rich."

I raised an eyebrow. "*Rich?*"

"Yeah. Onyx paid her close to a million dollars." She stopped speaking and stared at me. "You didn't *know?*"

I was feeling sick to my stomach. I got up and stood looking at the empty fireplace. The one person I thought was the exception to all the shit that went on in the world—was no better than the rest of the trash I dealt with. The mother of Carla. I turned to look at Kitty. The gun was still on the table. She was eyeing me.

"I could put a bullet through your head," I said.

She laughed. "Then you'd never learn the information I'm going to give you."

I was shaking. "*More?*"

She said, "Someone on the police force is running interference for the drug operations. Theodore Onyx is informed when the police are getting close. That's how his operation could avoid detection for so long."

"There's a snitch on the force?"

"There's a dirty cop in the lineup of the boys in blue. He's well-placed because he's never wrong."

"Do you know who he is?"

She shook her head. "I don't."

Kitty got up and poured another drink. She came and stood by me. I looked up, and she handed *me* the drink.

"You can't ever reveal where you learned this," she said.

I nodded.

"You can't tell anyone where I am, either. My life could be in danger. You understand?"

I took the whiskey down in one swallow. It burned my stomach. My first drink in ...

"Be sure to take your gun with you when you leave. I won't untie him for ten minutes after you're gone."

Outside, the sky was black. The pounding in my chest was just now slowing down.

Should I do the right thing and report this? Bring down justice on the drug smugglers? I realized that was impossible with a snitch in the NOPD.

I also realized if I exposed the crime operation, Jane's reputation would be ruined. It would forever stain the memory of Jane. And she would be forever linked with the drug money.

I debated with myself. *Would it be better if I kept my mouth shut?*

CHAPTER 74

As I drove away from my meeting with Kitty, my mind was fighting to absorb all information she told me. So, Bull *was* right. There was a stool pigeon passing information to the drug cartel. And to my sorrow, Jane was involved.

However, Bull was right on target, but he had no proof. It had all the earmarks of a whitewash. Someone had killed MJ. That made what Jojo Turner did, trying to arrest me for my friend's murder part of the conspiracy. It was after midnight. And I had been through so much in the last few days, that I couldn't be sure I was thinking straight. My heart was hurting as a heavy black cloud hung over me.

I still could not believe Jane was part of a drug smuggling operation.

Was this the truth that Dr. Fowler was referring to? I checked my phone. Bull had called twice. But when I called him, it just went to voicemail.

I headed back to my apartment and was almost there before I remembered the police probably had staked out the place. So I sped up, not sure where I would go. That's when I noticed a car following me. It hung back a couple of blocks and disappeared after I hooked a left. Was I getting jumpy, imagining things? It was not the police because they would have flashed their lights.

I drove back to my original route, which was going nowhere, to tell you the truth. The car appeared again. I took a right, then a left turn. This time, it stuck with me. I supposed I could drive over to police HQ and pull into the lot. That would get rid of them. Ha! Then I'd be arrested. That wouldn't work. The car looked like a late model Ford or Chevy. But Moshe's car had plenty of speed and agility.

Up ahead was the up-ramp by the Superdome and I sped to the I-10 ramp and merged into traffic, heading towards Metairie. I thought I had lost them. But within a mile of the Causeway exit, they were there again. I continued on straight and after half-an-hour, saw the Mandeville exit, past the Spillway. I put my foot on the gas and the car hit a hundred miles per hour. My heart was racing along with the car engine. If I lost control, there was no place to go except over the cement railing and a thirty foot drop into the swamps. They must have had a souped-up car as well, because they kept up.

I was putting a little space between us, when I spotted what I was looking for: The Middendorf's exit at Manchac. The two headlights behind me had fallen behind about a mile.

I killed my lights and slammed on the brakes and started a long skid down the exit ramp. I prayed no car was ahead of me, or stopped at the base of the ramp. My car started fishtailing, and I corrected the skid by steering into it, just as I'd practiced on the police force. As I hit the bottom of the ramp, my front bumper bounced off the street and I spun over both lanes of traffic. The back tires hitting the marshy soup of the pavement.

I jerked the wheel right and shot out of the slush back onto the service road and screeched to a stop on the pavement. *What luck!*

My heart was pounding in my chest. I glanced behind me. *Nothing.*

I took in a deep breath and exhaled it. I had gotten away.

But my relief was brief as I heard the screeching of tires and horns honking on the elevated highway. I saw a pair of taillights backing up.

I jammed on the gas just as a pair of headlights swung onto the ramp. *These guys were good.*

Middendorf's Restaurant was on my left as I shot past. The headlights of the car chasing me swung around, and I heard the scream of their engine. *Where to now?* On my right were deep ditches clogged with weeds and cattails. And on my left, the Lake. Straight ahead, I remembered a cutoff that led to a low bridge that passed over the swamps. It led to the old ground-level Highway 55, long abandoned after the elevated highway came in. Only fishermen and old retirees used it, looking for boat launches. And the Dixie mafia looking to dump bodies.

The car following me must have been holding something in reserve because, within seconds, it was on my tail. The bridge was up ahead on my right. I gunned the engine to get a little more space between us, then slammed on the brakes to make the turn.

The driver must have anticipated my route because he gunned it and slammed into my rear just as I was beginning the turn.

I started losing control.

He didn't let up, and I felt my car turning sideways as it jackknifed.

Looming ahead of me, I saw the side of the bridge. The next thing I knew, I was airborne. And I gripped the steering wheel to brace myself.

The front end went in nose first and a wall of water rushed up to greet me. KABAM! The airbag exploded in my face. But the seatbelt kept me from being speared in my chest by the steering column.

Don't panic—If under unlucky circumstances, your police cruiser plunges into water, don't panic.

Don't Panic! Are you fucking nuts? What the hell?

Water began filling the cab. *God, I'm going to drown!*

Then the water stopped. Of course, it was swamp. The tires had landed on the bottom.

Laughing with relief, I knew then that I would live. Not gonna drown today.

I unbuckled my seat belt to get out when the first bullet hit the air bag. It deflated in seconds.

A quick glance out the driver's window and I saw muzzle flashes from the bridge. Another bullet hit the roof like a hammer on a steel anvil. Those *motherfuckers* were trying to kill me.

I threw myself away from the driver's side. The next bullet shattered the window and buried itself in the dashboard.

I grabbed the passenger door handle and shoved with all my might. It moved only a couple of inches; I was pushing against water and mud. *Don't panic—let the water come in on its own.* I waited just another heartbeat. The water gushed in, and then I was through the door before I could even take a breath.

A couple of shots pinged off the roof.

It was black and cold. Disorienting. I swam, and with two strokes I was hugging the bottom, grabbing at swamp grass and branches. I had gotten turned around. *Where was the car?*

I stuck out my foot and felt the metal. I bent my knees and shoved off, pulling myself along the bottom like an octopus. My head bumped into mush. I had run into the bank. My lungs were burning for air.

Two more shots zinged into the water.

I couldn't come up yet. I began crab walking my way along the bank until I found myself in a jungle of grass. My lungs were screaming, and I had to reach the surface before I drowned.

The jungle was a clump of tall cattails, reeds, and swamp grass. I spit out mud and water and gulped deep breaths. My heart was pounding.

I heard voices bouncing over the surface of the water.

"Do you see him?"

"No."

"Shine that light over there."

I sank down till only my nose and top of my head were out. The light swung by and I thought for sure that I was a dead man. But the light passed right on by.

"Did you hit him?"

"Probably. He hasn't come up yet."

The light swung back and forth over the water for minutes. One said, "Let's get the hell out of here. These bugs are murder." "Wait a minute," the other said.

"What? Do you see something?"

"No, no. Just wait." The unmistakable sound of someone urinating off the bridge reached me.

After a minute, their souped-up engine revved up. It backed off the bridge, turned around, and roared off towards Middendorf's.

I sat in the water for over ten minutes with only my nose and eyes above water, making sure one of them hadn't stayed behind on the bridge. I swam my way back to the car to retrieve what I could. My revolver was under the front seat, but my cell phone had been lost somewhere in the marshy waters.

I shuddered with the realization that if the water had been deeper, I could have drowned. The water was only chest high here. In the commotion, I had lost my shoes as well.

The old Hammond Highway was deserted this time of night. Mosquitoes attacked me like kamikaze pilots as I started walking back. I had gone a hundred yards when I heard an engine. Were they coming back? I was ready to plunge into the big ditches along the edge—but this engine sounded different. No souped-up car this time. Instead it was the sputter and grumble of an old vehicle. In the distance, two headlights appeared, one in need of alignment.

It was an old Ford F-150, like my dad used to drive. I breathed a sigh of relief and held up my hands to flag them down. Fishing poles and a flat-bed aluminum boat stuck out the bed of the truck. It slowed and stopped in front of me, blinding me with its lights. I walked around the side. A hunting dog barked at me from the back, paws on the rail, tail wagging. A round smiling face poked out the side window and greeted me with a hardy, "How ya doin'?"

"I ran off the road," I said in response.

Both of them started laughing. "You ain't the first one. Get in the back, you're too wet to get in the cab. We'll drive you to our fishing camp and you can call your people from there."

• • •

Bull sat in a back booth at the Half Moon Bar and Grill off Magazine Street, nursing a beer when his phone chirped. He did not recognize the number. He answered.

It was Malone.

"Zeke, where the hell you been?" asked Bull.

"Tell you later. But, for now, I need a ride."

CHAPTER 75

Two hours later, Bull picked up Zeke from the fishing camp of the two friendly fishermen and their friendlier hunting dog, Leroy. Zeke swore them to secrecy, and in their good natured way, said they'd drink to that. But only if Zeke had a drink with them. It had only been hours since he took the drink from Kitty Fowler, and over two years before that. But he couldn't refuse their hospitality. Zeke downed a couple of beers to seal the deal and felt light-headed. They loaned him some faded bib overalls, an old Reggie Bush jersey, and a thread-bare terrycloth Sea World towel that he dried his hair with, rubbing out the swamp water. None of their boots fit, so he sat in borrowed socks, listening to Waylon Jennings sing about Luckenbach, Texas. The hound, Leroy, licked his hand and sat under his chair.

Bull pulled a towel out from the trunk and told Malone to put it on the seat. "Don't want it getting greasy."

Malone, already dry, said, "I don't think it can get it any worse. Besides, it will be the first time the seat got cleaned."

As they sped up the ramp to the elevated expressway back home, Malone related the chase and the crash.

Bull asked, "Do you know who it was?"

"No. Just that they were good. Kept up and drove me off the road. One thing's certain, though."

"What?" said Bull, steering into traffic headed towards New Orleans.

"They wanted me dead. I estimate they fired a dozen shots trying to pick me off in the drink."

They drove in silence over the elevated highway that spanned the Spillway.

Bull said, "I got a call."

"From?"

"My contact at the D.E.A."

"Okay, is that the one you called from the Half Moon?"

"Yep. The freighter, the *Santa Maria II*, is registered under a dummy corporation."

"We knew that. Fred told us that."

"Well, what he didn't know is that the *Santa Maria II* is owned by yet another company—a Caribbean holdings corporation."

"A real company?"

"No. Another dummy shell."

As we neared the end of the elevated highway, a passenger plane glided over the swamps to the Louis Armstrong International Airport. I could see the lights of the passenger windows. The 747 seemed to glide only a hundred feet above the tops of the cypress trees. No voters living in the swamp to complain.

"Hmm, let me guess," I said. "The Caribbean company is owned by yet another corporation?"

"Correct. And that one was owned by another, like an M. C. Escher staircase leading nowhere."

It was late at night with little traffic on the streets. We exited at Elysian Fields to pass by my office in the Bywater.

"Who's onto us?" I asked.

"I'm not sure. But there's a bullseye on your back, and those two guys had you targeted."

"With *pistolas*, no less." I said. "No, no, don't park in front." We made a few passes and parked a block away.

"Did you spot anything?" Bull asked.

"No, but no use taking chances."

We walked back to my office, pausing in the shadows, watching, before moving on. The flag-stone carriageway was pitch-black and I could see a dim light on in my office. We drew our weapons and held them at our sides. I led the way up the stairs; the door was ajar.

We stepped into the office. It was a mess: overturned chairs, desk drawers open, papers scattered on the floor, filing cabinets open. I peeked into the bathroom. *No one.*

"What do you think?" asked Bull, putting his gun away.

I righted a chair and sat down at my desk. I held out my hand and spread my fingers apart. Despite my best efforts, my fingers still trembled. "Too much excitement for one night," I said.

Bull roamed the office, toeing the edge of scattered files. "Well, one thing is in our favor."

"What's that?" I asked, fitting together the broken pieces of my Saints coffee mug. "Tell me, Doctor Pangloss, what good do you see coming out of tonight?"

"They think you're dead."

I looked up at him. "You're right, I gotta admit. At least for the time being. What about when no body shows up? And by that, I mean *my* body!"

"Chances are, they'll search for a few days. Maybe they'll think alligators ate you up."

"That's a comforting thought," I said.

"What about the two good-ol'-boys that picked you up?"

"I promised them two hundred a piece if they played dumb."

"Good." Bull rubbed his ham-like hands over the side of his face. "I want you to go underground. At least for a while, or until we can get a better bead on who is behind this."

"Just—play dead?"

"More or less. *Play* dead, so you won't *be* dead."

I nodded. That made sense.

CHAPTER 76

The ferryboat, crossing the Mississippi River from Canal Street to Algiers, always made a racket, so you felt as if you were standing next to a jet engine at takeoff. Bull felt the vibration and rumble from the ten ton engine in his eyeballs, stomach, and groin.

Bull's palms were damp as he parked behind the car in front, and jerked his parking brake, double-checking to make sure it was set. Though he'd ridden the Algiers Ferry hundreds of times, Bull never felt at ease on the river. In his mind's eye, he always saw the Luling Ferry Disaster from decades ago when a twenty-two ton Norwegian tanker T-boned a ferryboat full of women and children, flipping it over into the Mississippi River.

But Bull shook off the feelings of impending disaster, closed his eyes, leaned his head back, and took a deep breath. He unlocked the doors as the ferry revved up its engines, shaking the car.

After a few minutes, a dark figure appeared at the side of his car. The man paused a moment before opening the door and jumping into the passenger seat.

It was Zeke Malone.

They glanced at each other. "It's risky to meet," Bull said. "They found your car. But nobody knows where you are."

"I saw the news reports. Let's keep it that way. What else?"

"There's a warrant for your arrest," Bull said. "For murder. They think you killed MJ."

Both men sat silently as they each thought about the funny little man in his oversized lab coat and coke-bottle glasses.

Bull said, "And it's official. I'm off the force."

"Wait. Why?"

Bull told him about the disciplinary committee. He also filled him in on the DEA investigation. "We need to keep this quiet. If there's a snitch in the department, the entire operation could explode in our face. And we could end up in the swamps as gator bait, *for real this time.* We can't make any more mistakes."

The ferry reached mid-river, and the engine revved up as it fought the current. Bull clutched the steering wheel.

"It's going to be tough to get anything done," said Zeke. "With you off the force and me officially dead. What are we gonna do?"

"Lay low. Allow it to play out on its own. Hang in the background till the time's right for us to strike."

"Anything else?" Zeke asked.

"Nothing. I'll keep you posted," Bull said.

"Okay." And with that, Zeke jumped out of the car and disappeared between the other vehicles.

As the ferry approached the Algiers side, the decks bucked up and down like the back of a bronco. Taking a deep breath, he held it in. The ferry bumped into the pillars and the engines roared as it reversed. He waited until the men tied up to the wharf before releasing the emergency brake and putting the car in gear. It was then, he finally released his breath.

CHAPTER 77

Zeke strapped on a protective Kevlar vest that could absorb the force of a bullet up to a twenty-caliber. It could save his life. But the vest was useless against the newer, more powerful, steel-coated, armor-piercing rounds. He took a gunshot to the chest once, knocking him off his feet. The Kevlar vest saved his life, though he was black-and-blue for a month. But in the end, he did survive.

It was no surprise, Bull's old friend, Elroy Mandrix, led the DEA raid on Theodore Onyx's drug operation. Agent Mandrix had twenty years of outstanding service, gray hair on the side, a lined face, and a reputation for *getting the job done*. He and Bull were similar. Both tough men—both with a *Just Do The Job* attitude.

The agents uncovered an old map in the archives of the Louisiana Historical Society, dating back to when streetcars still rode on Desire Street. The map revealed a tunnel leading to an adjacent building.

Although Bull was *officially* off the police force, and Zeke still had an outstanding arrest warrant, Mandrix insisted on deputizing both men. After a quick swearing-in ceremony, both men received temporary designations: Special Field Agent. Bull was assigned to guard the tunnel.

Zeke was to go with Agent Mandrix to identify Onyx, since he had arrested and knew him by sight. Easy. Just find a short, fat, man looking like a well-dressed white Buddha. They wanted him alive.

Standing behind Mandrix, Zeke's heart was thumping faster than he liked, and he took deep breaths to slow its pace. Over a dozen DEA agents, with weapons drawn, crouched like a troop of simians in front of a green exit door.

Zeke said, "I hate to bring this up, Elroy, but ... "

Elroy stared back at him. "Something wrong?"

"I don't have a weapon."

Elroy pulled up his pants leg, revealing an ankle holster, and took out a pistol. It was a snub-nose Beretta, small in Zeke's hand. He checked the chamber. Loaded. Yet, still, his heart rate remained unchanged.

He waited for the signal to begin.

•   •   •

Meanwhile, a hundred yards away, in the abandoned building across Desire Street, Bull followed the map down rickety stairs to a sub-basement filled with broken wood crates and discarded furniture. His original expectations were that an underground passage would no longer exist. And to his surprise, he found the tunnel where the map said it would be. But for what purpose? Did they need escape tunnels a hundred years ago?

Unpainted wooden sheets covered the entrance to the tunnel. Tracks in the dust leading to and from the door showed recent use. He loosened the trigger guard on his revolver.

With a few good shoves, the wood gave way. A stiff breath of moist air hit his face and neck. His nostrils pinched against the damp, earthy odor of rotting timber. The shaft was about four feet wide, the walls and ceiling lined with plastic panels you might find in a do-it-yourself shower display from Home Depot. An inch of water stood on the concrete floor.

No use making himself a silhouetted target. With difficulty, Bull shoved the plywood back into place. Better to wait in the larger area if there was going to be a fight. There was nothing to do at the moment, so he found a wooden crate to sit on and waited for the action to begin.

• • •

At that moment, Agent Elroy Mandrix nodded to the man in charge of the explosives. The plastik on the doorknob ignited with a *WHUMP!* and a puff of smoke. The EXIT became an ENTRANCE. Zeke followed Elroy and his men as they stormed into a narrow stairwell. On the opposite side of the building, a second team of DEA agents entered the building, and Zeke heard gunfire as he barreled up the stairs, two at a time.

At the top, a figure appeared with an automatic weapon pointed at them. Zeke's heart leapt into his throat, but the gunman hesitated, and that was his mistake. A barrage of bullets hit him dead center, knocking him back. His finger must have death-squeezed the trigger because his automatic weapon sprayed into the ceiling. Plaster rained down on Zeke's head.

The federal officers leaped over the gunman's body, and two agents scurried down the hall. On the next level, they repeated the process, leaving two investigators to secure each floor. When they reached the top floor, only Elroy and Zeke remained.

"Theodore Onyx is here," the agent said, pointing his weapon down the passage.

They entered. A janitor stood in the middle of the hall, hands in the air, his eyes saucers.

Mandrix shouted, "Down on the floor! Don't get up until the police say so!"

He complied.

The last room took most of the top level. A penthouse, locked. "Stand back." And with two shots, it banged open. "DEA Agents!" he shouted. "We're armed! Show yourself!"

This was a critical moment. Zeke felt a jolt of fear as they entered. The only reply was the muffled voice of a sportscaster announcing a football game. The apartment was well-furnished, with mirrored ceilings, a gigantic well-stocked bar, crystal chandeliers, plush peach-colored sofas, and a monster-sized flat-screen TV.

Next to it was an elevator with gold buttons.

Mandrix shook his head and muttered, "*Damn!* They must have just put that in. Wasn't on any blueprints."

The door to another room, unlocked. Both men positioned themselves on either side.

Zeke wrinkled his nose. "Do you smell that?"

Elroy nodded. "Yeah. Burning hair."

After yelling another warning, they entered. Theodore Onyx sat in an expensive leather executive chair at a desk, and spread out in front of him were expensive bottles of wine, fluted glasses, and a pasta bowl. He was face-down in a plate of spaghetti.

"Jesus Christ," Mandrix said, doing a double-take.

Onyx had no face. The back of his skull had a large hole where someone had shot him—execution style. Judging by the powder burns, the muzzle was likely only inches away. Bits of brains, spaghetti, and blood dotted the calendar, pen set, and computer screen. The Saints' 2009 Superbowl victory was replaying on the flat-screen.

After a moment's hesitation, Zeke lowered his gun and sat in a high-backed Windsor chair, his mind trying to wrap around the number of deaths. *What the hell is going on here?* It started with Leslie Barrone, the female impersonator. Shot dead by Clive Bronsky. Then his mind flashed to the professional hit that left everyone in the Oasis Club, dead: Presley, Clive, the barman, and the five unlucky patrons.

And though he couldn't prove it, he was certain that Jane was also a victim in all of this mess.

Zeke glanced at the fat body slumped across the desk, half his head blown away. An odd twinge popped into his thoughts: *If Theodore Onyx was behind this and ordered their deaths ... ?*

Then who ordered Onyx's death?

•　　•　　•

Across the street, fifteen feet below street level, Bull heard the gunshots reverberating in the tunnel. After a few minutes, he heard two sets of footsteps running towards the exit, splashing in the water. Bull stood and aimed his pistol torso high. The plywood door flew open and two men burst through.

The first one through was the short, built-like-a-fireplug Nazi with the crew cut, pistol in his hand. Behind him, Bowling Ball at his heels.

Bull shouted, "Drop your weapons!"

The two froze for a second, but instead of dropping his gun, the Nazi raised his and fired. The bullet impacted in the wall above Bull's head, scattering mortar. A fraction of a second later, Bull fired, hitting the short man mid-chest. He fell backwards at the feet of the man behind him.

Pleasantly smiling, Bowling Ball slowly raised his hands. He was tall, taller than Bull, and outweighed him by forty or more pounds. "I have no gun, Detective Bull." He stepped over his fallen comrade.

"You know my name?"

"Yes. You've been trying to find the shooter in the Oasis Club." His shoulders were massive under his coat, like a row of bowling balls in a rack.

"*Okay,* you know me. And now we've met," Bull said. "So, were you the shooter? I saw the closed circuit videos. And the shooter sure looks a lot like you."

"You want me to confess?" He curled his lip and laughed. "The most you can get me on is running away from gunfire."

"Nonetheless, I'm bringing you in," Bull said.

"Not me."

"Look, you can make this easy or you can make it hard. I'd rather *easy.*"

"I'd rather it be neither," Bowling Ball said.

"Or I can shoot you in the kneecap and call for an ambulance. Your choice. But you are going in."

"I don't want that, Detective Bull," he said, drawing himself up to his full height. "And ... I think ... neither do you."

Bull tilted his head to the side. "What does that mean?"

"Look, I know you are a big dick, Detective. But when did they let the piggy grease of the mall, you sorry sack of *shit.*"

"What did you just call me?" Bull's nostrils flared.

"You heard me. You are big. But I am bigger. You are fast. But I'm faster."

Bull said nothing, but felt the heat flush through his body.

Bowling Ball continued, "So, let's make it an even match. No guns."

Bull laughed. "What is this? You expect me to put down my gun and fight you?"

"Why not? Let's see who is the better man. You aren't afraid, are you?"

Bull didn't respond.

"I'll tell you what. I'll sweeten the pot, Detective Shitbox. If you win, I'll confess to the Oasis Club murders."

"And if I lose?"

"Then I walk."

Bull leaned back and evaluated the big man again. He probably carried forty more pounds of muscle than Bull. But how much of it was gym-machine-manufactured and steroid shots? Bulk did not mean speed.

"I'll tell you what, Detective Bull. I'm going to make it easy for you."

"How's that?"

"I'm gonna walk towards you and stop at three feet."

"I wouldn't do that."

"You can either put the gun down and start fighting," said Bowling Ball. "Or you can shoot me. I've got nothing to lose." And with that, he began walking towards Bull.

"That's far enough," Bull said, backing up. But the giant continued walking right up to him and halted three feet away.

"What's it gonna be? Or have you gotten soft from all those damn Krispy Kremes?" Bowling Ball said.

Bull aimed the gun at his chest and fought the temptation to pull the trigger.

"I'll count to three and then I'm going to tear your head off. One ..."

Bull cocked the hammer.

"Two ..."

Bull hit him on the count of two with a left hook to the chin. It was cheating, but who's counting? Bowling Ball staggered backwards. The two eyed each other. Then Bull held up his Glock 22 at eye level, dropped the magazine, and tossed his weapon onto the crate. He smiled slowly and stepped away, putting up his fists. The two men faced off, circling each other. Bowling Ball smirked and put his meat-hooks up into a boxer's stance. That was his first mistake—trying to box with Bull.

Bowling Ball feinted with jabs to no avail, then appeared to grow impatient. He jabbed with his left before throwing a looping right hook, a real haymaker that Bull avoided by ducking and letting it slide by, into thin air. After it passed, with Bowling Ball off balance, Bull stepped in and smacked him on the bridge of his nose with two sharp rights. He heard bones crack as he threw his full weight into both shots. His opponent stumbled back, blood gushing from his nose. He straightened up, swiping the back of his hand under his nose, looked down at the blood, and seemed a little surprised.

He cleared his throat and spit out a glob of blood at Bull's feet and gritted out behind a bloody grin, "You ain't got me yet, boy," lifting his bulky shoulders in a show of force. They circled again, and

Bowling Ball threw glancing blows off Bull's shoulders. He hesitated about pitching another haymaker, and Bull took advantage of that delay and threw two quick jabs at his right eye. His brow cut open, blood streaming down. He staggered back, his sneer gone, squinting out of one eye. At that point, he changed tactics and decided to use a technique that had worked in the past, to overpower Bull with the sheer force of his weight and muscles.

After a moment's hesitation, he charged. That was his second mistake. Bull sidestepped to his blind side, tripping and shoving him into empty crates, toppling a stack of two-by-fours that were leaning against the wall. Bowling Ball got up like an enraged buffalo and charged at him again, head down. Bull stepped aside and caught him with a left uppercut to his chin as he passed, then crossed with a right into the side of his skull, making a sound like a cracked walnut. Bowling Ball toppled to his knees before falling forward on his face with a satisfying SPLAT!

Like a young Muhammad Ali, Bull stood above his foe. He retrieved his pistol, reloaded the clip, holstered it before taking his cuffs, snapping one end on Bowling Ball's wrist, the other to water pipes sticking out of the wall.

Then Bull called an ambulance, gave his location, and sat down on a crate to wait.

CHAPTER 78

Later that night, Kitty Fowler was preparing for bed.

She enjoyed sleeping in the nude, but tonight, *It's chilly. Summer passed so quickly.* So, she slipped on an XL T-shirt on her way to turn off the TV, toothbrush in her mouth. Suddenly, she let out a small *Eek!* Theodore Onyx's mugshot was on the screen.

She couldn't believe her eyes. Onyx looked slim, about twenty years younger, with a police plaque of numbers held beneath his chin. *Probably from the days in Angola.* He had allowed no photos since then.

On the news, a young woman reporter, in a too-tight dress and heavy eye makeup, announced that a powerful "Drug Smuggling Operation" had been busted earlier in the night. DEA agents stormed a warehouse on the 1900 block of Desire Street, near the docks, allegedly the headquarters of a drug cartel.

The announcer, looking very young, dressed like a model, stood in front of *Police: Do Not Cross* tape, giving details of the shootout. Behind her, the flashing lights of police cruisers and ambulances reflected off old brick warehouses. And policemen stood about in clusters, as they often do by the time cameras arrive. The report cut to footage of criminals, disheveled and handcuffed, being led and placed in patrol cars. The attractive reporter said, "Unfortunately, the head of the drug ring, Theodore Onyx, was not apprehended. Rather, he was shot during the raid and died on the scene."

"Well, I'll be *damned* ... " Kitty Fowler mumbled, too overwhelmed to grasp all the details. The TV report was over in a minute, and advertising for *"One Call, That's All!"* replaced it. She flopped on her bed, her legs feeling limp, and her head a whirlwind.

Does that mean I can come out of hiding?

She spent a sleepless night flipping through the channels, trying to get the full story. The next morning, in a state of near exhaustion, she scoured the newspaper for more facts. Finally, she came across the headline that read:

SIX DIE IN DRUG RAID

Over the next several days, follow-up stories reported another raid was executed on the offices of Goldenstein Accounting Agency off Lake Boulevard. Kitty was not surprised to see Zip Romero, attorney for Gilbert Goldenstein, telling the media his client knew nothing about any illegal operations. That he was just a law-abiding accountant that had done some peripheral work for Theodore Onyx. "My client is innocent," he announced.

Kitty re-read the articles to be certain she understood correctly and kept the local news channels on. The next night, she went to bed with a floating sensation, as if a burden had been lifted. If she had been religious, she would have made the sign of the cross before hugging her pillow and collapsing into a coma-like sleep.

It had been four days since the raid, and the story had moved to page eight. *It's foolish to go out in public again. Too soon,* she told herself. But by ten that morning, she had made up her mind to venture out. Where would she go? It was too early for bar-hopping. And she didn't feel like shopping.

A cup of coffee! That was it. One of her favorite pastimes, after a night out drinking, she enjoyed relaxing in a local coffee shop, sipping café au lait, eating *beignets* or savoring a French sugar-coated danish. Her mouth was already watering.

Although she had decided to leave, she still felt uncomfortable with the risk. Someone might recognize her. *Are they still out there? Still looking for me?* Staring in the mirror, she thought, she couldn't go out looking like Kitty Fowler. No high heels, no short skirt, no low-cut blouse. Must wear awful jeans, bulky shirt, and NY baseball cap.

She leaned into the mirror, examining her face, tucked as much of hair as she could under the cap, and tying the rest into a ponytail. Skipping lipstick, she slipped on a pair of aviator glasses. She stared a long time into the reflection, and a wave of sorrow swept over her, the futility of her marriage. Of her life. Reduced to sneaking around in disguise to stay alive. Finally, she left the apartment, stood on the balcony, her hands trembling. She almost went back inside. *"Don't be a chicken shit,"* she told herself.

Forcing herself down the stairs, she cut through several back streets before making her way over to a taxi stand near the Quarter. The taxi took her to Canal Street and dropped her off by the St. Charles streetcar line. Her timing was perfect—a streetcar heading towards Audubon Park approached, rattling and clattering on the tracks. It dinged-dinged, shuddered to a stop, and she ran to catch it. She jumped on, paid her fare, and took a seat on one of the wooden benches facing so she could check anyone getting on and off, front and back.

Near the river, where the line turned to go up Carrollton Avenue, she got off by the Camilla Grill but realized it was too noisy and public. Instead, she walked two blocks over to a small coffee shop where she and Jane used to meet before—before the explosion killed Jane, and before the cartel wanted *her* dead. The little cafe had a large storefront window with a huge hand-painted white flower. Surrounding that, the curved words *Magnolia Grill* and *Fresh Breakfast Guaranteed* formed a circle. It sat two blocks from the Mississippi River in a block of small shops—a bookstore, a clothing boutique, a dry cleaners. She scanned the small grassy postage-sized park across from the grill. A homeless woman sat on a bench by an overloaded shopping cart beneath a crape myrtle with gnarled limbs.

Kitty opened the restaurant door. The inside smelled of coffee, eggs, and greasy bacon. There was a counter and a narrow corridor leading to the bathrooms, a rear exit, and an emergency door to the side with a sign above it. Three escape routes. Only a few customers sat at tables, and she took one with her back against the wall, affording her a view of the street. She took off her dark glasses when the waitress, a middle-aged lady with a smile, approached carrying a water glass and silverware in a plastic sleeve.

"What ya have, Hon?"

"Uh, just coffee ... " But then she realized she was starving. The waitress turned to walk away, and Kitty said, "No, no, wait. I'll have the Big Breakfast."

She drank her coffee and devoured the meal. Yummy, yummy, indeed. Afterwards, pushing away the plate with a few leftover scraps, she took a third cup of coffee and leaned back, staring vacantly out the window.

How does a woman let herself go like that? Kitty mused. The homeless woman dressed like straight out of Woodstock. Multiple layers of shirts over sweaters, an ankle-length gingham skirt and a broad, floppy man's hat covering her graying, straggly hair. A relic from another era.

Kitty was raising her cup to her lips when her heart froze. She realized that the street woman was staring at her through the steamed glass windows. Her skin tingled. *No, it couldn't be—But it was.* The bag lady's unwavering gaze fixed on her.

Had they found her?

Beneath those folds of clothing, a knife or gun could be hidden. Maybe it had been too early to venture out? Trying not to appear frightened, which was what she was, she spilled coffee on the tablecloth, rattling the cup into the saucer. Her hands now felt limp and cold, and an icy sensation in her stomach made her nauseous.

Kitty felt her mouth going dry. She turned and gave a wave to the waitress, trying not to appear panicky. She paid the bill. Out of the corner of her eye, she saw the woman had not moved. Who was she? Maybe all she wanted was a handout. *Or maybe all she wanted was to kill me. Will I die when I walk outside?*

"Do you have a bathroom?" she asked the waitress.

"Yeah, just down the hall, Honey. Be careful, sometimes the door don't shut right."

Kitty locked herself in the bathroom. *How stupid to venture out so soon?* Her heart in high gear. *I can't stay locked in this bathroom forever.*

She cautiously unlocked the door, sneaking a peek into the dining area. Nothing. As quietly as possible, she shoved the bar of the exit door and stepped out into the sunlight. It was an alleyway with trash cans, stacks of pallets, and a dented, rusted dumpster. The stench made her want to go back, but the door had locked. A calico cat feeding on trash looked up at her before dashing off.

The alley was a dead end at one end. The open end led to a narrow side street and a row of boarded buildings. She saw the edge of the levee beyond. There was only one way out and she started sprinting when she heard footsteps running towards the entrance.

Before she got halfway, to her horror, the homeless lady turned into the alley.

Kitty froze. Trapped.

The bag lady started walking towards her, removing her floppy hat, removing the gloves with the fingers cut off.

She was smiling ridiculously. "Kitty, don't scream," the lady said. It was a voice so familiar that Kitty thought she was dreaming.

Kitty couldn't believe her eyes. It was like looking at a ghost.

"Jane ... Jane Malone? It can't be." Tears flowed. She choked back sobs. "You're supposed to be dead."

"Not hardly," said Jane, removing the gray wig and shaking out her hair. They embraced in the alley for minutes until a garbage truck rattled into the alleyway.

"Let's get out of here." The two friends made their way arm-in-arm to the levee overlooking the Mississippi River. They sat on the grass and talked for hours, watching the river barges and gigantic tankers steam by.

"Now, here's my plan," said Jane. "We must execute it with no *fuck-ups.*"

Kitty Fowler nodded.

CHAPTER 79

At seven o'clock, Lukas Spinoza cheerfully left the *New Orleans Art Museum*, locking his office door and stepping lightly down the museum stone stairs. He left after examining a new painting by a local artist, Martin Covert—the painter had only recently died, drowned in a freak boating accident. Demand for his paintings, purple alligators in the swamps, was growing, and the prices were skyrocketing. He was amused at how much the public would pay for a piece of art when the buzz started and the price went up. *Like buying stock.*

That morning, he was surprised to find a note stuffed beneath the door of his office at the museum.

I need to see you.
At the River Road Plantation.
Come at eight tonight.

He read it and smiled. There was no signature, but there was a lipstick kiss. It could only come from one woman: *Kitty Fowler.*

Spinoza guided his new, silver Lexus across the Mississippi River Bridge, enjoying the wind streaming on his face—how long since he made love with Kitty Fowler?—he fantasized her luxurious body beneath him, her moans like a whore. He exited the off-ramp and followed the twist and turns along River Road to the Fowler Plantation. The Lexus LC 500, with its 471 horsepower, was a beast, and he had to be careful not to give it too much gas. The curves on River Road sneak up during the day, but in the dark they could be even trickier. Like driving through a cave.

That crazy broad is taking an enormous risk inviting me to meet her—at the Fowler Plantation, no less! So was that where she'd been hiding? He should have guessed. Almost in plain sight. Much had been left unsaid between them when she vanished. In fact, the last time they were together, the last time he had sex with her, they were in the air-conditioned building attached to the glass greenhouse at the Fowler Plantation. It was her favorite place to get with him. *To get it on.* Spinoza preferred a hotel room for their romps, but she insisted.

Slowly, he pulled into the isolated driveway leading to the plantation. The gravel crunched beneath the tires. The burnt-out hulk of a main building was a black hole, swallowing up all light. He maneuvered his car around the ruins. The surrounding thick woods gave him a claustrophobic feeling, like being in a giant unlit auditorium.

The greenhouse was dark. At the sight of it, a thrill ran through him as he remembered her embraces. His heart rate upped a notch. However, he couldn't help but have misgivings. Glancing at the dashboard clock, he saw he had arrived promptly at eight. He gripped the wheel tighter, not sure what to feel: joy, dread, or excitement. The headlights lit the interior of the greenhouse. As the car sat idling, he wondered whether he should get out or drive off.

After a moment, the overhead fluorescent lights of the greenhouse flickered and popped on, illuminating the jungle of flowers and ferns. He chuckled to himself. *That old doctor sure took extra care of those plants. For what? So that others could bed his wife on a cot between the orchids?*

A minute passed before he saw her, and much like an actress entering the stage, she stepped out from behind a row of palm leaves, decked out in a red blouse and a sexy white skirt. Blonde hair hung down to her shoulders. Even from a distance, he could tell she had lost none of her shape, or beauty.

Being in hiding must have agreed with her. Probably made her extra horny. He expected taking her in his arms and satisfying her passion. And his own. He was giddy with excitement.

Spinoza killed the engine and shoved open the door. He could feel his own fire and was ready to take her, to caress that lovely body. His first impulse was to rush inside, but he gained control. *Don't act overeager. Let her start.* She must be ready after being on the run for so long. He hurried into the open doorway.

She did not move, but gazed at him. Unsmiling. Something was not right. He had expected her to run and throw her arms around him. Instead, she stood, arms crossed, with a frown. He'd come here for a tryst, but her expression said otherwise.

He tried to kiss her. "You've come back."

She turned her face so his kiss fell on her cheek. "I don't think so."

He stepped back. "But your note said you needed to see me?"

"Actually," she said, uncrossing her arms. "I came to say *goodbye* to you."

He hadn't expected that. "You called me all the way out here to tell me that?"

"You know *why* I want to say goodbye. The reason is you. I'm on the run because of *you.*"

Spinoza scratched the side of his nose. "Care to explain?"

"You're the thief, the mind behind the smuggling of artwork, aren't you?"

Spinoza narrowed his eyes, staring at Kitty hard. "You're just guessing."

"At first, I couldn't understand your interest in Jane Malone. You were using her to smuggle narcotics into New Orleans. It was all a very convenient set-up. You imported legitimate art pieces for the museum. What she didn't know was that the art had hollowed-out secret compartments."

"That's a pretty elaborate fairy tale you've concocted there, little darling." He started laughing. "Unfortunately, none of it is true."

"Oh, don't you patronize me! You're the one who ordered Jane's death!"

The laugh caught in his throat. He glared at her. "That's a pretty serious accusation to be made, Kitty. Besides, everyone knows that the boy with the explosives was a retarded kid. Who else would strap dynamite to his chest and demand a million dollars?"

"You've got an answer for everything. You and your cronies set Jane up to be murdered."

"Who's going to believe you? You're an ex-hooker with a drinking problem and you wouldn't make a credible witness. You hired a cross-dresser to cover your affairs." Spinoza shook his head. "You got it wrong. I'm through with *you*, not the other way around. You were okay for kicks! A good fuck. But let's face it, Kitty, you're *trash*."

"You mean trash like *you?* You're nothing more than a *son* of a cock-sucking *whore*." she shot back. "When I first met you, I thought: 'Here is a respectable professional—the head of a major museum.' But you're just a *fucking creep* like the rest of them. Only you dress better."

He snorted. "Kitty, still living in a dream world. Don't you know you were the one that got passed around?"

"I don't care! I'm going to the cops."

"Yeah, I wouldn't do that," he said.

"Oh, why not? You think I don't know there's a snitch in the police department?"

"So, I've been told."

"What you don't know is that before Jane Malone died, she confided in me. She found out about the smuggling operation. She suspected you, but wasn't sure. But *now*, I'm sure. Lukas, I know you. You headed the operation. And since I can't go to the police, I'll have to go public. I'm sure that Dan Milwaukee, with his EYE ON THE

CITY, would just love to hear how the director of our beloved museum was the mastermind behind a drug cartel."

"I can't let you do that." He stepped towards her and grabbed her arm.

She tried to step back, but his grip was vice-like, digging into the flesh of her arm. "You're hurting me."

His eyes blazed. "You will not talk to anyone," he said through clinched teeth. In one quick move, he lifted his hand to her throat.

She shoved him with all her might, pulling away from his grip. Her purse sat open on a potting table, hidden by ferns. She reached in and pulled out a small pocket pistol.

He pulled up short. It was a small caliber, but could still be deadly at point-blank range. His eyes moved back to her face, trying to evaluate if she was serious. She was serious. He stepped back and drawled. "Why are you *doing* this? There's plenty of money to go around. We can make a deal."

"What do I need with money? I married it. Now, he's on his last leg with terminal cancer. I'll soon be wealthy. What do *I* need with more money? Especially if I'm dead?"

"Nobody's talking about killing you."

"Don't bullshit me. You had Jane killed. And you're probably behind the Oasis Club massacre. And if that fat weasel, Theodore Onyx, was alive, he'd be singing for his supper, and you'd be the goose that gets cooked."

"He can't sing. Not now."

"So I read. The agents shot him during the raid of his hideout."

"No, he was dead before they got to him. I ordered the hit. My word ... " He paused as if to emphasize. "*My word* put a bullet through his head."

"I don't believe you," she said.

"Look, I knew Onyx was one of your lovers. He and I go way back. He needed to smuggle in the drugs and came to me to use legitimate artwork as a cover. You never knew this, but Theodore Onyx was the one that called me and arranged our meeting—*purely by accident,* you see. You were my conduit to Jane Malone. Onyx said I would like you. He was right. Onyx pimped you out." He was standing in front of her, staring into her eyes. "What I didn't know at the time was that I would develop a genuine passion for you."

"You're lying."

"Am I? A spy in the police department told me the federal raid was coming down. I knew they'd eventually get Onyx to roll over. I couldn't afford that. So he had to die."

"A snitch. Who?"

Lukas Spinoza shook his head. "That's top secret. No one knows but me."

"I don't care. I'm going to go public."

In a flash, his fist shot out and caught her on the chin. She stumbled back in surprise, stunned. This isn't the way it was supposed to end. When she recovered, she saw he had the gun in his hand.

He was breathing hard, eyes wide. "You stupid *bitch*. You aren't going anywhere."

And before she knew it, he pulled the trigger.

The report of the gunshots rattled the glass panes inside the greenhouse.

Blood spurted from her chest, and she fell backward. Her hands flayed at the limbs of a short ficus tree and a Boston fern as she collapsed between leaves, closing over her like a curtain.

CHAPTER 80

Lukas Spinoza stood with the gun still in his hand, arm extended, a ribbon of smoke curling from the barrel. He couldn't believe what he had just done. *Shot her pointblank in the chest.* He stared down at her legs sticking out from beneath the plant leaves, like the legs of the witch from *The Wizard of Oz.*

It was one thing to order a man's execution. Someone else always carried out the job. But to do it yourself? It was a high he hadn't experienced before, the adrenaline coursed through his veins. He was almost euphoric.

A voice said behind him, "Nice shootin', partner."

Spinoza whirled.

Two men walked in the doorway from the darkness outside. He recognized the shorter of the two—Zeke Malone, the ex-cop who visited him at the museum digging up information on *Los Tres Jeffes*—Jane's husband.

The other one was a gigantic bear of a man, with a mustache that hung down both sides of his mouth. Mustache walked calmly up to Spinoza and jerked the gun out of his hand.

"Lukas Spinoza, you're under arrest. Put your hands behind your back," he said, spinning him around, pulling a pair of handcuffs from his back belt.

Zeke hurried over to the fallen body of Kitty, parting the leaves of the ficus. He stared down at her.

"You all right?" he asked.

Blood oozed from her mouth. She opened her eyes and blinked several times. "Sure, why not? It isn't every day that a gal gets shot!"

Zeke took her arm and helped her to a seated position.

Spinoza did a double take. "I just shot you." His eyes widened. "You're dead." Kitty worked a wad from the side of her mouth and spit out a red plastic capsule. "Not hardly." Zeke helped her to her feet. She wiped her chin with the back of her hand as the front of her blouse still oozed blood.

"But I—"

Bull turned him around and shoved him against a wooden table before patting him down.

Zeke offered Kitty his handkerchief.

"Thanks," she said, wiping her neck and arms. She began unbuttoning the white blouse that was soaked in blood, untucking it from the red skirt. Bull took the gun and removed the clip and held it up in front of Spinoza's face. "Blanks." Kitty stripped down to her waist, exposing two perfectly shaped breasts and a large square flesh-colored tape covering wires. She peeled it off and said, "God, these things are itchy."

Zeke said to Spinoza. "Haven't you heard of movie props? Fake blood capsules activated by hand. Looks like the real thing, doesn't it?"

Kitty peeled off two more strips of tape, then pulled out wires attached to a small microphone. She handed the mic to Zeke.

Spinoza blurted, "You'll go down with me, Kitty."

Bull said, "She's already confessed to the DEA her part of the drug operation. For her cooperation, she gets immunity."

"Besides," she said, tossing her bloody blouse to the tile floor. She took one of Dr. Fowler's old denim work shirts off a hook and put it on. "I got the best attorney in the world to make a deal for me—*Zip Romero.*"

"You'll never make it stick," Spinoza said.

"Don't bet on it," Bull said.

Smiling, Kitty washed her hands off with a water hose. "And since we are coming clean with everything," she said, drying her hands with a towel, turning towards Spinoza. "You never were a good lay. I had to fake it with you all the time."

Bull laughed and shook his head.

Then she pivoted towards Zeke. "And since we are coming clean, I have something to tell you, Zeke Malone."

He frowned and held up the palms of his hands. "Need I remind you? We never went to bed, Kitty."

"Not that. It's something else."

Zeke said, "What else?"

"Oh, a lot more. But the best is yet to come." She beamed.

Zeke cocked his head and raised an eyebrow. "Like what?"

"The best part of the night."

"*What* are you talking about?" Zeke said.

Kitty turned and stared at the back door of the greenhouse.

Zeke turned and peered into the dark doorway. After a beat, a woman appeared. She was wearing an oversize blue workman's shirt and a baseball cap. Zeke froze, speechless, staring in disbelief. He couldn't be sure if she was a phantom or just his mind playing tricks. But there was no mistaking those grass-green eyes.

"Jane ... " he stammered as he reached out to touch her, to reassure himself. "Are you real?"

She smiled through her tears. "Yeah, it's me. And I'm real."

He didn't remember running to her. But then they were in each other's arms, embracing like two long-lost souls. It seemed like only yesterday that he had kissed and held her in his arms. That first kiss was beautiful and passionate, and so deep that it seemed he was tumbling down a rabbit hole into an alternate reality.

They kissed and he still could not believe it was her. He remembered the past two years of dreams. Of holding her. Of kissing her. His heart drummed in his chest, and his legs felt weak. He held tight, as if she might slip away. *Please don't let this be a dream,* he thought.

She leaned back and said, as if she knew what he was thinking, "No, I'm not a dream, Zeke. I'm real." Then she sobbed into his neck. Her athletic body, her straight back, felt unchanged in his embrace. There was a familiar warmth. The scent of shampoo and pixie sticks, the heat of her body, were all still the same. She looked older, tired but happy. Still beautiful. He brushed off her baseball cap, and it fell to the floor between elephant ears and begonias.

"You dyed your hair. Dark."

"Yeah, I was wondering when you'd notice."

He whispered, "Jane, stay with me forever?"

"*Always.*" She put her lips under his ear and kissed the curve of neck like she'd done a thousand times before, sending shivers down his spine.

Never let it end, he thought. *Don't wake me. Don't wake me.*

At that instant, the windows of the greenhouse exploded inward, spraying glass like confetti. Gunshots rang out.

CHAPTER 81

Zeke shoved Jane to the ground between the potted plants as bits of pottery and wood rained down on them.

Detective Bull knocked Lukas Spinoza to the slate floor underneath a flower table. Kitty Fowler leaped behind them. Shots continued to shatter the greenhouse windows.

Bullets snapped the stems of small trees, flowers, and shrubbery like a thrashing machine. Ceramic pottery exploded into thousands of pieces. Bull, using his broad back and thick neck, flipped the table onto its side to serve as a shield against the bullets.

Then, just as quickly as it started, the shooting stopped.

Zeke's ears were ringing. His heart pounded in his chest.

Bull grabbed Spinoza by the shirt and pulled his face inches from his own. "What did you do?" Bull demanded.

Spinoza laughed. "Do you think I'd come here alone?"

"Psst, Bull," Zeke whispered. "I need a gun."

Bull loosened a gun from his ankle holster and tossed a small caliber Glock to Malone.

A figure appeared in the glasshouse doorway with two pistols blazing, like out of an old western movie. Both Malone and Bull laid down a wall of fire. The man pitched backwards. Then silence until a volley of shots smashed the few remaining windows out. Suspended flower pots exploded, contents slamming the overturned table. Bull scooted over the floor, grabbed a long-handled rake and flipped the light switch off. In the eerie darkness, the only sound was water splashing on tile from a busted pipe.

Kitty peeked out from underneath the leaves. "You guys never told me *this* could happen."

Bull grunted, "Next time we'll know. *Keep down.*"

All five were breathing hard. Zeke whispered to Bull, "How many?"

"Five, maybe six."

Bull got on his knees and peeked up for just a second. Beyond the top of the overturned table, he saw only dark night, before hearing footsteps by the back entrance. Another guy rushed in through the rear door, guns blazing. Zeke turned and started firing. Bull was hit, that spun him around, but he got off two shots before hitting the floor. He cursed in pain. The dead guy by the backdoor said nothing.

"Bull, how bad are you hit?" Kitty crawled towards him.

He grimaced with pain.

More shots rang out. Then quiet.

Kitty examined his bloody leg. He was leaking blood. She undid his belt and fastened a tourniquet above the entry wound.

"How many you think?" Zeke asked.

"One less than before," said Bull between grunts.

Zeke removed the clip from the gun Bull had tossed him. Zeke held up three fingers and rammed the clip back in.

Spinoza crawled over to Zeke and said, "Look, Zeke, you and your partner are going to get killed. Take these cuffs off me and I can help you."

A shot plunked into the wooden table. They ducked lower. "Why don't you make it easier on yourself?" he continued. "I'll tell them to let you go."

"Right," said Jane, bashing him on the head with a clay pot.

Two men leaped through a broken window. Zeke shot one at point-blank range. The other assassin crashed into him, knocking him back, and his gun skittered away. They tumbled onto tables, pots, and gardening tools. The guy had a size advantage over Zeke. But Zeke was fighting for his life.

Zeke wrapped a garden hose around the guy's neck and twisted. The man kicked in desperation. Jugs and buckets of flowers (Moth Orchids), airborne as the rakes clanged to the floor. But Zeke wasn't about to let go—twisting it tighter and tighter until the man stopped struggling.

Zeke fell back in exhaustion. A terrible burning sensation throbbed in his shoulder. He reached up and felt blood. "I've been shot."

"How bad?" Jane asked, scrambling over to him. She examined his shoulder. There was only an entrance wound, meaning the bullet was still in his shoulder. He was grimacing in pain. "Overcome this, Zeke," she said. "Or we won't get out of here alive."

He shook his head and swore he would not lose her again. He searched the floor for his weapon.

"You looking for this?" Kitty asked, sliding the pistol across the floor. "You know, Jane was right about you," she said, "You're an okay guy. And you're not as dumb as you look."

Jane leaned in and whispered in his ear. "This will not end well unless we think of a way out. Why don't you try talking to them? Maybe you can figure out something?"

He nodded and checked the clip—one bullet.

Zeke looked towards Bull who was holding his leg in agony. Bull nodded.

Zeke crawled over to the blown-out windows. Nothing but the night lay beyond. "Hey, Jojo Turner!" he shouted.

Zeke heard muffled voices. Then silence.

"Jojo Turner! Talk to me, *fucker!*"

After a minute. "So, you figured out it was me?"

"Yeah, I figured it out!" was all Malone said.

"How?"

"I thought to myself," Zeke said, "Who's the biggest asshole I know?"

Turner's laugh cut through the darkness.

"So it had to be you," Zeke said.

"Hilarious," Turner called out, but it had an undertone of anger.

"Not only is it hilarious," Zeke peeked over the edge of the sill. "But everybody *knows* it was *you.*"

There was a pause. "You're bluffing."

Zeke pointed at Bull and gave him a *keep him talking* motion with his hand.

Bull nodded. Shuffled with pain to the window, Bull shouted, "Hey, Turner!"

"Bull! Is that you?"

"Yeah, it's me."

"Well, now the party's complete! Bull, you were told to keep out of this."

"Well, you know me, Jojo, I don't enjoy taking orders from a *shit*head—especially one like you."

While the two were exchanging insults, Zeke crawled out the back door, over a dead body, and circled around through the tall grass and scrub trees. The clouds had parted, allowing silvery moonlight to slant through. Zeke made out the grassy outlines of the grounds.

"That's too bad for you, Bull. Now you have to pay for covering for that loser Zeke."

Bull snorted, "I think you've got it ass-backward, Turner. The truth is going to come out about you!"

"They can't prove anything."

"Not only can they prove it, there's enough to put you away. Plus, we just recorded Lukas Spinoza admitting he ordered Onyx's execution. And you covered it up!"

In the dark, Zeke followed Turner's voice. His heart was pounding in his chest, and the pain in his shoulder intensified whenever he moved. His left arm hung useless at his side. The clouds parted revealing the half-moon and stars, that twinkled in the night sky. He saw Turner's outline, crouched behind Spinoza's Lexus.

About ten yards to the left, a movement caught his eye. A second person knelt behind a small hedgerow. Zeke figured they were the only two left. *They started with five?* His shoulder throbbed, making it hard to think clearly. *Or was it six?* He wondered if he could take out one without wasting his last bullet—*I hope there's not another one.* With only one arm, he might be able to use the element of surprise, and take one guy out, but two … ?

"Hey, Turner," Bull yelled from inside the building.

"What do you want?"

"You know the Feds are on their way here to arrest Spinoza. Thanks for showing up here and making it easy for them to find you!"

"I've heard that before! Don't forget, I'm a cop and I've used that bluff myself."

"Oh, yeah? Suit yourself then and sit out there till they arrive. Won't be long now!"

"If that's true … " Jojo turned and motioned to the shadowy figure. "Then we ought to end this now!" Turner stood in a crouch and started towards the door of the greenhouse followed by the other man.

It's now or never. Zeke raced the short distance towards the trailing figure, and cross-body blocked him. He doubled over with a grunt. Zeke leapt on him and with his good arm, whacked his face three quick blows with the butt of the gun. He rolled off, expecting Turner to be on him, but he saw Jojo was entering the greenhouse. Before Zeke could move, he heard a volley of shots and a muffled scream. *Damn it.* He rolled off the unconscious man, scrambled up, and stumbled towards the doorway.

But before he could reach it, Turner called out, "Hey, Zeke!"

Zeke pulled up, throwing himself to the side.

Movement came from inside. "Zeke Malone!" Silence. "Show yourself!"

Zeke's breath came in short bursts. *Never expose yourself in a gun battle.* "I can't do that!"

"If you don't," Turner shouted, "Jane dies."

Zeke couldn't answer, and his stomach knotted. Blood pounded in his ears.

"Bull is already dead!" Turner yelled.

The ringing in Zeke's ears seemed to get louder. *That can't be possible.*

"Do you think I'd hesitate to kill her?"

The overhead fluorescent lights of the greenhouse blinked on. Zeke rolled away from the light. He saw Turner standing amid the rubble with Jane as a shield. He had his arm around her neck and a gun pressed against her head.

No. No. Not again!

"Throw your gun through the doorway!" Jojo shouted. "Show yourself, and I'll let her live."

A fluttery feeling filled his chest and suddenly, all the fatigue fell away, but the pain intensified. *When faced with an adversary, never give up your weapon.* "I can't do that."

"Then, she dies!"

Zeke glanced around the edge of a window.

"Don't be stupid, Jojo! If you shoot her, you'll lose your cover. Then what'll prevent me from blowing your ass away?"

Jojo paused. "Okay, then keep your gun! Show yourself anyway." Jojo laughed. "That seems fair!"

Just do the job. Just do the job, he heard Bull's voice in his head. *When you can't think of what to do, just do the damn job.* Zeke took a deep breath and stuck his gun around the corner of the door, and then peered around.

Turner stood behind Jane, his body pressed against her, his face half hidden, lips only inches from her ear. His gun was now hooked under her chin, pointed upward. A quick glance around the greenhouse—Bull's body lay on the floor. No movement. *Can't think about that now.* Kitty Fowler was nowhere to be seen. *In hiding, good girl.* Zeke extended his arm farther into the room. He pointed the muzzle of his weapon at Turner.

"Zeke, don't be shy," Turner said. "Come on in!"

Zeke stepped farther into the light, his good arm pointing the gun at Jojo. His other arm hung at his side.

"All the way in. That's right!"

Zeke took a shooter's stance, knees bent, one arm straight out, gun pointed. He tried to bring up his wounded arm, but it only made the pain worse.

"That's better," Jojo sneered. "Well, why don't you take your shot, Zeke? Take. Your. Shot."

Zeke couldn't without hitting Jane. He shook his head. "I can't."

"I knew it. I knew it." Turner whooped with glee. "I knew it *then!* And I know it *now!*"

"What are you talking about?"

"You couldn't take your shot at Bomber Boy. And it cost Jane her life." Jojo blinked, cut his eyes to her, and pressed his lips to her ear. "Well, nearly." He smiled. "Since she's still alive. No thanks to you."

No. No. Not now. The dream that had plagued him for years flooded back in. Zeke sank into his nightmare, standing in the hallway by the elevator of the museum, staring into her grass-green eyes, Bomber Boy, explosives strapped to his chest, with arm hooked around her neck.

Zeke's hands shook. Sick to his stomach. Sweat beaded his forehead. The voice of Jojo Turner shouting, "*Take your shot!*" Again and again in his earpiece. *"Take your shot, asshole!"*

Zeke blinked hard and shook his head until he left his dream and suddenly found himself back in the greenhouse. But this time, instead of Jojo's voice in a dream, Jojo stood in front of him—with Jane as his shield.

"Looks like a stalemate," Jojo said.

Zeke stepped forward. "Tell me what happened?"

"What?"

"We know you were the snitch for Onyx and the drug ring. You warned them. Then you killed Onyx."

"I had to. The Narcs were closing in, getting too close." Jojo said. "I took care of him before they arrived."

"Tell me, why did you want to murder Jane?"

"Why should I tell you anything?"

"What you say here about my wife will never leave here. If you kill me, of course I'll be able to tell no one. If you kill her, it won't matter. 'Cause *you'll* be dead. I'll make sure of that."

Turner hooted and cackled with laughter as if it were the funniest thing he'd ever heard. "Ain't that the truth!?" He repositioned his gun under Jane's chin. "But why should I tell you anything, you *spineless* sack of crap?"

"Because you owe me. She nearly died last time. Tell me: was she involved in the drug operation?"

Jojo peeked over Jane's shoulder and shook his head before ducking back down. "Jane was not involved with the drugs. She provided legitimate buys for the museum. Onyx was using her. And he was blackmailing her."

"Blackmailing her? But ... about what?"

"Carla!"

A flutter started in Zeke's belly and shot up into his chest. Images of Carla popped into his head. He could see her blonde, curly hair. The freckles. He shook away the image.

"What do you mean?" Zeke shook his head. "Blackmailing over what?"

"You know, Carla is not her daughter, right? Onyx threatened to take her from Jane."

"Then, whose ... ?"

"She's the daughter of Kitty Fowler! You mean, you didn't know? You *stupid* shit."

His eyes darted to Jane. She stared at Zeke, her eyes blazing like green emeralds.

"That's right," Jojo laughed. "She's the offspring of Kitty Fowler. Go on, Jane." He jabbed the gun under her chin, hard. "Tell him."

She nodded. Her green eyes glared. Then, she shifted her eyes left and downward. She repeated the eye movement twice more. *Left and then down.*

Zeke stepped in the direction she had indicated.

She squirmed like she were trying to get away from Turner.

"Stand still," Turner commanded when they banged into a workbench. He turned Jane, so she was still between the two of them. He shoved the gun under her chin, pushing her head upwards.

Zeke kept his gun up. "So, tell me: what happened?"

Turner sighed. "Jane finally realized the scam. That the art shipments were to cover the drug-smuggling operation. She found out she was being used. Onyx threatened to take away Carla. But she still went to the police to tell all!"

"Did she?"

Turner cackled with delight. "Oh, yeah! And guess who she went to see?"

"You?"

"Oh, yeah."

Malone frowned. "Why didn't she come to me?"

"Who knows? Maybe to keep you from getting involved?"

"And the boy, the bomber?"

Jojo took a deep breath. "The crazy kid with the explosives? He was a setup!" Jojo let out a heavy sigh. "It was too easy. We promised him a house for his mother if he pretended it was a robbery. He wasn't all there to start with." He shook his head. "His detonator button was a decoy. It *wasn't even* connected."

"But the explosion?"

"We controlled it remotely. When the SWAT guys shot, we activated the explosives."

"Then Jane was the target all along?"

Jojo nodded. "*Hell, yeah.* We couldn't let her go spilling her guts."

Flashes of the nightmare loomed before Malone—her grass-green eyes—but he shook it off again.

"For what its worth, I'm sorry about trying to kill her," Turner said. "I was against it, but letting her blab was not an option. She brought it on herself."

Zeke saw her lips moving silently—*I love you.*

"But what about me? I was there. I talked to the boy. Was I part of the plan?"

"No, you just walked in at the wrong time. You always were a pain-in-the-ass. But I'm tired of answering your bullshit questions." Turner's voice was harsh now. "Zeke, if you're going to shoot, do it now! Take your shot. Shit or get off the pot."

Jane's eyes darted to her left.

"You can't! Can you? I knew you'd freeze then, just like you're doing now. Take your shot, Zeke, *if* you've got the guts."

Jane squirmed against the edge of the table. She worked her hand over the top of the workbench and slipped her fingers around a pair of garden shears.

Turner shouted, "TAKE YOUR *GODDAMN* SHOT, ZEKE! IF YOU GOT THE GUTS! *TAKE YOUR FUCKING SHOT!*"

Jane forcefully swung the blade down into his thigh, so hard you could hear the point hit bone. He screamed in agony and jerked away. Jane ducked to the side. He failed to pull the trigger and blow her head off.

Zeke Malone finally took his shot.

CHAPTER 82

THREE MONTHS LATER

Zeke sat uncomfortably, listening to the police chief in the same auditorium where they held the press conference for the Oasis Club Massacre. The dress suit felt heavy and stiff. Itchy. His tie seemed to choke him. As he applauded, the sharp pain in his shoulder where the bullet slammed still reminded him of that night.

This time, there was only one reporter from the newspaper doing a background follow-up to the GREENHOUSE MASSACRE, as the pressed dubbed it, to distinguish it from the OASIS CLUB MASSACRE, as if the public couldn't figure that out on their own. The sub-headline read: *Head of Homicide Dies in Drug Bust.* The NOPD Press Department's official statement was that Captain Jojo Turner led the assault on the drug dealers. Turner's full involvement in the drug operation was kept from the public's eye. To keep up appearances, he was buried with full police-military pomp, a slow hearse passing a half mile of men-in-blue saluting Turner in honor. The true story was interred with him, similar to the Bomber Boy's burial.

After the gunfight, Zeke thought Bull was dead, lying on the wet concrete floor amid the shattered pots and ferns. But Bull, true to his nature, survived the gunshots.

Chief Washington praised the gallant officers and detectives that had given full measure. On the stage, six American flags and six Louisiana state flags provided the backdrop. His raspy voice echoed off the back wall of the auditorium. "And with unbelievable courage, Detective Hugh Bulardeaux refused to back off the case. Like any good detective ... " the commissioner paused and smiled. "And like the best policeman—as Detective Bulardeaux certainly is—he pursued every lead. Even putting his life on the line. Even sustaining multiple gunshot wounds, he never quit."

The crowd of well-wishers and police dignitaries stood and applauded.

It had been touch-and-go with Bull for a while. None of the bullets had pierced an artery. "A miracle," the doctors called it. The press picked it up, and that was printed:

Detective Bull's Miracle Survival.

Zeke sat behind Bull, who had bandages on his neck to hide the recent skin grafts, his leg in a limiter walking-brace. The police chief was calling Bull to the podium. And with difficulty, Bull stood to his feet.

He walked using a cane to the front and up the stairs to the platform. The applause was loud and sustained. The chief and the new homicide captain extended their hands, and Bull gave each one an awkward, left one-handed shake.

Finally, Chief Washington held up his hand, and the applause died down. "It's with the greatest pleasure, I award the highest decoration for bravery and valor of the New Orleans Police Department to ... " He stopped and gestured for Bull to step forward, "To Detective Hugh Bulardeaux."

The applause exploded again as the chief pinned a ribbon on Bull's chest. Slowly, one then another stood, until we were all on our feet, giving Bull a standing ovation.

Zeke applauded. The chief had offered Zeke his old position back on the force with his retiring rank—if he wanted it. So far, Zeke had not accepted or declined. Still hadn't decided.

Scanning the audience, Zeke saw Carla and observed her. The older she grew, the more she resembled her mother—Kitty Fowler. She stood immobile, head down.

Mark and Doris stood next to her. He still was not friendly, but he finally agreed that Zeke was not responsible for Jane's "death." When the facts came out, Mark admitted Jane's murder, correction—attempted murder—was a setup. One that Zeke could not have prevented.

Zeke smiled and tried to savor the moment.

Also in the audience was Fred LaForge, the ex-clown. The past few months, he alone had run the agency while Zeke recovered. Zeke had made Fred a partner in the firm, renamed the agency Malone-LaForge Detective Agency. Fred had hired three more people to work him.

Throughout most of the ceremony, Jane sat next to Zeke, holding his hand. *Jane Doe Alberato Malone.* The real person, *alive* and warm and soft. *Not a dream.* She turned to him and smiled, and he wondered what she was thinking.

•   •   •

Now, he saw her in happier times of their marriage. Saw her smile. Her twinkling grass-green eyes, the aroma of her skin. Soap and pixie sticks. Her voice whispering, *I love you,* but not in a death farewell. He heard her in their intimate moments—when they made love, when he held her, in her gestures, in the clutch of her hand as they sat in the dark. Now with the truth, of her background and her innocence, revealed, his world had changed. Now that she was alive, the nightmares of blood and explosions mostly left him. *Or had they?* But Zeke still had two recurring dreams. Sometimes, in his nightmares about the Bomber Boy, he still saw the blood, and heard the blast, and awoke clutching the sweat-soaked sheets. He'd turn to her in the dark, reaching out to touch her reclining figure, reassuring himself that she was still beside him.

He still saw Dr. Lucy in the Sky occasionally. She said he was making progress. "Remember the stages of death. You might be approaching the last and final stage."

"And what is that?" Zeke asked.

She said, "Why, *acceptance,* of course!"

"But, Jane is alive," he said, "I accept that. She did *not* die."

"Maybe to you. In your *conscious* mind. But underneath, where all the gnomes and goblins live, in your *subconsciousness* doo-hickey." She tapped the side of her head with her fingers. "They still can't believe she's alive. *They* still think she's dead."

"That's a comforting thought," Zeke said.

"Give it time." She rolled back away from him, her wheelchair falling into the grooves of her rug. "Give it time, they'll come around. After all, to run a marathon, you still have to ... " She arched her eyebrows and looked at him expectantly, giving him the *come-on* hand signal.

" ... take one spin of the wheel at a time," he said.

"See, I knew you were making progress," Lucy in the Sky said, spinning in circles with her chair, laughing.

In his other dream, in the *Audubon Park Dream,* Zeke pushed Carla on a swing, higher and higher into the oyster blue Louisiana sky with fluffy white clouds. It was dangerous, but he couldn't stop himself. And she laughed with delight until the swing reached its apogee and releasing her grip, she went floating off into the cerulean sky. Flapping her arms like a bird, she circled above him, her French braid growing longer and longer like a kite's tail. He leaped as high as he could to catch them but he never could reach high enough, always beyond his grasp. She looked down at him and giggled before disappearing beyond the top of the cypress trees, disappearing above Audubon Park with the sound of lions roaring. In his dream, he stood dumbfounded, mouth open, "Now, how did she do that? How did she learn to fly?"

CHAPTER 83

It's been a year since Jane and I have been back together. Happiness fills our home. The three of us: Jane, Carla and Yours Truly. We moved to the North Shore of Lake Pontchartrain across the twenty-three mile bridge to Abita Springs, Louisiana. Life is slower here, and it suits me just fine. Uh, suits *us*.

Do you remember the million dollars the museum curator, Lukas Spinoza, paid to Jane for acting as the go between? The court ruled that she had earned it legitimately. Therefore, she was entitled to keep it. They call it *fees for honest services*.

To my surprise, it had grown to over a million and a half dollars by the time we touched it.

We purchased a ten acre parcel of land with tall pines, a small catfish lake, and a horse stable. Carla just loves the horses. A mare named Lola, her favorite, is *as gentle as they come*.

The land is only a few miles from *École de France* where Jane used to work under the assumed name of Alice Potterfield. She returned to work there and took up her duties again, only this time under her real name, Jane Malone.

But what I never figured out is why Jane enlisted MJ to cover up her death and how she thought disappearing would solve her problems. But it was her decision. She said she did it to save my life. I do think it cost MJ his life. As with many things in our marriage, we just don't discuss it. On that tragic day of the explosion, when she saw Jojo Turner outside the Whitney, she knew he was the snitch.

We don't talk about that either.

I seldom see my old partner, Detective Bull. It's like another life I once led—the life of a cop—but I think about it.

One day last week, he called me out of the blue and asked me to go have a beer with him, *like old times.*

"I still don't drink," I told him.

"I figured. Meet me, anyway, at the Half Moon."

I was uncertain if he needed my help, so I said, "Okay."

He hung up.

It was dark when I arrived at the Half Moon; once again, more of the electric neon letters were out and the sign read: HA—OD. Which, if you add another D, was what I was feeling—*How Odd.*

He sat alone at the long oak bar, nursing a mug of beer with a Hilton Hotel logo on the side. Jane's description of Bull comes to mind. He did resemble a bear, hunched over, guarding his drink with both hands on either side.

I felt a heavy feeling in the pit of my stomach. Everything was familiar, *but not really.* Like going back to your elementary school, and finding everything to be absurdly small. *Did I once sit in that chair? At that tiny desk?*

Once, long ago, I sat here drinking beer, chatting with Bull, playing the 20-Questions Death Trivia game with MJ, and shoving quarters in the jukebox to listen to outdated music. Now MJ was gone. Bull seemed depressed. Yolanda, the waitress, had retired. They had removed the Manet *Olympia* print from above the bar. It wasn't the same.

Bull looked up and waved his beefy hand at me.

"Hi, Bull."

"Hi, partner. Long time no see."

"Yeah, I've been kind of busy. What with the new house, and all. The grounds and the horses. "

"You're turning into a real country squire, Malone. Rural life really must agree with you. How's Jane?"

I explained she was back working at the school, and that Carla was going to an excellent school nearby which specialized in autism.

A cute new waitress, college-aged, brought me a Coke. She left to serve other customers.

We sat quiet for a few minutes.

"What happened to Detective Birdie?" I asked.

"Birdie? Aw, she moved on. She quit the force over a month ago."

"How come?"

"She met some dude. Took her to Los Angeles. He's a cameraman, or something like that, with a production crew that filmed in New Orleans—NCSI, I think."

"Huh. What about Kitty Fowler? You heard anything from her?" I asked.

Bull scratched the side of his head. "The old doc finally died, she collected all of his money, liquidated all of his assets, and disappeared without a trace."

I can't say I was surprised she ran off. I pictured her. In the nude, reclining like the hooker from Manet's *Olympia.* As I thought about it, Kitty Fowler was at the bottom of the whole situation. The death of Bomber Boy, Jane's involvement with Onyx and his crew, Leslie Baronne, Presley Baronne, Felix, the barman, and Clive Bronsky's deaths. And the five unlucky patrons. And I guess you could even say the death of Onyx, Spinoza, and that rat, Jojo Turner could be traced back to her. Kitty was responsible for so much suffering that visited many different folks. And she walked away, pockets full of blood money.

We sat a couple of more minutes, watching the new waitress bussing tables, her hips swaying to music from the jukebox.

"Want to hear something funny?" Bull said. "Not *ha-ha funny,* but something crazy. My doctor thinks I need to go on a diet. I could have told him that. The physician said I'm pre-diabetic. Can you believe that? Pre-di-a-be-tic." He pronounced each syllable as if conducting a class in Cajun French, motioning with his empty glass.

The bar felt cold, and the antique neon Pabst Blue Ribbon sign blinked on and off, reflected off the worn bar, creating an eerie red-and-blue halo around Bull's head.

"Well, *Fuck the doctor,*" Bull said. "What does he know?" Then he appeared to settle into a funk, slumping forward, arms on the counter, staring straight ahead. "My uncle had diabetes. *Bad,*" he said. "They amputated his leg up to the knee. He told me he could still feel his toes, though. Itched like the dickens. But there was nothin' for him to scratch. Where is that Yolanda?" Bull searched around before realizing Yolanda was no longer there. He waved for the new girl, the college waitress. I got a whiff of sadness coming off my old friend, much like waves of heat from a Bourbon Street sidewalk during the middle of Summer. "Another beer? I mean Coke?" he asked me.

"No, thanks. I better be going. Long drive back over the Causeway. And you know what it's like after dark." I slid off my stool. "Maybe some other time."

"Yeah, some other time." He scanned the room for the waitress, lifting his mug again.

Outside, the air was stifling muggy, just another typical Louisiana night. I stood in the orange glow of the half-lit, Half Moon neon sign, thinking of Jane. She was alive, and that was all that mattered. But try as I may, I still could not believe she was really here. The ache would not go away; I just couldn't get it out of my mind.

Phantom pain, they called it when you still feel the amputated body part. There is nothing you can do—except endure the agony and hope it goes away. As I started back to my car, I thought, what do you call it when you miss someone? I was heartsick and could barely stand it. Could it still be called *phantom pain?*

I still can't believe this all happened. I know Carla and Jane are waiting for me at home, but I still can't shake the feeling when I walk into the house ... *no one will be there.*

Walk into an empty house?

And the weird thing is ...

I wouldn't be surprised. *It would be like waking from a dream into reality.*

THE END

NOTES FROM THE AUTHOR

Word-of-mouth is crucial for any author to succeed. If you enjoyed *Mardi Gras Madness*, please leave a review online—anywhere you are able. Even if it's just a sentence or two. It would make all the difference and would be very much appreciated.

Thanks!
Xavier Desoto

ACKNOWLEDGMENTS

A lot has gone into *Mardi Gras Madness*. I never imagined how many people would be involved in bringing this novel to life. Like birthing a baby at a hospital, you never realize the troop of doctors, nurses, medical assistants, ward clerks, and even down to the janitors, that make it all happen.

I am grateful to all those that have helped me.

The fact of the matter is, when I first started writing this novel, all I had was a vague idea about who Zeke Malone was. But as I started writing, his personality shone through, and then his wife, Jane, emerged, and all the rest of the people who worked with him on the mean streets of New Orleans, and sat with him in the Half Moon Bar and Grill. Though I had plotted out the novel, things changed as I wrote and I had to go along.

Many times I wanted to quit, but certain people, like my wife and three sons, encouraged me to continue. So, I started again, getting Zeke Malone out of bed, followed by his naked, grass-green-eyed wife, complaining, "Zeke, someday you're going to get yourself shot." Thus the story began anew. Again. When most people think of Mardi Gras and New Orleans, they think of parades, marching bands, beads (*Throw me something, Mister!*), and gaiety. But there are darker undertones in the Crescent City, and I wanted to capture that mood. The story is about Death and Life and then Death again, and how easily we can be fooled by both. *Things never are what they seem.*

I want to thank several people for their patience and support.

First, I want to thank Oscar Ortiz, former New Orleans policeman, who read early versions of my book and made pointed suggestions about police procedure. Though all errors are my own.

As an adviser about writing, I am grateful to my great colleague and friend, Leah B. Erskine, author of award winning *CC's Road Home*, for never pulling punches. She was my greatest help.

To Kirsten Corby, Diane Watson, Lou Fuenzalida, and the members of my writing/critique group for their helpful comments about my writing. Also J. Moody and K. Fassl for their help. Thanks to Chris Smith in the Jefferson Parish Library system.

To David K. Lemons, my oldest buddy from Pasadena, Texas, for his unwavering friendship, and encouragement.

I want to thank Elan Tran, for teaching me about promotion and social media. I couldn't have done it without you.

Thank you, Laura Foust, for doing the tedious work of editing all of my writing, weeding out mistakes, for your good humor and patience. Errors are still mine since I seldomly listen well.

To my book publisher, many thanks to the entire team at Black Rose Writing, especially Reagan Rothe, publisher.

And for my family, Angeles (Cookie), Tony, David, and Timothy for their patience and encouragement. And for all my nephews and nieces, my grandchildren, Ethan, Brady, Parker, Emily and Skylar for lifting my spirits when I thought my story was a mess, especially teenager Ethan who is a computer whiz.

As I sit here in a coffee shop scribbling out my notes, (WE CLOSE IN TEN MINUTES! they shout), I know I have forgotten half the people who have helped and encouraged me along the way. To them, thank you and I'll catch you in the next novel.

For Alex Pate who left us too soon.

For the city of New Orleans, that inspired me to write.

ABOUT THE AUTHOR

Xavier DeSoto was born a stone's throwaway from "The Wall," the State Penitentiary in East Texas. That's when his interests in murder mysteries, and the psychology of criminals began. He has worked as a psychiatric orderly, a cameraman, a door-to-door salesman, and factory worker. He transplanted to New Orleans in his early twenties, working his way through college to receive his first B.A. in Communications, before serving as a copywriter, TV director, and program director. His hair started turning gray in his mid-twenties. Later in life, he returned to college for his second degree, and worked as an RN and ICU coordinator. He has written numerous short stories, and is currently working on his fourth novel. Xavier lives in New Orleans with his wife and a dog named Lola.

www.facebook.com/XavierDesotoWrites
or just friend me on Facebook if you'd like to!

Twitter @desotoxavier

Instagram @xavierdesoto

www.xavierdesoto.com

Or contact him directly at xdesoto8@gmail.com

OTHER TITLES FROM THE AUTHOR

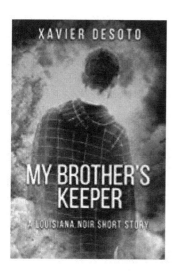

My Brother's Keeper

My brother, who hadn't said a word in twenty years, suddenly started to speak. What secrets will he unearth?

The Sisters
A Tale of Family Horror and Secrets

She was falling down a rabbit hole of insanity.

DISCUSSION QUESTIONS

Note to Reading Groups and Readers: These discussion questions can reveal important aspects of the plot line and outcome. If you haven't read the entire novel, I suggest you wait before reading these thought-provoking questions.

1) Jane, Zeke's wife, dies at the beginning of the story. And then, Zeke went into a deep depression and withdrew from his loved ones for over two years. Is that a normal response? How long after a death should a person take to get over their grief?

2) How does the city of New Orleans, Louisiana, play a role in his life? And in the novel?

3) By mid-story, when Zeke discovers his wife's death may not have been an accident—wrong place, wrong time—was he justified in his need to seek revenge and find her killer?

4) How does Zeke's relationship with Detective Bull affect his recovery?

5) Jane Malone kept her survival a secret. Was it necessary? What reason did she give? Was it substantial enough? Did she do it to protect her husband and autistic child?

6) Did the story come full circle for you? In the beginning, the captain of Homicide, Jojo Turner, shouted into Zeke's ear, "TAKE YOUR FUCKING SHOT!" Zeke cannot pull the trigger for fear of hitting Jane. At the climax of the story, during the showdown in the greenhouse, Jojo Turner shouted the same words, but the novel ends with different results. Were you satisfied with the ending?

Please email me your answers, comments, or questions to xdesoto8@gmail.com I look forward to from hearing from you!

We hope you enjoyed reading this title from:

BLACK ROSE
writing™

www.blackrosewriting.com

Subscribe to our mailing list – *The Rosevine* – and receive **FREE** books, daily deals, and stay current with news about upcoming releases and our hottest authors.
Scan the QR code below to sign up.

Already a subscriber? Please accept a sincere thank you for being a fan of Black Rose Writing authors.

View other Black Rose Writing titles at www.blackrosewriting.com/books and use promo code **PRINT** to receive a **20% discount** when purchasing.